OF STATIONS INFERNAL

KIN S. LAW

CITY OWL
PRESS

OF STATIONS INFERNAL
Lands Beyond, Book 3

CITY OWL PRESS
www.cityowlpress.com

Cover Design by Mibl Art. All stock photos licensed appropriately.

Edited by Heather McCorkle.

For information on subsidiary rights, please contact the publisher at info@cityowlpress.com.

Print Edition ISBN: 978-1-949090-20-8

Digital Edition ISBN: 978-1-949090-19-2

Printed in the United States of America

For the family who knows me.

PRAISE FOR THE WORKS OF KIN S. LAW

"As befits steampunk, Law fills the pages with exciting gear action and fashion...His prose includes some brilliant descriptions including the opening sentence: 'A black murder rose from the wound of a cliff'."
- Publisher's Weekly

"Adventure is what I expected going into this book, and adventure is what I got. The atmosphere was entrancing, the airships were captivating, the action was spot on. I can't wait to see what the author has in store for us next!"
- Mystery Author, M. W. Griffith

"A different take on the steampunk genre. Most stories tend to explore the contraptions invented had the Industrial Revolution taken a different path, and the world remained stuck in the Victorian Era. Using Mark Twain as a pivotal character will likely bring about a chuckle or two."
- M. P. Ceja, InD'Tale Magazine

"It's a fun story about a diverse group who comes together to save the world, something we've seen many times, but what sets this story apart is the quality of the writing- great dialogue, cool world building and wonderful characters, especially the women. Rosa and Vanessa are prickly, strong, smart, and capable, and couldn't be more different from one another. No damsels in distress in this Pirate story, I loved those ladies."
- GoodReads Reviewer

"The characterization of the four main characters is exceptionally well done. The plot is a weave of two quests. The first is to find out who is stealing famous landmarks like Big Ben and the Eiffel Tower, and of course to fight them and thus return the landmarks. The second is to find Albion's mentor, Captain Sam Clemens, and resolve the issues that caused their separation. The fantasy elements were quite interesting and the author has been very creative."

- ARC Reviewer

STATION 1

Ghosts of the Lonely West

THE INSPECTOR LANDED ON SOIL THAT HAD LITTLE KNOWN THE BITE of tuppenny boots, breathing the burned-wood scent that prevailed in the American winter. Her boots had been bought for a song across an ocean in a market in Camden Town, which seemed all too far away now.

In sight of the dim evening lamps of a small town, Vanessa Hargreaves, expatriated from her beloved England, looked back up to her steel guardian. It was a ways down from the cockpit, but his hip plate made for a sturdy footstool to hop the ten feet to the ground. Alphonse certainly looked out of place here, a knight far west of the castles of Scotland where he had been built. As out of place as Hargreaves herself. To think of it! An agent of Victoria III, Queen of Pax Brittania, in exile in the wildness of America with only a steel golem for company!

But Hargreaves knew too well that what lay in the box on Alphonse's back had the potential to destroy the world. There were forces high and low, standards under both the black flag and the Union Jack, that would do anything to get the Cook box. Though Hargreaves pined for the high streets and low alleys of their home in London, there were still dragons to be slain in the west. So she put the thought of merry England behind her and resolved to carry on.

Hargreaves rather thought she would be needing her steel friend before long. Sadly, his innards were starkly empty of fuel, and he would carry her no farther. Alphonse's belly wouldn't feed itself, which meant Hargreaves needed to impose on the local town for coal. The inspector supposed the papers might have exaggerated America's famed conservatism just a tad, but she didn't care to risk attracting her pursuers in any way by parading an automata down the streets. She slung her carpet bag over her shoulder and covered the bulk of Alphonse with canvas and branches. The covering served to protect her guardian from prying eyes and exposure to elements. The deep darkness of the giant's metal eye slits seemed to appraise her with a sort of inanimate loneliness.

"Don't blame me. It's your fault for being a great big shiny lump," Hargreaves admonished it, before covering the steel frog-head. From a distance, the disguise wouldn't be anything of interest even in the daytime. That was of special importance. Alphonse carried on his back a box that could unleash a plague of biblical proportions on the unsuspecting townsfolk. Nobody must touch the box!

Hargreaves gave a thought to herself. Her leonine mane whipped about, comforting in the cool of autumn. That would never do. She tied it back into a neat bun. Then, she set off down the path, trying to walk casually. Respectably. Her undercover instincts came alive. Soon, the spot where she had hidden Alphonse disappeared behind the trees, and some peaked roofs and a water tower came into view over the next copse. The tower had been painted with a huge red apple.

As she entered the town, a steaming omnibus rumbled down the nearly deserted main street. The rounded, riveted front marked it as an older model, not far removed from a locomotive. It stopped in front of the plate glass of an eatery that served double duty as a bus station. With her canvas bag and dusty clothes, Hargreaves easily blended into the group of harried passengers. There was a slight delay as the people packed on the sidewalk, apparently too polite to go onto the road. From the murmuring, it seemed there were more people than usual on the omnibus. One man mentioned something to do with the major rail lines being shut through the Midwest.

Hargreaves bought a paper and a notebook from a freeman's newsstand, taking her change from his dark fingers. As she turned, one of the passengers remarked on how lucky he had been to catch this bus, otherwise he would have been obliged to wait an entire week for the next transport. Another bumped into her and kept going, not even raising his cap in apology. She nearly missed the lewd look of appraisal as he glanced back.

"Why, I never!" Hargreaves breathed. Sometimes she missed the vestiges of Victorian England. Back in the reign of the first Victoria, men were responsible for any untoward display of the baser natures. Even being alone with an unwed woman or remarking on her ankles was considered untoward. Today, women of the Pax Britannia still enjoyed the trace chivalry of that heyday, as was only proper. She reminded herself this was America, and these people had bucked English customs as easily as English rule. But she definitely felt they had thrown the baby out with the bathwater on this one.

Hargreaves hoped there was an inn or a boarding house somewhere. Alphonse's seat was no place to weather the cold mountain nights. But the eatery seemed the only establishment open at the moment. Faint smells reminded her she hadn't eaten since leaving Rosa and the crashed airship 'Berry yesterday afternoon.

Hargreaves walked into the eatery and settled into a warm, plush booth. A patina of wear had descended on everything, and the air carried just a hint of frying grease. The fare appeared to be the ubiquitous soup and Hamburg steak. A row of taps dispensed a bubbling effervescence, with a smell like sweet engine cleaner. There was an awful lot of paisley, but besides this slight, the place was welcoming in every sense of the word. It was to be expected; airships brought more than goods, they brought ideas, and not all of them were used the way it said on the tin. Hargreaves suddenly missed Auntie, the 'Berry's resident matron, on a profound level.

"Blech," she groaned under her breath, watching someone consume something that looked worse than naval rations. She should have been more subtle, but the stuff was truly foul. Some sort of potted pork or beef.

"We don't have none of your fancy city grub," said an apparent local. The man was two seats away. Whenever he spoke, crumbs dribbled from a spotty beard. "But I got somethin' a lot tastier back here, legs."

Hargreaves was in no mood for his low brand of repulsive.

"Beg pardon? Have you escaped from the chef, you unbearable swine?"

Scattered chuckles sounded from the nearby diners. A cook tipped his hat from behind a service window. The sally seemed to rile up the repulsive man, who slowly creaked to his feet. Surprisingly, the man wore threadbare suit trousers and a vest under the grime. The overall effect was of a solicitor rising from the grave to settle an account. Diners nearby crinkled their noses.

"Why, you limey little whore!" said this repulsive character.

There were twenty-one different ways Hargreaves could have dealt with the filth, seven of which did not involve stepping in the man's aura of stench. Fortuitously, it seemed she required none of them, for another man stepped up and delivered a sharp left hook into the roiling swamp of the breathing hazard's face. He went down with an admirable crack, right onto the tile where a busboy began to unceremoniously sweep the rubbish out the back door.

"Huzzah!" the diners cried, and began to congratulate Hargreaves' savior. They looked meaningfully into the inspector's eyes. Etiquette demanded some response, but Hargreaves lacked the social vocabulary. At last, she spotted a waitress enthusiastically lifting a half-full pot.

"Might I buy you a cup of coffee?" Hargreaves managed, wincing as she said the word. It elicited another round of applause.

Her rescuer turned out to be a well-dressed man of middling means, with a kempt brown beard and remarkably pale eyes. As first impressions went, Hargreaves could find no fault with his. He struck her as an earnest fellow perhaps a touch older than herself. His name was Herbert Holm Howard, or Howard, as the townspeople seemed to prefer calling him.

"Thank you," Hargreaves managed, though she would have preferred a quiet meal and a soft bed to the drama. Her nerves were strained from imagined plots and actual danger.

"That was Wilford Appleby, one of Appleton's fallen sons. We take care of our own," Howard said, as he nursed a cup of black coffee. His knuckles, perched on long craftsman's fingers, were flushed red where he had decked Appleby.

"What happened to him?" Hargreaves asked, curious despite herself.

"In life? Failed in the city, slunk back to Appleton with just the clothes on his back. It's a common enough story. Jill, the waitress over there, tried her luck as an actress," Herbert said, wincing as he shook out his hand. A heavy, paper-wrapped cylinder fell from it with a thunk. "Just now? I was palming a roll of quarters."

Hargreaves laughed. Her food arrived then, a sad, limp bovine corpse on soggy bread and wilted salad greens. She was reasonably sure she had seen the chef take the patty out of a can before slapping it onto a grill. The chips were suitably greasy, but cut too small. The apple pie, however, was spectacular, and she was told it was on the house.

"I was under the impression America was a land of plenty, rich with industry, ingenuity and the fat of the land," said Hargreaves. "But there were an awful lot of people like Mister Appleby, coming up from New York. I hope you do not mind my saying so, but the reality falls short of the dream."

Hargreaves had passed shuttered houses and people destitute, living out of their still-warm jalopies. She had parked Alphonse by lots full of clacking boilers, with the windows blocked out by belongings, not yards from centers advertising the latest in clockworked home conveniences. As an enforcer of the law, she wondered where the destitute could turn if a woman amongst them fell prey to abusers. She wondered how many amongst them could afford to eat.

Howard glanced amusedly at Hargreaves' table manners. At a nearby table, another diner was holding his burger with both hands, tucking in with a bloody gusto. Hargreaves snorted, and continued her surgery.

"Do not forget: we are a nation built by people leaving the old world. We're stubbornly independent," said Howard. He looked toward the street where he had just thrown out poor Mr. Appleby. "Even when we are demonstrably sick."

Hargreaves suddenly felt like a right git.

"The coffee, at least, is strong," Hargreaves said.

"If you need to stay awake this evening, there's Miracle Drop at the fountain," said Howard. Where he looked, Hargreaves saw no statues or vaulted sprays of water, only the row of vile-smelling faucets.

"Miracle Drop?" asked Hargreaves.

"Maybe it is the old country that is backward, if you've not heard of pop. Here, I'll order us some," Howard said.

Hargreaves did, in fact, know of pop. She was accustomed to a lovely amaretto fizz in summer, at her favorite Italian café in Leicester Square. Sometimes she would treat herself to a dish of strawberries, inexpensive in season and matched with the nuttiness of the drink.

What the waitress brought roiling and whizzing to the table did not much smell like pop. In fact, Hargreaves rather fancied she saw the spilled droplets eating through the façade of the table.

"This is Miracle Drop," Howard declared, inserting a straw and drinking, to Hargreaves' horror.

"What does it taste like?"

"Err...red, I think."

"That is not touching my lips," Hargreaves declared. The stuff gave a protesting sort of gurgle, like mad science gone sentient.

"Amazing what our ateliers can do. The trains bring the raw material, and the contraptions turn it into a beverage on the spot. And for a fraction of the cost we used to pay for tonics," said Howard.

"Cost that was paid for brewers and vintners. Jobs Mr. Appleby might have done," said Hargreaves. "There's value in the human touch."

"But where's the money in it?" Howard said. He took another sip, before shrugging. "Somebody has to make a profit. And Appleby wouldn't take the work. He used to be a millionaire."

Hargreaves shook her head, speechless. It seemed beneath the fizzing red glitz of this nation, something was subtly rotting away. But she was one to talk—her own government was contemplating using disease as a weapon.

After the inexcusable dinner, Howard was the perfect gentleman, taking the time to lead her to a respectable boarding house in the center of the town. The signboard outside showed a merry sort of worm coming out of an apple and the words "Early Bird Bed and Breakfast" woodworked in cheerful copperplate. The worm was on a cam and a spring, so it poked its head out at certain intervals. The sign was nearly invisible in the dim light of a gas streetlamp, the only one on the street.

Howard insisted on helping Hargreaves check in with the elderly owners, who greeted Howard on sight. They looked identical, gray-haired and pearly, like a pair of matching porcelain dolls.

"Room 2D," said the elderly woman, the front desk half of the pair. Howard took the key and passed it to Hargreaves. "And the husband can take care of your luggage."

"Oh, no, I couldn't possibly," said Hargreaves. The elderly man looked hale enough, but Hargreaves had a deceptively heavy assortment of small arms and incendiaries in her carpetbag. The sparker alone would have caused a significant uproar. She struggled for a white lie.

"There are some delicate samples I can entrust to no other. In fact, once I purchase some coal for my engine tomorrow, I must get going."

"Didn't you come in on the bus?" Howard remarked.

"Yes. The driver found me waylaid on the side of the road, and was kind enough to offer me a ride," she lied. Howard nodded.

"A shame. Howard talks to so few women, let alone a nice young lady. All the nice ladies are gone," the elderly woman said, writing in the hotel's thick, mostly blank registry.

"Gone?"

"To the city, I imagine. Here one day, and not the next."

"And which city is that?" said Hargreaves, both flushed and endeared to the lady's remark.

"Why, New York City, of course. No other."

"Esther, Miss Hargreaves, I believe I will bid you a good night," said Howard. He tipped his hat as he went.

"See? A right gentleman. Although one does wonder what he gets up to, with no wife in the house," said Esther. Hargreaves blushed, as Esther looked at her pointedly. But eventually Hargreaves secured the room key and climbed the stairs to a small room, one of four on that floor. Curiously, the hall kept going for another few meters, and Hargreaves thought perhaps the other rooms had quite luxurious floorplans.

As soon as Hargreaves found her room, she quietly closed the door and fussed about, picking her heavy bag up and putting it down in different places. When she was sure Howard had gone, she went downstairs again and approached the front desk.

"Why, the room is delightful, just delightful, but I'm driving several hours in the morning, and I'd sooner not look on the road while I'm resting," Hargreaves explained as the innkeeper nodded empathically.

"Those dreadful engines! With their racket and soot. I understand, dearie. Here you go." Esther smiled as she handed Hargreaves another key. It opened room 2B, directly opposite her current room.

Hargreaves regarded such practices as second nature. Though idyllic Appleton had its charms, she had not forgotten she was being pursued. So she braced the door with the vanity chair, and confirmed she could climb out of the window if necessary.

Then she sighed, loosed her golden tresses, and settled into the quilted comforter with a depressed sort of poof. She wondered when she had even begun to have these habits. Was it when she became an agent of the Queen? When the pips had landed on her shoulder, making her a plainclothes inspector? Hargreaves suspected it was even further back than that, but before she could go there her mind drew a veil of sleep over the waking world.

Half an hour later, she was suddenly awakened by the sound of a floorboard creaking. Through the fog of sleep, she slowly worked out the sound was coming from the hallway just outside her door.

"Likely the innkeep's," Hargreaves thought. "Or a resident out to the loo." Nevertheless, she got out of bed, still fully dressed, and extracted her 9mm Browning from the carpetbag. She tucked the Browning into the band of her skirt and drew the Bowie knife. Then she looked through her peephole. The moon in the hall window was bright enough, and she didn't bother with the room's gas lamp.

Howard? thought Hargreaves. Kneeling at the keyhole of 2D, her savior was stealthily but vigorously picking the lock. She wouldn't have thought the pleasant man such a deviant, but there he was, kneeling in his well-starched trousers, intent on assaulting her in her boudoir. Hargreaves huffed. She might have stayed in the room if she'd known there would be an opportunity to thoroughly thrash a sexual predator.

The door to 2D swung open, and she saw the shadow of Howard go into the room. Her view was blocked by the edge of the peephole, but she heard the footsteps. With the full intention of confronting the dastard, she slipped open the door to 2B.

The blow was stealth itself, but the hard object across her temples hurt no less than if she had seen it coming. Her knife fell quietly to the rug in the hall. It would have been melodrama to faint straight away, but Hargreaves was no fragile blossom. She whirled round, her head stinging abominably, to see the vicious Howard somehow wedged into a blind spot behind a delightful bureau. His eyes were wide, the skin flush and wet, the lips open to reveal perfectly white, straight teeth. He had a knife, too, a long, thin switch that sprang cheerfully into the moonlight.

Hargreaves waited for Howard to lunge, before stepping aside and putting her knee into his abdomen. The knife snickered back across in a vicious slash, and the inspector's training took over. She grabbed the knife hand in a Roman handshake along the wrist, and struck at the heel, bending the arc into Howard's chest.

"Gahh..." said Howard, wheezing through a new and unnatural aperture.

Hargreaves took a step back, expecting blood, only to bite her lip as the head came up and clobbered her clean under the jaw. Her last sight was of the ceiling, and the empty hallway behind her, before her crown came down on something hard.

When the stars had faded from her eyes, she saw Howard stumble down the hall. When she followed, she found a dead end—and a secret door that had not been properly shut, leaving a hair's breadth of opening and a bit of a draft.

Wondrous. Hargreaves sighed. She had been in Appleton a day, and already the ghosts of this small town west of all she knew were swirling around her ankles, begging to be exorcised. She drew her Browning.

Time to get to work, Inspector.

STATION 2

In Maman's Footsteps

CEZETTE LOUISSAINT EXPECTED MAMAN TO BE DIFFICULT TO FIND. After all, Vanessa Hargreaves was a trained inspector of Scotland Yard, with all the familiarity with stealth, steamcrafts, and hand-to-hand combat essential to evading capture. And she would need all her skills now. Who had led Cezette and Hargreaves' friends this far? Who had summoned those ghastly metal spiders that so ravaged New York in Hargreaves' pursuit? And what was the spectral train that had pulled out of the station when Cezette saw her maman escape those spiders?

It was the airship pirates again who had saved Maman, of that Cezette was sure. But what had happened after? Not even Arturo C. Adler could tell. So here they were, driving by induction alone to find her.

Cezette perched her slim shoulders on the seat back and arranged her clockworked legs a little more comfortably, so she could look out the window. The roads in America were longer and straighter than Parisian alleys, and wider than God. Flat gravel rivers of tar turned to rounded paving in the towns. Untamed foliage threatened to undo civilization from the banks of the road. There could be a dozen whirring, clacking monsters in the greenery, and they would never know. That was how thick and wild this country could be.

Cezette took comfort in her maman's resume. Hargreaves had been made an agent of the English Queen herself, survived and befriended an air pirate crew, and had the help of an iron giant built by the best craftsmen in Her Majesty's service. If anybody could get away with the Cook box, her maman could. But Cezette didn't have much hope of catching up to her in their stolen New York taxi leaking steam from a dozen cracks, bullet holes and seams. And though MAD—Hargreaves' hand-picked unit—had become like family to her, Cezette wasn't particularly fond of sharing a steaming sedan cabin with four older men.

Wait.

What was that?!

Merde!

Suddenly her maman's trail proved all too easy to follow, or so Cezette hoped. For a moment she thought the blisters of police lights were the ones from her past, when Mordemere had laid waste to her beloved Paris. But though they resolved into American patrols, there were too many of them, and their markings reflected several different authorities. Jean Hallow, her tutor dozing in the back seat, had taught her to tell the difference. But even had she not known, and even with the dense coverage, it was difficult to miss the flocks of screaming, steaming police lorries tearing down the road, leaving rooster tails of gravel and panic.

"*Alors!* Look, look!" said Cezette, rousing the napping pile in the back seat. Uncle Cid, who was driving through what seemed an impenetrable gray beard, nodded that he had seen as well.

"Deuced loud, those American rozzers," Arturo grumbled sleepily from the backseat. "What're they on about?" The detective who had insisted on MAD following Vanessa Hargreaves to America had seemed less keen on the idea when he discovered the sheer distances the country was full of.

"Those patrol *chasseurs*, they are all headed to the same place. Do you think another of the spider contraptions is loose?" said Cezette. Her voice drew huge, bleary looks, but there was recognition in Arturo's face, at the least. The toff had lost some of his glitz on the trip, but preserved a remarkable amount of lace. Jean Hallow, on the other hand, emerged from his torpor as he always did: like the undead. Hargreaves had selected him for his skill, not for his charm at society soirees.

"And what if Hargreaves has already gone on ahead?" grumbled Arturo.

"I think we all need a respite from this dreadful cab," said Hallow.

"Consider it done," said Cid in his usual basso profundo. "None too soon. My nethers feel like they've been clamped in a torque vice."

"Cid!" said Arturo. "There is a lady present!"

"I also feel as if I'm carrying a *bébé* in my petticoats," said Cezette, to the detective's mortification. Cid exchanged a conspiratorial wink.

"I could also use the facilities," agreed Hallow. Arturo huffed.

"Well, carry on then!"

Despite the levity, there was a sort of grim note to their exchange. None of them could forget the destruction the metal spiders, some as big as houses, had wrought. And where chaos was, Hargreaves and her metal guardian would be. After all, MAD had followed her by trailing the casual destruction left by her dastardly pursuers. Ominous and nebulous, their enemies had caused several pitfalls to appear in downtown Manhattan, and also flattened a small town.

The group took the closest turnabout and followed the sound of yowling cats to an exit, where the road deteriorated into a two-lane country track and thence into a five-street small town. MAD found the wailing sirens of the constables crawling all over a small shop. It was flanked on every side by fire engines and steaming-hot police vehicles.

And as Cid pulled around the spot to look for a place to stop, Cezette corrected herself; those were police officers, and the shop was a general store. Jean Hallow had been coaching her on proper nomenclature, and the effect it had on "the common people." Linguistics and psychology were subjects the archivist seemed strangely keen on. He had stressed the importance of using them, particularly around figures of authority in foreign places.

Cezette applied her learning as soon as they had relieved themselves at a nearby eatery. She walked down the road, up to one of the stern, uniformed men and tried being as direct as she imagined Americans would be.

"*Mon dieu!* Officer, what happened here?"

The straitlaced uniform looked to her, then up past her as if he had never seen such a strange assembly of characters. She followed his gaze, to find Arturo a ways back along the road, intent on staring at everything dramatically, his spiky platinum hair quivering as he did. *Merde!* Cezette had hoped her modest clothes would make a good impression. She had made sure not to show any of the machinery of her legs, which were not flesh and bone but lacquer and mixed metals.

"Run along. A crime scene is no place for tourists," the uniform began, but when he saw Cezette more curious than pale, he relented. Perhaps he figured it was safer she go away, morbid interest satiated. "There's a lot of blood in the hallway of the inn. We're trying to find the body now."

"The body. You are sure they died?" Cezette inquired. Then the implication took her— what if it was her maman? A surge of Arturo's detecting lessons pumped into her head. "Was there gold hair? The time frame? Is the blood dry? *Les preuves, monsieur!*"

"The what? You got some wild ideas in your head. Did you see it in a picture? Crazed directors these days, making all kinds of oddness. I blame those plains-crawler dirigibles. Traveling always gives folks strange ideas." At this point, the officer found he was talking to himself.

Cezette had already turned away from him, intent on the rest of the scene. The others had also moved on, Cid drifting toward a nearby cafe for his morning cuppa, Jean loitering by the police vehicles. Arturo was casually conversing with the lead officer on the scene, but he soon stopped. His face announced it was a cut-and-dried case, or in Arturo's vernacular, boring. He seemed distracted, or nervous, glancing at the police vehicles as well. It seemed she had a little time to poke about, as it were.

Cezette felt quite odd. Something about this little town smelled of Maman. The place was certainly in range of Alphonse's loping limbs, if a bit toward the west. His pistons were not so different from those below her thighs. For a moment, Cezette thought back to when Maman pulled her from a clockwork horror, only to find she had emerged without her legs. Uncle Cid had given her new ones, with the stipulation she learn to maintain them herself. Cezette didn't need to be told twice. She loved her regained freedom. It was a gift that meant a lot to a girl who used to be trapped all her days; so she used them now, stepping lightly onto the crime scene, being careful to leave no trace. Her heels tended to press harder than any young woman's ought to.

When all four police officers had their heads turned, Cezette pirouetted on smoothly oiled knees and slipped into the inn, barely ruffling the cordon of thin crime ribbon. Inside, sunbeams lanced through dust motes, peacefully lighting up an abandoned front desk. Cezette instinctively took the stairs, remembering her maman's teachings about high ground. When she got there, it didn't take any detective training to see the ugly splotch of red, darkening to a mauve brown at the edges. It was dramatic, still wet at the center, but not nearly enough to kill. Cezette knew that much. The stain dripped away across the carpet, and around a corner.

Arturo had been teaching her the craft of detection in spare moments on the airship across the Atlantic. She looked around, trying to get the feel of the place. There were drops scattered some distance apart —two people? Scuffed rugs. An unlocked door, and a recently picked one, that was clear from the scratches. But the rooms themselves were empty, without a single sock even in the wardrobes.

There was also a lock of blonde hair caught on a door hinge. Cezette smelled it carefully: airships' aeon steam, and the faint perfume of lilac, some days old. Even though she hadn't mastered the art of detecting completely, she knew one thing immediately: Maman had been here! But where had she gone?

"If there's been a theft, follow the money. If there's a body, follow the blood." Arturo's maxim. She followed the blood, leading her around the corner and smack dab into a dead end. The hallway terminated at a little nook, with a decorative table set against a blank wall.

"*Sacre bleu!*" Cezette cried, but softly. She rubbed her knee where it had banged it, though it didn't hurt. She was simply rather protective of Cid's gifts. But as she looked down, she observed the droplets of blood go right up to the wall. Tellingly, one of the tiny, perfect circles was cut in half by the edge of the wainscoting.

Cezette felt around. Under the lacy edge of the table's doily, she discovered a tiny toggle switch made of brass. When she tripped it, there was no visible change or sound, but the wall felt just a little bit looser, as if no longer part of the inn's firmament. Cezette pushed. The section of wall fell back, taking the table with it to reveal a secret passageway.

"Alors," murmured Cezette. "Won't Arturo be jealous?"

She slipped inside, her lithe body finding the crawlspace quite spacious. A man would have trouble with the low ceilings, she surmised. Once between the bare slats, she found there were cunning slits in the walls to let in the light. At the moment, they were showing scuffs, drag marks, old tears in the wadding of the wall. Cezette gasped, but she kept her head, looking for the fresher blood. And it was there, now outlined in a footprint. No, two. There was the trace of a large shoe. Heavy tread —a large man? Or someone struggling...

Cezette followed the crawlspace well past the physical limits of the inn. At this point, she must be in the adjacent building, which was, as she recalled, a mixed-use residence with a general store on the first floor. What she would call *une epicerie*. She was about to feel for a door seam or catch when suddenly the space opened up into a room about the size of a large closet. The wall simply ended, slats sticking out of the plaster like ribs. She was looking at a room with white walls and a single object in it.

When she got close, the object turned out to be a wooden horse, dark with old blood. Not the kind she looked for in a toy shop window, but the kind Cezette only knew from a book on medieval torture her tutor Jean Hallow had accidentally brought her. Victims would be sat, naked, on the sharp triangular block and given weights to hold. The torture took days, and it would be agonizing, until the person simply died from the blood loss or infection. How much of the torture was simply the knowledge that, even if the tortured survived, they would never be the same again? Why did Hallow have such a tome to begin with? Cezette hadn't dared ask.

Now Cezette covered her mouth, feeling her gorge rise. Had Maman been subjected to this?

The fresher drops led around the horse, thankfully. Cezette stepped carefully around the terrible thing, trying not to let it touch her pinafore. She arrived at another blank wall. Puzzles upon puzzles...but the person who was bleeding had been careless. A splatter of blood showed where he had stumbled, and Cezette placed one dainty shoe against the board outlined there. The wall fell back, again impossibly quietly, and there before her was another tiny, cramped crawlspace.

As she passed by a cleverly hidden panel, a bear trap tripped on utterly silent, oiled hinges, its teeth glinting cheerfully in the dark.

"*La vache!*" cried Cezette in surprise. *The cow!*

Steeling herself, she looked down—to find she was quite all right. If she were all flesh and blood, her ankle would have been crushed. But she was steel and enamel below the knees, and the teeth of the trap merely made her stumble, biting ineffectively on her shin. Cid's steel was better —it chipped the rusted teeth of the trap. Clearly, the thing had been meant to maul, not to sever.

Gingerly, Cezette extracted herself, careful not to snag her long, raven hair on the edges of the walls. Pulling the trap out of its hiding place, she tossed it forward down the crawlspace. And it was a good thing too. The contraption triggered two more traps: a cutting wire that struck sparks against the bear jaws and a deadfall sandbag that dropped from the ceiling, swinging back and forth through the passage. As the bear trap landed, it crashed through a false floor and made a clattering noise. When Cezette moved carefully to the lip, passing a few other rooms, she saw there were sharpened stakes on the next floor down, ready to impale someone who fell through. The place was a house of horrors. What sort of perverted mind would build something like this?

She didn't know what to expect after that, but she picked carefully forward, with her toes first, and discovered a convoluted passageway full of blind corners and dead ends. Ladders ascended toward the roof, and parts of the hall sloped disarmingly. On the other side was a steep metal slide leading down to the first floor, or more likely a basement, where the fresh blood made a wet skid on the surface. The steel dropped away into the darkness, and there was a foul smell, like bad eggs and pennies.

Cezette placed herself at the top of the slide and looked. She was no fool. Cezette was well aware there might be more traps below. But her days of being trapped in her room above the Rue Fremicourt had honed her sense of danger to a fine edge. Even so, when she slid carefully down the slide, she became aware of something else in the room and gasped, nearly falling over her own feet.

Just beside the bottom of the slide was a body.

Voices and a rustling above caught her unawares. A door somewhere was opening!

Startled, Cezette's heel fell on something uneven on the floor. She felt the weight shift through her hips, her legs unable to compensate, and she caught a nearby shelf for balance. There were unsavory things on the shelf, brown with old blood.

"What was that noise?"

"There's somebody downstairs!"

The loud shifting brought the voices closer. A basement stair? She had surely slid for more than two stories. But in the time before the voices arrived, Cezette quickly took in the dim room for anything useful. The smell was stronger, choking in the enclosed space. The body was a man, his chest a ragged wound, but fresh—the smell could not be from him. His head looked wrong, misshapen, and there was a wet-looking hammer shining at his side. Signs of a struggle: an upset workbench, scattered tools. And, *mon dieu*, were those rags, or bodies? More blood, old, some of it on the shop stair. There! A second stair, with daylight peeking through the trap door at the top.

Just before she ran to the stair, Cezettte managed to scoop the object that had tripped her off the floor and into the front of her pinafore. Maybe it was instinct, or a vindictive sense of needing to know what had befuddled her beautiful prosthetics, but she did it without quite knowing why. Then, she confronted her only means of escape.

It was locked. A heavy brown chain linked the handles of the trap door.

Cezette wasted no time. She took off her shoe and kicked with her hard metal heels. The chain crumbled into rust, and she was outside even as the basement began to fill with the footsteps of officers. She closed the doors behind her quietly, put her shoe back on and walked casually around to the front of the building.

Then Cezette disappeared, blending into the crowd.

Cid had just come back with coffees for everyone in pasteboard cups plastered with some obnoxious green branding when Cezette sauntered up to the old cab.

"The tea they serve up here is beastly, some faded ghost of a Keemun or a Ceylon. But the lattes are not bad. What do you have there, Cezzy?" said Cid. He said it with concern, but Cezette appreciated the fact that he didn't make a grab for it. She was visibly flustered, she knew, and her leggings on one side were chewed to threads. But Cezette managed to climb into the cab, and they eased off down the road even as the officers began to pile out of the front of the general store, some of them vomiting into the bushes.

"A notebook, I think," Cezette said. "From the crime scene."

"Hum," Arturo said. He shifted a blind inside the cabin of the taxi, and a beam of light lanced into his lap. "Give it here."

"What happened?" asked Hallow.

Cezette filled them in, trying to keep to the facts as Arturo had taught her. But their conclusion was the same as her own.

"This man in the basement must have been killing people for ages with his beastly torture house," summed up Cid, clearly disgusted. "Funneling people from the inn. A hotel where you check in and never leave."

"And for once it went horribly wrong," finished Arturo. "My, my, our Inspector Hargreaves would have beat seven bells out of a serial murderer."

"Is it Maman?"

"We shall see," said Arturo, opening the notebook.

Inside they found a few torn pages, a scribble of some aborted poetry, some lists of numbers and calculations done in a hurried pencil. The rest of the book was blank.

Cezette slumped back in her seat, disappointed. It was *merde* like this that convinced a girl her instincts were useless, she thought to herself.

Arturo's amused mumbling brought her out of her slump.

"Well, hullo, Inspector. I believe we are not far from you at all," he said.

"Show me!" Cezette demanded. She lunged out of her seat, and her skirt rode up over the part of her leggings that was ripped.

"Girl! What did I say about taking care of those legs!" shouted Cid.

There was a moment when the whole cab shuddered with Cid's angry piloting, and everybody else tumbled about inside the cabin. The notebook went flying out of Cezette's hands.

Once things were put right, Arturo explained he had been on the receiving end of Hargreaves' missives before. Once he pointed out the straight, clear strokes and the no-nonsense block print, her handwriting was as plain as day. The calculations were promising. It was Cid who proposed they could be fuel and distance figures. Arturo pulled out their map.

"Assuming your maman was there in the shop, almost the victim of a current-day Pit and Pendulum, and further, managed to dispatch the torturer, she would want to put as much distance as she could from it as soon as possible," Arturo said. He pointed to a wriggling India ink line he had drawn, one of several highlighting various routes. They wound through mile after mile of untamed lands, wild forests and proud mountains surely unfriendly to any steam crafts.

"If she started one night ago, she may be on this road here," Cid filled in. "The grade is level, and it has short intervals between towns where she can find coal, water, and food."

"Those figures are enormous," said Hallow. "Hundreds of miles at the least."

"We will never reach her in time," Cezette bemoaned. She thumped the side of the poor suffering taxi.

"Where the devil are you going, Hargreaves?" Arturo asked. "Where are you dumping the box?"

His finger traced the map routes spread out between them in the cabin. Cezette imagined his gentle digits flying over the pines, giant, manicured tips brushing the rocky heights of the Appalachians, and into the vast flats beyond, the plains and the desserts. There would be no automata there, just lengths upon lengths of endless distance to keep the world from the terror riveted inside Maman's iron box. Only waystations marked the interminable distances, beacon towers that only existed to field the vast plains dirigibles on their slow crawl from one middle of nowhere to another. Cezette looked at the veins spread out over the vastness, and the capillaries below them crawling where Arturo's finger lay. Then she looked over the coast, to the Pacific, and past it, towards the gray veil hiding the interminable vastness of the Lands Beyond.

The perfect place to dispose of the Cook box.

Arturo's face spread into a roguish grin. The grin soon spread to Cid's lips, and the two of them sat there, teeth bared like baboons. Then they both looked outside, to a road sign just coming round the bend.

"What is it about Britons and trains?" Cezette said aloud, and sighed pleasurably.

They might have missed Maman in New York, but she could feel their reunion coming now, like the undeniable rush of a locomotive engine.

STATION 3

Montana

VANESSA HARGREAVES' BREATH CAME IN A RAGGED WHEEZE, SO LOUD she was terrified of it bouncing over the mountains and into keen ears.

She risked a glance out of the stand of trees; nothing, no more gunshots, though because this state had legalized hunting with silencers, the quiet was far from reassuring. The last scream had come from at least thirty yards down, difficult to gauge with the thick temperate arbor pressing in on all sides. It was pitch black, even though in the day she would have been in sight of the town. The town's leaders hadn't wanted to make it easier for bandits, and had installed no gaslights along its streets. An antediluvian attitude at first unbelievable, until the sun set and she was left with the blanket of night that had comforted cavemen so many eons ago. It made staying hidden a cakewalk, but Hargreaves imagined she saw the shapes of wild things, restless spirits perhaps, abandoned idols cantering with eagle-feathered antlers.

She considered making a break over the next ridge. It would be an ankle-breaking climb over rocks, in the dark, sliding down the slippery rot of leaves. In this part of the country, the snow had not descended across the plateaus. Alphonse was waiting for her behind a ridge near the road, an impervious titan. The only problem now was running through those wolf-infested woods without getting shot to bits by her pursuers.

How had she arrived at this unenviable pickle? She hadn't stopped asking herself since coming to this confusing place, this mournful place, so at odds with itself, this town of Spelter, Montana.

After the dreadful business at the waystation, Hargreaves took the next woolly bear out as far as it went, over the desert, and then took off on Alphonse alone. She couldn't risk being connected to a murder, or running into the Ripper. Following a dim notion of keeping the Cook box from seeing the light of day, she turned west, where the world stretched out and the distances between places were still full of places to hide. She hired a man with a lorry, loaded Alphonse on the back, and at the first opportunity drove away alone, leaving the driver on the side of the road. It had been easy—she had simply asked him to close his eyes and take off his trousers, then turned and walked quickly to the cab. She had felt little guilt, which in itself made her feel terrible.

And so, eventually Hargreaves reached the beautiful state of Montana, which seemed to her an open ocean on land: miles and miles of murderous golden desert gradually fading to rolling waves of hilly green grass in the western part of the state. Majestic plateaus skewed across the endless horizon, vast, flat ships of slate braving the waves. Roving schools of wild horses and bison occasionally came into view. Hargreaves had been reading on the Red Indians who lived here, books snatched from waystation parlors mostly. It was easy to see where their idea of a Great Spirit had come. Winter had come, but the life hadn't gone from the lowlands. She wondered if the spirits knew her mission, if they would aid her in her quest.

Eventually she entered those mountains and plateaus, larger than any she had ever seen. And here she saw the majesty of the American spirit for the first time, for there were signs of life clinging to those naked rocks. It showed itself in the bright green of garden plots high on the cliffs, basin-like scaffolds that irrigated and watered the crops, and the slab-like homes wedged into the crags of the cliffs. They had long, smooth roofs to catch the sunshine for the boilers inside. The whole flat table of the mountains was their home, and on the roofs stood tall, spire-like balloons ready to fly in the clear sky, their rounded tops shaped with wagon-wheel frames of spry wood. Aeon farmers, by the look of them. And by hearsay. Hargreaves could only deduce at a distance the great condensing sails that drew the stratosphere down along the narrow envelopes and the great tanks that would hold that fortune, just like the waystation pamphlets had advertised. As they filled, they would slowly draw the balloons back to the mountaintops, where the tanks could be unhitched and the balloons fitted again. In the distance, a slew of tall balloons were descending on farther peaks, and the stone framed the brilliant blue horizon with stark ruby beauty. As she watched, an airship drifted slowly by on spinning square sails, like a great windmill that had torn loose from the rolling green hills.

The inspector turned her eyes from the spectacle with difficulty and tried to keep her mind on the small roads. These were a challenge, meandering, rocky paths bravely cut from the great American wilderness. She fancied there were bears and wolves peering out at her from the bushes. But when she looked closer, she instead came upon herds of penned-in cattle, gleaming with velvety brown flanks and shining, well-kept hooves. Perhaps one in ten glinted with the unmistakable rust-red of steamworks that had been left in the rain for some years, though the cattle did not seem to mind. They were hard to make out, but Hargreaves found a cow quite close who had a shoulder covered with a pitted, rust-dappled plate. The thing seemed to be riveted onto the animal's shoulder bone, though it displayed no discomfort as it chewed its cud placidly.

Hargreaves discovered just what they were when she stopped to buy a cannister of milk and some finely ground cornmeal from a farmer who was stopped with his cart. A cow and an ox grazed nearby, unhitched from their yoke. The heifer was a lovely caramel red, but the other bore a hodge-podge of metal in lieu of his back leg. When the animal's rump settled on the leg, it hissed softly through a round copper valve. The farmer laughed when she asked about it.

"Ruby and Copper? They've been with me for, oh, six seasons now. Copper ran into some coyotes and lost his back leg two summers ago. Time was we would have shot him on the spot for the meat." The farmer struck Copper's meat buttock cheerfully as he trod closer. Copper paid him no mind.

"So what did you do?"

"Well, I need him to pull my cart, don't I? The scrap yards are full of broken horse, and it's easy enough to hammer out a fit."

"Doesn't it just stop when the coal runs out?" asked Hargreaves. Automata horses needed to eat fuel, or their furnaces would stop.

"No, we just shovel his pies into the chute, and they burn well enough."

"Pies?" asked Hargreaves, but in a moment she received a most unwelcome demonstration, which hastened her departure.

"Wait a moment," said the farmer. He whistled, and Hargreaves looked on quizzically. But she didn't wait long, for in a few moments a man appeared from behind a dip in the road. He had straw in his hair, and was quite handsome, with a strong aquiline profile. It looked like he had been taking a nap in the sun. Hargreaves drew in her breath. His strong, muscled stomach peeked out from between the buttons of his white shirt.

"This is Funny Goat. The name is on account of he's a half-Blackfoot," said the farmer. "Some sick sort of joke by the tribe, I thought at first."

"No joke," said Funny Goat simply.

"Hello, Mr. Goat," said Hargreaves, a little at a loss. "I'm Vanessa Hargreaves."

Funny Goat tipped his head to her and a little straw drifted to the ground.

"He's been helping me with the harvest, but I think he's fixing on going west. Why don't you ask the nice lady if you can ride in the back?" said the farmer.

"Oh, no, it's quite all right. The cabin is much more comfortable," said Hargreaves hastily. She didn't want Funny Goat poking around and discovering either Alphonse or the Cook box.

"Thank you," said Funny Goat. "The back is fine. I have a little money, and I am used to hardship."

The way his big brown eyes looked at her made Hargreaves feel the blush start to creep into her neckline. She just hoped her tan would cover it.

"No, it's no trouble," said Hargreaves, who had known more than a little kindness already on the road. "Are you sure you wouldn't like the cabin? There's buckwheat cushions, and we could get to know each other," Hargreaves wanted to say, but the words choked tight.

"Down that way's Spelter," said the farmer with a strange cadence to his voice. "Those folks don't take kindly to Injuns. Or Blackies, Mexies, Chinamen. Anybody not your pretty color, to be honest. It'd be better if he hid in the back for a spell."

"Oh," said Hargreaves. Before she could protest, Funny Goat climbed the back of the lorry and hunkered down low under the cloth canopy. She tried not to stare at the backs of his legs pulling his chaps up. "I suppose I could sneak him past the town. There's a blanket in the back there, Mr. Goat."

A hand came up and waved in acknowledgment.

"You're a good egg, miss," said the farmer. "Not often you see a woman traveling on her own in the country. Let alone one with the gumption to help a man, 'specially a red man."

"Everybody needs a helping hand once in a while," said Hargreaves. "Truth is, I don't believe I've been a very good person of late."

"I think this will help put your accounts right," said the farmer. "Funny Goat's led a hard life. He's been waiting for a ride for a week, but the moment people 'round here see his Injun nose, it's like he's got the pox on him. It's those papers, talking about the Blackfoot threat all the time. Half those raids are white men dressed up in feathers and making damn fools of themselves, you mark my words." He started cluck-clucking around like the birds in his cart.

Hargreaves laughed, nodded enthusiastically and took her purchases to the cabin. She made to give Funny Goat one of the corn cobs she'd bought, but turned only to see a wide-brimmed hat pulled over his face and his chest rising and falling evenly. She shrugged, left the farmer to his cart, and drove on down the road.

The meandering back roads took their toll on Hargreaves' coal and water stores, and she didn't much feel like scraping the dry, grassy mounds from the road to refuel her lorry. Funny Goat seemed comfortable enough on the old straw bales Hargreaves had used to hide Alphonse, though. Eventually she was obliged to use a main road, in the hopes of finding a town. Well paved and free of the old spirits of the West, it took her unerringly forward until it stopped abruptly at a checkpoint placed across a bridge. Hargreaves slowed when she saw it, and pulled over to warn her passenger.

"Hey, Funny Goat. There's a checkpoint here," said Hargreaves, turning to knock on the wall of the cabin. She could see into the lorry bed from a small window, but still started when Funny Goat sat up from the pile of hay. He seemed to become swallowed up in it very easily.

"It's all right," said Funny Goat. He seemed oddly calm. "Just drive up to them."

He could hardly know about Alphonse, disguised as a pile of scrap and some bales of hay. Hargreaves didn't want to draw attention to her own secrets. So she nodded, and soon enough they were on their way.

A double row of sandbags and one horse-drawn phaeton barred the near side of the bridge. There were four patrolmen, who initially seemed quite normal under their practical coats. Each man wore rifles on their shoulders. None of them wore a uniform, nor anything official. It was only when one of the men swept his coat aside to spit out a wad of sick brown tobacco that Hargreaves felt the chills march down her back. Under their coats, every patrolman wore a suit of clanker armor. The spitter strolled amicably toward her window.

"Miss, this here's a routine checkpoint, by order of the Militia of the State of Montana," the man said as he arrived at her elbow. Hargreaves shook off the memory of being chased by hordes of senseless monsters and instead took in the ill fit of the suits, and the slapdash way they had been put together.

"All right," Hargreaves said to the militiaman. "Will you be needing my license and papers?" Of which she had forged a copy, carefully splicing her warrant card photogram onto a legitimate license in the goggle compartment. The papers were in a folder on the passenger seat, but Hargreaves made a show of rifling through some bric-a-brac on the console so she could get a bead on the disturbing armor.

Once she took note of the rusted joints and general air of ill maintenance, she let her breath out in a slow, calming exhale. It was the gait that gave them away, she decided. No, these weren't the cursed hauberks of piston-powered cruelty designed by the mad alchemist Mordemere. She recognized the familiar grates and riveted plates originally designed for plodding livestock. These men had cobbled together suits that surely would be useful against highwaymen with guns, but they would never be driven insane by their corrupting presence. Still, if they looked in the back, she might have to shoot them, and her .22 rounds were never any good against clankers. Alphonse would pass as some automata horse parts. Funny Goat was another matter. If worse came to worst, there were always her trusty feminine wiles.

"Gosh, no." The militiamen laughed. Hargreaves relaxed. "Them Feddie papers ain't worth shit. Pardon my French. Possession is nine-tenths the law out here."

"I have no other papers," said Hargreaves.

"That's all right. A good white gal like you's all right by us," said the man, leering just a bit. Hargreaves could only smile.

"Once we take a look in the back."

She froze, trying not to let her panic show.

But the militiaman was already gesturing to the other two men in clockworked suits, who were just climbing with softly whistling joints into the bed of the lorry. Hargreaves could see them in her mirror, a little. Her foot hovered over the throttle. If they found Funny Goat or Alphonse...

The man jumped into the lorry bed, setting the springs squeaking, and the sound of his steps paused. Hargreaves felt the lorry bounce as he jumped off the back again. Then the first man appeared once more at her window, which was a little like having her heart jump ticking out of her chest. Those damned suits!

"Looks like you're headed to town to trade some scrap," said the militiaman amicably. "Listen, once you're done, the militia like to visit the Corn Hole on the east side. I'd be happy to buy a lady a drink."

"I'm sure," said Hargreaves with what nerves remained to her. She tried to look inviting as she drove off, and was so concerned with getting away and checking on Funny Goat, she nearly missed the tattoo under the man's collar, just peeking out of the makeshift clanker armor. For a moment, Hargreaves thought she saw a treacherous hound.

Two miles past the bridge, she stopped in a deserted side road. She jumped down and walked to the back of the lorry, but Funny Goat was gone.

Instead of the handsome burnished man, Hargreaves found two sturdy feathers joined by a glass bead. A gift, she supposed. She braided the ornament into her hair, admiring herself in a mirror. She hoped Funny Goat would be able to find his way through Spelter unharmed.

Once she reached the town, things began to come more than passing strange. As she turned down the main avenue, a pile of sandbags at the corner made the road difficult to pass. From the milkman to the meter maids, everybody had a characteristic lump in their belts. Hargreaves gasped when she saw a small boy, no older than six or seven, sauntering down the street clutching a brightly painted, child-size rifle. She caught a newspaper that was stuck in a fence nearby, which seemed almost jubilant about the civil unrest that had enveloped Wiliston and Watford City back in the Dakotas. Hargreaves frowned. She had boarded a plains-crawler a few days ago from Sidney, not two towns from those places, and there had been no news of unrest. Not to mention those towns lay on the other side of the ether desert she had just crossed. Where would the news come from then?

There was no shortage of space in the wide streets of Spelter, so Hargreaves left the lorry in a quiet alley and entered the town proper. She wanted to match records from Burgess' books to the town hall ledgers. The numbers were suspicious. For a dealer in gears, Burgess was regularly buying equipment usually used for food processing: grain mills, industrial grinders, tons and tons of salt. If she was passing through, she might as well look into the capacious pantry Burgess was building. But in her darkest heart, Hargreaves also knew what such things could also be used for. The manufacture of boiled hams, yes, but also disease mediums. Pestilence in a can. And Spelter, with its age-old automata horses and its brand of provincial xenophobia, seemed just the innocent sort of place that would produce such things without asking too many questions.

When she reached a Greco-Roman courthouse, she discovered the book she had copied the numbers into was gone, along with some other small notes. Fumbling about, she cursed. Was it still in Alphonse? Or dropped, at the waystation, or at Appleton? Thinking she might telegraph the waystation at least to check, she found the nearest townsperson, a matron on the arm of a large, bearded man who scowled at Hargreaves. Before she could speak, the man interceded rudely.

"Excuse me, I was speaking to the lady," said Hargreaves, affronted.

"I speak for her," said the man. "And she ain't no lady."

Recovering quickly from the rudeness and the double negative, Hargreaves asked for the nearest telegraph. The man pointed to a small general store before hurrying the woman away by the arm. He mumbled something under his breath, something that sounded like "foreigners."

In fact, most of the passersby seemed insulted by her very presence. They kept staring at her corset, worn on the outside, when she walked into the general store. When she addressed the men in it, they wouldn't speak to her. One of them muttered behind her back. She caught something that sounded like "off her leash." She asked the front desk for coal, and was told rather reluctantly that there was a depot within walking distance.

For Vanessa Hargreaves, Scotland Yard Inspector, a pattern began to emerge: a woman out and about on her own was in very poor taste. Despite the bile bubbling up inside her, she had to concede things would go more easily if she was not the subject of the town's ire. The inspector was no stranger to disguise, and it took merely one trip through some untended laundry lines to emerge with trousers, a cap to conceal her golden hair, and a thick vest to hold down her ample bosom. Undoing her corset and modest bustle was a guilty pleasure. As soon as she stepped into the street, her figure instantly separated her from the womenfolk.

"Men. Such dolts," she murmured, with some bitter satisfaction.

A horse-and-four passed by drawn by automata horses. It stopped not far ahead, and two men got out with a crate of magazines. One of them began to display them to passersby, while the other put on a square wooden pack jingling with change. A third man appeared with a long pole that unfurled into a banner depicting a severe-looking man with a priestly collar. Several people appeared to offer custom.

"The latest from Reverend Deveraux on the evils and arrogance of so-called ether science!" the man with the banner advertised.

"Blackfoot scalpers seen south of Missoula! The Ghost Train sighted in Cooperstown, Rugby, and Bottineau—citizens unaccounted for! Is Spelter next? Congress talks soot tax! Coal miners threatened! That'll be a nickel," The second man joined in, as he made change for a customer from his pack. There were switches at one of the straps, which he depressed to produce the change jangling down to a slot at his waist. "Troop ships off the shores of Milwaukee!"

Hargreaves bought one, a twenty-page sheaf about the size of a penny dreadful. It was about as enlightening, the same sort of tripe as the official news. She was just wondering who in their right mind would believe it when she heard another customer gasp.

"They bombed it! They even got to New York!"

Curious, Hargreaves turned the pages of the pamphlet and found a small, blurry photogram. Though she hadn't seen it before, she knew it instantly for what it was; the wreckage of the streets of New York after the great tarantula automata had wrecked the sewers beneath it. The shot had been taken with the iconic shape of the bridge in the background. Shockingly, the headline beneath claimed that foreign powers had collaborated with the Indian nations and conceived to attack. Exactly who those powers were was a matter of some speculation, but the article was not shy about pointing fingers at everyone "from the blacks to the gypsies."

Hargreaves, had had enough of this mockery of journalism. She left the little knot of people surrounding the cart and soon found herself at a market, where she could enjoy her newfound gender freedom somewhat. The collection of stalls was located on a wide green, full of autumn melons and golden corn with tumbling, untrimmed beards. The farmers treated her as if she were a young, beardless man, but at least they smiled and did business. She wondered how they would feel if Rosa or Captain Clemens walked through the market, given the sorts of headlines they were exposed to. It was hard to find a single person not of European descent in Spelter, but easy to see why people who lived out their lives in such plenty would be afraid of losing it to things they had never seen.

More of the automata horses were tied up at some public hitching rails. They got along with flesh-and-blood horses even through mouthfuls of sparking coal chips. Rust tinged the plates of their shins and their bellies. Clearly, the horses had known the sound of automata for a long time, perhaps even grown up as foals scampering about steel flanks. They did not find those clockworked horses strange or terrifying.

"I have to bugger off out of here as soon as I can," murmured Hargreaves to herself. She had been expecting a steamworked utopia when she touched on American shores. Instead, this place seemed rife with ancient ills.

The trains, like they were in every other city she had passed, were not running through Spelter. At the station, she found the ticket office shuttered and the news boards quiet, the long lines of ticking letter tablets flipped to their blank place holder faces. There was some ether traffic at the telegraph office, but with the trains not running across the ether desert to Minneapolis, there was nothing to carry messages from the East than lines buried more than a century ago.

Only the Fred Hornby's next door seemed to be doing well, supplying good food to bustling group of locals. Hargreaves enjoyed a clandestine pastry while she consulted a map behind the counter for the fuel depot. She smiled at the two men behind the counter, a pair of twin brothers she told apart by their demeanor. One stayed behind the service window, a shy man whose dark skin made him almost invisible. The other ran the counter with a smile, a flip of his neatly tied dreadlocks, and a grin. Hargreaves watched him bring food to a pair of ruddy-cheeked ladies sitting near a window. She could just read their lips.

"What in tarnation! You watch where you're putting those thar hands of yours," said one of them.

"Maude, the boy doesn't know any better. And look, he's got the plates on a towel."

"How can you stand people like that?" asked Hargreaves when the waiter came round.

"Hmm? Oh, them," said the waiter as he got Hargreaves more coffee. Truly, she was beginning to see the appeal. "The town's full of them. We'd make no profit if we turned every racist away. And the rail doesn't just bring business, it brings more civilized folk every day, shipped in with every balloon."

"Why ought you care? It's not like it's your place...oh," said Hargreaves as she caught the ocean of meaning in the man's eyes. "Duly chastised, Mr...."

"Cormac. Fredrick, and my brother William. We just bought the franchise a few days ago. Truth be told we're hoping nobody finds out we own the place, and don't just work here," said Frederick, a touch more ominous than Hargreaves cared for.

"What will they do if they find out?" asked Hargreaves. "What would you do?"

"Honestly? Hope the racists don't run very fast."

When she left the Fred Hornby's a little while later, Hargreaves felt more than ready to leave, and headed straight for the fuel depot. She was able to barter for some cans of water and a few bundles of coal. It would get her through the thin part of Idaho and into the gold rush towns of Washington. From there, she thought she might book passage on a ship bound for the Lands Beyond. If the fare was too dear, she could go south where adventurers and explorers congregated more often. Crescent City, or Fort Bragg. But not San Francisco, where she had discovered the Ubique western headquarters had been built. If Officers Ortega and Ferrera were right, Burgess had dark dealings with that seller of sundries, and Hargreaves did not know how far his reach would be. She could see one of their cam and cog markings in that very depot, advertising quality steamworks right over her head. San Francisco would be the belly of the beast, and she would be delivering the Cook box to the enemy.

As she finished her fuel transaction, she overheard two men leaning against a truck, unshaven but otherwise quite civilized. Their truck had been patched with canvas and other impromptu but sturdy materials. One of them was leafing through one of the onerous pamphlets.

"...don't give a damn about us. It's wild out here."

"Don't tell me you believe Devereaux's bupkiss."

"The Blackfoots coming out of their reservations on raiding parties? Nah. But that Ghost Train? I'd rather be safe than sorry. They say it pulls in at the witching hour to let dead men aboard. Its boilers are full of blood, and its lines are strung with the bones of the damned."

"The mayor is saying we shouldn't have repealed all Washington's gun laws. He thinks we can defend ourselves perfectly well even if we wait for a telegraphed check."

"And pay their fees and taxes in the meantime. No, we need our guns now against those Blackfoots and pirates and ghosts and God knows what else. Lazy Mexies taking all the jobs up north, I hear. Uppity niggers too."

"Hey, now, I don't stand for that kind of talk. My cousin is married to a freedman, a decent feller up in Traverse City. Trades in furs, proper businessman he is. T'ain't his fault he's blacker than a kettle."

"Sorry, I knew it. I knew it."

Hargreaves nearly retched. She had been in town for most of a day, and hadn't seen a single Red Indian or blackamoor about in the open, let alone an Arab. Now she knew why. But this talk of the Ghost Train had her attention, though it didn't seem to be the time to think about it.

The attendant had barely finished loading the lorry and unbuckling the water hose when a ringing alarum tore through the air. At once, the space in the fuel depot was a flurry of activity. The two chatting men jumped into their truck and steamed away, rusty pistons clacking up a complaining din. The attendant rushed into the depot's small shop and depressed a large lever. Hargreaves instinctively ducked for cover, thinking she was under fire, but the loud clanking sounds were coming from every water pump and fuel dispensing machine. Experimentally, she tried a hose, which only regurgitated a few hot drops before going dry.

Hargreaves dashed after the attendant, who was trying to lock and bolt the heavy, riveted door. She jammed her boot into the gap. Inside, Hargreaves could just make out a second worker, a rail-thin cashier who had been stocking tea sandwiches. Now these were all over the floor, their paraffin paper wrapping wounded and leaking. The cashier was standing there like a lump of wood, her knobby fingers knit together, lip trembling.

"What's going on?" Hargreaves asked.

"Get out, get out!" said the attendant, trying to pull the door closed. He wasn't very fit, but he was absolutely terrified, and it lent him strength.

"Tell me!"

"You don't want to be on the streets when Commander Scream calls a raid!"

"Scream?" Hargreaves asked. But just then a lock of gold hair slipped out of her cap, and the blood drained from the attendant's cap.

"Wilhelm Scream," he said in a quivering voice. "Now get!"

The attendant was not very strong, a rather corpulent young man with just the beginnings of a beard. The man gave a wheezing shove, looking like he would cough up a lung. Hargreaves let the door go, which promptly slammed shut. There was a metallic groan as a deadbolt was ground heavily into place. The entire depot was armored in heavy bars, the machinery in the lot caged in. She got the hint, and hurried back to her own lorry, with its precious cargo in the back.

She put her hand on the pressure throttle and all the needles buried themselves in the ground. Hargreaves nearly kicked herself—she had let the boiler go cold.

"Bollocks, bollocks, bollocks!"

Precious minutes crawled by as she sat willing the little red needle in the gauge to climb, listening to the alarum sound and the noise of something approaching from the west. A klaxon? A machine howl. She hadn't liked the sound of the name: Wilhelm Scream. It sounded like something from the black forests of the Old World that didn't belong in the wilds of America.

When the gearing finally caught, lurching the vehicle to life, she chortled an exclamation of triumph.

"Yes! Oh, you brilliant bucket of bolts!"

She pulled into the main road just as the street before her lit up orange, as if the sun had set early. In her mirror, a plume of black smoke rose over the town's hall.

This was no business of hers. Hargreaves had no jurisdiction here, and the last thing she wanted was to become more visible to her pursuers. Besides, she was one woman, towing along a great big lump all the forces in the world wanted to get their hands on. What did it matter if the idyllic, oddball people of Montana succumbed to some bandit raid? The road was invitingly empty as she pulled onto the fork leading out of town.

Something clutched at her mind, the precision cogs there caught on some niggling piece of motivation. Instilled by years of service and the Queen's favor, where someone needed help, Hargreaves had always been the first to appear. If she passed someone drowning, she would dive in without removing her corsetry. Her stomach clenched, and it wasn't even her time of the month.

"Bloody Nora," she spat, and spun the lorry's wheel violently.

Hargreaves managed to run the lorry under a concealing ridge. The tires bit into the gravel at the side of the road, chewing them into a gray plume. There was a terrible clunking noise, but she was satisfied the bend completely hid the lorry from view. For a brief, mad moment she thought of ripping the cover off of Alphonse and heading back to town encased in an iron titan. But if anything happened to her, Alphonse and the Cook box would be left to whatever sickness had gripped this place...these people. This...Wilhelm Scream. Formless but oppressive, the shape of the malady escaped her. But she saw it in the eyes, and the ridiculous preparations at the fuel depot. No, better to leave her charges under the ridge for the next strong rain to bury in the American wilds.

It took her only a few minutes to return on foot, but by that time two more plumes of black smoke had sprung up in the midst of town. Her man's clothes did little to keep her own body from working against her, and she had to stop and button the thin coat tightly around her front. For once in her life, she wished for some sort of supportive undergarment to hold down her assets.

Hargreaves had nearly run back into the town proper, and was only one alley away from the smoke and din when in the darkness two black pupils blinked open. Startled, Hargreaves's heels scraped to a halt, and her hand instinctively reached for her gun. She, could not believe she hadn't seen the woman hiding in a corner of the alley where the brick met a wide wooden facade. She would have run right past her if not for the whites of her eyes. An arm appeared with a torn-off board in it, and the fingers that gripped the splintery wood were pale beneath skin as dark as the encroaching night.

"Oh!" said the voice. There was a pause, and then, "You're a woman, aren't you?"

"Where the devil did you come from?" said Hargreaves. She could hear the heavy footfalls of suited militiamen in the street. Why hadn't the woman gone to them for help?

"Hush. They're right around the corner. Lord knows what they'll do to you if they find you in man's clothes."

Her eyes began to adjust, and Hargreaves took her hand from her Tranter's grip. Even from an outline, she could see the woman hiding in the partially boarded up alley was unarmed and clearly unused to violence. Her clothes were old and restrictive, the heavy, the durable linen cumbersome around her ankles. Her long, bundled hair was partially hidden under a shawl. She seemed to have shrunk into herself, a pose that did not suit the regal form of her wide shoulders or her high, clear forehead. It was now furrowed in impatience, and the woman gestured with one hand.

"Come, come!" said the beckoning fingers. Hargreaves slipped into the shadow, which was quite spacious enough to press in next to the woman. To her surprise, there was a small, dark child about four or five years old hiding behind the black woman's skirts.

"Never mind, Emory. It's you, noisy white woman, that should worry," said her nook mate.

"Pardon?" said Hargreaves, her accent leaking through.

"Oh, and English too. They'd get rowdy, those Screamers," concluded the other woman as she pressed her eye to the splintery surface of the boards once more. "So hush!"

For want of understanding, Hargreaves hushed, and peered through one of the cracks in the wooden facade before her. Two of the militiamen were visible, standing clustered around the Fred Hornby's. A clockwork horse stood calmly nearby. As Hargreaves' eye stoppered the light in the frame of the board, a third man stepped out of the cafe, his steps landing heavily into the street. He clomped slowly into view, so at first Hargreaves didn't see the rope he was leading with one armored hand. With a shock, Hargreaves saw the shape of a terrible hound come into view as he turned and the back of his garish red coat swept into view. The hound man let the rope drop to the street and struck one of the other militiamen's greaves with his own, striking bright sparks in the twilight that was falling. As he did, the odd man out gave the horse's flank a hard slap, and the horse began to trot forward.

The rope grew taut, accompanied by the worst caterwauling Hargreaves had ever heard. And soon, even in the dim light, Hargreaves could see the dark-skinned man who was dragged screaming out of the cafe.

"No!" hissed the other woman, though her grief was touched by a clear desire not to alarm the child. Hargreaves stepped back into her alley, covering her mouth to keep from screaming. Her second, more noble instinct almost took over, and she had taken one step into the light when the black hand clutched her wrist.

"What are you, slow? Scream's gang will do unspeakable things to a woman on her own!" the woman whispered.

"Wilhelm Scream is no highwayman," said Hargreaves. "He is a keeper of the law, a sheriff. Are you saying he condones this travesty? This...barbarism? I don't care what that man has done, this is not law!" The militiamen would have caught her right then and there for the outburst, if not for the continued screaming. Now a second voice joined the first as another dark-skinned man joined the first, who had been tied up in a bundle in the street.

"We shouldn't talk. We're like two black tails before the coyote. It's not safe here," hissed her companion. Seeing Hargreaves continue to bristle, she added, "I'm Constance. Constance Lamb. Who are you?"

"Vanessa Hargreaves," said Hargreaves.

"Now see here," said Constance, "Miss Vanessa. If you'd be coming along with me in a moment after those boys lead away that infernal hay burner, we can be getting away and I can explain everything over a nice cuppa tea."

"Really?" said Hargreaves, raising her eyebrow. Constance grinned, a black sort of humor in several ways at once. But there was a sudden, different kind of uproar from behind the alley facade. It was the sound of a steel horse rearing and snorting embers, ready to gallop. Constance whipped her face back and forth, then shoved Hargreaves hard.

"Quick, in the borrow pit!" said Constance. "Boy, you get in with her!"

"The what?" cried Hargreaves, but allowed herself to be shoved, suddenly finding herself in the ditch just under the alley facade. The bulge of two warm bodies crammed in next to her, followed almost immediately by the thunder of hooves striking sparks from the stones in the alley. The heavy tread struck deep gouges almost right where

Hargreaves had been standing. Then a second and a third horse followed, the last dragging its screaming, horrible burden after it. Hargreaves reached out at the last second, bringing little Emory's leg the rest of the way into the ditch before it could be crippled by those biting hooves. She heard the sharp gasp from Constance as she did.

When the dust settled, Constance dragged herself out of the pit, followed by Hargreaves. They both helped Emory up, who seemed upset, but not about to scream. Constance hugged the child close.

"You did good, Em. You did really good," said Constance, in the practical way of someone terrified herself.

"Who are they?" asked Hargreaves.

"Montana shoeshine is what they are," said Constance, and spat. "It should be safe enough now."

They walked together into the Fred Hornby's. Hargreaves braced herself, not knowing what to expect. She had just been in there earlier in the day. But as she walked in, the worst thing was the sameness of it. All the rail station cafes looked the same, from their high, painted ceiling arches to their patterned tile floors. A sign told customers "Everything Will Be All Right!" in cheerful copperplate. This one was in a state of some chaos, the usually neat, clean tables cast aside in a clear and dreary pattern of abduction. The restaurant was deserted, but it still carried the comfort of Fred Hornby's that was now monstrous and alien. How could anything ever be all right after what she had seen?

Constance reached over the counter and retrieved a bottle of milk from the thrumming cold closet. She handed it to Emory and fetched two coffee cups, filling them from two boilers along the wall. Then she turned them off, pulling the heavy levers between them to set the valves grinding closed.

"It'd just go to waste," said Constance sheepishly. "Somebody ratted out the Cormac boys who were running the place. Not going to leave the rigs to boil away until Seamus comes back. That's Roger Seamus, the regional manager."

"You work here?" said Hargreaves from where she had sat Emory down at the counter.

"I was just starting my shift when I saw the smoke. That's the other black folk, fighting back. A signal telling the others to let her buck.

Town's no good for us," Constance managed before slamming back the cup of coffee. "Wish I had something stronger. Once we meet the others we'll catch the next train or woolly bear coming through. Some of us may even have found a place on the morning train by now."

"There are more places like this?" gaped Hargreaves.

"Too many," sighed Constance. "William Cormac said this state wasn't friendly to us. But a cousin of mine went through Shelby and said it was all right."

"I'm sorry about your friends," said Hargreaves. "I met Frederick. He seemed a decent sort."

"Brothers," said Constance, and Hargreaves knew she didn't mean family. "You get used to losing them. But the freemen will find our place. Plenty of land in America."

"Shelby's near the Blackfoot territory," said Hargreaves, who had studied up. Right in the corner of this restaurant, actually. "They probably demand respect with spears and arrows. You ready to defend what's yours?" Constance gave her a long, hard look.

"You're pretty sharp," she said finally.

"For a white woman?" asked Hargreaves.

"For a copper," said Constance, but she was smiling. Hargreaves smiled too.

"Not anymore."

Hargreaves would have said more, but just then the plate glass of the Fred Hornby's shattered into a million pieces. Constance screamed, a banshee howl that resolved into a storm of expletives. A split second later, the coffee urns burst in a tattoo of droplets as the second brick struck. Only it wasn't any brick, but a bottle full of fuel oil that spread in an eerie blue wave as the flames danced over the wet tile.

Hargreaves turned toward the open window now pouring the cold of the street into the warmth of the restaurant. The Tranter was in her hand. Instinct took over, and she let fly blind through the window, pop-pop-pop. But then she saw the woman's leg, twisted at a sick angle where the third brick struck her ankle.

"Constance!" said Hargreaves.

"Go! Just go!" cried Constance. She thrust Emory at her. "Take him!"

Sight and sound ran together. Hargreaves picked up the child and thrust her .22 into Constance's hands. The woman, now befouled with ash, looked up and shook her head once. In that moment Hargreaves understood: a gun was just another excuse for those brutes to give no quarter. Hargreaves nodded and, thrusting the Tranter into its holster under her vest, turned and tumbled over the flames and through the back door. Emory reached for his mother, but was smart enough to stay mute, save a squeal or two. Had he no words?

Furious for a reason she could not name, Hargreaves burst onto a narrow field bordered on one side with gravel and clinker. She was on the tracks when the first cries of capture came over the singed breeze. Emory cried out once, and Hargreaves clutched him to her bosom.

"God have mercy, you'll see her again," she said, and began to run. She hadn't gone fifty yards before she heard a cry from further up on the tracks. Hargreaves saw a dark hand come groping out of the shadows of a boxcar further up, along the platform of the station. What had Constance said? That some of the freemen might already have found the morning train?

"Miss! White miss! Here! Bring the boy!" cried a voice. Hargreaves felt the brush of her hair against her shoulders. Her golden mane had come loose from her cap. But now wasn't the time for it, and the boxcar before her spelled salvation of a sort. At least it was a place to hide. Hargreaves thought.

That was the last thing Hargreaves knew before a sharp pain flowered in the side of her head. She was still Yard enough to avoid the worst of the blow, and she caught sight of the ruffian emerging from the darkness between boxcars. Then came the false night of a burlap bag, descending over her face, though not before she counted three of them, one smeared in furnace soot all over his arms and face. She felt Emory wrenched, screaming at last, from her arms. For that reason alone, she let her limbs fall limp. Hargreaves feigned unconsciousness, even when she felt the ropes bind around her wrists. For a brief moment she thought she saw an aquiline profile and tan skin through a tear in the burlap. A red man amongst these militiamen? Only a fleeting dream, a false hope.

Hargreaves stayed perfectly still. She felt her thespian's instincts descend upon her, and tried to convey the limpness and helplessness of a recently dead corpse. The brutes had no interest in her face, though they certainly pawed about everywhere else. Amongst the fools was someone with a sound head on his shoulders, however. They damn well made sure to check her for a gun before they hefted her onto someone's armored shoulders like a bag of potatoes. But they didn't find the razor-sharp pin tucked in her hair.

By and by Hargreaves managed to get her eye to the rip in the burlap, she saw mostly the backside of the militiaman who was carrying her. She smelled the machine oil and felt more than heard the hiss of pressure shifting the riveted plates under the leather coat. Moments passed into minutes, and her soft parts grew sore. It felt like they walked for about ten minutes, though of course the suited man who carried her felt no fatigue. The other two men exchanged jibes about her raised backside in the first few minutes.

"Say, Hayworth, can't we just drop by the saloon a spell? Wouldn't even need a bed. Stable's good enough for the filly," said one of them. She felt a brushing sensation as someone touched her hair.

"Second that," said the other voice. It sounded familiar, somehow, but Hargreaves couldn't place it.

"She's not some negro speed goat you can rut in the back of a barn. We take her to Scream," said the one carrying her, Hayworth, and that was that. Whoever Wilhelm Scream was, he was fine and terrible motivation.

Soon enough the trio reached wherever they had been going, and Hargreaves felt herself being dumped through into a cooler space and down onto something soft and musty, like a coach seat. She waited until the din of the men subsided to a dull roar before peering out of the rip in the burlap. Only a dark, somewhat dusty buckwheat cushion filled her vision, and from the angle of the quivering firelight, it seemed she was in a coach with the doors shut. She slipped the burlap loose only to find her wrists bound with rope, not cuffs. Blast. The pin would be little use.

She was able to wriggle up to the rear window, and the sight there was shocking to say the least. Firstly, she made out the low wagon hitched behind the coach. Even under a sheet she recognized the newsboys' equipment from earlier in the day. There was room behind the clockwork where a number of shapes were piled, wriggling slightly but still bound. Hargreaves looked for Constance, but the light flickered too wantonly for her to see. She didn't want to think about what the militiamen had said about the free women they caught. And Emory. What of Emory? She could not see the child, either.

The coach door slammed open before Hargreaves could make an attempt to feign unconsciousness. Instead she whirled, fixing her eyes in what she hoped was wet panic. She almost breathed a sigh of relief when she recognized one of the men from earlier. One, not three. Upon closer inspection, he was one of the newsboys from the afternoon. He had chestnut hair that might have been handsome on someone less loathsome. Like a horse.

"Don't think I missed you when we were giving out the pamphlets. I don't know where you come from, the Feddies, the Wisconsin troopers, Burgess's men," said the chestnut. "I've got three inches of steel that say you ain't going anywhere."

"What? What are you—let me go!" said Hargreaves, hoping she wasn't selling the farm. She twitched her legs as if in fear, but placed them in an angle to show off her rear through the boys' trousers. Then, lowering the pitch of her voice, she said, "Your...your leader, Scream. You're to take me to Scream. "

"That's what Hayworth thinks. But no, I think you're too dangerous to let go. No blackies have got out from Spelter in three months, and nobody would believe them if they did. But a limey white girl...that's different. So you're not going anywhere...but first, I'm going to have some fun."

With a snarl, the man climbed into the coach. Hargreaves loosed a scream, high and loud enough to carry through the closing door. She clenched her teeth as she bore the militiaman's attentions, which were clumsy and thick-fingered. But it hadn't escaped her attention that he had said Burgess' name, nor that his slapdash clanker armor was hanging half off his chest and legs, ready for whatever foul deeds were on his mind.

Hargreaves waited until he had pulled her trousers to her knees and his face was buried in her sex. She took time, waiting long enough to know her scream hadn't brought anyone running. Why would they, in this crazy little burg? Then, when she was quite sure, she trapped his hands under her rear and clamped her muscular thighs shut around his neck.

"Mmmph!" said the man, his face turning bright red as he lifted it from her sex fast enough to leave rug burn. His legs kicked at the padding of the coach. His teeth were a concern, but it wasn't her first rodeo, and she rode tight under his chin, looking calmly into his eyes as the light slowly left them.

Hargreaves waited the few minutes for him to fall unconscious. It took a long time, and longer still for her to recover her breath, perhaps twenty minutes from when she had first been thrown into the coach. Then she shoved the limp body off her, and shimmied her pants back on as best she could. Kicking one boot free, she felt with one foot for the knife the militiaman had bragged about sticking in her.

"Damn! You bloody wanker!" She couldn't believe it. She couldn't fucking believe it. Hargreaves kicked the man's head, hard, and checked again. But no, she had been quite thorough. The man didn't have a knife on him. Either he had left it outside the coach, as was prudent, or he just liked his victims terrified.

"All right then. No knife, no guns...come on, Vanessa, think," said Hargreaves. But any attempt to escape would have to wait, as she caught the sound of a clockworked horse clopping closer. Thinking fast, she grabbed her would-be rapist with her feet and crammed him under the coach seat, where the baggage racks usually lay. There was a poncho or blanket draped over the forward passenger bench, which she was able to use to cover the man's drooling face. Then she retrieved her boot, though her clothes would have to stay disheveled, and lay down on the seat again to listen for the horse to come closer. The stink of the militiaman was still on her, and she wished dearly for a lavender-scented bath.

"The hood!" said Hargreaves, nearly when the men were upon the coach. She wriggled close enough to it so it would seem as if the burlap had fallen off. Then the door opened and Hargreaves concentrated on keeping perfectly still.

A moment passed, then another, as the muffled sound of conversation and a huffing, sparking horse drifted in. Then a body came flying in and landed on the other seat, hard enough to jostle Hargreaves feigning unconsciousness inside. She risked a peek. It was Constance! But her clothes were ripped, and her neatly piled hair was now ragged, sticky, and draped over her nudity. Part of her head looked like it had been shaved. She seemed barely there, her eyes dull and unseeing. There were marks upon her, marks that were hard to see in the dark but to Hargreaves' trained eyes clear indicators of at least three men. Bile raged up into the back of Hargreaves' throat, not the least of which bore the bitter taste of survivors' guilt. Because she had been a white woman and Constance was dark!

For a brief moment Hargreaves wasn't sure she was lucid as a witness to this horrific scene, but the moment passed and the doors closed on her, leaving her in blessed quiet. She could hear the men outside busying themselves, but she did not deceive herself into thinking they would leave her alone for long. Surely one of them would decide there was a much-awaited main attraction in the coach.

Instead, the coach gave a rattling lurch, and Hargreaves nearly pitched onto the floor with the unconscious man. Had she killed him? She didn't hear breathing. But she found she didn't much care, and when a choked gurgle came from below, she found herself disappointed. That was when she saw the glitter of the knife that had tumbled out onto the floor.

"Now?" Hargreaves hissed in frustration. It must have been slipped into a hidden part of the armor. With a groan and an epithet, she took the next hole in the road and tumbled down next to the knife, getting her teeth around the handle though all the while a little voice in her head was praying she wouldn't bite through her tongue. It didn't take much effort to pull her bound hands over her legs, and then a moment of fury as she sawed through the ropes.

"Constance! Constance!" whispered Hargreaves as soon as she could cast the rope away and sit up. The driver's compartment window was shut, but she heard the motions of the driver and one other man in the passenger seat. She kept her voice down as she inspected Constance, who did not answer. She had dipped into the sandman's realm, overcome by her injuries. Hargreaves felt her body, and cursed the brutes once more. There was certain to be some internal bleeding, and her left eye felt like they had fractured the orbital. Most of all Hargreaves felt the cold realization that she was alone.

Alone, but not overcome. Not yet. Hargreaves didn't try to open the door. For one thing, the coach was still moving. For another, how would she take Constance? Or the other freemen and, plausibly, women, in the back wagon?

It didn't take much to redo the knots so they looked tight, but could be easily slipped off. Then she tucked the knife into her boot and laid back down to wait. Almost as soon as she was still, the driver window slid open and a militiaman peered into the gloom. Finding nothing untoward, he turned back to the front, leaving the window open. Hargreaves bit her lip and tried not to mind the bollocking those hard seats were giving her backside. Better a seat than a lout, she thought.

By and by, the coach did stop, though Hargreaves was starting to doubt the possibility. The coach doors opened, and Hargreaves expected to be thrown into the horror Constance had faced already. But no, it was just Hayworth, who grabbed her roughly and started to carry her out. He didn't seem to notice the burlap that had slipped off.

"Those are some nice boots," said one of the men nearby.

"Go on then," said Hayworth. "Your daughter would like them."

And so she lost her knife, as well, though she didn't hear the sound of a blade drop to the ground. It was very dark.

Sneaking a peek here and there upside down on Hayworth's back, Hargreaves made out a rolling range, like the many she had observed when she rode into Spelter. She only just made out the side of a large manor house a few yards away and the knot of perhaps eight men gathered near it. One of them pulled an armored gauntlet off and she saw the tattoo of a great hound upon his arm. Then her vision was swallowed up by the eaves of a barn, then by the hard boards of a wall and the scratchy comfort of what felt like a bed of dry straw. Something creaked, loudly, and then there was the distinct groan of a huge set of barn doors closing.

As soon as the voices had faded away, Hargreaves dashed forward and stuck her hairpin into the barn door, but cursed a blue streak as the pin snapped in the lock. It was old iron, sheathed in rust, and she had botched the job in her haste. She let rip with profanities. Her feet pricked with numbness, though she would likely feel the hard ground soon enough.

Attempt foiled, Hargreaves took a step back and regarded her surroundings. She was alone. Unbeknownst to her, the men had put the empty wagon in after her, though she could still make out the bloodstains. The stacks of pamphlets and the change backpack still sat covered in the wagon.

Hargreaves broke the lever off of it for a weapon, but almost as soon as she had it, she heard the soft crunch of a footstep outside the barn. Not a clanker, just a man, but the foot was clear enough in the crisp evening. She dove for the hay pile, looping the rope over her wrists again and tucking her new truncheon under her body. Just before the door opened, she shifted her legs so her best side was in view, but dipped her head so it looked as if she was afraid.

Moonlight snuck in as the smaller door in the barn's front opened. Someone came in the barn, and stood there. What were they waiting for? Hargreaves clenched her jaw. Come on, you bastard, she thought. Come on and Inspector Hargreaves will show you a good time.

"Your tricks will not work," a deep voice said calmly. "I know you are awake. You have been this whole time."

Hargreaves snapped her eyes open. Then she whirled, and sat up, not caring that her poor abused page's top was flapping like an untethered airship sale.

"Funny Goat?" she hissed, not daring to believe her luck. "What the bloody hell are you doing here?"

Under the cloth cowl draped loosely over his head, the Indian looked as handsome as he had by the farmer's stand, and oddly not at all harried. A single feather clung to his long hair, pulled back into a neat fall framing fine aquiline features. Hargreaves thought she might feel improper objectifying the man, but when he came close, he smelled like clean sweat and forest floor. It was hard not to stare, but Hargreaves was certainly in no mood for romance just then. He was a sight for sore eyes, though.

Funny Goat had brought her some water in a basin.

"Oh, you bloody marvelous billy, come here!" said Hargreaves, and plunged her head into the basin, drinking deep. It was crisp, cold, and brought her back to life. Hargreaves was acutely aware of what the splashing water was doing to her front, and remembered suddenly that she hadn't any proper underthings. Corsetry never seemed more welcome. To his credit, Funny Goat did nothing except hold the basin and try to keep his eyes on hers, which just made it easier to see the discomfort in them. After a bit, she could stand the silence no longer. "I don't suppose you've got a cuppa tea?"

"You should run," said Funny Goat.

"No tea? That'd be a proper treat."

"You aren't running?"

"I was brought with others," said Hargreaves. "I suppose you followed me here. Perhaps you didn't see the back of the wagon. But they've got others here, people you would call freemen. People of African descent. Scream and his men are hunting them, gathering them up in Spelter."

Funny Goat just regarded her quietly.

"You will help me free them, right?" said Hargreaves, all the joviality seeping out of her voice.

"I would not," said Funny Goat. "I...would be caught. And I know what men such as these would do to me."

Hargreaves was about to berate him for being a coward, but paused with her hands smoothing back the spun gold of her hair. He was right, after all. How could she ask him to join in her madness, to risk his own life and body for her stupid arrogance? Hargreaves wasn't police here. She probably wasn't in England anymore either. If she was smart, she would run like Funny Goat said, and tend to disposing the Cook box as she had set out to do. If she was smart...

But the sight of Constance's eyes and Constance's smile haunted her still, as if they had been painted onto Hargreaves' own blue pupils.

"I would make it worth your while," said Hargreaves, thrusting her chest up in that particular way. That special way she unleashed when she was undercover as a barmaid, or wanted to distract a man from the gun she had in her skirts. My, my, thought Hargreaves. You're getting lewd in your retirement from Scotland Yard. But she needed an ally, and she hadn't missed the sizzle of his skin and the quickness of his breath as he looked at her. Now or earlier, when he snuck out from the back of her truck. The louder part of was saying she could knock him upside the head when his pants were down, the same way she had dispatched the poor lorry driver. But there was a quiet part of her that pushed her bottom out a little farther than necessary.

"I do not enjoy taking this thing by force," said the Red Indian, frowning in offense.

"You don't want my body?" Hargreaves feigned insult, covering her front. It was a nice touch, she thought.

"No, I want your body," said Funny Goat, flustered. He backed up slightly, his firm footing unsure for the first time since she had met him. "I mean, you're very attractive. You have long legs. And your soft breasts, I would enjoy them very much, and you would enjoy it also...that is...I mean...I've probably already helped you too much."

"You're not very good at this, are you?" said Hargreaves, feeling her eyebrows rise.

"No, no. I'm sorry," he said. "I haven't spoken to women very much. Either with the Blackfoots or the white women."

"Oh," said Hargreaves. "Well. Let me tell it to you straight. Listen, Goat. Goatie. There's well on twenty souls trapped somewhere on this accursed farm, and I don't think the plan is to cook them a nice dinner. One of them helped me out of a pickle, her and her boy. I'm going to go find them and set them free, and you're going to help me do it."

"And for that you're offering me...recompense?"

Hargreaves didn't know if he was as innocent as he claimed or if he was puzzled. His foreign Indian's face was inscrutable even to her keenly honed senses. But she had had a horrid, no-good, very bad day and she just wanted to get on with it.

"Yes, yes, it's not like I have any money left on me. If we live through this, you can bloody well have a shag. I daresay you'll find it easy to take me to Bedfordshire, with that sweet nancy." The last hung on the air, slipped off her tongue in her haste. Funny Goat simply looked at her as inscrutably as ever. "Well? I'll be well and truly offended if you refuse." Damn it, Hargreaves realized, she would. She felt her face turning red.

"I will help," said Funny Goat. Hargreaves fancied he might charge money for people to look on his blank face: here be the Red Indian, carved out of wood. He was like a daguerreotype come to life from pictures of the Old West. But he simply turned to gather up a sack he had brought with him. Inside it were Hargreaves' Tranter, her Browning, and even her boots with the knife still in them.

"You marvelous, clever little caprine." said Hargreaves, amazed. Recovering, all her things, she said, "Carry on then!" They slipped out into the night.

It did not take long to find the place where the other people were hidden. The stars were out over the flatlands of Montana, and Hargreaves could see the wagon tracks as easily as if they had been painted. Strangely, it seemed Funny Goat could too, and headed straight for a low cellar sunk in the back of the house. They had to be careful, for firelight shone in the front parlor, and the dire militiamen were still awake. But eventually they found the cellar door, which barred on the outside with no lock. Hargreaves lifted it and gently set it to the ground.

"If anybody's inside," she said quietly through the crack in the door, "stay quiet. We're getting you out."

They pulled up the doors as quietly as they could, nearly abandoning the effort when the hinges squeaked loudly. But then they lay on the ground, and the darkness of the cellar yawned below them.

"Oh. Oh, God," said Hargreaves when she smelled it.

"By..." and Funny Goat uttered something she didn't know, but sounded like "Koh-Koh-Mi-Kee-Sum." But whatever gods he swore by, they couldn't help these people now.

Hargreaves stepped further into the darkness, among the chains and the cramped spaces barely big enough for one body. She felt her boot push into a thick, congealing pool, like primal mud that filled her nose with iron. She felt a hand clasp tightly around hers.

"I have to be sure," said Hargreaves. And Funny Goat let her go, to walk through the blood to the forms in the darkness. It was only later, in the moonlight, that she felt the wetness on her cheeks, so different from the wetness in that hellish cellar. But thank God for small favors. There were no small bodies in that accursed hole.

"We must run. And run now," said Funny Goat after a moment. "There is no one here alive."

"Yes. Yes I know," said Hargreaves. "But not until I find the child."

"Ah," said Funny Goat. He seemed to consider something. "He will be in the house."

"How do you—" Hargreaves started, but thought better of it. Instead, she shot a venomous look that said clearly, "I'll have it out of you later," and crept toward a set of stairs. She couldn't hear him, but she felt Funny Goat follow across that sick floor.

The basement door slid open smoothly, unlike every penny dreadful Hargreaves had ever read. They were thankfully in the back of the house. She paused, uncertain, until Funny Goat slipped past her and led the way through a back hall, past a number of open rooms that looked like barracks. None of the rooms were occupied except for a number of clockwork frames like costume hangers, most of them hung with the makeshift clanker suits. They made a soft hiss as they pulled steam from the house's taps through long hoses and into cannister-shaped capacitors.

"In here," said Funny Goat, and he nudged open a door in the very back. Hargreaves drew a sharp breath when she saw Emory there, lying beside a large and snoring man in his fifties or sixties. The man was naked, but thankfully, Emory still wore the clothes Hargreaves had last seen him in.

"Here. Emory," hissed Hargreaves gently nudging the child. She thought he was asleep, but the stark whites of his eyes opened as if he had been waiting for her. He was as quiet as she had ever known him. "Come on now. Let's go."

Emory opened his mouth and said something that made Hargreaves' heart break.

"Yes, yes, we'll find your mother. Come, before the man wakes."

Emory got up, and with agonizing slowness, padded over to Hargreaves. She knelt with her arms out for what felt like an eternity before he got close enough and Hargreaves scooped him up.

"It's all right now. It's all right. You're safe. Come on and let's go home to Mother."

"Gehh?" was the only reply.

"Yes? Yes, Emory?" said Hargreaves, but even as she said so she realized a simple truth that made a cold something dribble down her back.

The sound wasn't coming from the child. The man was awake.

Even before she saw the man in the bed open his eyes, Hargreaves turned and shot him dead as he rolled toward them. He managed to loose a deep, hearty grunt before his throat became a ragged wet hole, ripped through by those nasty .22 rounds in Hargreaves' Tranter.

"I'm sorry," Hargreaves said to Funny Goat, but he was already pulling her out the door, ignoring the mewling from the little dark bundle in Hargreaves' arms. She clung to Emory tightly even as her front grew warm and wet again. And still, he didn't scream, did not cry.

When the first man appeared in the doorway, his bald head turned into a red flower almost before Hargreaves saw Funny Goat draw on him. The half-Indian was fast, even with an enormous Bacon six-barreled gun that barked like a mule. Then everything became a blur as they backtracked through the hallway, using the heavy clanker armor as cover and shooting their way out. They made it as far as the back door before Hargreaves saw the endless sea of grass that might as well be an actual ocean for how far they would have to go to get through it. She could hear the others rousing, screaming, gathering to come and kill them.

"Goat!" cried Hargreaves.

Funny Goat turned and whistled, and from seemingly nowhere the drumming hoofs of a clockwork horse came thundering around the house, running down first a barrel of water and then a man who got caught in that billowing cloud of steam. It whirled around the equine, wreathing it in a mystic fog that seemed to catch at the ankles of their pursuers. Funny Goat caught the braided reins as his mount swung by, and he held Hargreaves as she and the child swung on. Then he climbed up himself, pressing in tight behind the inspector.

"Go, go!" said Funny Goat, and made an odd sort of click. The horse reared, almost bucking, and then they were off, charging into the woods before the will-o'-wisps of their passing had time to fade.

The horse had no care for unsound ground or where branches threatened to cave their heads in, which made for careful riding. On the other hand, the metal horse was indifferent to brambles, and the embers in its eyes lit just enough of the darkness to see, which made their going easier.

Funny Goat communicated his directions almost preternaturally to the horse, without visible spurring. For some reason it reminded Hargreaves of Rosa, steering the *Huckleberry*. By and by Hargreaves asked about the Scream men, anything to forget they were running from the monsters that had wrought the abattoir in the basement.

"Beneath the mask, Wilhelm Scream is the Reverend Francois Devereaux," Funny Goat said, as calmly as he said everything else. "His men do not know this. His power comes from fear and misinformation, and the things the Ghost Train sells him. The deputies do not ask questions. They are taken in by his charm, and his promise of kicking out the blacks, the gypsies, the aeronauts with their worldly acceptance of the different...the Indians."

"But he allows you to be with his group," said Hargreaves. Funny Goat did not deny it, and rode forward in furtive silence.

Strangely, this outlook did not surprise Hargreaves. She'd seen too many on the road with many strange and sordid problems. On Funny Goat, it seemed as if this stoicism, this quietly borne cross, was his birthright. She thought she might have finally tracked down a quintessential American attitude, to those who had inhabited it first.

Goat started out reluctant to speak, but she told him something of her life growing up in the English country, and her father the chief constable of their little town, how she played with his badge and his pips. She told him about her difficulty entering the service, and the drive to prove herself, so much that she was recognized by Scotland Yard for exceptional service. Being given undercover assignments, and resenting it, both because she was so good at it and because it was considered a woman's specialty. She did not tell him of Maple Cross.

Something she said must have moved the Indian, for he began to speak. Hargreaves learned he was the child of a French colonial mother, who had come south escaping a bitter cold. She had not one thing to her name save fine, high cheekbones and milky skin, so found refuge with a wealthy caravan man, who put her to work singing in his traveling caravan's tented saloon.

The caravan man was very fond of her. When the swell of her belly made it inconvenient for them to travel farther, Goat's mother had convinced the owner it was his. Whether or not it was true, when the squalling babe was born Goat's older brother looked enough like the caravan master for them to lay down roots. Later, Funny Goat was born, but came dark, the new moon to his brother's full. Goat's true father was a sideshow Indian in the caravan, a master of the throwing tomahawk.

His mother hid him as best as she was able, and that very night his true father smuggled him out to live with his own people. It was understandable then to Hargreaves why Funny Goat approached the fairer sex in so inadequate a fashion—his mother had in infancy dealt him a cruel hand so they all might live. He must expect all women to be so practical.

Funny Goat grew up with the Blackfoots. He had gone back as a younger man to try to find his mother, in the city where he had been born. It was there he learned of Devereaux, the company he kept, and the opportunity to make a life for himself. As for his mother, the town was full of people who could recount the nice caravan owner's wife, who died of the dreaded consumption far too early, and perhaps left too much of her son's schooling to his carny father. Her grave was atop a high hill, laid to rest by his elder brother. And Funny Goat had only one family in the world, so he had gone to him, not knowing what he would find.

Funny Goat seemed to know the country well, and when he grasped for a tree it almost grasped him back, like an old friend. They did not go quickly, but it seemed they were suddenly quite far from the barn, and quite near to the mountains. When the moon was high in the sky, they reached a stream, with still, dark pools along the edge. There were thick stands that hid the stretch of rocky beach from view. Funny Goat tied up the horse on the far side. Emory had fallen asleep. Hargreaves took the opportunity to tidy up her shirt, all the while aware of her arrangement with present company.

When she stepped in the river it was crisp, bracing, and it made her acutely aware of how her hips swung when she walked. And she wasn't totally oblivious, not in shock. She had enjoyed his long legs, and his taut chest stretched over strong ribs. She wondered how she would do with a man shorter than her and a bit thicker round. Hargreaves needed this as much as he did.

"Through the water. And the shirt. The dogs will make easy work, with the child's scent on you."

"Yes, I know," said Hargreaves, and stripped off the garment unthinkingly, unfeelingly. The water was a rushing cold like silver in the dark. The woods were dangerous, but they dared not light a fire. The militiamen had the clanker suits, and would not tire. But they would not tread too far in the darkness, either. By the crackling, dark belly of the clockwork horse, the little bundle that was Emory lay, terrified but finally asleep after many hours of riding. Hargreaves shivered. Her body was sore, but they had put many miles between themselves and that accursed place they had saved Emory from.

"Quickly. We'll use Baccarat for warmth," said Funny Goat a few steps away in the river. Somehow, she was happy he had taken a peek, though he was just a shape to her outlined in starlight.

"Baccarat?" said Hargreaves. Her skin felt numb, and it wasn't for the cold of the Montana evening.

"The horse. You're in shock," said Funny Goat, and suddenly he was there by her. Hargreaves didn't even step back or cover herself as he led her out of the river and sat her on a log by Baccarat. They were on the other side of the horse from the child, but hidden beneath some bluffs.

Slowly, she began to regain some feeling, and after some moments realized it was because Funny Goat was wrapped around her, his arms crossed over hers and rubbing her shoulders. A rough blanket was wrapped around him and folded over them both. She felt his skin on her back, and he was breathing hard, but he didn't seem to be doing anything but warming her up. Hargreaves was acutely aware how close their bodies had come.

"Oh," said Hargreaves, starting, but there wasn't much to do but inch herself forward. It was cold, after all, and there wasn't much room under the blanket. Her first instinct took over, and words tumbled from her lips. "This isn't proper."

"Proper is a white man's word," said Funny Goat. "Out in these lands, I suspect this might be more proper and right." He clutched her closer, and somehow Hargreaves turned under the blanket, holding his bare chest back with her hand, just an inch from her own front. It was strong, and muscular, and slightly musky. She liked it far too much to trust herself so close to it.

"And what is this? Are you asking for recompense now?" said

Hargreaves. It was only after she said it that she heard the bitterness and sadness in her voice.

"No," said Funny Goat simply. "I did not fulfill my end of the bargain, after all."

"But you came with me," said Hargreaves. "And we saved Emory. All those people...why would someone do that, Goat?"

"I know," said Funny Goat. Then, perfectly understandable to Hargreaves, "I don't know."

They sat quietly for a moment, and Hargreaves slowly turned back around, letting their closeness ward off the cold in the blanket. Funny Goat resumed his rubbing, but slower now, with his fingers, keeping his movements from shifting their covering. Hargreaves saw their clothes draped on Baccarat's back, slowly steaming dry. They had shared an unspeakable horror together, and Hargreaves needed this too, this closeness and the feeling of another's pulse against hers to dry out the damp in her heart.

"Are you cold?" asked Hargreaves, though she knew he couldn't be.

"I'll have that recompense now," said Funny Goat, and his voice was hoarse with lust. He moved slowly but with purpose, and then his lips were there, finding their way across her cheek. Hargreaves mumbled some weak protest, but soon she tasted him darting about like a furtive animal, felt her wrist clutched in his strong fingers, and returned the favor as savagely.

Ordinarily, she might have said no. She might have told him what he could do with himself that would leave him ruined for other women, or gone with her original plan to knock the bugger out. But at the moment, Hargreaves didn't have much respect for herself. She felt incompetent, she felt lost, and she felt guilty letting all those people down. Most of all, she felt the long stain of corruption by her betrayal of the Queen. The death of the man in Appleton still clung to her like an oily slick, and the blood of the others in the house just now were on her hands too. She felt it filthy between her fingers, and she wished for some pure flames to lick them clean.

At last Funny Goat broke from her, his face opaque with the breath rising from their bodies. His fingers dug into the top of her trousers. They had chafed slightly during the ride, and his fingers seemed to burn with need against the tender swell of her hips. There was no pretending she was a man, not with those.

"I have seen too much death tonight," said Funny Goat, and Hargreaves knew what he meant.

"Yes. Yes, oh God. Show me life," said Hargreaves.

She grabbed his large, strong hand and pressed it to her backside, where she felt it grasp tight. She slipped off the log, and felt her bottoms catch and slide down as the pair of them slipped to the soft forest floor. And as they danced the first steps of this much-needed waltz, the events that had just happened came rushing back to her, as if the experience had been jostled loose. As Funny Goat's breath feathered along her ear, she felt for his desire under the blanket, she arched for him to taste the sweetness pooling at the base of her neck.

Funny Goat proved a perfect gentleman, and when his fingers set her to moaning, he stopped, letting her come down from that shining spot. When she finished, they talked, naked under the blanket, Hargreaves teasing him by holding his unrequited desire loosely in her fingers.

Hargreaves nestled tighter into the wideness of Funny Goat's chest, though her long legs threatened to poke out of the blanket. Sod it, she thought, and slipped her knees around his hips as she kissed him deeply, feeling her warmth press against him. Her golden hair fell loose and wanton about her shoulders.

Funny Goat began slowly, though his desire was clearly at zenith. She could feel it up on her stomach, throbbing insistently. He writhed with her, sliding up and down, and Hargreaves groaned, barely noticing him draw closer to her with every pass. And getting more imposing as well... where was he hiding all of himself? When Funny Goat slipped suddenly low, she took his strong neck in her hands, as if it gave her some symbolic control. He made no complaint, merely looking at her with the barest hint of amusement.

"What? I am no prude. You're just, well..." Instead of admitting her sudden shock, she shimmied under the blanket, kissing and tasting smooth, burnished chest. She felt hands at her thighs, not letting her stray too far. She felt his firmness against the downy skin between her thighs and gasped, fearful. The thoughts in her mind were of duty, and abandonment, and of murder. Maybe she wanted the pain, as if it would cleanse her of the doubt, uncertainty and guilt dogging her journey. Perhaps if she had spoken with her Queen more, understood what was wanted of her...Then he put one hand on her back and reached behind her, underneath him, and there was no denying Funny Goat from possessing Hargreaves, and no denying her from him.

"Oh! Oh yes!" gasped Hargreaves, no louder than Baccarat's breath rustling the leaves. Her first impression was of a terrifying fullness. In the first moments, she did not think herself equal to the task, but she made the attempt anyway. He stroked her golden hair as she worked at him, and she cupped him gently. The chiseled rear she had admired from afar was firm under her fingertips. His smell was clean, making her think of the wild open country. Vast vistas seemed to cross her mind, images of infinite blue skies, roaming herds of bison, gold plains that stretched from horizon to horizon. His fullness took her breath away, but his sweetness made it bearable, a warmth that suffused her like flaming fairy floss.

She had been on the pull once or twice, certainly, but not with anybody like Funny Goat.

As promised, he enjoyed the softness of her breasts and her legs. She had large breasts and Vanessa sometimes thought of them as unwieldy, needing quite a lot of cramming and handling to fit into corsets and dresses. But his hands felt like impossibly well-made underthings, soft and supportive even as their dance made the silver of the river before her jostle like a plucked string. She didn't have to pretend, didn't have to go knockers in special knickers. Funny Goat didn't need anything but a good shag.

Then he was insistent in a way that could only be described as the linguistically vulgar 'turgid,'so often in penny dreadfuls, but so much more satisfying when experienced. She was being gobsmacked by something turgid, and that was just ace to Vanessa Hargreaves. At one point she looked down at herself and thought her legs went on forever, and she was the flatlands of the universe, and there was his rippled, burnished abdomen with its cloven tattoo and white scars like the sky to her earth. She remembered seeing the steaming automata horse upside-down, and by the time she regained her faculties the horse had cooled, pinging itself quietly to its metal sleep.

By her reckoning, Hargreaves was in a safe time of the month for this sort of thing. She knew it was no guarantee, but in the wilderness and on the lam, the patch of tacky wetness she found on her stomach in the morning was nearly high society. Funny Goat had somehow woken before her, or maybe he did not sleep, so before Emory could wake they did it again propped up by a tree. Hargreaves tasted him this time, enjoying the look of rapture on his face.

Best of all, she felt no guilt, no remorse. Instead, there was a lightening, as if a burden lifted from her shoulders. No devil had appeared in a puff of smoke to claim her. To those in so-called progressive Britain who would say so, even the occasionally prudish Hargreaves had to say "bollocks!" Behind the facade of a clean-cut conservative place like Essex or Spelter, folk were having a good old time of each other. Vanessa Hargreaves felt herself entitled to a little every now and again.

Once Hargreaves had it clear in her head, she saw no reason not to utilize Funny Goat for all he was worth. He had been very resourceful, even catching some small fish for breakfast before their impromptu social. If she explained the urgency of retrieving Alphonse and the nature of her mission, Goat would be all too willing to assist her. So she asked, but before she could tell this part of her story, Goat stopped her.

"Goat, do you think...I'm going west, and I could rightly use some help. Where I'm going—"

"This place holds nothing I cannot leave behind. I will come with you," he said.

"But your family?"

"The Blackfoot, they do not see me as one of their own. And I have met my brother. We did not have good words. I would much rather travel with you," he finished, and kissed her. It was sexual congress, just physical pleasure, thought Hargreaves, but his frankness made her think of the future. Being alone wore dreadfully. No, it was not impossible for her to imagine traveling with him, getting to know his secrets, finding out where her knee could reach...

"Your brother...Devereaux..." Hargreaves said. Funny Goat looked dour, an almost imperceptible sadness, but in that moment all the guilt in the world seemed to settle on his shoulders.

"Yes. He is in league with devils. But he is my brother," Funny Goat said. Then he looked about, at Emory's breakfast freshly cleaned and roasting by Baccarat. "I would just as soon be gone from this place."

As if the revelation tore away some protective veil, Scream's men found them not long into the day. Funny Goat and Hargeaves were coming back to Spelter via a roundabout route, trying to get to Alphonse. In the woods the sound of clanking boots was like hearing some dread hellhound coming after them trailing bloodied chains. It was more terrifying than the actual dogs.

"They will not bring fire," Goat said. "The town's wealth comes largely from logging and game. Devereaux knows this well, and will not risk burning it down."

"Splendid," said Hargreaves dryly.

They were in a sort of pass, between some large rocks that bridged a fearsome gorge. Funny Goat looked left and right, and then Hargreaves felt something hot and wet splash across her face. When she touched there, her fingers came away red. She heard a wet thumping noise.

"No!" said Hargreaves, whirling.

Funny Goat had fallen from the horse. He lay splayed across the sharp rocks, and his back was a red carnation of blood—he'd been shot. Hargreaves grasped for the reins, barely catching them.

"Goat!" she cried, but he was already pulling himself up, gingerly, careful of the stones.

"More men will be coming on foot. I will lie in wait here, where they must pass. They will fall," he said simply. Already the wound seemed less than nothing, just a scratch. His face was flat as he worked his knife from his boot.

"But you are one man! There are surely—"

"No more than four," Goat interrupted. He smiled, briefly, a gash that made his implacable face look unnatural. It wasn't for him. It was for her. "And their armor will only slow them. My blood will draw fiercer things." And then he took a nut from the backside of the horse, as if he were plucking a flower. The effect was as if he had slapped a flesh horse —it lunged forward, bearing Hargreaves and Emory quickly away.

"You tosser!" Hargreaves cried, watching as long as she dared. But she didn't try to dismount, not with Emory clinging to her. She saw the first of Scream's men appear, and the normally stoic Funny Goat suddenly roar with bloodlust, bestial and furious. She had barely gotten a few yards before the first of the men fell to Goat's thrown knife, and she heard the screaming as his enormous gun barked warning. Then they disappeared behind the close of the forest.

The clockwork horse gave out perhaps a day's hike from where Hargreaves had hidden Alphonse. It had run pell-mell, without stopping despite her best efforts. Only with its water gone and the last spark of life vanished from its eyes did it slow and finally stop, an iron statue in the wilderness.

Hargreaves dared not return the way she had come. Not with Emory, anyway. Wilhelm Scream was a scourge upon his own people, burning and ravaging in his own backyard. She thought of the Ghost Train, and what fell cargo they were filling the dread apparition's hold with. She dared not think on what might happen if they got their hands on her again. So she set off on foot, still smelling the scent of tree bark and sweat on her skin. The men were not far behind her. But they were much lessened, and for that she had her paramour to thank. By the afternoon, the tears had dried to seasoned trails down her cheeks.

In the light of midday she found a cool deadfall to rest under, with not too many bugs and a nearby stream to disguise her scent. When she was sure the men passed her by she wept into a blanket, trying to quash a sudden and inexplicable grief welling through her. Who was Funny Goat? Someone who had extorted her freedom for her body. Normally such men made her sick. The thoughts helped, for a while, but soon enough her tears drained her fury, leaving her feeling sodden and cleaned out. And the child, Emory needed to be fed, with what fresh berries and some hardtack Funny Goat had left on Baccarat. That was when she heard the fallen boughs break, perhaps a mile back where she had come. And she had flown from that place on wings of haste and the knowledge that she was likely as close to Alphonse as she was to the militiamen.

Hargreaves had almost made it when she sensed something in the darkness. She froze, letting her gaze adjust, until an eye stared out at her, a thin sparkle of madness. The shadows parted for a moment, drawing back like a curtain as the clouds overhead moved before the moon. There was a cloven hoof, the thin scythe-shape of long horns, and impossibly, a long, thick stream of milky breath against the blackness. The swishing of a pronged tail lashed through the impenetrable dark, and the thing opened its mouth, a hole full of gnashing teeth and hellfire.

There, in the blackness, a devil had come to claim her.

Vanessa almost turned and ran, but the crashing through the brush had drawn her pursuers. Instead, she tripped and fell into a ditch, which dumped her into a long slide that came out under a familiar ridge. Behind her, she heard the unmistakable sounds of screaming, gunshots, sounds of people falling over themselves.

Alphonse was right where she left him. The truck had taken more damage than she thought, bleeding a pool of its vitals into the dry brush. She scrambled onto the automata itself, with the Cook box on its back, and tucked Emory tighter in the seat. She felt no doubt, no hesitation now. It was strange, but she felt as if the open prairie, the smell of the woods were fortifying her. What devil would take her, feeling as rarefied and pure as this?

Later, when the sunlight came lancing through and sanitized the landscape into its idyllic scenery, she realized what she had seen, indeed, what had saved her. She should have known—they were common enough. It was one of the refurbished livestock, with perhaps most of its front end replaced with machinery, invulnerable to the bullets of fanatics. The bastards had fallen to the frenzied kicking of a stud with iron flanks. Except it had been no bull, Hargreaves thought. She felt certain that in that moment of panic and murk, she had instead seen the wicked horns and strange eyes of a chuckling billy goat.

She felt certain she would see Funny Goat again. He was as tough as any of these animals, and this land was in part his land to begin with. It would take care of him. She wondered if perhaps there had never been a Funny Goat, if those old spirits had sent one of their own to help her through this madman's paradise. But the comforting wheeze of Alphonse's boiler and the soft breaths of Emory sleeping made it easy to put the whole thing behind her.

STATION 4

Roadside Attractions

A ROAD GOING FROM ONE HORIZON TO THE OTHER.

Arid, windswept plains.

A lone lizard sunbathing on a rock.

Vanessa Hargreaves' Feint flatbed rumbled through a tiny spit of land that might have been Anywhere, USA. Woolly bears crawled low over the rolling landscape. There were stretches of boundless prairie only passable by these plains dirigibles, cloud-like balloons slung with gondolas, full of steam-set society in the suites and emigrating settlers at the bilges. But down on the ground, the sun baked any normal steam engine dry within hours, and rendered any identifying scrub a monotonous portent of doom. That was the problem with this part of America, Hargreaves thought. One place looked pretty much the same as another. The spit-shined fixtures, the monotonous straight roads, the inedible roadside food with not even a Fred Hornby's to attend her coffee fix.

Hargreaves had doubled back through Idaho and down Nevada, through the desert and the hellish heat, to avoid any pursuers who might be following her trail. Not even the woolly bears ventured too far, so she was forced to jump from waystation to waystation, following their airship routes by watching the dirigible bellies. Sometimes she thought she saw the shark's fin of a pirate airship, far out on the dry mirages.

One thing she had to give credit for, though: her arrivals with an enormous metal titan at the waystations raised no alarums. It seemed the wildness of the country made it easier to accept the strange and outlandish. Some of the junctions were just a few mooring towers raised up from the desert. Others existed in a pall of mystery, full of local gurus, Red Indian tchotchke sellers and pan flute players. Perched on cliff sides, sunken into lakes, even stretched across the tops of forests, the stations sprung up wherever someone had a still for whiskey and a steady source of coal. At one of them she found a group of freemen who had known Constance, and recognized Emory in her arms. At first, they thought she had stolen him, and the plausibility of that as a common occurrence shocked Hargreaves more than the accusation. Hargreaves left Emory with his distant aunt, who clutched him to her with a look equal parts suspicious and glad. That was all right. This child was dear to her, but he reminded her of her lost lover too well.

The plains pirates traded in every currency, even English poundage. In this way she had crossed rocky Colorado, flat Kansas, and wet Missouri, somehow veering South. Not that the stations were always safe. There were stories. There were rumors of spiders that would lay their eggs in sleepers' faces. A hook-handed killer who preyed upon promiscuous women. Travelers sometimes found bodies hastily sewn into mattresses.

Sometimes it was difficult to tell if she had fallen asleep and ended up coming all the way around to where she had begun—the waystations and towns were more or less alike, and waking in one foul-smelling canteen was much the same as waking in another. The important thing was to keep the Cook box moving, like a can kicked melodramatically forever further down the road and away from evil. If she looked at the little memorials that cropped up here and there, she got the feeling that a single carpenter had come through and raised every single plaster structure, put up all the fences and sprinkled in the waystations just to give the illusion of hope.

So when she spotted a distant billboard way off on the horizon, Hargreaves' spirits couldn't help but pick up a bit. She pressed the throttle, mindful not to melt her tires on the hot dirt of the road. Soon the board resolved into an advert for the biggest ball of dirigible cord known to man. Some miles later, a derelict shack supported a hand-painted sign for a religious personage whose claim to fame was threading snakes through his nostrils. After that, the adverts came hot and heavy. There were unusual sculptures by the dozens, enormous pastries surely hardened to stone, and animals carved out of the most unusual mediums. Strange births. Martian visitors. Eldritch stones. Bodies of notorious killers preserved in pitch. Whimsically shaped houses were advertised as the apex of teapots, of tires, the largest bison boneyard in North America. Indian everything proliferated, with nary a turban or comforting curry in sight. Burlesque parlors sprouted by the score. At least, Hargreaves' rather British mind translated those vulgar slogans into "burlesque." It looked like the world's biggest everything had been gathered in America.

At a Kansas City style barbecue joint far from Kansas City, Hargreaves watched a man nearly finish a five-pound brisket sandwich in twenty minutes, only to collapse vomiting to the floor as the establishment cheered. One of the attractions was interesting enough for Hargreaves to pull into the dirt track. It was a stone claimed to be fallen from the Laputian Leviathan that turned out to be an irregularly shaped boulder in a carved hole.

Eventually the deluge of adverts culminated in a series of extravagant placards placed at twenty-five degree angles to the road, a gauntlet of color and riotous rattling of the swill bucket. They all said the same thing.

Come One Come All! said one.

The Most Rollicking Show In Four States! said another.

Jugglers, Clowns, and a Gentleman's Club! said a third.

And the very last of the series:

The Jango Brothers Rodeo and Circus. Exit Six off Route Thirty-Six!

"Why not?" said Hargreaves, for whom the endless straight road and unwavering scenery was a scouring purgatory from her own dark regrets. She took the exit indicated, feeling Alphonse roll against the straps with the sharp turn.

Some ways down the dirt track, the signs of festivity were already in evidence. A long rancher's fence snaked down along the road to a small clump of trees, which hid what appeared to be a pewter statue of a Union soldier complete with ancient rifle. It was only when Hargreaves drew close that the statue came alive, pointing the way toward the distant fizz and bang of festivity. She made to continue on to the broad track lined with vehicles, only to find the statue had quietly taken up a post before her Feint's grinning grille. She made a sound equal parts sigh and chuckle, before depositing a dollar and watching the Union man scurry back into a handsome salute.

Although the placards had advertised a rodeo and circus, the hubbub Hargreaves pulled into was less three-ring entertainment and more a loose collection of upstaging magicians, performers, and charlatans. A man boasted being impervious to pain. There was a woman with four teats. In one booth, a man sold copies of haunted photograms. Cowboys in various stages of nudity lassoed middle-aged women into their greased embrace, and there was a cowgirl, plopped onto a stage, dancing to some flyaway honky-tonk. To Hargreaves' eye, the double-exposed haunted negatives were obvious forgeries. The four-breasted woman was simply well-endowed and familiar with belts. But the thrill each elicited from the crowd was real.

In the distance, the circle of train cars that had delivered the circus were clustered around three that had been converted to carnival rides. The boxcars were wider than most, and unfolded like charming puzzle boxes to reveal the whimsy within. There was a merry-go-round, naturally, a double-decker with miniature dirigibles and fanciful cavorting pegasi. A winsome pirate ship swung riders back and forth, pausing at the peak of its parabola. In the far corner was a two-part ride that made Hargreaves gasp. At one end of the train a cannon shot a capsule with a rider inside of it over the fairgrounds. At the other end an oversized martini glass caught the capsule in a flowing water slide, delivering it to a shallow pool. Barkers rolled the capsules merrily back to the cannon as their riders emerged from them.

"Only a nickel, miss!" said one of the barkers in passing. "Gyroscopically stable! Enjoy the lofty heights!"

"Not on your life!" said Hargreaves, laughing.

Deeper inside the circus began to make a little more sense, with magicians' criers barking at the door and fortune-tellers telling of calamity and celebrity. Calliopes tinkled a merry tune. A juggler suspended the contents of a tea trolley in one corner, and another held aloft a rather dazzling selection of luminescent spirits. Fairy floss floated like little moons, glowing in the shimmering arc light hung high around the fairgrounds. Hargreaves found herself enjoying the spectacle more than she'd care to admit. The Ferris Wheel! The Ring Toss! The Strongman's Bell! The hugeness of it made her feel small, childlike.

A series of high tents had been erected around three rings in the center of the attraction. The first two rings were flat ground bordered by wood, but the third was recessed, a pit dug into the earth. All three were empty. A number of pavilions had been erected to shelter an audience around them. Stepping through, their multicolored exuberance revealed a bar under the stands, and an impromptu whore pit, where Hargreaves was mistaken for an employee. She didn't know whether to be flattered or insulted, until she tried to buy a drink and a large, foul-smelling swine began to snuffle after her posterior. Before she could react, one of his trotters closed on her ample bottom and squeezed possessively.

"An English rose," he said. "But needing a prickin'."

Hargreaves struck him hard enough to set her hand throbbing. She felt something crunch under her knuckles. There were far too many people in the brothel to shoot with impunity, so she participated in that noblest of traditions, the better part of valor. She turned tail and ran.

Which drew her molester and his friends out with her. Obviously.

She knocked over a collection cup and a brief havoc of scrabbling for coins followed her wake. Dodging left and right, the louts flowed through the circus like serpents in the garden. Hargreaves dispatched the first one by ducking into a blind corner, door-prizing the running man with a heavy strongman's hammer leaned up in one corner. He went down hard. The second she managed to lead into an ongoing parade. Naked women with painted breasts cast batons and waved balls of fluff about, riling up the crowd. Behind them marched elephants, lions in cages, and floats full of peacocking people. Seizing a bag of gumdrops from a nearby stall she cast them behind her. Her pursuer slipped and slid right into the painted women. Hargreaves winced, as the batons and high heels fell upon the man. A nasty way to go.

"Hello, rose...."

"Bugger." Hargreaves thought as a straight length of chrome appeared at her throat—a dirk. The man's breath was foul, heavy, and likely a hundred proof. His beard scratched. Her hiding spot now became a dangerous niche where nobody could see.

"Gave us a merry chase, didn't you?" He growled now, his voice gravel. "Open that mouth and I'll slit your tongue out. Now guess. What happens to a rose when it gets plucked?"

The cold knife touched her neck and Hargreaves gasped. It slid like an icy trickle into her laced bodice. He slipped it up, fast, precise, and one side of her chest was hanging out. Hargreaves felt herself being flipped around, pushed, and she threw her arms out so she wouldn't fall —winding up bent over, with him fumbling at her. It took a moment for him to notice she had got her lighter from where it was tucked into her boot. Still more precious moments before he realized the clicking sound and the smell were the trousers at his ankles, now aflame.

"What the—"

It was ballet itself, delivering the elbow to his face. She idly wondered if her skirts were aflame. She had acquired a plain rough-spun skirt that hid her .22 Tranter, but the edges were a cheap, durable trim lace. Seeing a stray ember, she beat at it until it went out.

Hargreaves certainly did not expect the lout to rise to the occasion of fire with a soprano lilt, stumbling to put himself out, lurching into the crowd. But she followed him anyway, in case she had killed him with her little act. Her stomach gave a groan of protest.

"That will never do," said a voice nearby, and she almost lashed out again. But it was only one of the ladies from the parade, decked out in red, white and blue. Feathers at her crown soared high up, bowing and waving. Under the paint her skin was a rich sienna, her eyes kind. Hargreaves tucked in her elbows, in case she touched the woman's front by mistake.

"Did you know him?"

"Don't you worry about him, there he goes now into the horse trough. Crowd thinks he's a clown. No, look at the state of you, honey. Come here," said the woman, and she fussed over Hargreaves' torn bodice. With a firm yank, she pulled it the rest of the way off.

"Oh my word!"

"My name is Jocasta Santiago," said the woman. Behind her, a man in purple and yellow motley appeared with jars of paint and a brush. He had his eyes covered. "And that is Shanks." Jocasta eyed Hargreaves' assets. "He juggles."

"Oh, but I'm not—" Hargreaves protested, but the woman was already tucking Hargreaves' bodice up into a bustle, and rolling the boots down for more skin. Shanks handed over the paints, and once Santiago began to apply them, Hargreaves was held rapt.

For one thing, the paint made it hard to move without smearing it around. For another, Santiago was turning her skin into an inspired canvas. Stars appeared in deft strokes at her side, and stripes too, covering her front and up one shoulder: an artistic rendering of the American flag. It was too late to request the Union flag, Hargreaves supposed. Santiago put up her hair, so her neck rose swan-like and cool in the desert air. Then she felt herself being summarily pushed out into the parade, which had dispersed to let folks talk to and take photograms with the painted women.

It was exhilarating. After a while her undercover training and the reflection in mirrors made her stand tall, push her chest out, and even preen, a little. People came by and offered her money to stand, and look magnificent, and smile. What few hecklers arrived were quickly dispatched by burly strongmen from the parade, so quickly it must have been according to some prior compact. The jugglers and clowns stood near, ready to receive the currency, which made it about the guests, not the money.

Shanks the juggler wandered the outskirts, tossing aloft bottles, bright balls, and knives. "A hair under a pound," he said, when Hargreaves asked him if they were difficult. "The bottles. The balls, lighter, half a pound. The knives, a quarter. But they're the hardest."

Quite contrary to her own very Victorian sentiments, the enterprise of public nudity seemed natural and beautiful. Soon enough her smile was genuine. She didn't think it possible, but the instant she found herself in the crowd, she understood why Jocasta Santiago had done it. Her clothes were hopeless, sliced too badly to be decent. But painted and part of the show, she was not only accepted as normal, she was revered. Celebrated. Amongst them, she was protected. Untouchable.

In the distance, the dim glow of the rodeo's lights lent a pagan air to the shouts of encouragement, like a May Day festival. The lights of the fire breathers lit up the night. A bull bellowed, in rage. Really, a spectacle was always a sort of sacrifice, she thought idly. Her aching feet were a testament to that, slotted into borrowed high heels after one of the girls remarked on the inspector's excellent calves.

Later in the evening, the performers counted the day's substantial takings. A good percentage went to the strongmen and the jugglers, enough to be appreciative but not enough for them to have any power over the women. Jocasta Santiago counted the money, comparing it to a meticulous ledger in her head. Hargreaves accepted her stack of coins and bills. That small fortune would take her at least to the next woolly bear junction at Dodge City.

The juggler Shanks raised his glass in toast, which Hargreaves gladly accepted. His full name was Cole D. Shanks. He was a lanky fellow, youthful, with old gray eyes. Old scars dotted his hands, whether from his profession or his peers, it was hard to say. As they ate, the food and beer and the money loosened their lips, and Hargreaves found herself sharing her trip across America with Shanks, who took it as if it was the most natural thing in the world. Of course, she mentioned nothing of her betrayal of Her Majesty, or the dire lumps sitting in her lorry out in the field.

By and by they spoke again of the day's haul, which even by an old hand's standards was a fair lot.

"I don't mean to bite the hand that feeds," said Hargreaves through a chummy bite of smoked turkey leg, "but the spectators are awfully loose with their money."

"It's always this way. Doesn't matter the season, they come in droves. This year, perhaps more...there's a rumor afoot, you see," said Shanks. He seemed a practical sort, but it would be wrong to say there was no bitter bone in him.

"A rumor?" Hargreaves answered. Shanks had an air of showmanship telling a story.

"Yes...The rails are humming with a story...a story about a ghost train bearing the souls of the recently deceased..." Shanks went on. "Stand at midnight at any station in the country, and you'll hear its keening wail across the desert. Stand too close and it will take you with it—barreling through like a bat out of hell. They say it's no mere engine but a fortress of iron, its smokestacks huffing brimstone and its cars bristling with the *skeletal arms of the damned!*" Shanks made a wobbling howl, as of a lost soul.

"No!" Hargreaves gripped her heart, and put her hand to her forehead, feigning a spell.

"Absolutely! Why do you think the streets are so clean of vagrants? Ain't Christian charity," said Shanks. He turned and helped serve the arriving tankards from a passing hand. The clowns and strongmen did their own cooking and serving. The ale was good and river-cold.

"Why are Americans so keen on traveling?" said Hargreaves, feeling the chill from the ghost story blend with the ale. She wanted to talk about little nothings instead.

"Most of them are just passing through, on their way to some other place," said Shanks. He made a sort of flapping shape with his hands, to indicate greener pastures far away.

"Why is that, you think? Don't they have anything better to do?" asked Hargreaves.

"People out in flyover country, they get a little crazy," said Shanks, between sips. "Fly-over, because the woolly bears generally take folks over without stopping by. Nobody here wants to live here, but folks stay for the freedom, and the lawlessness, and the sheer stubbornness of having a piece for themselves."

"That explains the spectacle, the sideshow feats. The enormous novelty."

"There's so much space and wealth and time—who knows what to do with it?" said Cole indifferently. "Look at that horizon. It doesn't go anywhere! The airships close everything down real small, maybe a few days apart, but down in the flyover, the west might as well still be endless."

"Scrappy plains from nowhere to nowhere. Rolling hills full of coyotes. Fruitless woods thick with murderous lions and tigers and bears," said Jocasta, coming to sit with them. "And nary a good man in all of it…save this one."

Hargreaves started. The woman was voluptuous, top to bottom. She had the wild beauty of the plains Indians. An equestrian's body, an aquiline nose, but the olive complexion of the Spaniards. Up until then Hargreaves hadn't noticed her own nudity. Jocasta went on.

"Lots of people don't belong here. They came in their ships with their guns hundreds of years ago and still think they own this place. They haven't earned this land, and the land knows it."

"It'd be the stupid man who can't sit still and appreciate all that natural beauty," said Shanks. "But the conveniences of the Steam Age make it hard to. The looseness of the girls in the big city, the wealth and power, and the height of the towers. Seeing airships crisscross over their heads day in and day out. Anybody would feel inadequate."

"You're the last one to feel inadequate," said Jocasta, nudging him with her elbow. The smile she extracted seemed a little forced, but it clearly satisfied Jocasta, who held on to Shanks possessively. Hargreaves brought them another round from the tent's stall, and Shanks went on as if there was no interruption.

"There's something going around this land that taints everything. The ether is always jabberin' about limeys waging war in South America, beggin' your pardon. About the Mohammedans killing everybody. Two hundred pounds at a time, receiving a nitroglycerin blessing and up! In the air. They fear the prairie pirates coming to take their daughters. They fear our way of life coming under fire, of killers falling from the clear blue sky. Meanwhile, the people doing the most killing are born and bred right here. The senators and congressmen don't see, so far away, fighting amongst themselves, deciding the lives of the soldiers without ever setting foot on foreign soil."

"As if you vote," said Jocasta, looking away. She looked like she'd heard it before. Probably Shanks himself would be swallowed up in his flyover country, if he didn't have Jocasta.

"People feel powerless, they feel small, so they get in a rickety cart and they ride, like their folks used to on the frontier. For any ounce of hope. On the bleeding edge of the frontier, because they'd got to where they were going, where the edge of the world was. What else was left?" said Shanks.

"How about a family? Building something for themselves, like a house, or a town?" said Jocasta.

"But that's not what they do. They wind giant balls of string, they build unlikely architecture, and they fuck, yes, and maybe that makes them happy, for a time. Maybe they feel like their tiny flyover world opens up into something big and they're free from that terror for a while."

Shanks fell into an introspective silence, sipping at his suds. Jocasta looked into the sideshows, at the bright lights in the darkness. A weariness was settling into Hargreaves' bones. Dancing was hard work. The chill of the night crept inexorably in. As she got up to go, she nearly missed Shanks' slurred mumble, deep in his cups.

"The folks who have the most? They're the nuttiest of them all."

Vanessa Hargreaves spent the night, at Jocasta's insistence, in the small train car that housed the performers' bunks. The others bolted the thick doors against the calliope music and the shouting. The train walls were solid steel, covered by soft, colorful weaves, and made a comfortably quiet place to rest. She had been invited to stay and join the revelry, but Hargreaves was weary from the road. As it turned out, that was her salvation.

Hargreaves only found out what happened the next day, but knowing didn't help her guilt. She hadn't known what had happened to Shanks or Jocasta. Neither of them had returned to the bunks, and Hargreaves had stayed as long as she dared, long into the day. But the red-soaked ground at her feet had been terrible portent for their fates, and she'd remembered her own pursuers, certainly not far away. So she had pulled her Feint away from the circus, surprisingly untouched.

That night, the circus had gone on, sleepless. Clowns had appeared, chucked a few pies. Handsome cowboys had ridden, with just the right blend of simpleton charm and not giving a damn. Fun was had by all. That is, until they brought out the Brazen Bull.

Its muscled surface gleamed in shades of bloody gold and yellowed bone. Grates held back the fire of its loins. Its hooves raised a fine dust that burst scintillating into a thousand sparks, rising up from its steaming, rumbling flanks. Most terrible of all, its golden horns twisted out and forward, a yoke tipped with carved images of sacrificial rites and a pair of wicked points. The builder, an unknown man with rather Latin mustaches, demonstrated their sharpness by holding out an inflated canvas balloon, a sturdy stabilizer common to airships as counter-ballast. Snorting, the Bull reared, its head twisting in the direction of the target, and the balloon became rags on the ground.

All this Hargreaves heard later, driving her Feint away and chatting with the folk at waystations on the road. One of them had a poster depicting the animal, though it did not look nearly as terrifying flattened on paper. Hearing the storytellers reiterate how the Bull snorted and tore through the ring, how the challenge was issued, and how the freemen who roped the livestock fled from it like a black tide. She fancied she could still detect the faint thunder of its footfalls. The shining spurs of the rider, as he mounted against the handler's protests. She could envision the fine weave of his showy spats against the tiny pistons of steam work. The glint of the Bull's hooves, stomping the remains of its rider to pulp. And then it had torn its way out, trampling the rest of the rodeo.

Of course, none of the storytellers had actually seen it for themselves —but they had seen the bodies in the morning, gored through by the thing's horns and bloody upon the ground. And, remembering Cole D. Shanks' words, Hargreaves did not forget to look at the faces of the storytellers: flush, animated, lively with lust and novelty. Perhaps the accident had been some tonic for their otherwise gormless lives, but Hargreaves did not care to repeat the experience. The thing she was towing in the back of the lorry was terrible enough. She did not need to seek a golden calf to feed an existential wanderlust.

But she found she hadn't yet tired of the sideshow quality of the American highway. The roads were rough, and the going bland. Any distraction was better than the endless stretches of rolling plain, dotted here and there with disturbingly adorable roadkill. Hargreaves did wonder; was the moping Shanks right? Did the infinite land and cruel wildness make the natives go mad? Mad enough, perhaps, to lavish their unblinking affection onto a clockwork folly even as it speared them on its horns.

In a dive somewhere on the plains, Hargreaves cheered as a local man heroically tackled twenty-one Hamburg steaks (bun and lettuce included) to win the local championship eating contest.

She stopped at a grotesquerie housed in a humid lean-to. Featured attractions included a three-headed sheep, an aborted cow fetus, an allegedly haunted doll, and a man with six fingers to each hand, who turned out to be the proprietor. The curator's doe-like smile belied something sinister that Hargreaves could not place; she found him the most unnerving specimen of all.

At length a tornado sent her far north off her regular route, where she came upon an enclave of recluses made up of musicians, nudists and mushroom fanatics. They lived high on a plateau where they held saturnalia in rock chambers that overlooked the plains below. Hargreaves dimly remembered changing into something not quite decent, joining the group in a dazed catatonia. In her sweet madness, she thought she heard a long, low whistle come tearing over the plain. When she peered out over the shadows of the country below, she thought she saw a long, thin shadow writhing over the land like a wraith trailing its cloak of pestilence. Shanks' ghost train? But the stone room had no substance, and the world was topsy-turvy. Her eyes could not be trusted. Hargreaves felt a bit like Alice falling down the rabbit hole.

The next day she quietly crept off the plateau, recovered her clothes, drove away, and watched a man eat twenty-one pies only to vomit all over a diner. He did not win the contest.

Wandering felt good. Distractions felt good. If Hargreaves stopped to actually get on with her mission, she would start thinking about Her Majesty again. The mission weighed heavily on her. Operating without a formal briefing and trusting to the Queen's nebulous moral authority to justify her actions made Vanessa want to run into the nearest waffle house & challenge the local record, stuff herself to bursting and vomit out all the bad. Maybe Shanks had been right. Maybe the people around here built themselves grotesqueries and Brazen Bulls out of clockwork to distance themselves from the horrible dry void of their lives. If Abraham had had the Golden Calf near when asked to kill his own son, he might have chosen the brilliance of the material distraction over the immaterial God. What was Hargreaves' idol? Who was her God?

Back on the road, she was waylaid by a Red Indian uprising. The Comanche had journeyed far north, or Hargreaves had ventured farther south than she'd thought, or they were highwaymen dressed in Comanche colors. Hargreaves had come to learn this was a common enough diversion tactic.

The maybe-Indians had derailed a locomotive, a big Squamosa hauling a train of thirty or forty cars. Raiders quickly plundered the passengers of their small valuables and left the ravaged train sprawled across the county road, blocking it off. The engine itself lay wedged across the pass, sixteen wheels to a side, her great bellowing vents screaming useless against the unfeeling stone. It wasn't a violent derailment, but it was a mighty inconvenient one, which was surely the point. With the roads blocked and the law busy freeing up the Squamosa, the thieves could get away as quick as they liked.

The train behind the engine had stopped across the road in a valley, blocking up the way ahead. Hargreaves was left trapped behind a long motor caravan, in a valley that allowed none of them a way around the train. The drivers took it in turns to yell at the mostly-freemen engineers, and the pale authorities that showed up from the other side yelled at everybody. From inside the train came the braying of asses, the roaring of tigers and the lowing of bison—the circus was here, recovered from its horrible night, shipped away from its rings and packed into its colorful cars. Hargreaves supposed it must be a traveling act, with many different stops to entertain.

With the Squamosa straining to hoist herself back onto the track before the next engine came through, there was an atmosphere of urgency with the workmen. They scrambled forward and backward, connecting cranes with tall sprockets and frantically loading fuel pods from the fuel car. Not a single relay allowed the signaling of the oncoming train, barreling along at ungodly speeds toward them. If it collided with the rear of the derailment, even at braking speeds, it would wrest the remaining cars off the track and turn the valley into a bonfire.

"Dammit!" one of the workmen said, as a fuel pod tumbled off his cart, striking a stone and leaking a sticky, bluish slick.

The deputies and engineers were understandably nervous. The passengers and trapped drivers, less so. Onlookers milled about, conversing, peering curiously as more and more official-looking cruisers approached, crowding the narrow throat of the road and furthering their entrapment.

Several of the younger train passengers commandeered a wide, flat high ground invisible to the valley below. The drivers below looked on enviously as these well-off society ladies collected themselves and headed up. The menfolk came to Hargreaves and asked if she might ascend the lofty heights to discern if the girls were safe from bandits. It was natural, she supposed, as there were few women of an age to hold no truck with such frivolity yet still hale enough to climb the rocks. At first, she had refused point-blank, but she began to fear some entrepreneurial youth would climb the rocks himself, so she took it upon herself to get rid of their excuse. The louts spared not a glance for Hargreaves' own statuesque figure and leonine mane, though they had watched the young girls climb. Granted, she'd been slotted into a dun traveling dress and trapped in a hot sweatbox for hours, but the sting was sharp, nonetheless.

At the top, Hargreaves found the ladies had opened parasols, and sent for extravagant amounts of teatime victuals, and were sunbathing as if they were on the beaches of the French Riviera. The view over the valley was quite beautiful, stretching away a golden vista to either side. Hargreaves accepted a biscuit and some lemonade before heading down.

Once she reported the situation, the menfolk seemed to lose interest —out of sight, out of mind. Parlor games sprang up on the roadside. The conductors revived the attendants, who engaged the spirit of opportunistic capitalism with cases of lemonade, cakes and other victuals now salable to a larger audience. All the while a group of engineers, naked to their dark waists, wrestled with great chains and other heavy equipment to put the Squamosa to rights. Hargreaves thought the division of labor didn't have to be quite so chromatic, but she was at a loss as to where to start fixing the problem or what the problem even was. It was not her place to question it.

In fact, in the riot of recovery, deploying the crane and sorting out those passengers who would surely never see their heirlooms again, and the amiable picnic atmosphere now permeating the afternoon, the murder might very well have been overlooked.

The girls were returning from their plateau, save one or two stragglers. Lord knew why they had stayed—for a glimpse of the sunset, perhaps? It had grown dark, but the warmth of the sun was still in the rocks, when the cry rang out.

Hargreaves immediately knew the scream of death and raced toward it, only to smack right into a panicked young woman. She had not finished restoring her dress from the sunbathing, and her underthings showed. It was hard not to judge the menfolk, who seemed more shocked by the sudden whiteness of her petticoats than the screams.

"Men," muttered Hargreaves. By the stations of the cross, they were only underclothes!

"Oh my God! Bernadette, oh, she was only just there, by the rocks. She fell. She's still running!" said the girl, her shock infectious.

"Here, take care of the hysterical lady," said one rather strapping fellow, who felt compelled to ascend before the frowning Hargreaves could help. A few others lit portable arc lanterns, and in the harsh light, the strapping fellow looked much the cad to the inspector's eye.

"Oy, who do you think you're speaking to?" Hargreaves protested, but she was weighed down by the nervous bundle in her arms. "Hi, what's your name? Penelope? All right, come now, sit there, everything will be fine. Yes, Bernadette will be fine."

Hargreaves foisted the lady onto a rock, where she could look after herself reasonably well. The inspector did not see why self-reliance had to be a solely male virtue, nor why she was the designated nurse. The strapping fellow pulled out a rather large pistol, with a far too clean chrome inset. Then he flew up the trail.

Once the girl's protests were overcome, Hargreaves put a foot onto the path just in time to hear the bang of a firearm. Casting aside her presumptions, she dashed up the pebbly slope, nearly getting her head blown off in the darkness by a second volley. Only her Yard instincts saved her at the last moment, preserving her behind the cover of the ridge.

"Blast it, I'm the woman, the one from below!" she cried. She thumbed her lighter, which lit the scene before her in a comforting sphere of firelight, and held it to her face.

"Oh! I'm so sorry. He's gone behind the brush!" The strapping fellow said. His voice sounded as if his suspenders were on too tightly. "There's a lot of blood," he added, too loudly for Hargreaves' taste.

Looking about her, Hargreaves saw the scraps of vegetation indicated, and rolled toward it. Dry and crumbly, they offered little cover, but the pile of rocks they stood upon were good enough against any slugs dulling themselves against their bulk. She was also dimly aware of another girl, slumped against a rock, and a man, spread-eagled, tinting the air with the copper of blood. She pulled her gun and held it together with the lighter, with her fingers splayed to protect her eyes. Hargreaves was mindful the flame did not touch the cylinder. Then she ducked over her rock, all in one go to blind whomever was out there.

A deeper shadow shifted, spitting out the figure of a man.

Hargreaves caught the dastard in the shoulder with her .22, just as the figure emerged from a clump of brush. He was colorful, standing out from the desert in flickering gold. As he fell, something tumbled from his hand and stuck deep in the earth—a vicious boning knife, long and curved, with a sturdy wood grip. The man's face turned into the light.

It was the juggler, Cole D. Shanks.

There was a queer expression upon the juggler's face, a grimace owing no small part to pain, and all to some possessing hate. Another spectre, Hargreaves could not help but think. But she had loaded her gun with .22 bullets that were never intended to kill, and Shanks was only stunned and bloodied.

She was upon him in an instant, kicking the weapon away, and a tussle followed. But high ground was high ground, and boot heels were boot heels. Shanks rolled, as if he could escape, perhaps, but came to a painful rest against a sharp stone. Dust coated the blood on his colorful costume, and the wound must surely have stung abominably. The man was lucid, with no sign of shock, hissing in pain.

"Why?" Hargreaves asked, leveling her gun at the performer's chest. They were both breathing heavily, and even the one word was considerable effort. Her flame flickered, dangerously.

Shanks, wheezing, mumbled something. He grinned, his lips moving impossibly farther toward his ears.

"What?" gasped Hargreaves. She was starting to see red. Perhaps she was wanting of water. The last of the mushrooms? But that was hours ago. Shanks' colors were running together, the handsome suit blurring into chevron shapes, like tiny horned diamonds in the flickering light. They looked more like scales than anything, and when she focused on his face, that too was strange, as if its surface crawled with a thousand golden insects. When he spoke, his mouth was a gash in the surface of the moon. The words she could make out were gibberish.

"A hair under forty dollars," he was saying. "The kidneys. The eyes, dearer, half a Benjamin. The heart, a quarter thousand. But they're the hardest..."

"Ugh!" Hargreaves shrieked, and heard an answering call. It set Shanks to shouting.

"The girl! I got so close! Close enough so you smell the perfume off her skin and you realize she's just made of meat. Fat and skin, nerve, and gristle, and meat, meat, meat. And meat, you can buy by the pound..."

Shanks snarled, springing forward like a cornered beast.

Hargreaves shot him, one-two-three, in perfect Yard form. Because she didn't stop shooting until she put down the threat, and this time the bullets hit at point-blank range, pricking the juggler full of holes. He went down like a sack of bricks.

Or a pound of sausages, thought Hargreaves.

She felt whatever dark thing that had taken Shanks grip her for a moment, and she thought maybe, just maybe, she heard the shattering noise of a doorknob-sized glass orb break on the rocks.

She looked at the other man sprawled upon the ground. His clothes were good, but not flashy. She touched for a pulse—none. When she went to check, the girl was still breathing, probably just out from the shock of seeing blood. The man, an attendant? A paramour? It did not matter. He was dead.

She had no doubt, then, that there had never been a Brazen Bull at the circus. At the rodeo, perhaps there had been some clockworked attraction that had later been incorporated into the visitors' stories. But the thing that had killed all those people that night had been Shanks. Shanks, with his easy smile, and his fast hands. The way he had tripped her attacker back at the circus into the horse trough, thinking nobody had seen. Even armed, a person might not see him coming, with the darkness and the tantalizing lights of the circus. And there was his trailer, with so many places to hide contraband, and so many chances to meet with the Ghost Train.

Hargreaves spared a thought for Jocasta, whom she had cared for—what had become of her? There were no easy thoughts to be had there.

Later, as she descended the rocks of the plateau with the girl in hand, she heard the others calling to each other that the body was gone. The clown was no longer on the plinth of rock, and in fact was nowhere to be seen. Search parties were organized, more lanterns got from the authorities' stores. As Hargreaves sat in her Feint, watching the officers remove the girl to an ambulance on the other side, she thought of another story and checked the back of the flatbed, where Alphonse sat in the dark. Alone, by the light of her flame. Good.

But that was of little comfort. Even after the deed was done, the grimace would not leave her; the feeling of madness in Shanks' round eyes. It was inside of Hargreaves, something that maybe had almost caught her as well, clung to her by its fingernails until it was violently jostled aside by this baptism of blood. There was something roaming the ether, perhaps a demon loosed upon the land, but nothing virgin or native. No, no, this was not a wild thing, but a warped, imprisoned creature Hargreaves had known most of her life, that had found freedom in the wide-open Eden of America.

Due to either gross negligence or sage cunning, the local police did not arrest Vanessa Hargreaves. Vanessa herself was not sure which. At any rate, too many people were out looking for the murderer Shanks to bother stopping her. Later, with the help of an officer, she managed to back out of the valley. He wanted nothing more than to be rid of her in their jurisdiction. One less mess to tidy up. She passed a hearse, a landau, its boxy carriage final in its utilitarian shape. Then she was on her way, and yes, definitely, there was nobody in the back seat.

About an hour later, she heard the thunder of the other train colliding into the back of the Squamosa. Thirty tons at least, plus animal, human, and cargo, righted by a massive effort onto tracks two yards apart. The engineers had forgotten to get the train going, held rapt by the spectacle of the murder.

STATION 5

America the Beautiful

FROM UPSTATE NEW YORK, INSPECTOR HARGREAVES' MOBILE Automata Division took the train west, in roughly the direction the fearsome tarantula automata had been traveling. Arturo's spending account only came as far as the telegraph stations, that is, somewhere between Ohio and nowhere. Past that they had to rely on hard currency. So they peddled the weathered cab, and as the journey went on, their last possessions. Cezette, for one, felt the loss most keenly, but also wholeheartedly—some of the sold things were for her legs.

Yet as they crossed the golden mountains and into the rolling forestry of America, a smile also crossed into her face and stuck there, as if spirit gummed. It wasn't long before they caught the whispered rumors of some giant metal man traveling the highways of America. MAD followed, from the foothills of the Appalachians across the southern reach of the Great Lakes.

Through Chicago and across Iowa.

Making the connection over the plains' dirigibles past Montana. These were great balloon clouds floating in orderly lines over the plateaus, as if foreshadowing a storm that would never come. It was not significantly quicker than a locomotive, but benefited from being totally indifferent to the landscape, though storms grounded them twice. Also, half the lines had been closed off and no engines ran the Northern corridor. Guardedly, the clerks spoke of something prowling the tracks, some kind of roaming menace that preyed on travelers. One intrepid paper had a staked out a position and photogrammed something terrifying: a vast shadow spilling over both sides of the tracks at a pass, dark eyes shining in the dark. Whatever it was, it was big. Cezette thought proper Ghost Trains had no business being so corporeal.

Mountains and lakes came and went beneath MAD as they flew west, the great canvas of America reduced to mere scenery. The main entertainment seemed to be watching two fighter escorts bristling with riflemen. They swooped over the ever-changing landscape, the only protection against air pirates. They could be seen sometimes, the shark fins of their sails stark against the rolling yellows and greens below.

"America, she is beautiful!" Cezette proclaimed, as one wild beauty to another. Arturo felt a sudden pang of paternal feeling, though she was no child of his.

South, and always west.

As they drew closer, the rumors evolved into articles in the local papers. Hargreaves' trail seemed clearer and clearer with each way station. Once they passed Utah, however, the trail grew cold; there were no articles about the mysterious traveling automata, nor rumors about its operator. It was as if the vast salt flats had swallowed them whole. Even Arturo's information networks diminished to a dribble of telegrams, often two days late and of no use anyway. It was all they could do to ride the trains and ask the people on them, like some sort of Luddite. Here, past the breadbaskets, the rails had opened up again, connections available at Salt Lake City, Grand Junction, and Cedar City.

On a routine way station stop, they learned of a town called Midland, a gateway between the heartland and the ports of the Northwest. A successful mining town turned fuel hub, Midland was destined to become one of the great western cities in Washington territory. That is, until an accident lit the coal mines beneath the town. Their great drill tunneled too deep, or hit some sleeping geological titan, and the next thing they knew the mines were aflame. Smoke began to issue between the cracks of the Earth. Water became contaminated, bursting aflame at the merest touch of a match. A gray murk covered the town in ash and acrid poison. Buildings crumbled in sudden sinkholes. People fell through gaping maws in the street, swallowed by the hellish inferno beneath.

Arturo had said he suspected Hargreaves still wished to drop the box into the Lands Beyond. Nevertheless, if the inspector had word of Midland, she would know that was as good a place to dispose of the box as any, and closer than the Pacific. Of course, these destinations were only a product of his inductions, but they made sense. Hargreaves merely needed to drop the box into a sinkhole, where the flaming abyss would hide it forever. The periodicals had published numerous photograms of tall, thin drilling spires erected over a blasted inferno, and Hargreaves likely would have seen them

It was cheering news to Cezette, and it made the picturesque scene scrolling past them more beautiful. Their train was a handsome one, its windows like gilt picture frames. Even in a pinafore, clicking legs churning up an uncomfortable heat inside the wool, her enthusiasm could not be contained. Now she leaned out of the train window, holding her hat and watching an eagle wheel over the rusty plateaus.

"Look at it! Oh, is there nothing so grand?" Cezette cried to the wind.

"Yes, if you can forget about the underground slave economy, the barely concealed militaristic isolation, the perversion of the democratic ideal..." Jean Hallow trailed off as Cid and Arturo both gave him their best searing looks. A dark cloud came over his brow.

"How uncharacteristically grim of you, my dear Jean," Arturo said, settling on one of the plush couches in the spacious sleeper car. He tore into a waxed bag of Spud Chips. "Curses! These are crisps!"

"Didn't you live in America for a time, Hallow?" Cid said, in his usual kindly grunt. He sounded like a French horn trying to play a waltz.

"Yes. I attended private school and university here," Jean said. He huddled deeper into the lapels of his greatcoat. "I apologize. The scenery is beautiful, I would not want to spoil it for you."

"*Oui!* Look at all the space! You can see for miles!" Cezette cried. She started to shift sideways, for a better view, but her foot froze as she shifted her weight. Cezette began a slow topple into the opposite couch.

"Your leg!" Jean said.

"Careful, girl!" Cid said.

Both of them reached out for her at the same time, Jean opening his arms to catch her, Cid reaching for her outstretched arm to steady her. There was a slit through the skirt for her clockworked legs to stride more easily, and now they came jerkily through, tearing the slit further. Cid pulled on Cezette's arm, and she fell sideways into Jean's lap. Her legs came up and bashed Cid across the brow. He fell beneath them, pinned like an insect. It was the perfect time for someone to come in and misunderstand the situation, so of course the paneled train door slid open.

"Excuse me, I was wondering if you knew where the conductor was, I have some baggage to look after...Oh, my!" It was a young woman, wrapped in a colorful garment none of them could name. Though the brightly dyed silks covered her from neck to ankles, they were billowing cool, and the brown skin of her face was smooth and dry. She looked much more comfortable than Cezette.

"My good miss, this is not what it appears to be," Arturo attempted to waylay the new arrival before she could summon the conductor. Instead, she lunged forward, nimbly pulling the French girl to her feet, away from the two men.

"Don't you try anything, or we shall call for someone. Conductor! Conductor!"

Cezette took it upon herself to cover the new girl's lips with one finger. The soft gesture was more effective than gagging her with a palm, as the menfolk were sure to do. With her other hand, Cezette calmly closed the door.

"You misunderstand. They are merely trying to assist me," Cezette said. Before anyone could protest, the girl slipped her skirt up, sliding her opaque footwear down far enough for a glimpse of sprocketry to show. The brown girl's eyes widened, but she said not a word. She sat down.

After a reasonable interval without the conductor making an appearance, Cezette sat down herself and, after a hesitant pause, removed the rest of her shoe and sock for Cid to make an inspection.

"I see you finally know to clean these regularly," Cid grumped. He held the leg by the foot and calf and peered through the space where a normal leg's Achilles tendon and the bone would be, oblivious of the wide-eyed young woman. He groped about with a tapering pair of tweezers. "There, a piece of the fabric is caught in the suspension spring. Damn ladies' fashions...if these were in trousers, nothing would go wrong."

"My bonnie Cid, *je suis Française!* I will look horrid in your stovepipes!" Cezette protested. She fished about in her small tote, until she found a floppy hat to jam defiantly upon her head.

"Bah!" Cid said.

"I suppose, where you come from, having steamwork legs is quite normal," the girl still on the train seat piped up. The tenderness and skill Cid used in manipulating Cezette's legs around their porcelain fittings had seemed to hold her rapt.

"Rude," Jean Hallow coughed. He seemed to take the new arrival poorly. The lanky scholar sat resolutely staring at the blur of lush, wild country outside the window.

"Costly, but normal enough," Arturo replied. Ever the accomplished liar, he made up a story on the spot. "Our Uncle Cid loves his niece so. I'm sure your elders are as affectionate to allow you the freedom to wander about without a chaperone, Miss..."

"Jade. Violet Jade," the girl said quickly. "I am traveling in the car behind yours. With, ah, my father."

"That is Arturo C. Adler, my guardian," Cezette replied. "Cid Thatcher, my machinist, and Jean Hallow, my tutor. I am Cezette Louissaint, late of Paris. Arturo and Jean are lovers."

Having been sequestered in a tower much of her young life, Cezette lacked the finesse of society more than she lacked English, and it showed sometimes. The sudden accusation sparked an instant din of quarreling; both men protested, insisting they were no item of any kind, became offended at the others' protestation, and began to bicker with enough sass to drown out the North of England. To make matters worse, Cid was uncharacteristically progressive, repeating his grinning mantra of "it's a new England; such things are as common as tea time," with increasing variations of smuttiness and innuendo. But Cezette saw Violet Jade pale, as if she had never met a homosexual before.

"What brings you here, Miss Jade?" Cezette said as soon as she found a gap to slip out of the crossfire. She was curious about the new girl, since she hadn't been allowed friends her own age in Paris. The constable in Hargreaves had flatly refused to put Cezette in a public school with the hooligans, but could find no private school willing to take a girl of little-known origin from a common household, so Jean Hallow had taken up the cause of her education.

"My father...he took a job at the plant up by the Falls," Violet Jade said. As they chatted, Cezette fished needle and thread from a pocket to mend her skirt with deft strokes. She was becoming quite good at it, and it reminded her of her maman. Both of them.

"Yes... I have read the Indians are quite adept at steamcrafts," Cezette said, remembering one of Jean's periodicals. Jade frowned. "Or is that just an English presumption?"

"I am afraid so. But, I am not Indian," Jade protested. "I was born and raised Bristol. My father is a moor of Sicily, and my mother an Italian and Russian performer. They met when she was touring his port of call."

"My own mother was an artist of some renown," Cezette said. "It is part of the craft to travel for one's patronage. Anything could happen."

"And your father?" Jade asked, but the expression on Cezette's face was sufficient. Jade took her by the hand, a gentle, feminine gesture the French girl hadn't known in quite some time.

Suddenly the little train cabin filled with a shimmering light—they were passing near another body of water, a rushing torrent nestled between America's verdant curves. A train conductor's voice came through the vacuum tubes, announcing the view and the beginning of tea time in the dining car.

"I apologize," Arturo suddenly emerged from his row, which until this moment had been continuing in a politely hushed murmur. "But Jean and I must settle our differences in the adjacent cabin."

The two of them got up and left the room. There was an audible bang as the adjacent cabin opened and shut. Cid looked around, then pulled out a small machinists' journal and a sandwich he had procured from the train's trolley.

"What? If you wanted something, you ought have spoken up. Here, go have some fun in the diner car," Cid grunted. He held out a small sheaf of money, a crisp fold he must have slipped out of Arturo's pocket when he wasn't looking. *Old habits die hard,* Cezette thought.

"Thank you, Uncle Cid," Cezette said, giggling, and the two girls left to make their way to the diner car.

Once there, Cezette was glad she had come. The diner car was well appointed, with a spacious triple-decker seating arrangement. A grand chandelier had been cleverly strung, immobile, between the gap of the top decks. Cornflower-blue and marigold tassels made the place feel almost Parisian.

When a serving man seated them at a bolted-down table in the middle deck, they discovered all the tableware was fine bone china edged in gold. Cezette was sure they would be destroyed with the first significant turn in the rails, but upon lifting one delicate cup, discovered a thin ring of clear rubber holding it fast to the saucer. Other locomotive conveniences were in use, including an ornate panel of toggles one could depress to discreetly summon the waitstaff, or to activate a small gramophone to play the train schedule and some light music.

"*Quel d'ommage!* They only have classical and this American jazz. Cid would have a ball," Cezette remarked.

"It's a shame. Habanero Aftershock have a new single," Jade agreed.

"Is that some American group?" She asked.

"Yes!" Jade giggled. "The accordion player just takes the piss! Haven't you heard them yet?"

"No, but the Heinous Anus was very good." Cezette pronounced it "ay-noos."

"The cafes were playing their cylinders all the time when I left London. Oh, and the bassist, he has the cutest bottom..."

"Tell me more about this...bassist..."

The ladies took their tea, or rather, the bottomless coffee everyone seemed to be having, and chatted pleasantly. Dense curtains gave them some measure of privacy, and contained their high-pitched giggling as well. Cezette had never done this with a girl her own age before. Questions came pouring out naturally, things she had burning in her head but was always too embarrassed to ask Maman. She was curious about the latest fashions, the newest music, the secret parties happening every Saturday amongst the progressive social set. But at that moment, the dining car announced it was shutting down to prepare for evening service, and the conversation drew to an end.

"I will be very happy to see you again," said Cezette.

"As will I," replied Violet. "I will bring my gramophone cylinders." They giggled, thinking of the bassist and his bottom.

The engine chugged north, through Idaho and Oregon, winding around Nevada to descend the spine of California. Over the course of the next day on the train, the girls stuck together, having few others of an age and temperament to talk with. They got on very well, and at the next tea time Violet got back around to the underground parties that seemed to happen in every fashionable city in Europe. Under Prague's fairy-tale streets, in the ossuary warrens under Paris, even the old church of Padua, where it was said Romeo and Juliet made their union.

"There is a Venice here as well, in the new world. We could go to a concert while the train refuels," suggested Violet one day at tea.

"Oh, we are not staying long!" Cezette protested. "We have some business, and then we will be gone. I am sure your father would protest, as well."

"Why?"

"Why? *Une femme* traveling in California, going to a social gathering... I was told polite society is not yet ready for something so bold. What if you found a *paramour*?"

"Hah! I should like to see father stop me," said Violet, her lip curling taciturn. Then, as if not meant for Cezette to hear, "Besides, I am promised to another..."

Cezette took a polite sip of tea, allowing Violet to return from her reverie.

"I am sorry, but I am here on a mission, and as much as I would love to, I am afraid it is not meant to be."

"That is a shame," Violet Jade said. "I was so hoping I could have—I say, what is that racket?"

Cezette and Jade pulled back the curtain of their dining booth, expecting perhaps an upset passenger or badly cooked cordon bleu. Instead, they found the diners out of their seats. The more assertive gentlemen were standing, peering around the chandelier at a uniformed conductor conversing tersely into a private speaking tube. They mumbled amongst themselves. Cezette accosted the nearest, a bespectacled gentleman with a paunch.

"Word from the forward cars is," the gentleman said, "there's been some disturbance farther along the line. The conductor is intent on clamming up about the subject."

Cezette turned to Violet whose face was twisted in abject horror. Her rich brown eyes bulged from skull like rotten cherries. Her full lips stretched tight over her mouth, frozen in a silent scream.

"Violet, *c'est* a small disturbance, likely some wild deer on the tracks. The conductors have it well in hand." Cezette tried to reassure the girl quivering in her bright silks, but she would not be consoled. Some childhood trauma, Cezette considered, remembering Jean Hallow's lessons.

"Cezette, you do not understand!" Violet said in an exasperated whisper. "We must take cover; we must find shelter!"

"Where? We are on a moving train!" Cezette began, before she was cut off by a piercing cry from a higher deck.

"What is going on?" A concerned woman shouted from the third level. She had a husky, smoke-rough voice that would brook no refusal. It echoed through the diner car, prompting the more old-fashioned men to take charge and make for the conductor's spot by the car's entrance. It was certainly the gentlemanly thing to do, but Cezette was pleased to see several of the ladies place their napkins on the table and set off to find out for themselves what had happened.

Unfortunately, it was perhaps the least opportune time for the husky madam to make herself heard. As the investigating diners reached the front of the car, the first of them seemed to jump, and the others shortly followed, in a wave. But when they came down they crumpled, like paper.

"Hold on to something!" Violet Jade's voice was something between a shriek and a bellow, and it caught the next throw of the train. The assorted tableware flew sideways, shattering like mortar against banister and skull alike. Cups smashed. Fobs winged past like deadly missiles. The husky woman tumbled head over heels like a circus performer in the center of the car.

Strangely, Cezette felt no panic, only a sort of detachment as if she were watching a piece at a picture-house. Her teacup gave a little hop, cup and saucer all of a piece, spilling a single drop of coffee in an inertial arc, right into the milk. It was an uncanny sight that more than anything brought Cezette's wits into focus.

Cezette hadn't forgotten the ways and means of her misadventures quite yet. She knelt. One of her hands flew to a rail, while the other depressed a spot in her leg, hidden by her skirt. There was a faint click, and Cezette suddenly found herself the rock in a deluge, anchored by the grip of her wrist and her heels. The claws in her soles held the material of the deck floor, and locked her ankles so she would not fall. Her sprung heels absorbed the shaking as a sort of disorienting vibration. There was a faint sensation of vertigo, as up became right and down became left and a tray of biscuits whirled about somewhere in the vicinity of her ear.

She threw a hand down to intercept Violet Jade, but her fingers were wet with coffee, and her grip loose. She might have been able to save herself, but her new and only friend tumbled headlong into the calamity.

STATION 6

It's Like Looking at a...

UNBEKNOWNST TO MAD, VANESSA HARGREAVES WAS HURTLING along nearby, having a grand old time. Having been cooped up on a woolly bear with only debutantes and country ranchers for company, she had taken to the ground with abandon, selling the Feint and crossing the naked country on Alphonse alone.

Despite the presence of her disquieting cargo, the journey through America was proving most relaxing. Most of the towns she came across were quiet, sheltered, and lacking deranged killers. They were oases in the wild, free country. In fact, she had learned traveling by engine or clockwork horse was something of a pastime, and some wanderers never settled down at all, choosing careers moving goods from one far-off town to another. Hargreaves found it freeing, which was surely the point.

The worst thing about the whole trip was having too much pie, and tending to Hargreaves' monthly needs. Decent manufactured goods were scant, save the ever-present Ubique-branded canned hams and beefs, distinct in their green wrapping. Just as she was contemplating the difficulty of purchasing sanitary items, she heard the derailment as a clamorous din not two miles through the forest.

"You have a mission...you have a mission..." Hargreaves tried to remind herself, but she knew it was of no use. She changed course and began moving swiftly toward the distant clamor. Alphonse responded lightning-quick, his steel arms thrown out for balance, legs digging furrows into the path. The dirt and rocks flew behind his wheels, spraying debris in every direction. Alphonse was made of surer stuff than Hargreaves, taking the occasional pebble with hardly a ding of complaint. The inspector worried for the Cook box, hoping it would withstand the shaking from its position on the automata's back.

It was not difficult to find the derailment. A plume of black smoke marked the place where it lay violently burning. The engine at the front had jumped the track and crammed itself into a small mountain pass like a book on the shelf, the one that clearly doesn't fit but is made to anyway. The other cars of the train had fared no better—the momentum had dragged the first cars into the inferno, adding fuel to the fire. Hargreaves counted; five cars, most likely first-class by the melting gilding and what markings remained. She resigned herself to the fact that those people were doomed.

The densely packed steerage was in the middle, and had merely skidded off the tracks, digging great trenches into the surrounding greenery. They'd slid up to the front of the train, and people were struggling to climb out, away from the burning engine. The boiler was still in one piece, but making rather distressing sounds.

Hargreaves urged her iron titan closer to the burning wreck. Alphonse leaped down the hill, tires shredding on the rough rocks. No matter; his lumbering steps took her down amidst the rent sides of the train, and his lobstered armor came between her and the occasional rivet, fired hot from its seat like a bullet. Quickly, she identified the nearest tragedy; an overturned car, closest to the burning hulk of the engine. Passengers in various states of injury were struggling to climb out of the windows.

"Tally-ho," Hargreaves whispered, and toggled all the pressure into the automata's legs. With a groan and a hiss, Alphonse answered by leaping completely over the car, his feet crushing out a coal fire about to lap at the plain washed wood. They were suddenly before the wreck of the train engine, waves of burning wind squeezing through Alphonse's gaps.

Hargreaves toggled pressure once more, flipping a line of switches that made pleasingly efficient clicks. She dumped it into Alphonse's arms to give her the most torque possible around his shoulder joins. His limbs shot forward, punching dents into a thick boiler plate—but holding the sheet in place, even as its rivets gouged dents into his chest and shoulders. The trembling wall of steel threatened to loose all the pressure of the ruined boiler onto the passengers behind Alphonse.

Heat from the burning engine and Alphonse's own interior was overwhelming. Hargreaves stripped off her duster. She removed a piece of ribbon from her neat bun, tying it securely round one of Alphonse's levers to keep him holding the plate in place. Only then did she climb out from between his head and shoulders, shielding the cockpit cavity with her duster as she did so. She heard it singe where hot sparks landed.

"You three!" Hargreaves called toward the nearest people, two men and a stout looking matron gazing at the wreck, their mouths agape. They were scorched from their escape, but did not seem hurt. "Help me pull the injured from the car!"

Hargreaves must have been a fright, with her leonine mane flying, bellowing orders like a general. The three survivors leaped into action, the men tackling a family just emerging from a broken window. The matron heaved herself at a bloody gentleman and hauled him out on her own. Hargreaves jumped down and helped to pull an elderly chap from the window nearest her before attending to the bloody gentleman.

"A nasty gash to the head, nothing too horrible. Can you walk? Head for the line of trees, there, and help guide others to you. You there! Support his head; he's got a neck injury!"

As more and more passengers emerged, Hargreaves was able to commandeer more assistance. In the second car, she found the train doctor diligently binding wounds with makeshift tourniquets soaked in grain alcohol. He must have raided the bar meant for the first class. The locked cabinet doors swung from broken hinges nearby.

"Zachary Methuselah Price, MD, at your service. I see you have first aid training?"

The young, curly-haired healer put the patients Hargreaves brought through triage, but he was far from businesslike. Instead, the doctor spent more time asserting his authority, treating Hargreaves as a nurse, even when the panicked patients around him looked to her confident direction for assistance. The inspector knew this would not do, and grabbed Price bodily by the collar, lifting him up.

"I am an inspector of Scotland Yard, and I have seen worse disasters than this. Make yourself useful. Tell these men to move the triage to the trees!" Suitably cowed, the doctor began to do so.

Bashed skulls and sprained ankles were common, but some patients required immediate attention. Their makeshift triage soon ran out of the precious grain alcohol. Hargreaves bellowed bloody murder when she discovered why: some of the gentleman passengers had taken to drinking it.

"What do you need them spirits for, eh?" the nearest of them protested when the inspector snatched the bottle out of his hand.

"Haven't you ever heard of germ theory, you backwards lump?"

"It's a conspiracy! Like coal-soot warming!" another lush declared drunkenly.

"Don't waste your breath! There's more liquor in the dining car!" Doctor Price yelled over the general din of suffering.

"Ugh," Hargreaves said, as she hurled the sturdy bottle at a man who was still sober enough to try beating her to the dining car. The glass shattered against his crown, putting him down. "Head trauma!" she cried to the doctor.

By now, they had recruited enough of the passengers, and the train was crawling with rescuers. The extent of injury did not abate as they moved down the line, it merely changed; there were more shattered items here, and more cuts and bruises. By the time Hargreaves reached the dining car, the train was not the Jacob's ladder of toppled cars near the front, but a more manageable queue of upset second-class cabins. Some of them were still upright, and the more enterprising passengers were using those beds to seat some of the steerage patients.

For a second, Hargreaves thought she saw a spiky Roman candle poke up from the cacophony, but she denounced it as a disaster mirage. She was tired, thirsty, and beginning to see things. Her chemise had long soaked through, the stays of her undergarments showing through the thin white fabric. She had chosen a reasonably thin spring skirt from a small shop some miles back, but to hide the gun tucked in a garter, she required the material to be opaque. The garment clung, itching like the dickens, until she had a moment to tie it up by her thighs. As for her ruffled top, she simply ripped the sleeves up to the bicep, tying off the excess. There were no complaints about decorum in the disaster; most of the older gents were simply glad for the sight, both of Hargreaves coming with first aid and of her long, shapely calves.

When she got to the dining car, she discovered a scene of utter chaos. The train had taken the brunt of the impact in the engine and first cars, but the shock had traveled down the remainder to end up in the rearmost cars. Like a whip, the force of the crash had run down the line of cars throwing the caboose and the dining car completely off the rail. Even from a distance, Hargreaves saw blood. Quickly, she climbed through a roof access into the car. Only a few decorative gaslights were still operating.

"Oh, God...Are you hurt, ma'am? I have field training; you're going to be just fine..."

Hargreaves was so involved in extracting the lady trapped beneath a heavy tea trolley she nearly did not see the man behind her. She turned to ask for assistance, but found herself suddenly under attack from a heavy truncheon. It was take the hit or drop the woman, so she turned her head and took the blow at her cheekbone. Stars swam into view.

"You ruffians!" the woman under the tea trolley screeched, rousing Hargreaves, as the pain started to dull her consciousness. More importantly, she got an arm free, bracing herself. Hargreaves threw up her hands to catch the next blow before it could connect with her head. Her block was clumsy, but effective; instead of knocking her unconscious the blow merely slid her down the aisle.

Hargreaves howled in pain but collected herself well enough to parry the next attack. The limited space made it difficult to avoid her attacker, but Hargreaves managed to avoid his advances long enough to get in a lucky punch to the figure's face. She felt wool—a mask? In any other fight she would have pulled her .22 and fired into the assailant's knee, but some foggy part of her recognized the smell of gas from the smashed lights. One shot might set the whole place ablaze.

Instead, the inspector went in for a sweep, taking out the man's leg from under him. Hargreaves felt the man fall, and also hesitate, not used to his prey fighting back. She was all ready for a punishing kick, but something hard struck her in the back of the head—a second villain!

The inspector was known through the Yard for being hardheaded, but even Hargreaves' thick noggin could not withstand repeated hammering. She went down like a sack of bricks, the world spinning around her. A dull lead weight in her side was a hateful boot. Dimly, she heard her assailants speak, but she found she could only weakly reach out, both depth perception and breath gone.

"Nubs, you lecher. Could have left the blonde well enough alone." A man's voice, deep and gurgling from a barrel chest.

"Look at the gams! The tart is asking for it in that outfit." A second voice; reedy, whispery. Probably the first assailant. Were they opportunistic bandits? Had they derailed the train? The voice gave her chills. Hargreaves was suddenly very aware of the open button on her chemise, the way it clung to her front.

"Get on with it, then. Stroke of luck she left the box with her gear," Barrel said. "Otherwise you wouldn't have the time to have your fun." Reedy giggled. There were heavy footsteps, leaving the car. The inspector could hear the tinkling of broken glass being trodden.

Suddenly Hargreaves felt hands on her. Realizing what was happening, the inspector managed to roll her eyes up, thinking, "Not again!" before her ankles were picked up. Didn't the menfolk have anything else on their minds?

"Scoundrels! Demons!" the tea trolley lady began to scream. She was certainly in pain, punctuating her accusations with groans, but whatever injury she had was overridden by the outrage of what was happening to her rescuer. Hargreaves herself busily swatted at the fleshy vices at her ankles, but the angle was all wrong, and her head still swam with mollywobbles. She heard someone, a man, come to investigate at the door, and receive a harsh rebuke.

"I say, why aren't you helping with the—what are you doing to that woman?"

There was a crack, and Hargreaves would bet her last shiny penny the Good Samaritan's jaw had been broken.

The hands at Hargreaves' ankles stopped dragging her and pulled her roughly to her feet. They stood her up and slammed her over onto her stomach on some surface, likely a dining table. She felt a boot slip between her toes and start pushing apart. There was a crash—the ruffled lady had thrown a teacup, or a saucer, with very poor aim.

Hargreaves felt the first pangs of fear. Certainly, sexual congress was nothing new, but this was not of her choosing. She was tough, trained, toned, deadly, a lean peacekeeping engine, which somehow made it worse. Every skill was a brick, every moral mortar holding together a fortress. The thought that low scum could best her was anathema. It made everything she had built seem worthless.

But the moment passed, and she rallied, fighting back with renewed vigor. She experienced something like what gamblers must feel when they back a good horse but still lose. Training, experience, even rage she had, but because she had been caught off-guard in a moment of kindness for others, this simpleton was about to have his way with her. She growled in frustration, but the beast simply redoubled his efforts.

Hargreaves was about to give up when all of a sudden there was an odd metallic thunk, and a cry of pain. She felt the weight fall from behind her and inhaled, hoarsely, drawing in all the hot, scorching air in the room. The edge of the table had been pressing on her stomach, and now her head cleared in a great rush. Coughing, she whirled round to see her attacker laid out on the debris of the floor. His head was caved in, obscuring whatever grotesque features he possessed before. He had been a thin, swarthy cretin. His penis lolled, still partially engorged.

When a supportive arm came round her, Hargreaves nearly threw her rescuer to the ground. It was only when she looked a second time did she see the unbelievable phantasm of Cezette Louissaint, holding her up with some difficulty.

"Maman! It really is you! Are you hurt?" Cezette gasped. Another look showed the girl was limping, one of her shins was bent at an unnatural angle. Her face was scrunched up, and she appeared to be twitching. Could she feel what went on in her legs?

"Cezette, how...? Why? Your leg, it's..."

"Do not worry, Maman. I broke it hitting that...*cretin,*" Cezette said. "Do you think I killed him?" For a time, the two simply stood there, standing over the limp, crushed form of the would-be rapist. They held their breath, Cezette, out of innocence, and Hargreaves, out of nausea.

Then the body shuddered, and a great wet snort erupted from it, and the women let out a long breath together.

Hargreaves' clothing was in disarray, but it was unimportant, a breach of decorum easily mended. She thought she would cry, in relief, or fear, or something, but the moment juddered to a halt as the tea trolley woman groaned once more.

"Your English, it is much better," Hargreaves managed to Cezette. "Sit over there. Let me help that poor woman before the trolley crushes her further."

"I had a friend..." whispered Cezette. She looked around, but nobody besides the corpse of a couple occupied the diner car. Evidently, the others were already evacuated.

"Had I known my end would come by afternoon treats, I might have ravished the lemon cakes with more gusto," the ruffled woman in question interrupted, with as much dignity as she could muster. The trolley had a small boiler for hot teas, and it was doing quite the number on her lower body. After some inspection, Hargreaves estimated if the matron's conservative skirts hadn't intercepted the blow, the trolley might well have broken the leg.

"You are very brave, my good lady. Now hold still," Hargreaves said. She waved Cezette over, and after bracing the young girl by the shoulders, used her powerful artifice leg to heave the trolley aside. The ruffles woman screamed, but it was a scream of panic, and the leg appeared only sprained. Hargreaves helped her up, and suddenly the three of them were looking at each other, marveling at the fact they were unharmed amidst the destroyed diner car. Hargreaves' temples were beginning to clear, and now the ringing was no worse than the migraines she got sometimes from her monthly dues.

"We must do something about your hair! *C'est quel horreur!* Was there a fire? Your chemise, it will not do," Cezette finally broke the silence, feigning a quibble over Hargreaves' attire. Her bottom lip wobbled. "Maman, we have been trailing you in America for weeks! Arturo thinks...oh, what is it...that, 'someone lit a fire under your *derriere.*' You simply disappeared!"

"Fire...fire! We must leave, quickly! The gas!" Hargreaves gasped. "My lady, I am afraid the two of you must help hold one another. Be careful picking over the glass!"

"And you?" the ruffled matron asked with urgency.

"I must take this ruffian outside. You've done quite a number on him, 'Zette, but he is still breathing," Hargreaves answered.

Hargreaves was aching all over, but her breathing came steadily, and she was quite hale still. She looked down, delivered a sharp kick to the lout's side, then grasped one of the prone legs and began to pull, careful to hit every patch of sharp china or broken lantern along the way. Her steadfast ethic required her to rescue him, but she certainly did not have to make his awakening pleasant. Besides, she doubted anything would penetrate the many layers of grimy clothes. The hodgepodge aesthetic was vaguely familiar—an air pirate? A plains pirate…perhaps.

A second, well-manicured hand reached to grasp an offensive appendage.

"Petunia Arnold," the ruffled woman said. "Very good to meet you."

"Inspector Vanessa Hargreaves, MD6 Scotland Yard," Hargreaves replied automatically. Then, more sincerely, "Thank you."

Just before they reached the exit, a shattered deck-to-ceiling window, the ground shook with some inexplicable boom. The three women halted, looking around for an explosion. The remaining gas flames flickered alarmingly, but they were well contained in their glass tulips. A second boom sounded, and a third, in regular succession.

"The louts had an automata!" said Hargreaves, recognizing the sound of metal footsteps.

They finished dragging their unfortunate baggage outside, tossing him summarily into a bush. It did not take long to spot the hulking engine in question, for its foot nearly came down on raven-haired Cezette, limping about like an injured blackbird.

The automata had been some ways behind the last car of the train, and was now walking to the front. The ladies rushed away from the car, and finally laid eyes on the beastly contraption; one huge cylinder of black iron sprouting thick, round limbs in a rough analogue to human form. Stovepipes bled a thin stream off the back of the torso where a gap in the plate allowed a collection of cogs, chains and cams to spin freely. In fact, there were gaps all over the walking engine where armor had been supplanted by moving parts, like the giant had been cobbled together from a dozen different machines.

Cezette made to follow, but her leg suddenly gave a twitching motion and dumped her in a bush along the rails. "*Merde!* Never mind me, Maman, *allons-y!*"

"I will mind your child. Go, Inspector!" Petunia Arnold said gamely.

"Madam Arnold, she isn't—oh, bugger it all!" said Hargreaves. She began to lope, a little lamely at first, but picked up speed. The automata might be large, its gait long, but it was also heavy, and it had to pick its way through the debris of the wreck. Hargreaves caught up with it two cars up.

"Hey! You! Stop!" Hargreaves yelled at the top of her lungs. They hurt from the dry, smoky air. When her hoarse croak received no response, she drew her .22 and left a few tiny dents in the carapace far above.

"The blonde?" a tinny rumble rolled down from the top of the automata. The hulk turned, just enough for Hargreaves to see the pilot behind a layer of steel mesh in the front of the cylinder. "Look, I'm real sorry about Nubbins, but with your outfit, it's hard to blame him."

"His name was Nubbins? I was about to be...by a Nubbins?" Hargreaves was astounded, both by the ridiculous situation and the callous objectification. Everything felt just a little surreal, like she'd been having mushrooms again. "I'll wear whatever I damn please! Never mind! You're headed for the Cook box, aye?"

"Aye..." The driver, Barrel, seemed confused by the sudden pirate mode. His voice was a little different, plains pirates a different species, Hargreaves supposed. "'Tis the job, miss. Now if ye will pipe down, I'd much rather act the gentleman and not crush ye with this here Gear."

Typical, Hargreaves thought. The man was being paid to do a job, and didn't much mind what his cohorts were up to. Such men were oblivious to the casual chauvinism and outright violation happening right before them.

"Don't touch the box! I left my automata holding the engine together. If you move it, the boiler will explode!" Hargreaves called, desperately trying to convince this mercenary pirate of a critical situation.

"Now, miss, if ye were in my place, would ye believe such a load of claptrap?" Without further ado, the metal giant began once more to lope over the ruins of the train. It reached the relatively undamaged middle section and began to run, hissing steam from its knees.

"Stupid git!" Hargreaves roared, but it was hopeless. There was no way she would catch Barrel now. Still, she made a heroic effort, seizing one of the ladders aboard a car so she could run over the smooth top of the train. There was nearly no debris, nor any injured passengers to dodge round. She spotted Doctor Price, now setting bones in the relative quiet of the trees next to the rail bed.

All of a sudden there was a terrific clap of thunder, and the entire train shook. Her knees gave out from under her and Hargreaves cursed as she cut them sliding off the roof. She managed to cling to a handhold, slowing her descent, and swung off it onto the soft loam. The smell leaped up at her: good dirt, grass, and the sooty patina of clinker.

"Bollocks!" she cursed, forcing her abused legs back into a run. The rail bed was deserted, and she picked up speed despite the trickle of blood on her shin. She knew the Cook box contained a terrible plague, and any explosion was like to vaporize it into the surrounding air. She could almost feel the movement of it now, warm, dry and downwind off the engine. Any second now someone would cough out a death-knell of red spots. Or her skin would erupt into boils. Or she would start melting, who the bloody hell knew? The thought floated around, looking for a panic toggle, but the inspector's mission drove everything out of her head. She had to contain the disease before it spread further. Where was the nearest town? What lay downwind?

She reached the first cars and began to climb over them, around them, hastily trying to get by the destruction. There was a cracked, rounded divot where Barrel's automata stepped onto a train car, and Hargreaves leaped for the crushed gilt with hardly a thought for splinters. She scrambled over it. When she reached the top, the sight stunned her into a full stop.

"What in the Lord..." Hargreaves uttered, unable to comprehend what lay before her.

All around the edge of the clearing, the signs of the explosion caught her attention first. She had been trained to assess threat, and there was certainly a lot to assess.

It was a pressure vessel breach, she was sure. The train car nearest the engine was burning when Hargreaves left. Now it was extinguished, the walls left holed and gutted from the shrapnel like the husk of an insect. A characteristic clean smell permeated the air, like a sauna or a fresh rain, pushing out the green pine smell of the forest.

Alphonse had flown clean away, where he sprawled on his back not two yards from her. Perhaps three yards from him, the standing silhouette of Barrel's automata gave Hargreaves a shock—until it groaned, and fell backward to reveal a pitted, scoured front. The steam had taken the paint and rust right off.

Hargreaves had seen the touch of steam before, felt it from the 'Berry's pipes. She nearly turned to retch when the cockpit of the gear came into view, but the angle was wrong, and she could not see anything inside. She could smell it, though, just a whiff. She could imagine driving the auto, pushing to get at the box, then having the sudden shock of a thousand streams of hot vapor come through the viewing mesh like a swarm of angry wasps. The force would have scoured the flesh from bone, and the inside of the engine was surely an abattoir.

What happened next drove the unsavory thought completely from her mind.

As the automata fell, one of its arms dropped off. The other toppled backwards, and the Cook box it clutched hit the ground and cracked open over the seared ground.

Cezette's leg wasn't quite broken, as she tried to explain to Petunia from their perch on a nearby rock. The only thing wounded about the girl was her sense of adolescent independence.

"But dear, it is really quite horrific! We must set the bone, or something," said Petunia. She wasn't fainting or fanning herself, but the matron seemed anxious to help something, someone. The woman smelled of strong coffee, from the upended trolley.

For the second time in a day, Cezette found herself lifting the hem of her pinafore, showing off her souvenirs from Mordemere. She was not accustomed to thinking of the legs this way. Their viola-like trim, the subtle variation of ebon varnish, copper, and red brass had always reminded her what a beautiful gift Cid had created. In the light of the wreck, it was difficult not to think of the kobolds, and the clankers, and the terrible thing Maman had pulled her out of.

"Oh my..." Petunia finally fanned herself, and, seeing not much else to do, tied a pretty ribbon from her own parasol round the worst of the breakage. She propped the parasol itself firmly against the glare of sunset. A sound like some gigantic flatulence rolled down the tracks, turning both women to behold the deserted diner car finally catching flame.

Cezette's good leg tapped a rhythm against the rocks, some modern number from the diner car's gramophone. If she were whole, she would have been hot on Hargreaves' heels.

"I hope my friend Violet Jade has found safety," Cezette murmured in a restless way.

"Oh, but she has."

Cezette whirled around, unable to believe her eyes; Violet Jade stood there, her silks bloodied and torn, but seemingly whole. Between the various bright hues, the tight winding of a bandage showed around her middle. Had she been injured? The winding looked tight, but the stains were old blood.

"Stand. You are coming with me."

Cezette had never seen a sparker before, but the bright conical object in Violet's hand was too ridiculous a threat to be anything else.

"Violet! What is the meaning of this?" demanded Cezette.

"I tried to warn you, poppet. The derailment was not supposed to happen. I had this all in my pocket, but those...those buffoons!"

"Dearie, whatever is the matter?" Petunia stepped before Cezette, and stretched out her hands, as if Violet was a child to be comforted.

"Shut it!" Violet screeched, and before anyone could stop her, a bright lance shot from her hand and into Petunia Arnold's rather rotund middle. There was a smell like pennies in the mouth. Petunia jerked in place, glowing for a moment in a halo of lit dust motes. All her ruffles stood on end, and then Petunia Arnold fell to the ground.

"Ah. Hair trigger, what. Rather sorry about that; these things sting like the dickens."

"Violet!" Cezette gaped in horror.

"*Tranquilo!* Sorry. I traveled in Spain with the caravan, picked up the jargon. Peace, peace, she is merely stunned," Violet said. She tripped something on the sparker with a click, rather too expertly for Cezette's taste. "Now, it shall kill. Stand!"

Cezette stood, with difficulty. After fumbling about, she managed to secure Petunia's parasol, which was a good length for a makeshift cane. Violet seemed unperturbed by the possible weapon, but she stood well away from Cezette as she got to her feet. Her hair swung in a raven wing behind her, clipped in a barrette. Violet whistled.

"How I always wished to look like you, Cezette. Skin like milk, hair like the night." Violet sneered down her extended sparker arm, a rich coffee color splashed in black soot. "The world worships people like you, did you know? Our picture houses may play in sepia, but the screen behind it is white."

"Why are you doing this?" Perhaps inspired by the reference, or distracted by hobbling, Cezette found herself spouting picture-house dialogue as if by rote.

"And the accent! *Sacre bleu, c'est magnifique!* In a year you'll get better breasts, and the boys will be falling all over themselves." Violet gestured with her sparker, and they began to walk beside the rail bed, hidden amongst the foliage. Cezette had to pick her way between the virgin brush. "What will they say when they see your legs, Cezzy? You show them easily enough. Some gormless deviant will want to see how they connect to your mangled stubs. I bet you'll love his bad touch. March!"

"Stop this! You are my friend, Violet!" said Cezette. But she knew that for the falsehood it was now, though she wouldn't let on. She was at Violet's mercy, and her spite. The small girl suddenly seemed much older, twenty, even twenty-two to Cezette's seventeen.

Despite the clichéd penny dreadful appeals, Cezette was clever. She had been around Jean Harren and Vanessa Hargreaves long enough to learn the basics of criminology. Violet needed Cezette, otherwise she would never have shown herself. Therefore, Cezette had to keep Violet talking long enough to discern some information from her, or until

Violet slipped up. She was also aware the more Violet told her, the more likely Cezette would be killed. The knowledge did not perturb Cezette overmuch; she had been in such a situation before even Mordemere, in her little room over the Rue Fremicourt. It might not have been her mortal coil at risk, but perhaps what was salvaged was even more important.

"Yes, yes, it was fun for a time. Did you not wonder what I was doing, a lone girl wandering the train by herself?" Violet continued. "This is America! No doting father would allow his child to wander around on public transport!"

"There was no father," Cezette guessed. Violet was lonely, just like Cezette, and with a drop of empathic guilt, Cezette played on those emotions. It was hard to walk leaning on the parasol. Had Cezette weighed five more pounds, the gingerbread and lace at her fingertips would have crumbled long ago.

"Of course not! Nor any conductors in the car, after my sparker had its say. The last one was hard, I had to strangle him in the crook of my knee. Still, the derailment was not supposed to happen until later. It was only to convince those meddling Incognito you were dead," rambled Violet.

So! The infamous pirate populists were involved somehow. Cezette began to put the pieces together.

"I would have all the time in the world to find out where the box was, although now I have you, it should be easy to convince this rogue inspector to give up the goods. I really should speak to my employer about the quality of his henchmen," Violet finished, then was silent.

They were approaching the head of the train. The rail bed was deserted now, free of the prying eyes of survivors and rescuers, though in the distance the squeal of emergency engines could be heard. Violet prodded Cezette down the slope, and through a gap between train cars. They threaded between, and suddenly were upon a great, messy crater, where it was obvious some calamity had occurred. It smelled oddly moist and clean. Across the crater, Inspector Vanessa Hargreaves knelt. Her fall of blond hair obscured the rectangular metal object she was working on.

"Maman!" Cezette cried, unable to suppress a well of emotions. There was embarrassment at being so easily coerced, as well as anger, empathy, but paramount was her love for the woman who had rescued her out of Mordemere's nightmare machination.

"Cezette!" Hargreaves squinted. "Vera?"

"Yes, yes, inspector, the very same," Violet Jade replied. She waved her sparker. "Hands up, where I can see them. Throw away your gun, there. Cezette, dear, go over to your maman. Back, away from the box."

They crossed to Hargreaves, now an arm's length away. As Cezette came close, she saw the inspector shift on her feet, but not away from the box behind her. It was a clever waltz, creating the illusion of compliance.

"What is the meaning of this?" said Hargreaves. "Stop playing games, Vera Jasper. You were well aware how carefully I handled this box when we traveled on Ivanov's airship. Now it is open, and we are all in danger!"

To Cezette's surprise, the short brown girl doubled over in laughter, the sparker weaving dangerously all over the place. Before either Cezette or Hargreaves could lunge for it, Violet, or Vera, was pointing the weapon at them once again. She pointed menacingly, a rather comical gesture from such a diminutive form, and now Hargreaves had to really move away from the box, with Cezette in tow.

"Poppycock," Violet said. "You've seen it for yourself. The Queen lied to you. There's no plague in there." She noted Hargreaves' surprise. "Only Victoria III could have engineered such a brilliant tactic. Have a trusted agent turn rogue, and conveniently deliver the package away from our agents and into the wild blue yonder of America. Stay there, yes, that's fine."

Violet reached the large oblong box. A seam in the front panel was split, trailing gummy crumbs of sealant. Armatures within partially propped it open, like a cabinet where some idiot child had hidden. With a surprising strength, Violet stomped on the panel. It slid smoothly open, both halves into grooves within the casing. Cezette recoiled, but when no cloud of pestilence emerged, she dared to look.

It was a mistake. Her gorge awoke into the back of her throat, memories of being attached to greased pistons rising to meet the sight of the wet, sucking flesh. What lay inside was no ordinary corpse, that much was certain, but exactly what it was defied comprehension. Cezette had the fleeting impression of pink petals overlapping one another, of a thick fleshy column constrained by metal rings. From the inspector's face, she already knew what was inside.

Violet shut the box with a clang, and removed an odd device from her pocket. It looked like another sparker, but the tip was a glass bulb with what appeared to be a wad of steel wool inside. She pointed it at them momentarily, with a sneer, though Hargreaves was unmoved. There was a panel of mesh in the body of the gun. Violet held down a toggle and spoke into the mesh.

"Orb Weaver here. Rendezvous Pagliacci, repeat, Pagliacci. Your stupid clowns cocked it up."

Violet pointed the device straight into the air and pulled the trigger. A crackling boom sounded, followed by a flash of light, and then the tinkling of glass showered the girl.

"Dashed inconvenient, ether flares, but the only sure way of getting a complex message across distances," Violet complained, brushing glass from her silks. The blue smoke drifting from the device reminded Cezette of being aboard the *Nidhogg*, but also of her short time aboard the *Huckleberry*. She recognized artists' charcoal, the green scent of the Champs de Mars park, bordello champagne, and sweat. Aeon particles smelled differently from person to person, she knew.

"It was you! At Temple Mills, and killing Feerick at the Yard. The contortionist Orb Weaver," Hargreaves said calmly. "You tailed me all the way from England."

"Ah, ah, ah," Vera, or Violet, the Orb Weaver, said, leveling the sparker once again. She touched the bandage at her back, bending in a most unsettling manner to do so. "It wasn't personal, at first. I'm afraid I have a score to settle with you, and that amateur detective you consort with, for Temple Mills."

"Consort! I'll not die with a relationship with Arturo C. Adler hanging over my head!"

"You have no choice in the matter," Orb Weaver repeated. She grinned. Her finger twitched, but Cezette threw herself in front of Hargreaves, leg jerking spasmodically, parasol forgotten.

"Violet! Stop this! Maman was only doing her duty!"

Hargreaves threw Cezette back behind her, putting herself into the crosshairs once more. Ceztte's abused leg finally gave out, and she tumbled back onto the ground.

"A noble gesture," Orb Weaver said, and pulled the trigger. Cezette, unable to run or defend herself, screwed her eyes shut.

When the crackling sound of the sparker passed, and Cezette found herself unburnt, she immediately believed the worst. She thought Vanessa Hargreaves had taken the blow for her. Cautiously, fearfully, she opened her eyes to find Maman standing still. Her hands were at her sides, shivering with shock. The smell of burnt hair hung in the air.

"Cezette, are you all right?" Hargreaves said, turning to look on the girl's prone form. "We must go, hurry!"

"Violet...Vera...*Merde!*" Where was the Orb Weaver? Where was the sparker?

"There!"

Incredibly, the colorful silks of the Orb Weaver were quivering some five yards to their left, splayed but not splattered on the ground. Cezette turned to look behind her, and discovered a streak of black just to their left. The sparker blast had left a trail from the Orb Weaver all the way to the edge of the clearing.

"*Pourquoi?*" Cezette gaped, but when she looked for the Cook box, she found her line of sight blocked by a thick sheet of steel. It was dented and marked, but the shape was still familiar. Alphonse's right arm, the fingers clutched into a fist. He had struck at the Orb Weaver, knocking her to the ground.

"I don't know. Alphonse just moved," Hargreaves said. She helped Cezette to her feet, and together they limped their way to the metal man. Alphonse's cockpit was empty. "I am surprised Alphonse even survived the explosion," Hargreaves remarked, feeling the intact controls. They sat in the cockpit, a little cramped for space, but ensconced safely. There was a bit of torn ribbon inside. Had it given way, sending the iron giant's arm hurtling forward?

"I am not shocked," Cezette replied. "Cid and I maintained Alphonse ourselves. He is repaying us in his own way." Perhaps the movement was simply the result of some damage to his intricate clockworks, but Cezette did not think so.

"We'll work it out later," huffed Hargreaves. Clearly she thought it was a load of guff. "Right now we must secure the Cook box."

Alphonse moved stiffly, but there was still plenty of pressure in his boiler, and some scraps of coal to fuel his furnace. The indicators were intact, their glass tubing bubbling reassuringly. Just above the bank of gauges and toggles, the cockpit opened onto a thin slit between the chest plate and Alphonse's chin. With both women inside, the slit was hard to see out of, but serviceable. Hargreaves reached out to manipulate the controls and winced.

"Ahhh...I may have pulled something during all that running around. We need to pick up the box."

"I can do it, Maman," Cezette said, and squirmed forward to take the controls. Hargreaves' smell filled her nostrils, a clean scent of old sweat covering the traces of a nostalgic perfume like a rare bloom. Probably her maman was a little embarrassed in the tight spot, where she had been traveling for days, but Cezette found it comforting.

"All right. Gently does it, the seal is broken," Hargreaves said. "The finger toggle is very sensitive."

"I've done it before, Maman!"

By degrees, Cezette was able to stand Alphonse up. The Cook box was not far from them. She had not expected it to kill them outright, but there certainly wasn't any regular corpse inside the box. Further, Cezette had a disturbing sensation the thing inside the box was not deceased, but very much alive. She could imagine the thing watching them through the lid of the coffin. Cezette cautiously guided the iron giant's fingers nearly around the lip of the box.

WHAM.

Alphonse was suddenly thrown aside as if swatted. Cezette and Hargreaves screamed as they were tossed about inside the cockpit, suddenly both blind and deaf inside the close space.

"What the blazes was that?" Hargreaves hollered. Cezette, in control of the automata, found herself blinded. Alphonse's viewing slit was pressed against a train car. Rotating the controls instinctively, she pushed off against it, whirling Alphonse's hips round until the clearing came back into view. Amidst the gnarled tracks and cliffs, something crouched over the pass.

"I have seen it's like before," Cezette murmured.

"So have I," said Hargreaves.

It was unlikely they would mistake it for anything else. Hovering on eight legs, albeit much smaller than the one that had devastated Frances Derry's home town, the machine tarantula picking its way over the Cook box was built on much the same lines. Cylindrical abdomen, glass eyes, and wicked mandibles clicked at them across the box. It looked sleeker, more refined than its larger cousin. Behind it, Cezette could just make out a dark shape on the other side of the pass, a thing of riveted walls and great churning pistons. Some kind of train? Or a castle on wheels?

The Orb Weaver was climbing up one of the legs of the steel spider, a flurry of silks disappearing into one of the glass eyes. The eye closed with the Orb Weaver inside.

"Don't let it get the box!" said Hargreaves.

Cezette did not need to be told twice. She launched Alphonse forward just as the spidery automata began to fire cables at the Cook box. Cezette recognized the spinner-like device, and the way the tips stuck to the box without damaging it: magnetic clamps.

A claw struck out of Alphonse's blind spot. Cezette barely registered the offending appendage: green, with purple stripes, before the world shook. Everything loosened, raining lubricant and metal shavings. Fading twilight spilled into the cockpit. It was a savage hit, nearly taking Alphonse's head with it, and now they were outnumbered by a second enemy.

Cezette flailed, knowing Alphonse's arms were steel-plated truncheons. Any automata driver would be a fool to leap into that smashing hurricane. She wished to buy time, while she engaged the leg assembly into motion, and so she quailed when the next blow struck almost immediately, punching out a cone-shaped divot in the metal almost at Cezette's wrist.

"Their legs are longer than Alphonse's arms!" shouted the inspector. Cezette looked into a sighting mirror to see her maman peering out the rear slits in Alphonse's armor.

Cezette was unprepared for this, fighting an unseen enemy from within the enclosure of a steel titan. She had to turn to look into her blind spots. It was hot, and sticky with sweat. The controls jammed with the moisture, and metal ground with ear-splitting shrieks. She felt like she was being cooked alive in a great kettle.

These foes were quick, and sprang like real spiders fore and aft. She grasped the arm off the other automata, the barrel-shaped one already fallen and pitted with steam, lashing out in wide arcs only to be thrown by a pair of red legs tangling Alphonse's ankles. Alphonse's armor crackled when the enemy's sparkers struck. Cezette had to take her hands off the wildly flailing controls, gauges roiling in glass tubes, every needle swinging as if possessed. It hurt to touch the toggles. Sharp stabs rained on Alphonse then, and Cezette could only clutch her maman, screaming together while their loyal metal guardian fell to pieces around them.

As suddenly as the battle began, it was over. Every gauge had boiled over and shattered. Every control was jammed tight or twitching loose. Ragged holes cast a patchwork of flickering light over the women within. Through one of them, Cezette saw Alphonse's arm tossed a yard away, amputated neatly and leaking dark fluids. The train or castle that had been in the pass had gone, also, leaving empty sky behind the cliff pass.

"Maman, they've gone," Cezette said. She wanted to know what to do next, how to pursue the villains, how to exact justice on Orb Weaver. Above all, she wanted the nightmare to end. She wanted to be held, to be comforted. After all, it had been ages since Vanessa Hargreaves set out on her lone mission.

When Cezette reached for her maman and found her hand glistening red, she thought she had torn her machined leg again. It was only when she touched Hargreaves did she find the jagged hole in her side. Maman lay slack against the controls, her creamy skin frightfully pale.

Inspector Vanessa Hargreaves was dead.

STATION 7

A Sundry Interlude

How Albion Clemens escaped the great sewer flood of New York amounted to following the trail of shit.

When the 'Berry took off over the opened lock, and a wash of water began to overcome the bedraggled Dragonwell, Albion washed out a side tunnel too small for his enemy to enter. The eight-legged monstrosity lunged anyway, its bulk practically squeezing Dragonwell through the tiny round hole and into the deluge. Albion's battered Gear was barely able to float, much less fly. Albion flipped a couple of toggles, venting as much pressure as he could spare to flush the water from Dragonwell's innards. Suddenly free of its burden, the pair shot out of the flow, crashing through a locked grate to arrive at one of the many large waste channels of the city.

"Note to self: invest in full-face wear, instead of only goggles," Albion thought, spitting, and immediately regretted it. He had a canteen of clean water, which he used to clean off his face. A folded bandana made a thin defense against a true melting pot, the foul reek of a dozen different cultures' refuse.

He shook a flameless lantern to life, a simple sealed jar of aeon water with a waxed paper packet of minerals taped to the lid. The smooth, bubbling glow showed up the worst parts of the tunnel. Vermin-covered walls came scurrying alive in the flaring light. Gingerly, the pirate captain climbed down Dragonwell's leg, expecting a scaly jaw to reach out from the water at any time.

A spot check of Dragonwell confirmed he was relatively undamaged by the flood, though the battle with his strange assailant told a different story. Shavings came out of every joint, dents covered every panel, and the cape so vital for Albion's pirate image was torn completely off. The proud helm was cleaved, but Albion thought it lent a swashbuckling tilt to Dragonwell's face. Thankfully moisture coils mounted on either shoulder would provide clean, engine-ready water in time. Coal was a different story. Although the aeon shard needed very little fuel to function, it did need some. Albion had precious little remaining. He did not trust Dragonwell to fly, and in any case there was not enough room in the tunnel.

Knowing every waste pipe fed into water, he set off on foot. The tunnel branched off into smaller passages, enough for a man, but Albion did not intend to leave his loyal steel companion behind. Besides, they led deeper underground and showed traces of habitation. Coded marks on the walls served as garish signposts for underground dwellers. Like heads on a post, warnings not to come further. He touched the space just under his rib where he had once been stabbed in Belfast. Gangs, they were the same everywhere.

Around a bend in the tunnel, he found a dog scavenging in a gory pile. It looked at him for a moment, and Albion kept his eyes on the haunches, not its eyes. He saw its swollen teats, clipped on to a scrawny rack of bones. An arclight, sudden and harsh, would have spooked the bitch, but his lamp, like a little jar of fireflies, merely perked up its ears. Albion held the pose, muscles relaxed, until the dog turned and padded down a side tunnel.

Downstream, the tunnel terminated in the solid foundations of a waste facility. It would have been little issue for Albion to tear the various filter gates asunder with Dragonwell's cutlass, but he felt perhaps their pirate band had done quite enough damage to New York's infrastructure already. He might be a pirate, but there were rules.

Decency. Honor amongst thieves. Somewhere behind the cavernous walls, a train rumbled through with its characteristic swooshing vacuum sound.

When he returned to Dragonwell, the tunnel already felt hot and oppressive. Albion did not wish to strip in the dense stench. It was thick enough to cut with his hands, and maybe later he would toss his clothes into Dragonwell's furnace. So he got into the Gear again, fired up the boiler and began to explore upstream in long plodding strides. The pipe was wide, but old, and there was a lot of erosion in the center. Albion was careful where he placed Dragonwell's weight, distributing it against the walls with the Gear's canvas-covered fingers.

As the pipe gradually narrowed, Albion grew worried. Suppose the passage dwindled away to nothing, or was blocked off by another wall? The darkness played tricks on him, spurred his fears, rusted the steel trap of his mind. His reasoning said the pipe must have been built with engines of considerable size, and likely to accommodate lorries or maintenance engines similar to Dragonwell in stature. There were ventilation gratings every few feet, so the gas wouldn't build up. There must be tunnels like the one he came by to get out. There must be.

Reason was a double-edged sword, however, and Albion also knew there were things worse than human waste in the water. There were steamworks factories above this section of Manhattan regularly dumping vitriol, solvents, and other, nastier things into the sewers. Corrosives alone would strip Dragonwell's feet of their paint and get to work on the delicate pistons in the ankles. The waste in the water might have built up toxic levels of methane, choking Albion to death or worse, blowing them to kingdom come. It had been sheer luck Dragonwell's tiny furnace hadn't set off a bubble already, roasting them alive.

Him alive. Albion was alone down here.

Eventually, his fears passed. By Dragonwell's barometric instruments, they had been steadily ascending, and ought to have come out at street level some ways back. Albion's lantern showed yard after yard of narrowing tunnel, until suddenly he realized his was not the only light.

Albion headed toward it, and when a fenced gate blocked his way, he shot the lock off its hinges with Victoria. It shook open what must have been years of caked filth. He wondered how his prodigious guns had made little difference against the tarantula contraption. They had gored the thing through, and it had kept moving, as if possessed by some malevolent spirit. If Dragonwell was a fraction slower...Only the slight delay of the tarantula's gearing had saved them. Dragonwell had an almost preternaturally fast response. The crystal at its heart had once been inside of Albion's shoulder, and he still felt connected to the Gear's mercurial moods.

Though the air pirate yearned for blue daylight and white clouds, the light filtering down farther along the tunnel was cold arclight. Albion's path emerged as one of seven runoff tunnels from a large cistern or reservoir. Water flowed placidly from a large tank, big enough to drop a skyscraper into. Catwalks and protective mesh crossed it. Machinery in a faraway corner blithely turned a large cog.

Not a soul was in sight, but there was a secondary engine lying dormant, and blessings of blessings, a large store of dry coal in wax paper. There was even a rudimentary workshop, full of tools necessary for the maintenance of the engines. Albion broke the lock with an iron bar from the railings, and helped himself in true pirate fashion.

It took an hour to wrench into Dragonwell and refuel, but when he was done Albion flew the trusty red Gear up along the pipe to emerge in another water treatment area, this time for the distribution of clean water. He could tell, from the clear fluid flowing through charcoal filters, that they were the same sort of filters in Dragonwell's condensation coils. Odd. Why did a municipal facility require such high standards? The stuff he had briefly sampled from the taps above were potable, but not Gear-grade.

In one corner stood a high door. As Albion had guessed, an access route for large machinery. Beyond it, he could smell clean air, or as clean as New York could get. He thought of Rosa then. Had she found her way to the outside? What of Hargreaves? He grew anxious to get on and find them.

Albion was about to leave, but something inside told him to take a second look. Long halls stretched to his right and left, more sections of the plant unexplored. Workers in the distant high ceilings of the plant perched on the catwalks and operated the equipment. He didn't believe they had spotted him yet. If Rosa or Cid were around he would have made a joke about ninjas and Oriental magic.

Albion hid Dragonwell under a thick overhang of large pipes. The automata's occasional rumblings were easily masked amongst so many of its gargantuan cousins. He had been so thoroughly soiled by his explorations, there was no worry about being seen. At least the smell had desisted or he had gotten used to it by now. Thusly camouflaged, he was free to move about and satisfy his curiosity.

Like a ghost, he slipped through the pipes and the ducts, finding his way to a vantage point high in the plant's left hall. There, he observed the workers as they hauled about pallets and adjusted machines. Between the antiseptic smell overlaying the bitter, sour odor of rotten meat, Albion's impression of the facility was a mix of a cannery and hospital. The workforce seemed oddly mixed. Several of the workers wore faded boiler suits with secure caps and work gloves while others pinstriped suits. The suited men would not have been out of place at a cutthroat banking firm. Draftsmen, or more plausibly, overseers. The machinery was no less unusual.

Albion had gleaned enough knowledge of hydraulics and engineering from Cid to know there should be an exit near. He followed the pipes from the filter mechanisms, along the wall to a center distribution pipe back down to the labyrinth below. At the mouth of the tunnel, he found what he was looking for; a small divergent channel, leading through to a smaller doorway.

What he found beyond it defied description. It set him to retching, the scent from behind the door quite overpowering the scene before him and making him retch again. Albion wiped away the filth and backed away slowly, carefully pushing aside the cold slabs and trying not to slip onto a slick, rust-colored conveyor belt. There were high ceilings in the room, and blacked-over windows. A machine in the corner was busy stamping out a mark, with a shaped die. When he saw what the terrifying mark was inscribing in each piece of product, Albion knew what he had to do.

"I have to get to Vanessa Hargreaves," he thought, and turned to run for Dragonwell. That was when he realized the daylight had blinded him.

The door was mobbed with orange masked men. Wrenches and other thick weapons filled their hands.

Albion grinned, and showed them he was double-fisting Victoria and the Red Special. Then the screaming and the exploding began in earnest, and it was mostly not his.

STATION 8

Live Fast, Die Young

ARTURO C. ADLER WAS STILL EXAMINING THE GREEN AND RED SHARDS when the surgeon emerged from the operating theater. Hastily he swept the pieces off the table and into a satchel. When he stood up, the surgeon's sanitary mask startled him. The doctor took it off. Beneath the chitinous mouth and bulbous eyes lay a weary, smiling face.

"Your friend was dead for a minute and forty-two seconds. If there wasn't already a physician on site, and ready donors, we would have lost her for sure."

Arturo had been awake for nearly twenty-four hours, but he could still recall Doctor Price dashing towards Hargreaves' prone body, and the volunteers trailing behind, most of whom Inspector Hargreaves had pulled from the wreckage of the train. With the gravitators ready for the train patients, the Doctor simply attached Hargreaves to a glass jar of blood, tightly bandaged her, and put her on one of the ambulatory engines arriving on the scene. The volunteers who were strong enough took turns with the needle while they waited for rescue, swapping fresh needles, veins, and whirring germ filters. Price tested them for compatibility with a tiny ampoule. The filters were oddly shaped, like small whiskey stills unpacked from sanitary suitcases. They spun the blood and separated the components, removing the bad humors before it sent the blood to Hargreaves. At least, that was how Arturo understood it.

"May we see her?" Cid's usual grumble was subdued. Arturo recognized a sort of respectful gravitas in the old engineer's voice. Jean and Arturo remained silent. The two of them had become trapped in their car for most of the calamity. When Arturo finally jimmied the door open, they ran toward the loudest commotion to find Alphonse and the two spider automata already up in arms.

"She is stable, but cannot speak to you yet. We've given her something to help her sleep."

"May we see her?" Cid repeated.

The group filed into a side corridor, calm now compared to the hustle and bustle of the hospital. Arturo admired the efficiency with which the institution was run, but could not help noticing something subtly amiss about the staff. The nurses darted swiftly from room to room, but more often than not they were haggard, sometimes dropping things in haste. The doctors seemed learned and friendly, but their cheekbones stood out under red eyes. Arturo recognized the signs of substance abuse, and not the generally harmless hashish, but some far more abusive stimulant.

Before Arturo could investigate further, they reached a large room with twenty beds, partitioned from one another by swaths of white cloth. The more seriously injured train victims were here, many in slings or armored in great iron lungs pumped by engines in another part of the hospital. "Iron lung" was a colloquial. Arturo had no idea what functions the mechanical organs supplied in lieu of the patient's own body, but his medical knowledge was not quite on the level of a surgeon's. The glowing fluids coursing through their surfaces did not look particularly pleasant.

Gleaming silver equipment burbled near Hargreaves herself, but nothing was attached to the inspector except some gravitator tubing. It was dribbling clear serum, not blood. Her wound was invisible, hidden under a blanket, and her normally radiant mane looked damp and unkempt.

"We shouldn't tell her," Arturo said, standing at the foot of her bed.

"We have to," Cid rumbled. "She will want to know."

"The mark was obscured by the damage, circumstantial at best,"

Arturo said. "In a couple days, the evidence might decay further, become unrecognizable."

"Do you really want Maman to be like this for another day?" Cezette protested. "She will wake, and she will want to know."

"Fine! Why don't we all just push the inspector out into the crossfire, have her give everything for Queen and country?" Arturo's wrath suddenly exploded, a flaming geyser the others hadn't known existed. Hallow reared back like he'd been burned. Despite his apparent detachment, Arturo was extremely protective of his few friends. The sight of Hargreaves helplessly laid on a hospital bed was anathema to him. It was an insult. Bulletproof Hargreaves, struck down? Poppycock.

The group fell silent, and eventually drifted away from Hargreaves' bedside, leaving Cezette slumped at the foot. The hospital was a fine one, with a common dining hall notable for its pleasing lack of cleanser smell and constant supply of coffee. It was no Cid-contrived gourmet espresso, but it was bracing, and the benches were comfortable enough to weather the night. Arturo retrieved a newspaper from the shop, which told him nothing, and a telegraphed missive from his account, which told him even less. His head ached terribly.

Sometime the next morning, the inspector awoke and dispatched Cezette to retrieve the members of MAD. Cid had contrived a spot repair for the girl's leg, and though she wasn't the agile ballerina any more, she could handle stairs. She found Arturo on the rooftop, a cold cup of coffee beside him frosted with pipe ashes. From Arturo's spot, they could see the various hospital engines below, neatly parked beside a web of hot steam ports. The velocipede and sidecar he and Jean appropriated from a transport car in the train sat in the visitors' lot, its terrible cargo lashed down with tarpaulin.

"Time to face the music," Cezette said, following his gaze. Arturo stood up, and without a word, followed her down. Their steps clicked uncomfortably fast.

"Inspector," Arturo said hesitantly, as he entered the door. The curtain was drawn, and Hargreaves was sitting up, reading a discarded paper and scowling at the hospital's idea of a continental breakfast. She looked up, surprised, and arched an eyebrow. "Detective," Hargreaves said cautiously. "What's the matter, had a tiff with Jean?"

Arturo shot a dark look at Cezette, who was grinning like the Cheshire Cat. Soon Hargreaves dropped the icy stare and smiled warmly.

"Oh, come here, you silly man," Hargreaves declared. She set aside her tray, and pulled Arturo forcibly into her arms. "Thank you for coming for me."

While they waited for the others to arrive, Arturo filled Hargreaves in on their journey, and what was going on in the world at large. It was difficult to strain hearsay from the simple news of the day. The Falklands conflict had escalated since they last heard of it in New York, and Arturo's missive indicated Parliament committing as many as four Balaenopterons to taking the islands back. The papers were in the dark about the Ottoman retaliation, but everyone present knew of the Mordemere weapons the Empire possessed. Kobolds and clankers and ships equal to the Knights of the Round in size and firepower now threatened Her Majesty's forces.

"As far as we can tell, it's the threat of the Cook box that keeps the Ottomans at bay," finished Arturo. "They don't dare escalate for fear of it."

"But once the Ottoman agent Orb Weaver delivers the box, the jig is up," said Jean Hallow. "The Queen can only bluff if the Ottomans do not know the Box has no plague."

"How do we know she is working for the Ottomans?" said Cid. "Arturo was attacked, we were helped by a third party. Burgess is invested somehow. There are too many guests at this table."

"I should have delivered the box directly to the Queen," said Hargreaves, her face drawn with guilt and pale with injury. "One decisive strike, and all of this could have been avoided."

"You should not be so hard on yourself," Arturo said. He suddenly felt differently about showing Hargreaves what they had found. She was not ready. She would insist on acting straight away. "You are still alive. The box had no plague."

"Whatever was inside must have been of equal importance," Hargreaves reasoned. "Her Majesty would not have entrusted it to me otherwise. I have failed her, and worse, betrayed her. I am a traitor."

"Perhaps the Queen knew you would run off?" Cezette suggested.

Hargreaves seemed desolate, defeated. And that was not the inspector Arturo knew. He couldn't stand to see her like this.

"We found something...in the wreckage—" Before Arturo could continue a doctor arrived. Although there were still sixty minutes left before visiting hours for the day were to begin she made no mention of Hargreaves' guests. Instead she suggested the inspector would benefit from another few days in the hospital. Arturo saw a spark returning to the inspector's eye. She'd heard him. She knew he had something up his sleeve. Sharp as a razor, as always. And soon enough...

"I'm fitter than the devil's own fiddle. Cezette, I will require clothes. Arturo, fetch me coffee. Real coffee."

By afternoon they had fetched the things Hargreaves required. The outfit Cezette found in the hospital's Salvation Army donation center was a little too conservative for Hargreaves' taste, but the plain linen and saloon-style skirt accommodated her .22 Tranter holster reasonably well. A logger's coat and a jaunty, wide-brimmed hat lent her a frontiersman's wildness, and then they were off, hobbling away right before an assemblage of nurses.

"I say, Cid, is Alphonse ready to go?" Hargreaves asked, striding across the lot as if she hadn't just been gored like Christ on the cross.

Cid grunted, eyeing Arturo pointedly.

"Actually, that was what we wanted to tell you," Arturo said delicately. They had reached the visitors' lot, and now the moment was quite inevitable. Arturo flapped his mouth for a bit, then decided no quip was appropriate, and simply ripped off the tarpaulin's cables.

Jammed into the sidecar, Alphonse's severed arm clung, ruining the upholstery of the seat with black ichor.

"Right. I sort of expected this, Where's the rest of him? " Hargreaves said. When the silence stretched too long, she sighed, resigned. "Did you have to show me quite so dreadfully?" Before anyone could stop her, she reached out to touch the thing.

The fingers wiggled.

She leaped back in shock, nearly falling on her crutch. The arm shook the whole velocipede, springs creaking and squealing in protest.

"Look closer," Jean prompted. Was there a dark edge to his voice? Arturo could not tell for sure.

Hargreaves had been backing away from the flailing limb, but now the thing slowed, she peered closer, at the stump where forearm had been cut at the elbow. The movement had loosened some fluid, and now the lot was filled with a rank, sour smell.

Instead of steel and oil, Alphonse's frame was laced with silver skin and bleeding the unmistakable garnets of dark red blood. Hargreaves could not bear to look inside the frame, broken open by titanic forces, but when she dared, the horror of the damage faded in comparison. Inside the broken bones of her Alphonse, partially obscured by the break, the cog-and-cam mark of Ubique was distinctly visible.

Vanessa Hargreaves clung to hope like...well, like hope. Nothing else quite had the skin-of-the-teeth desperation that drove people to drink or religion. She remembered seeing the ghostly train behind the pass, like a fortress or a castle. A fort on the rails—a rail fort. But such things were still dependent on the tracks that crossed the country, and that was what she clung to. They had hope of catching the box.

Hargreaves could not shake the feeling of urgency. If this elusive, ghostly locomotive had an atelier for extracting the box contents without making berth, the game was done. If the train's master berth was close, all was lost. If it gave over the box to a dirigible, all was lost. Where was she now? Nevada? Washington? California? Her only hope was to overtake the rail fort before the trail grew cold.

But, as they rocketed along the road in the last direction the rail fort had gone, her hunch seemed to be paying off. For one thing, the Gear that trailed them from the hospital still showed no signs it knew they had noticed its presence.

"Where is it now?" Hargreaves called over the rushing of the wind, as they sped down an unbelievably wide, paved road on their velocipede. The air felt bracing, cutting any exposed skin, except the gap between the hot engine and the sidecar's mounts, where it was pressed into a formidable torrent. Her voice had to badger past a thick riding scarf and a pair of riding goggles. Its baffles restricted her vision, but it was that or be blinded by wind and road grit. The sidecar seat beneath her fingers and lap was still sticky from Alphonse's fluids.

Arturo adjusted his mirror slightly, the clutch loose, the throttle fully opened in his other hand. He hooked a thumb over his shoulder, to indicate the large covered lorry not far behind them. Hargreaves had a mirror on the corner of the sidecar, next to the wholly ineffective windshield. There was a momentary glimpse of something clinging to the back of the lorry.

The machine in question was small enough to hide behind lorries or in the outgrowth of Pacific forests. Their pursuer's gentle footprints left ripples in the ground, subtle vibrations Arturo C. Adler listened for when they stopped for fuel. He put his head against the earth, sometimes with a glass drinking jar, and the sound came rumbling along, terrifying in its eight-beat tango. It had begun to follow them almost immediately from the hospital.

There had been a brief argument, but in the end Hargreaves had yielded the driver's side of the velocipede to Arturo. The detective was the best choice for tracking their prey swiftly, given its immense head start. There was some discourse about who ought to go, but in the end Arturo's obstinacy and Hargreaves' stubbornness won out. Jean Hallow assured them they would find transport and catch up with the velocipede later, and went to find it himself. That was comforting. Hargreaves hadn't liked the way Cid was eyeing a nearby ambulance, loitering from a recent patient delivery.

Now she watched the lorry in the mirror, hanging on to her riding scarf, until the barest glimpse of a green and purple limb hovered into view, scrabbling for purchase. The abomination was clinging like a wen to the side of the lorry.

"Look there," Hargreaves indicated to a rest stop about a mile on. Her eyes were drawn to a cog-and-cam beneath the American symbols for fuel, lodging and food, but now was not the time to cherry-pick her opportunities.

They pulled into the fuel and water depot. It had been covered with thin slats and rough spun, to resemble a native tent. The coarse, sturdy-looking beams were shoddy and thin. They hid the real supports, rusty steel and panels drilled through with dozens of holes to save costs. A thin catwalk looped from the facade to the water tank, a steaming behemoth of thin steel over a furnace.

Arturo climbed out and drew a corrugated hose from above. A separate hopper supplied fresh coals, tumbling out in rods when money was inserted. Lighting embers could be scooped, a penny apiece, from a roiling furnace at the depot shop. There were a couple of pots of coffee on top, with paper cups, also a penny apiece. And of course, there were the facilities, surely a horrendous cesspool. If Hargreaves hadn't been cautiously looking for their tail, she would never have seen the flash of purple disappear into the tree line, the colors blending into the foliage.

"Arturo, go into the woods and lure it in," said Hargreaves. "When it gets close, I'll shoot at it, then trip the furnace hopper release and dump those coals atop its beastly head."

"A fine plan," agreed Arturo, "save for the part where you send me into the woods to die."

"More believable," Hargreaves countered. "It is unsightly for a lady of good breeding to do her business in the woods. Besides, you wouldn't step in a fueling stop lav if your bladder was exploding, you toff. Now go, you filthy man. Go."

Arturo shrugged, but sauntered off anyway, hips swaying. Meanwhile, Hargreaves played at visiting the shop, at least until she was quite sure the shopkeeper had his head turned. Then, she picked the lock at the back, took a look behind the door, and ascended into the wobbly catwalk holding the fueling apparatus over the roadsters and lorries below. There were certainly many pleasure riders about. This part of the country seemed infested with them. Good weather and unspoiled nature, she supposed.

The ladder was shaky, and Hargreaves was not fully recovered from her ordeal, but she put one boot over the other and soon she was watching Arturo walk into the wood. She clung to a riveted strut, careful of the hot boiler not two inches from her back. The embers scorched her hair.

Artruo climbed a low ridge. Hargreaves looked on from above with wild abandon. Where was the automata? She should have been able to see it. From her vantage point, it should be impossible to keep the inspector's keen eyes from detecting the machine. Where the blazes was it? Hargreaves barely registered the rumbling coming from the boiler behind her. Even in this age of advanced steam power, machinery was notorious for being noisy for no apparent reason.

When the boiler began to shake intensely, the inspector became alarmed. The rapidity with which the catwalk grew from a tremble to a bucking jolt left no doubt there was soon to be a boiler rupture. Now? With her side stitched up? In her condition she doubted she could descend the ladder before it burst. Hargreaves wondered if she should jump and if the trees would cushion her fall. It was a good three stories from the top of the platform, and no insurance against a boiler explosion. She caught the purple limb in her periphery a split second before it was too late.

With a metallic twang, the spider's claw arched through the space where her head used to be, a stake of gritty paint and chrome. It looked like a scorpion's stinger, dipping into the metal like it was the skin of a juicy milk bug. A cloud of searing steam sprayed into the crisp, dry air. Screams came from below, and shattering glass from shrapnel falling onto engines.

"Blithering idiot!" Hargreaves cursed from the floor of the platform, but it was reflective. She ought to have known, ought to have tracked better!

She rolled as the metal below her curled, the world coming about all shaky from the impact. It was clear the stalking tarantula had caught on, and instead of allowing the trap to close, decided to turn predator. No, not a tarantula—it was built like a daddy-long-legs, balanced precariously on stilts. The legs were telescoping slightly, slotted one length into the next like a pocket glass. Their reach was deceptive. She could also see Arturo running full-tilt to her rescue, hollering from below.

Hargreaves ran as best as she could along the catwalk as it began to buckle and twist beneath her feet. The spider clung to the supports, stabbing at her with its free limbs. As the spikes pierced the boiler, steam scoured the paint off the walk. The long-legs' body blocked out the sun. Inside its smoked glass eyes the pilot moved within the spider almost like a part himself. As if the skeleton movement that made up the creature's guts had a hold on someone eaten very recently.

The metal below her gave a wrenching groan and collapsed, throwing her tumbling through the air. Her hands scrabbled for purchase, the skin under her gloves scraped raw against the rough metal. . They caught on something. When she screwed her eyes open, she found herself dangling from a rail still partially attached to the tower, like a worm on a hook. From this vantage point, it was easy to see one side of the station was crumbling from the shifting weight. Bolts flew like bullets from the stretching metal, and the log façade had caught fire.

"Hi! You great lout!" Arturo shouted from below, carrying on struggling to catch the automata's attention. A stone whipped from his hand, clanging against the spider's carapace.

"Bumbling fool!" said Hargreaves. The automata was, indeed, turning to address this new threat, but not only was Arturo as defenseless as she, the movement pulled the dense, sloshing boiler more to one side, crumbling the steel below with audible moans. An orange rain spilled from one side of the scaffolding, the embers cratering and melting the luxury engines below like tiny, flaming meteors. A loose beam fell on their velocipede, crushing the big front wheel and sending it rolling into the countryside.

Something green spit violently from the front of the automata. Arturo dove for cover, and the glob enveloped a tree just behind him, reducing it to a hissing, splintery puddle within seconds.

"A vitriol-thrower!" Hargreaves said, horrified.

She had little time to act—the automata was reaching forth with two limbs, balancing itself on the other six. Rearing like a real spider, it lined up horrible mandibles two stories over the ground. A second shot spurted, melting a boulder not two feet from Arturo to a beastly puddle. The shots were becoming alarmingly accurate.

Hargreaves was unsure how long the abused supports below would hold, but she would not trust her, nor Arturo's, life to them. Instead of clambering atop the catwalk, she began to swing, throwing her weight along the rail until it ripped from its mooring. Huzzah! With all of her strength she held onto the rail as it shredded along its failing points, ripping in a line that sent her on a long arc.

Vanessa Hargreaves sailed through the air. Scarf flying, trees whipping past, she delivered a mighty kick to the spider automata's side, denting the metal where her foot struck. Her leg instantly went numb, prickling with the vibration despite her perfectly executed blow. Her wounded side was another matter altogether. It all but exploded with pain. The shock loosened her hold on the rail. Flailing wildly, she plummeted two stories before landing on something hard. Despite being painful, she found she was not seriously hurt from her fall. Even her stitches held up, though blood oozed through to her pretty saloon dress.

"Bollocks! Fuck! Bloody Nora!" Hargreaves wheezed, but she didn't feel as improved as she normally did.

She found she had landed on the back seat of an engine parked just below the tower. The hard landing was due to the ribbing of the seat. Recovering quickly, she poked her head over the edge of the paneling, anxious to find the spider. Her flying kick, while structurally nothing more than a fly's bite to the automata, set the thing off balance. With its weight already shifting the fuel depot, all its legs scrabbled for purchase and yanked the heavy machinery into a great searing landslide. She watched in horror as the beast struggled to steady itself on its precarious perch, only to come crashing to the ground, taking the tower with it. The earth shook with the impact. The boiler hit like a raw egg on rocks, exploding in a deadly plume.

"Arturo!"

Hargreaves launched herself out of the seat, dashing painfully toward where the depot had fallen. The ground was hot, sticky oatmeal, miring her in the mud. She hopped over the worst of it, though the steam made it hard to see. Soon she found Arturo at the edge, clearly shaken but otherwise all right.

"I hear mud is quite good for the skin," Arturo said calmly, lifting his fine glittering shoes out of the muck. They fell apart immediately in a waterfall of suede. "Oh dear. At least my pipe is in one piece."

"You silly bugger!" Hargreaves said, reaching to help him out.

The hot water from the boiler flowed into the road, distracting the drivers still whipping past. They seemed only momentarily interested, their destinations still more important than this roadside curiosity. Steam cleared just enough for her and Arturo to see the wreck of the steel spider, sprawled in the lot. Its glass eyes were mostly shattered, revealing a prone figure within.

"You should get on," Arturo said. He got up, without any of his usual flair. "We've lost time as it is."

"What about you?" Hargreaves said. "Our velocipede is crushed under that steel beam."

"Take the Lamia," Arturo said, pointing to the engine Hargreaves had fallen into. "I saw the driver get in with some others in a van and ride away. He'll think it was crushed in the fall."

"Why that's..." Hargreaves stopped short. She had committed enough crimes already, one more would not hurt.

"Go. I can catch up. Once this one's driver fails to report in they will flee with all speed. Perhaps I can find something of use here, but unless you get going we will lose the Cook box once and for all."

Hargreaves hesitated, not sure what to do.

"GO!" barked Arturo.

The inspector turned on her heel and loped towards the open-roofed engine, hopping neatly over the door and into the driver's seat. She whirled once, her golden mane fluttering, before pulling out of the lot, over a grass divider, and down the road.

"Godspeed, Inspector," Arturo said, watching her go. He winced, gripping his leg where a shiny red burn gleamed. If he had let Hargreaves see, she would have insisted on taking him to a hospital, and lost valuable time. Besides, there was something else that needed doing here.

Arturo hobbled along, avoiding the scalding mud as best he could. Ducking under a crumpled automata leg, he briefly inspected the spider. Upon finding the cockpit hatch, Arturo pried it open with a dislodged piece of the water tower's railing. Inside he found the driver's badly scalded body still strapped into its chair. As he hastily unstrapped the corpse and shoved it over the edge, a trickle of blood spilled from its mouth. Blithely wiping at the stain with a handkerchief, Arturo sat at the machine's controls. They glittered, invitingly, all shining toggles and glass-fronted chrome. Some of the labels had been scorched off. Excellent. A mystery!

"Now then...reveal your secrets to Adler," he muttered, tucking in.

Hargreaves' hair rippled in an unruly sail behind her, but she paid it no mind. She shifted more fuel into the engine's furnace. Surely the pressure could not rise much further into the red before some vital component blew, but she kept the flames roaring inside the Lamia's belly. Six long tubes of glass showed the pressure inside each of the pistons, a roiling blue hell trapped in bottles.

The Americans had built into this piece of machinery the heart of the west. Inside the long, gold-rimmed bonnet beat an unyielding rhythm that pushed her along like winged Hermes himself. The Lamia roadster was eggshell white, upholstered in red, with that classic wide, open front grille like the mouth of a great white shark. Sticking out from either side of the bonnet were oiled, naked steering mechanisms, holding out the front wheels like striking paws. She found the other drivers quite willing to acquiesce, seeing that maw opening up in their mirrors, giving her the right of way more often than not.

She shifted more fuel, as the previous rod burned through, showing in a weighted gauge on the panel before her. The mechanism rotated another rod onto the furnace pile, in a motion that dumped the spent ashes into a pan at the bottom of the engine so her passing threw up a comet's tail of sparks on the road. The colloquial was coal, or even peat, but these rods were far and removed from such primitive fuels.

Hargreaves steered round a slow four-trailer lorry, a long string of square boxes, and the driver pulled on the horn. The camaraderie was pleasant, until she saw the flashing lights in her mirror. A long black police cruiser tailed her, using its arc signals to flag her toward the side of the road.

"Sorry, constable. Normally I'm the most law-abiding person," Hargreaves mumbled. She dipped the nose of the Lamia toward the shoulder, as if to pull over, then abruptly wrenched it to the left, diving between a cabriolet and sedan that closed the gap behind her. She felt the movement keenly, an unpleasant, unfamiliar gesture—after all, she hadn't driven on the right side of the road for long.

Trapped, the police engine gave a frustrated wail of anger. Hargreaves opened the throttle further, weaving the Lamia through loose traffic at as close as she could figure over a hundred miles an hour. The speedometer had broken in the fuel depot. So had the windshield, and the gale tore at her scarf. If her goggles weren't on she would be tearing up, blind.

"There. Now I've gone and done it," Hargreaves said. "I wonder what the bounty for my head will be?" Actually, she found she cared more about whether they would get her leonine profile right for the wanted posters.

STATION 9

Ronin Memory

SOME HOURS LATER, HARGREAVES' DETERMINATION PAID OFF. AS SHE came to a long, languid dip in the road, the land seemed to open before her, and in the distance she saw the chugging, smoking bulk of the rail fort, churning along at a frightening speed. It was still a ways off, and she suspected it would have left her behind long ago if the terrain weren't as wild and untamed. America herself was helping Hargreaves.

The meeting was a chance occurrence. Had she gone any slower, or much faster, she might have missed the ship entirely. Because of the dip in the road she could see far ahead of her, where a set of four train-roads crossed beneath the paved asphaltum under the Lamia's tires. Likely as not, she could intercept the rail fort there!

There was little time to ponder the machinations hanging overhead. Even at the Lamia's tremendous speed, and the heavy load of the rail fort the dastards would soon overtake her and be lost. The road bent visibly before her, crossing the river valley and continuing on past. She would have to think of some means to halt the train before they reached the crossing.

"Come on, Vanessa! What have you? Your bollocks are so big you have to wear them on your front, now think! Be daring!"

"Shut up, Clemens!" Hargreaves shouted, but of course she was alone.

The fact she was hearing voices spoke to her growing suspicions about her sanity. or maybe her doubts had finally reached a head and taken audible form. Vanessa had been letting herself grow reckless, getting hurt with the Orb Weaver, letting her appetites have their day with Funny Goat. Then there was the murder in Appleton...she thought of it as murder, even though she had struck in self-defense. The smell of that slaughterhouse still haunted her at night. But most of all, she had been pushing back her increasing dissatisfaction with her mission and Her Majesty. She felt it like cloud at the back of her mind. Why it chose the pirate captain to impersonate was disconcerting.

The crossing was approaching fast, and Hargreaves skid the Lamia to a halt on the side of the highway, on top of the spot where the rails met the road. Small stones jumped at her feet as she hopped off the roadster. She could see the rail fort approaching now—her first real look at a wall of churning metal that spanned two train roads. For a moment Hargreaves just gaped. The rail fort's wheels caressed the tracks in a death grip, supporting a wide toothy cow-catcher between engines. In the middle, a platform held what looked to be a ship's deck, with raised castles and rounded cannons perched atop stocky, bulldog-like haunches. Most terrifyingly, the wet skull of a recently slain longhorn buck had been roped to the front of the left engine. As Hargreaves stared, the rail fort passed under the highway and shook the world.

All she had was a peashooter and some good old-fashioned British pluck.

The great double engine of the rail fort passed below, followed by long trains of cargo cars and linked platform cars that held covered loads. The train passed away into the distance on both sides of the road. Suddenly she found herself without doubt or compromise. She jumped back into her roadster and turned the steering wheel hard, sending The Lamia into a slide. She backed up, almost all the way to the edge of the other side of the road even as other drivers honked and cursed all around her. Other vehicles slid to a halt but Hargreaves ignored them. She opened up the engine completely, shifting rod after rod into the furnace, throttling the bellows to burn the fuel at a furious pace until the tires ground themselves into vapor, slipping and sliding in place. Then she let go of the brakes.

Something exploded behind her. The pipes at the rear of the Lamia belched a flaming cloud sparkling with metal shavings. Hargreaves' heart shot into her throat. The piston gauges began to burst, one by one, showering her coat with hot spray and glass shards. The tree line rushed at her. There was a smell of crisp damp, mineral and green, the smell of river and mulch churned up in a rooster tail behind her. Then the curb hit, off the road, and off any sort of guidance. That felt familiar.

Hargreaves felt exhilarated, if a little stupid. She felt at home in this wild land. She continued to feel it even when the bit of curbing ended, and the Lamia suddenly found her wheels churning the air, rushing forward with a tremendous momentum. The river of train cars surged below her; she had come down on the right side of the rail-fort, over one of the trains of cars and not the intermittent gaps between rails. She heard the boiler rattling dry, moments away from bursting.

Oh god. She had a thought. What if the train ended just as she landed?

But she had done the thing properly, and the Lamia came crashing down on a sturdy deck of some kind. She leaped clear of the Lamia even as it skid across the deck, running out of landing strip fast. She rolled, and when she came to a rest saw the Lamia foundering over the edge of the rail fort's prodigious deck. Then there came a tremendous crunching and the flatulent sound of an exploding boiler as the rail fort's wheels chewed her little roadster to bits.

"Hello Ghost Train. So, you are corporeal after all," she said, knocking on the varnished deck of the beastly great train.

She stood, brushing her clothes off, and found herself standing upon a wide landing platform that had been erected between two cargo cars. There was an exposed loading berth and a scavenger's dirigible lashed down to one side of the platform. It took up the space of an entire train car. Hargreaves recalled the *Montmarte Express*, and noted the dirigible's powerful salvage claw. On the other side, there were a number of the daddy-long-legs automata, docked inside the frame of a shipping cradle that looked like it had been meant to transport roadsters like her poor Lamia.

A linkage platform between cars led to the rest of the rail fort. Hargreaves headed to it. She was out in the open, a sitting duck on the huge platform. In the short time she crossed the deck, about ten or so small trees that had sprung up between tracks were flattened by the rail fort's passing. How the blazes did this monstrosity cross the wilds of America without being discovered? Hargreaves thought perhaps some money had crossed palms, or those horrible cannons at the rail fort's front were even more frightening than she thought.

When the first man appeared on the linkage, she clipped him with a .22 bullet to the shoulder. Her gun shoulder ached abominably from the spider attack, but she shot southpaw from the hip, a fast-draw trick she had seen one of the circus carnies do and practiced in her evenings. Now she could hit a whiskey bottle from a hundred yards. The man, much closer than a hundred yards, fell screaming to his death, mangled under the iron wheels.

Her hands trembled, her heart pound in her chest, and her fingers felt numb. She expected the other crew members to come investigate the commotion, but none were forthcoming. She continued to try to convince herself she wasn't a cold-blooded killer.

Inside, she found the jarring specter of the Cook box sitting in the middle of the car. Some part of her wanted to open the cargo door nearby and push it right over the edge to be destroyed with whatever was inside. But was the horrid thing still inside the box? Hargreaves threw open the lid, anticipating what she would find even as her hands stung from the wind-scored coldness of the metal. The lids banged open, clanging against the claws holding it in place.

She hadn't been sure what she had seen inside back at the train wreck, but thankfully, the box was empty. Now the box was just a box, huge and heavy and filling the boxcar. Hargreaves sighed, her chest heaving with something like relief.

Reloading her pistol, Hargreaves strode back outside toward the spider automata. With a shock, she discovered the train was now composed of one single line of cars, chugging through some hilly country. The platforms bridging the two parallel trains had been retracted, and at a casual glance Hargreaves would say the landing berth had been folded underneath the cradle car, just over the wheels. In the distance, some of the boxcars looked like they had been shuffled over on a see-saw like arrangement, tipped to one side of the train to make room for the bridged castles, cannons, and other large, centrally mounted components. The rail fort must have used a switch-over to run the left half of itself behind the right half, hardly slowing as it did. It made sense—few tracks ran parallel to each other, even in wide-open America. Whatever machinery noise had occurred had gone unnoticed by Hargreaves, who had been about the business of killing.

Within a short while she found what she was looking for: a series of long levers at one end of the cradle. She stepped up to them, squinting against the wind. With a feeling of deep satisfaction she pulled each of the levers until they clicked. At once, the spider automata shifted, groaning on their bearings, before sliding smoothly off their cradles. One after another they lowered gently to the ground and promptly tumbled off into the countryside. They smashed to bits on the quickly moving rocks.

"No running now," she thought, but whether it was the thieves' escape or her own, she could not say. She tied her skirts into a knot at her back and squared her shoulders. Gripping her .22 Tranter and 9mm Browning, she took a deep breath and kicked down the door. She cleared the corners. Her mind sharpened to the task at hand.

The train's steam lines were not, in fact, strung with the bones of the damned. She stood on a landing between two decks of a double decker car. She saw down the upper and lower hallways. Both looked deserted.

Hargreaves passed through the lower level—what appeared to be a barracks or sleeping car—doubling back to clear the upper level. Her drill officer would have been proud of the way she efficiently cleared each room. She found nothing save a wide gun belt and pouch stuffed with 9mm ammunition, which she appropriated. The belt was too cumbersome to wear over her shoulder, so she looped it twice over her hips, feeling quite the bandito. Then she stuffed the Browning into the holster, so she could crank open the door on the other side one-handed. The wind buffeted her again between cars, but there was some overlapping guards over the passage here, shielding her somewhat, and found a second barracks car, also deserted.

After that came a common area car, sparse, and a few storage cars after that, but no one else appeared to threaten her. Some held crates of Ubique Canned Beef, others bars of soap, even more soybeans, lentils, and various sundry. She seemed to be passing through the more mundane areas of the rail fort. Hargreaves guessed the sensitive areas of the fort were farther forward, where the other half of the train had joined in a long serpent.

Only when she threaded through a vast fuel car and ascended a short stair up into an engine room did she discover the first of the crew; a hearty, bald Red Indian covered head to toe in mercenary tattoos. The engine was one of the two great steaming behemoths at the head of the rail fort, now in the middle of the train. When the Indian spotted Hargreaves he lunged at her with a wrench as tall as she was. Her Tranter barked fearsomely, but only rang a staccato beat with ricochet. The tiny bullets were meant to be fast and accurate, not to punch through railroad steel.

Spotting the handle of a knife, she made a grab for it and hamstrung the man as she rolled under his wrench. A gout of blood spilled across the shaking deck. The man crumpled, and Hargreaves knocked him out with a heel stomp. When she stepped around him, she found a few other engineers; a mix of freemen and Orientals with long braids. They looked at her but did nothing to stop her, looking curiously at the Indian before returning to work.

"*Daaaamnn,*" said one of the freemen. Clearly they had no love for their boss.

"Good knife," she remarked just to be sure of cowing them, wiping it on a napkin. The Indian had been eating an apple and some jerky with it. The handle was wrapped bone, quite sturdy.

The next guard was farther along in the next car. Hargreaves walked out the front of the engine, through a notch in one half of the fearsome cowcatcher. The next car looked like the caboose for the other half of the train, appointed as a basic mess car. Like the rest of the fort, it bulged with riveted armor and featured multiple gun ports, with one rear-facing rotary cannon.

Hargreaves suddenly had to duck behind a bulkhead to avoid a sideways rain of motor gun bullets. About time, too, she thought in passing. Besides another man, there was a woman with a short, violently azure haircut tucked inside a bandana. Her shots gouged fist-sized holes in the wood paneling; a scatter-gun, loaded with lead shot. Thankfully neither were very bright. Hargreaves simply counted the shots until the motor gun rattled empty, and the scatter-gun fired twice. During the brief pause, she darted out of her spot and shot the first man through his gun arm, inside the elbow, with two tightly spaced 9mm bullets. It reduced the limb to bloody rags inside the sleeve. *Bollocks*. The owner of her new gunbelt had been cutting crosses in the bullets. She hadn't wanted to do that. But her guilt had to wait. A lolling arc sheathed her new knife into the woman guard's abdomen as she raised her scatter gun to fire. Chunks of the deck blew away as it howled harmlessly into the floor.

"Mercenaries?" Hargreaves wondered, as she watched the first man fade dead away, clutching the ragged ruin of his arm. As she turned, the woman reared up with a vicious stiletto. The blade connected with her upper arm, causing searing pain. Hargreaves flailed open-handed at the bone handle still stuck in the woman's stomach, extracting a scream of pain as it ripped sideways out of the wound. Hargreaves closed her hand upon it, but the azure woman slumped motionless in a puddle of blood.

"Christ," breathed Hargreaves, shaking. Not ghosts. Living, breathing people.

She winced as she finished tightening the belt over her arm. The scratch was not serious, but she wouldn't be wearing anything frilly for a long time.

At the end of this car she found a stair up and a riveted, locked door. She tried the door first, but it was too thick to force and the lock was a complicated cryptex of rolling drums.

Hargreaves climbed the stairs instead, and found herself amidst the fortifications and high castles of the rail fort's top deck. The wind hit her like a whipping, but it was possible to cross. A narrow catwalk led across the top of the train. The sounds of the rails were very loud, but she thought she heard activity farther up. Mindful of an ambush in the warren of pipes and tall castles, she hurried ahead until she was perhaps five cars from the engine. There she found a vast pit-shaped cargo boxcar, open to the air that appeared to be a staging area. It held barrels of pitch, oil, and water. A smaller crate held traces of pure aeon stone on a padded cushion, as precious as white truffles. Boxes full of sawdust filled the center, as if some delicate equipment had been recently removed.

She walked over the staging area on a center catwalk that spanned the length of the car. At the far end below, a door shifted back and forth with the movement of the train—a second car, but with its door closed. Now she looked around, seeing the toothed edges of the bulkheads' top edge. This car was built to load and unload from top, so airships could make deliveries of the heavy crates. Walking in a crouch, she approached the following car, her gun at the ready. But this car's roof was closed, the ceiling panels clenched together like a bear trap. Whatever the men were building seemed to be inside. She heard frenzied activity, and the walls hummed with arc power. Carefully, she stopped at the linkage between cars and took the ladder there down. She cracked open the door just enough to see.

Inside, was a high-ceilinged space like the car she had just left. An intense arclight filled the space, but through the tiny crack she could just see a stave-like fixture, planted in the middle. The top looked like half an egg topped with a cluster of sprockets and shining machinery, about as big as a cask of whiskey. As she watched, a figure walked up and placed something inside the egg. She couldn't quite see what it was or the figure's face without drawing attention to the door.

Then the figure did something very queer indeed. He produced a thin instrument from a suit pocket and pricked his left index finger. He squeezed a few drops of blood inside. Suddenly, the egg whirred into motion, closing over itself until it was a smooth, seamless orb. The man took the egg, with an effort, and gave it to a nearby workman.

Hargreaves carefully closed the door, and wanting to get out of the wind, stepped inside the staging area. There was a reflective bit of bulkhead and she caught her reflection in it. Her hair was a horror, a bird's nest of blond. *Proper decorum, Hargreaves*, she thought.

Stooping, she started to fix her hair in the mirror. Not a moment too soon. Something rippled through the air where her ear had been a moment before. An ambush! She instinctively rolled into her stoop, over her shoulder and up kneeling, her gun at the ready. Instead of scalping the inspector, the blow overshot her and cut a tall crate in half, turning inch-thick boards into a pile of firewood. Someone stepped through the wreckage, crushing the timbers underfoot. He had a long rusted cutlass.

"You! You were at the...the *Nidhogg*!" gasped Hargreaves.

And so he was. Hargreaves had never known the name, never seen the man under the mask, but had the tale from Rosa and Albion. It could be no other. Hikawa Shoutaro of Okinawa, who had fallen to Rosa Marija on the edge of the Red Square, and survived to deliver the *Nidhogg* its ill-fated heart. He still wore the remnants of his flaming robe, an Oriental affair that seemed more at home on a society belle. His distinctive mask hung down at his neck, the horns cracked and broken, and square wooden shoes propped up his feet. Rolled down on his hips and layered with belts, sashes and other garments, his attire looked all the more like some overly large bustle. The folds bulged with long, narrow shapes, which Hargreaves speculated were swords. The variety of lengths and thickness to the bulges implied he had a myriad of blades at the ready. The most shocking thing about him was his face; half of it gleamed with copper and oiled leather, framing a swiveling, twitching glass eye.

What was more, according to Captain Clemens, this man standing before her ought to be dead, killed by Valima Mordemere on the eve of his downfall after surviving Rosa's fearsome tarot deck.

Hikawa lunged at Hargreaves, surprisingly nimble on his wooden shoes. Instinct took over and she dove, rolling clumsily under a cutting wind. Uncomprehendingly, she saw a strand of gold float down before her, as if the sky was raining treasure. It was her own shining hair, sliced in two in the moments the blade drifted over her head.

The inspector scrabbled to her feet and opened fire. Amazingly, the strange Oriental was deflecting her bullets with sword strokes almost too fast to see. Blades simply appeared where the bullets would be. The glass eye spun wildly in his skull. His sword flaked and sparked, then finally broke. Unfazed, he drew two more from his robes. One rippled in the light like water. The other grinned cheerfully, its edge a saw blade of toothy nicks. In Hikawa's passing crates exploded into clouds of sawdust and barrels gushed, decapitated.

"Wait! Wait! You don't have to do this! Whomever you're working for, they're not who you think!"

With a gasp, Hargreaves put up her knife in time to take the cutlass, feeling it bite into the hammered bronze. Somehow, the Oriental had come close enough to strike.

"Bloody Nora! How did Rosa even...?" Hargreaves said. Her prior wounds were hurting abominably, and she suspected a torn stitch. She spun, using her best weapon, her legs, to sweep the Oriental off his feet. The swordsman hopped nimbly away, up onto a barrel.

"Curses, Clemens, can't you even make sure a man is truly dead?"

The swordsman hesitated. He glided off the barrel, coming to a stop a ways from Hargreaves. Both blades spun in his fingers, and the inspector expected some blasted Eastern trickery. Instead, the swords slipped gently back in their sheaths.

"You know...Captain Albion Clemens-*dono?*" he asked quietly.

His voice was clear and deep, yet inexplicably jarring. Hargreaves puzzled at the words, until she realized the queer sounds at the end of the sentence was something akin to a title, and she was merely thrown by the redundancy. The man himself seemed straightforward, and in truth Hargreaves was glad of the reprieve. Black of eye and hair, stern and stoic, he reminded her of a thinner, shorter, older Albion. Yet, he possessed a worldly weight Albion did not have.

"Yes," Hargreaves replied. "Vanessa Hargreaves..." Inspector? Agent? Traitor? She decided to opt for facts. "I was with him all last year. We stopped Valima Mordemere together."

"M-*dono,*" the swordsman murmured. "What do you want here?"

"These men," Hargreaves began, indicating the other car. "They have something of mine. I am here to get it back."

The whole fight had taken less than ten seconds, and with the train's rattling, Hargreaves had not been discovered. They stood there, looking at each other. Hargreaves breathed heavily, but Hikawa seemed untouched by exertion. What had happened to him in Mordemere's ateliers?

The swordsman seemed to come to a decision.

"Hargreaves-*dono*, I am Hikawa Shotaro *to mosu*. If you take me to Captain Clemens-*dono*, I will help you take back what was stolen."

"Pardon? What?" Hargreaves gaped. "Aren't you a..."

"I am not what I seem," the swordsman declared. "I am in the employ of those you call Incognito. Most shameful for a *samurai*, but I am *samurai* no more."

Incognito! Hargreaves started. What could the secret powers of the

Pirate Parliament want with the Cook box? No. Hikawa had seemed to want to keep a pretense of protecting the workspace. The Incognito must have infiltrated this ship to keep an eye on these box thieves—which meant they were hopefully on Hargreaves' side. Hikawa Shotaro seemed just the agent they would send. A fish out of water, but highly skilled and hard to read.

"Well, I can't promise when I will see Clemens again, but I suspect it will be soon," Hargreaves said honestly. "The bugger tends to pop up now and again. Why, exactly, do you want to meet?"

"We have an agreement?" the swordsman Hikawa said, ignoring the question. His face was implacably blank, the way some Orientals could do. Perhaps his reasons were as mysterious, ones only Captain Clemens would understand.

"Why, yes, I suppose we do," Hargreaves said cautiously.

"Then all is well. I will help you." So saying, the swordsman walked calmly to the next car. He opened the door, and then came sounds of screaming as he lay into the workers there with his swords. Hargreaves gaped for a moment, before rushing in herself, mindful to clear her corners.

Inside the next car, the space was full of machinery. The bulkheads were lined with writhing, welded piping and churning cams. The workmen wore full head masks with thick telescopic goggles, but their surprise was unmistakable. Crates were dropped and cries of pain rang out. To their credit the workmen scrambled for weapons, but Hikawa was far too quick for them. Snicker-snack, neat as tea-time. Hargreaves admired his deftness and speed, but questioned the wisdom of allying with him. A moment ago he had been ready to murder her, then on nothing but her word he had turned on his comrades. But then, it fit; the Incognito were known to be devious and fickle.

I may regret this later, she thought. Probably an understatement.

She clotheslined the man nearest her, toppling him mid-run. Instead of shooting him, she slammed the butt of the pistol into his temple as he scrambled to get up. Her stomach felt taut, smooth, and painless for the first time since London, save her large wound. Now that she was no longer an inspector she was not beholden to police protocol and could dispatch her assailants however she pleased. But that made going for the humane option more important. Soon, the aeronauts outside the canvas wall and those who had come running were laid at their feet.

"Where did you learn to fight like that?" Hargreaves asked of her new ally. As she spoke, she tied her hair back with a cloth from one of the crates, some kind of packing wrap, and settled her hat more securely.

"This? This is nothing," Hikawa said. "Compared to..."

"But you saw those men coming even from behind you. Was it the eye?"

"This?" Hikawa touched the rim of his brilliant blue-glass eye. Intricate frames, like the gyroscopic rings of a velocipede, swiveled in it when he looked at things. "This is only an eye." He showed her the flat of his cutlass, polished to brilliant mirror sheen.

"You see around you in the reflection of the sword!" Hargreaves deduced, drawing a smile from the grim swordsman. It was a fine trick. She felt a little better about her impromptu alliance.

"Come," said Hikawa. He gestured to the middle of the workshop car, where a tarpaulin had been drawn across the middle, partitioning the space. The car was very long, about the size of a warehouse.

Hargreaves nodded, plucked a saber from one of the guards and parted the curtain with the tip, hesitant to go too close. In Hikawa's sword, she caught sight of herself. With the wide hat, sword in hand, she was becoming far too comfortable playing at air pirate.

Inside the canvas, even harsher arclight momentarily blinded her. She stood behind the covering a moment to adjust. Hikawa had no such problem, and advanced into the space. The crack of a gunshot sounded, followed by the familiar sound of the swordsman's parrying. Then came a sound that chilled Hargreaves to the bone.

"Oh, it's you, the Oriental we hired. Hi...something, wasn't it? Good, you can take care of the interlopers. I'm almost done here."

The words were of no concern, meaningless, but Hargreaves recognized that voice. As much as she did not want to admit it, she knew it well.

It was the voice of Jean Hallow.

"Honestly, I might have a word with Stevie about the quality of henchmen this organization accepts," a female voice answered. Hargreaves knew this one, as well; the Orb Weaver, Vera Jasper.

"He...Hi...Harry, just nip on out there and take care of it." Hallow's normally calm subdued tone was now high and cruel, as if he did not mind who in particular was going to be cut down. There was a quiet moment. "Oh. Well it's you then. All right."

More gunshots, but the sound soon stopped. Hargreaves recognized the chilling silence of tactics, and she darted her head in to take a look. At the far end of the shop, lay a shape covered by a tarpaulin, filling the bulkhead to the top of the car. Something white peeked out the bottom. Not being able to make sense of it, she sighted Vera Jasper about to flank Hikawa's position, and acted with the closest thing at hand. She threw her saber at the devious little spider's head.

With a heavy clang the sword was snatched out of the air, shattering into thousands of pieces. The handle stuck by its broken point into the wall of the castle, quivering, and still Hargreaves could not see what had done it. A fluttering of the tarpaulin sounded, that was all.

"Orby, you mustn't let your guard down!" Hallow's voice rang out, but Hargreaves could not see where the skinny Englishman could be. Hargreaves raised her .22 at Jasper, who was wielding a wicked looking knife. No, the blade was strapped somehow to her wrist, like a stinger. The rest of her was wrapped in dark blues and blacks, veils and shawls, much as she had been at Temple Mills when she attacked the inspector.

"Jean! Stop this at once!" said Hargreaves. "Show yourself! What have you to say for this?"

"My, my, but that would take far too long," Hallow said. "Why don't you take a look?"

Before Hargreaves could react, pale, swooping fingers reached from under the tarpaulin and closed in about her, each a needle claw as long as her arm. An automata, surely, but one much faster than any she had encountered before. Suddenly she was rising, turning in the air as the metal hand brought her face to face with the machine. The fabric slipped, ruffling to the floor, and now she saw the automata's face was a sallow off-white, like the skin of a corpse. Its eyes were huge empty slits. Below the face, a second pair of eyes peered at her from between the collarbones of the machine. They were unfamiliar, though they should not have been, the face they were seated in a twisted gray mask of cruelty.

"Hallow!" gasped Hargreaves.

"In the flesh!" yelled the usually quiet Hallow.

Before the fingers could tighten, Hargreaves squeezed off a shot at the cockpit of the strange machine. She merely intended to disable what controls she could see, a panel strangely bereft of levers or control mechanisms. The shot went high, sparkling off the white enamel armor of the automata.

Perhaps Hallow had not expected Hargreaves to be quite so violent. Perhaps the shrapnel found its way into the cockpit. Perhaps Hallow was simply shocked by the burst of gun smoke. Whatever the reason, the fingers loosened just enough for Hargreaves to shimmy out of them, falling five feet to the floor of the train car.

"Hargreaves-*dono*!"

She barely registered the voice as Hikawa's. Instinct took over and she rolled across the floor. Vera Jasper's wrist knife dipped into her jacket's furred collar, missing her neck by hairs. It pulled out immediately as Hikawa's swords became a scintillating hurricane, forcing Jasper away. Freed, the inspector scrambled to her feet.

"Hallow! What did you do with the box?" Hargreaves screamed.

She fired a couple rounds at the automata, aiming for any exposed workings. A rippling collar started to extend, unfolding like a round, stepped accordion round its neck. Presumably some sort of guard, the collar made it difficult to shoot Hallow in the middle. The giant's flared joint armor and lobstered pauldrons were a parody of Alphonse's knight aesthetic, but the collar reminded Hargreaves of Elizabethan clothes. A jester, almost, with the terrible grinning rictus slashed across the machine's face. It gave her chills.

The monstrosity seemed to recoil as if it could feel the shots fired at it. Then with a lazy wave it swept her aside like a gnat. She hurtled into the side of the car, her body aching from the blow as if she had been run over by a Squamosa engine. The bulkhead buckled, and something in it gave, crumpling. She had hit a sliding door in the side of the car, and now there was a crack where the door met the wall. The fresh scent of pine and also smoky coal clinker filled the air. Her Browning clattered to the ground and bounced out of the train, lost to the tracks.

"Dear inspector," Hallow's voice tinkled from overhead. "Did you really think your little peashooter could harm the Grimaldi?"

The automata's limbs darted toward her again. Hargreaves turned to dodge them, but they were too fast for her. She felt a shooting pain across her chest as the automata swatted her aside again. The floor grew slippery under her. When she tried to raise the Tranter from her hip, her sleeve was red. Her stitches had torn, and she was bleeding a slick down her trousers.

Meanwhile, the white automata, Grimaldi as Hallow had called it, was standing up, its gormless grinning face close to the ceiling. A thin hiss of gas announced the ceiling bay doors opening, the sky peeking through in a crack of cheerful blue. Below, Hikawa and Orb Weaver dueled still, in flashes of metal nearly too swift to see.

"You have to give it back!" Hargreaves wheezed. "The box is going to kill a lot of people!" With the wind knocked out of her, she could barely talk. She hoped the hissing in her ears was from the airship's balloon and not from a punctured lung.

"Seeing as you're dying, I might as well tell you what I'm doing," said Hallow. The automata rose, using its great arms to shift the gate open the rest of the way. "I would not want you to go to your end not knowing the depth of your Queen's betrayal."

Hargreaves lay motionless, wondering how many of her bones were broken now. Desperately she wondered what Captain Clemens would do. She recalled how he had kept Valima Mordemere talking long enough to buy the time to destroy the dread ship *Nidhogg*.

Hargreaves regularly gave the captain guff about mouthing off to a madman. Now she saw why Clemens had found the last conversation an ordeal. Quite aside from the massive physical trauma, it was difficult to wholly disbelieve what Hallow was saying. She had known The Queen hadn't told her everything. She had in fact suspected she was being manipulated by the matriarch, maybe even put in a situation that very likely would be the end of Vanessa Hargreaves. What was it that kept her from believing Hallow now? It was hard to pin down.

There had been the conversation in Her Majesty's tea parlor. Amongst all the finery of the Empire where Her Majesty was in all her rights to simply order Hargreaves about, Her Majesty had poured

Vanessa tea. The Queen of the Pax Brittania, Empress of India, Bastion of the Lands Beyond, had poured the inspector tea. It was silly, stupid, and utterly naïve, but Hargreaves seized upon the memory of the Queen's agile fingers, the fragrance in the cup, of the sunbeams lancing through the mangosteen flowers. Above all, she remembered Her Majesty's youthful yet sagely calm face, her gentle smile hiding unfathomable troubles.

"Your Queen sent you running after a weapon," Hallow began.

"Yes, I know," Hargreaves wheezed, impatiently.

"But not the one you thought," Hallow continued. "Shall I show you?" The Grimaldi stood fully erect on legs thicker than Hargreaves' torso. The anatomy of the thing seemed impossible, with hips flared huge over thin legs.

The train was beginning to pitch with the thing's steps. It leaned over Hargreaves, and now she could see its long, narrow torso, a gilded cabinet in white enamel and gold trim. Slowly the fluted metal opened along a seam, revealing a sight so wretched that she nearly turned away. There was no engine or boiler like a normal automata. Instead, Hallow's face and shoulders peered out of a steaming, roiling mass of flesh. Strings of flesh were nailed to great orbs of gunmetal, peeking from the mass like caps of bone. Glimmering alloyed rings spun freely through, like celestial cartography, or coiled like a snake. They dipped in and out of the flesh, one with it, as if their substance was all part of some equation that made her head hurt. Whatever it was, it was pure nightmare fuel.

"Do you see?" Hallow's voice echoed strangely. After a squelching sound Hallow's pinstriped torso emerged from the gelatinous mass like a currant from custard.

"That is sick," said Hargreaves. "Sick and wrong."

"No, I'll tell you what is wrong," Hallow said as the rest of him slithered out of the fleshy blob. His foot made a popping sound as it came out. Despite no longer being inside the machination, the lumbering titan seemed to continue obeying his will, mimicking his movements. The tumorous mass pulsed and throbbed within its shadowed cavities. "What's wrong is Mordemere and I built these things to remake the world, and the Queen intends only to preserve it as it is: rotten!"

"What are you saying?" said Hargreaves, horrified.

"Isn't it obvious?" Hallow said. "Did you think the engines of the Empire were so advanced as to move such an intricate thing as this Grimaldi? Your Alphonse? Those automata we faced, Priser and Driver... weren't they slow and clumsy, compared to MAD automata? Did they not suffocate and kill their drivers?"

"But this is monstrous!" said Hargreaves, looking at the writhing thing in Hallow's shadow. Even as she did some part of her guessed at what Hallow had done, why he had come into the service of Her Majesty's government.

"I conceived and offered up these innovations," said Hallow, now free of the Cook abomination. He paced the deck. "I worked with Mordemere in his atelier. Did you think he could achieve all his wonders alone? I had Alphonse built in secret, to see how my works did in the field. And I have been lying in wait, until the Crown in its greed and fear helped to build the last part of my masterpiece!" Hallow gestured to the deathly white cliff behind him.

But that meant within Alphonse's black boxes...Hargreaves knew this instinctively, could feel it as deeply and with as much hurt as when she stood in the core of the *Nidhogg*. Every time she had taken Alphonse for a leisure ride, every time she had sat in that warm, close space...

"This is tomorrow," continued Hallow. "This is the innovation even Mordemere himself was too frightened to make use of, but your Victoria, oh, your splendid Victoria. She is no pushover. Once her soldiers found the plans in Mordemere's atelier, she knew it was the only chance she stood against the Ottomans. But of course, such a thing had never been built before. It had to be tested, and what better place to do so than against the nationalists of India and the sepoys? Plenty of test subjects, and plenty of raw...materials."

Hallow sneered. Hargreaves marveled at how different he was from the person she thought she knew. Normally patient and taciturn, Hallow now seemed condescending and loquacious, quite eager to prattle on about his master plan. She fingered the bronze knife at her waist, but Hallow was much too far away. She had to keep him talking.

"Materials?" she wheezed.

"Harvested, of course, from those foreign undesirables England is so fond of sweeping out of the way of progress. That has always been the way of it. The Queen's predecessors plundered India until it was a desiccated husk, just like she is doing now in Argentina. Only now, Victoria III has the benefit of airships, those cataclysmic angels on high. My Grimaldi, my Conqueror Worm eats only dead flesh, and those lands had been thoroughly killed."

"I won't have you speak of Her Majesty that way!" cried Hargreaves. Amazingly, patriotic fire remained in her belly. "You've created a monster!"

Hallow kept talking. It seemed he couldn't stop.

"Inspector...though you never caught on I had been sending missives to my agents from your very department, I can see the comprehension in your eyes," Hallow allowed. He began to laugh, his voice cracking. "Oh my, it is nice to have someone understand. You know why picture villains monologue? Because they're never allowed to just talk. To just take the piss. Maybe if we had an outlet for change we wouldn't have to go to all this dramatic tosh. We're always cut off before we get a chance to—"

"Ah, so that is your intent."

The voice of Hikawa Shotaro was a shock to both of them, but the sight of his blade cleaving the air was a greater shock to Jean Hallow. It stoppered his words before he could finish relating his master plan. One second he was striding about, gesturing with his scarecrow arms. The next, his hand and forearm up to the elbow went arching through the air, some three yards away from his body.

Hallow let out a long, high scream of pain. He whirled, spraying blood across the deck. Tears streamed through new furrows in his usually smooth, pale face.

"Orby! Help me Orby!"

His cry of help went unheeded. Vera Jasper lay prone some yards away, crumpled and unconscious. But she hadn't been of no use; Hikawa moved much slower, limping over a fresh leg wound.

"Your assassin will not save you," Hikawa said as he lunged, uncharacteristically clumsy with his leg, to finish Hallow.

The clang of the blade rang across the blasted deck. Hikawa's blade came down as a glowing arc, only to be cut off by the Grimaldi. The infernal machine put itself between Hikawa and his target with deft swiftness. Then the white chest plate swung open, crashing into the swordsman and sending him flying. The Grimaldi turned on Hallow, engulfing him whole into its cavernous trunk.

The train wobbled and pitched at an angle too steep for Hargreaves to stand. Not that she could, with her wounds. They were rolling, pitching fast into a turn as the train picked up speed. Hurt and straining, she felt her body tip, the door to the boxcar no longer supporting her on ruined hinges. With a terrible, slow foreboding she began to succumb to gravity's hold. She reached out, scrabbling for purchase.

Her fingers closed around a bit of unbroken bulkhead. Almost there!

And then she found herself in free fall. She watched the white form of the Grimaldi crouch down once more, the car's ceiling doors closing over it. From afar, the thing had a terrible beauty, all fluted posture and deathly finesse. It looked like some angel of the apocalypse.

That was the last thing Hargreaves saw before the blurring tree line enveloped her.

STATION 10

Terra Incognita

FOR THE SECOND TIME IN AS MANY DAYS, CEZETTE FOUND HER MAMAN in dire straits. She had whisked her to the hospital, clutching an appropriated toolbox while Cid made some last minute adjustments to the velocipede. The inspector was determined to continue fighting, even though she was broken and in need of patching. Now, Cezette seized upon Maman's familiar scent of goldenrods, cherishing it, committing it to memory. She did not know why, but she had a terrible urge to clutch Maman close. But it was not to be, for the moment they had her stitched back together again, Maman prepared to set out.

In the lot of the hospital, Maman asked, "You're sure you're not coming with us?" Alphonse's torn arm sat discarded next to the purring velocipede.

"The velocipede seats two," said Cezette. "Uncle Cid and Jean will take care of me."

"You're trying to reassure me," said Hargreaves. "Which means you're planning something."

"What other choice is there? Sit and do nothing?" Cezette answered simply. "Go catch the box, Maman. You can tuck me in when we get home."

"Silly girl. You're a bit big for that," the inspector said. She sighed, and held the girl to her breast. "Keep those legs working. Listen to Cid."

But Hargreaves was right: Cezette had been planning something. A germ of an idea had been growing in the clever little French girl's head. Finding her maman, making and suddenly losing a friend, it all felt like some roller coaster ride, with a deadly drop behind every hairpin turn. On the one side were the bright, shiny attractions of America, and finally being outside of MAD. On the other, there were the real dangers of murderous automata and shadowed forces she could barely glimpse, let alone control. Who had given them the cab? Who had warned them of the men in the hotel room? Questions plagued the girl. The whole journey was an emotional whirligig, but she wasn't about to get off the ride.

Cezette's plan was actually Cid's plan as well. She had run into him hiring a car when she went to the hospital's front desk. All the better—she hadn't been sure she could hire a car at her age. She also had little in currency. Cid, the old graybeard knew better than to question Cezette if they made too much fuss, it would give away the plan to Hargreaves. The inspector would never have allowed her ward to poke around in the sharp, rusting wreckage of a train, not even to piece Alphonse back together.

"I have the left leg!"

"And I the right arm!"

Cezette and Cid fully expected the derailment to be scoured clean, and every piece of Hargreaves's metal companion carted off to a junkyard or evidence lot. The prodigious amount of wreckage meant that hadn't happened, not by a long shot. The local authorities had brought in a steamer crane, to start hauling the wreckage from the rear of the train first. Additional lines needed to be diverted, compounding the inconvenience of so many trains already being rerouted for the Ghost Train. Days after the accident, the locals had only begun to excavate the middle cars. There was simply too much wreckage to sift through, and downed engines were known to keep burning for hours, sometimes days. Best to leave that end for last. Cid intended to retrieve Alphonse's corpse before those dread steamworks could be exploited by an immoral entrepreneur.

As the unlikely duo dragged the detached components to the bulk of Alphonse's torso, they found a rather large Latin man sitting on Alphonse's knee where they had left it on a pile. Cid dropped the leg he had been dragging with a clunk.

"I expected the inspector herself," the man said to the panting, sweating duo. Like a proper gentleman, he took off his fedora and stood up. Though he had a large paunch, the man's arms and shoulders were thick with muscle. He looked over the rickety bones of Cid, and sized up Cezette. "Unless, of course, you're more of Burgess' goons."

"Like the Orb Weaver," said Cezette. "Violet Jade, or Vera Jasper."

"If you're implying you're not one of Burgess', then who are ye?" Cid grunted. Seeing no recourse than to deal with the Latin man, he squatted on the chunk of leg and took a drink from a hip flask.

"Our mutual friend believes, of course, I am a detective in the ranks of New York's finest." The Latin man replied. "Vanessa Hargreaves is a magnificent woman, and a fine specimen of Scotland Yard, so it gives me pride to say I was able to deceive her. Sancho Ortega. I work for America."

"American intelligence. Secret Service?" said Cid

"I work for America, not the American government," Ortega said simply.

Cezette came to stand by Cid, searching his face for how to respond to this unexpected intrusion. She got the impression Ortega did not want anything from them—not that there was much to take besides their lives and Alphonse. Still, the automata was still there and they were still alive. She concluded this "detective" was here to help.

"Don't buy it," Cid said. He offered the Latin man a drink from his flask, but Ortega declined. Cezette thought she saw decades of heartburn in the momentary grimace. "Why would you haul your bollocks all the way from New York and not deliver our metal friend to your masters?"

"Because my masters do not will it," Ortega said amiably. "We are many."

"For we are Legion," answered Cid. His entire attitude seemed to change in an instant, not relaxing, but regarding Ortega with an analytical gaze instead of a threatening one. His grizzled brow wrinkled. "Why are you here?"

"What is this?" said Cezette, confused. She looked from Ortega to Cid.

"The little one is not initiated," said Ortega. "No, but we ought. She is...resourceful," grumbled Cid in his usual way.

"Uncle!"

"An old pirate like me would not still be alive if he did not have some connection to the Incognito," Cid murmured quietly.

"*Sacre Bleu...*"

Cezette had heard the tales from Maman, both her birth mother and Hargreaves. Her natural mother had read her penny dreadfuls in bed, while Hargreaves had spoken of them tersely. The Incognito were elite rogues, the most honorable of thieves. The Pirate Parliament, those who dwelt in the shadows, striding the line between brigand war-princes and aeronaut lords. Those foolish enough to cross their black sails or fail to pay their protection soon found themselves at the mercy of ten thousand cutlasses. Trade route blockades, inexplicable missing cargo, raging stock house fires in monsoon season, nothing was beyond their power. The Incognito were the only authority at waystations like the *Straight Hook*, and their dark hand could be felt in every world-changing deed. Air pirates with the Incognito's mark could fly mostly unpoliced, without fear of the gibbet, though it was said the mark did not come cheap.

"The notes! And thee convenient cab!" said Cezette. "Arturo's belly!"

More loudly, Cid continued, "There is no such thing as a member of the Incognito in good standing, but you seem to be one of those uppity-ups in a great deal of power. What is the meaning of guiding us this far? Nearly killing us?"

"I do apologize for this," Ortega said, gesturing vaguely at the blackened carnage all about him, and presumably, at Arturo's stabbing. "I had nothing to do with it, but it was not well done. The Ghost Train and the Orb Weaver was near. By putting Inspector Hargreaves' friends into our care, my agents hoped to secure the Cook box before the Ghost Train arrived to take them. It was bad luck the inspector herself arrived with the box."

"Those poor sods," said Cid, looking at the downed form of the barrel-shaped automata nearby. He had some fellow feeling for the plains pirates.

"Even the Orb Weaver thought those saboteurs were working with her and Burgess when they derailed this train, which is often the way we prefer it. We make small changes in others' plans to facilitate our ends. I, for example, specialize in social mediation. I tell a cab driver to meet you at your hotel. I keep tabs on Mister Arturo's informants. I employ agents where to find you. Sometimes we must employ agents who are...heavy-handed, let's say. The Incognito is not what it was."

"Pirates," said Cid, rolling his eyes.

"*Putos, pinche pendejos*," Ortega agreed. "I saw the ether flare Orb Weaver sent up. I presume the inspector is hunting them down? She was injured. I am, again, very sorry for that."

"You seem awfully eager to share. Won't your secret club kick you out?" said Cezette.

Ortega gave a deep, bellowing laugh. "Regrettably, the situation did not turn out as we hoped, and we require a...better hand of cards. The Ghost Train now holds the box, for whatever nefarious purpose, we cannot say. I assume you know what is inside?" Ortega asked.

"Of course. The instant the box arrived at the Yard, I poked around with an echogramoscope," Cid answered, snorting. "That thing is a menace."

A menace? But surely it is much more than that, Cezette thought. They could not all be fighting over a thing simply because it was dangerous, as if it were a gun or a bomb.

"Cid Tanner. Also known as the Oxfordian, and the Bull Shark. I always wondered if you were one of us." Ortega sounded impressed. "The job with the Sultan's jewels, how was that done?"

"Why are you here?" Cid growled as he drank the remainder of what was in his flask. It sounded alarmingly empty.

"I am going to help you. Well, not you exactly," Ortega said. He reached down, below his knee, and with one knuckle, rapped against Alphonse's punctured chest plate. Was Alphonse integral to the Incognito's plans? What would they want with fixing him?

"With what?" Cid said, gesturing at the ruin of Alphonse. "It's a longshot at best. You would need a fully kitted out manufactory, access to a forge, machines to shape and form metal. Or, anyway, an airship to bring him there."

Ortega simply smiled. As if on cue, there was an answering whistle from the other side of the pass. The instrument did not sound like a train's call.

STATION 11

Do You Like Camping?

ALBION MADE IT TO THE WEST COAST DURING THE WILD BEAUTY OF twilight. Orange and purple clouds splashed across a dark blue sky and the mountains lit up like huge embers, flaming on one side and scorched shadow on the other. His travel fatigue momentarily forgotten, he watched twilight fall over the land. Actually, the sundown soothed more than bodily aches. He had been traveling and searching ever since getting out of the water plant in New York, and he felt the world weariness in his bones.

Part of the experience was his ride. Dragonwell needed little in the way of fuel, and Albion himself was hardy, so he had expected to catch up to the *Huckleberry* in little time. They had planned to consult Burgress's documents at length, but there was no rendezvous, no plan to meet before the sewer attack happened. They were pirates, used to sudden upheavals. Albion recalled something Hargreaves had said about the Niagara, and so he headed north for some days. But the skies near the Canadian border proved unusually full of airship traffic, and there was the business with the New York State patrol. After what happened in the city, the roads were full of police cruisers with high-altitude rifles. The North was bristling with danger, but if it hadn't he wouldn't have come down far enough to see the wreck.

Albion took to flying by night. Rosa had taught him to listen in on pirate ether channels in America, and their soundings rippled through the receiving array in Dragonwell's console. If he tweaked the dagger-shaped device, he could just hear their voices. It was enough to gather something big had left a trail of destruction through New York and torn into a small hamlet looking for Hargreaves. The ether rang with rumors; some thought a wendigo had come out of the forests and decimated it, others said the dead had come back to life and the end times were coming. The ether net was entertaining, but not very helpful.

Albion might have lost the way back to his companions, but he was nothing if not resourceful. So he did what he always did when he was lost: he went to a bar. This far inland, pirate bars were rare, but the waystations were plenty, offering connections in the form of grizzled lumberjacks, small town gossipers and the usual rumor mill. The east coast waystations were forest cabins and old Indian nation meeting places, more often than not. Sometimes they were treehouses nailed to wide old trees. Once there was an old seafarer anchored in the middle of a lake, like it had been dropped there.

The waystations featured a species of freight airship Albion had never seen, a pig-nosed, long-bodied type of tug that could take several containers lashed together like buoys, each one floated on its own balloon. Thusly loaded, the tugs flew cross-country delivering goods in a relay, one tug to another trading containers as they went. The tuggers were hard-drinking types who loved a good story. Several tankards later, Albion had a lead on a ship that could only be his own, and boarded a tug headed south by southwest. Some trepidation nagged him. The tuggers said the ship was damaged, and was limping along uncharted routes. It posed some danger to the regular freight lanes, which were charted over uninhabited places. The tuggers were happy to take him, though. They had never seen the like of Dragonwell, and just having carried it made a story they could brag about later.

In Pittsburgh, Albion tuned in to another set of ether nets, and determined the 'Berry was flying west. The direction could only be related to Vanessa Hargreaves' unmentionable cargo. If he knew Hargreaves, she would want to get rid of the box as quickly as possible.

Albion did not think the hermetically sealed box could be easily destroyed. What was out West that could help her?

By skimming the autumn fallow in the dead of night, Albion made all speed toward the West and the gray veil of the Lands Beyond. Dragonwell was an excellent traveling companion, with a comfortable seat. Even so, Albion had to stop occasionally to sleep and eat, and to keep an ear out for news of his ship or Hargreaves. There was the occasional tornado or dust storm to worry about. If he took to the ground at certain places, he could parley with the woolly bear captains, making deals for supplies. His Morse lantern came in very handy, phrases he thought he'd forgotten resurfacing like old wrecks. The oppressive heat of the Nevada desert threatened to dry up Dragonwell's water coils, leaving them both to bleach in the sun.

He might have continued to fly west past where Hargreaves had fallen if Dragonwell's engine didn't give a worrisome shudder between his legs. Albion at first paid it no mind. Unexplained noises were a common occurrence with all automata. Dragonwell was battered and barely being held together with gaffer's tape. Every moving part rattled, and the rips in the canvas joints whistled maddeningly. Its ragged cape billowed, catching the breeze like a loose sail.

As he flew on, following the rail tracks below, Dragonwell's rattling picked up an urgency that was not just the air rattling through its bones. Over the weeks, Albion had learned to trust the big fellow's instincts and listen to its desires. The shard at the Gear's heart had once been inside of Albion, and sometimes he felt a pain in his shoulder where the crystal had lodged at high speed. Perhaps a piece of it still rested inside of him.

"All right, all right!" Albion said aloud. It echoed in the cockpit over the engine noise. His ears were full of Cid's words. On the day he left the 'Berry, Cid had cautioned the captain as only an old hand could—gruffly, yet tenderly.

"Be mindful of this," Cid had said, patting Dragonwell's exposed engine. It had not been completed yet, and the tin man's bones stuck out every which way. They had just fitted the shard into the engine's carriage, and already it was whirring and glowing furiously.

"Cid, you helped me build the damn thing. You helped bring me up from a tyke, you watched me climb all over your clanking engines. Now you're saying you built something I should be careful of? Why would you hammer together my gallows yourself?"

"Mindful, not scared," Cid had answered. "This thing was in your body, lad. We've never seen anything like this aeon crystal, let alone one that was inside a human body. You know I unwrapped it expecting your blood all over it, but there was nothing, not a drop. The blasted thing was clean and glittering."

"What are you saying?"

"If the old analytical engine is right," Cid went on, tapping his noggin. "And if I didn't cock up the tests, this Gear needs only minimal fuel, very little pressure, and only a little fine tuning now and again. The condensers will give you water enough to carry the aeon stream. Can't say for the rest of it, but Dragonwell's engine might very well run indefinitely."

"That's all right then," Albion said, relieved. "The Lands Beyond are wild and uncivilized. We might not be able to find fuel or water where we go." That was their plan, Albion, Rosa, and the 'Berry, to venture out in the wild frontier beyond the gray veil. The thought of it made him smile. That was why they had spent so much time staking out Burgess for parts, building Dragonwell—the automata that could fly, that could clear the way for the 'Berry in unknown lands.

"I don't know." Cid had said, picking up after his tools. "I'm saying I don't know what it's capable of, so you better watch yourself. It might be this here was what Mordemere was trying to build, before he went nuttier than the last bite of figgy pudding. If I were you I wouldn't finish building this at all."

They both looked up to the Gear's silent, unfinished face, grinning at them with its one eye, really a scope for the pilot. In the other hole, the gaping muzzles of a triple-barreled gun stared hungrily.

"A future that never was," Albion murmured. "A world without want."

"Lad," Cid had said while looking at Albion very carefully, "If you're not frightened by the notion, you're a fool."

Albion had only piloted Dragonwell a couple times before taking him out to battle, and only to test the parts they commandeered from Burgess' stores. Even then, the machine seemed to anticipate his movements. A lever stuck in exactly the right place sometimes, or a gauge might gurgle to show him a hidden patrol. Other times, the Gear had a mind of its own, stepping a little ways further than intended or not always staying exactly where it was left. Albion knew aeons reacted to the people around them. But there was a ghost in this machine.

Albion had an ear to listen now, when Dragonwell made itself heard, whatever the thing's motivations were. Albion had long ago decided to work with it, not against it. As he drew nearer the shape of a riverbank appeared from under a canopy of trees, and now Albion saw a swatch of land that sloped from the tracks to the river. The slide was full of smooth clinker and soft, rotted leaves. He picked a spot and landed Dragonwell.

Albion's boots splashed down in water. He looked around. What did his big metal friend want to show him? For a moment he felt silly, as superstitious as the old augurers back in the Kowloon Walled City. How could an assemblage of clockwork and steam engine parts want anything? But as he turned in a slow circle, he could make out the traces of something that had come rolling down the slope, dislodging a long slide of dirt. And at the base of it, there was something gold floating in the water.

"What the blazes—Hargreaves!" he cried out.

Vanessa Hargreaves did not respond to his calls, continuing to float face-down in a little eddy. She was starting to get pulled out into the main current. Albion splashed deeper into the river, and that was when he saw the cloud of darkness Hargreaves was floating in—blood! He knelt in the water, turning her and holding her up by her armpits. Amazingly, she was alive, her pulse weak, but still she breathed. Despite being unconscious her knuckles were clenched white.

"You're hardier than you look," said Albion, and pulled her onto the bank.

As the sun set slowly over an indifferent west, the river was treated to the splendid cacophony of Hargreaves waking.

"Bluh..."

"Ah. Glad to see you're awake, Inspector. I'm afraid I plum forgot the tea, but there's roast trout."

Captain Clemens sat across a glowing fire from her, a sight for very sore eyes.

Hargreaves looked about, groggily, and then her blush spread like wildfire. Beneath Albion's swashbuckling jacket, not a stitch covered her.

She picked up the closest missile she could find; a river rock. "Why... why you lout!"

Dodging the rock, Albion held up his hands in submission. Hargreaves's cheeks grew hotter. . The bloody pirate was naked as well. The next rock hit him in the right temple, knocking him for a loop. Colorful curses flew from her lips.

"Mind the gap," he said, pointing and holding his head.

"What gap?" shrieked Hargreaves. Looking down she saw Albion's coat edging into the ditch of the fire. With a start, she saw she was well covered by it, and quite dry besides. It didn't comfort her very much.

"Don't move around too much. You lost a lot of blood, from the look of the water. I put the stitches right, but they're temporary at best, wire meant for Dragonwell," said Albion. He hooked a thumb over his shoulder, indicating the hulk behind him. "It will still be numb, from the spot anesthetic. You must have been hit hard, the needle did not wake you. "

He showed her the needle: a fishing hook. The chrome syringe for the anesthetic was an altogether more terrifying affair. It was a foot long and had to be disassembled to fit in its tin box. Focused on those, Hargreaves nearly missed the looming shadow at Albion's shoulder. She turned dully until her eyes focused upon it, and she saw the Gear's bulk. Grimaldi!

"Get that monstrosity away from me!" she shrieked. With all the laundry hung drying on his steaming flanks, the automata's silhouette was freakish, otherworldly. For one terrible second she thought she saw the manic rictus of Hallow's creation.

"Whoa, whoa!" Albion said.

He threw a flaming branch at Dragonwell's feet, the shifting light glinting off the tricorn helm. Hargreaves calmed, pulling the coat closer over her. Albion walked over to take his shirt off the lines. The rictus faded back into the pirate grimace of Dragonwell's own face.

"You had quite a scare, now just sit back before you bleed out again," said Albion.

"I...I..." stuttered Hargreaves. But as much as she hated to admit it, Albion was right. The stitches holding her together was a dull hurt. Hargreaves slumped down, dizzy. The captain sighed, brought over a canteen of fresh water, and a leaf with a skewered fish with some late-season blueberries on it.

Hargreaves grabbed for the canteen, and tilted her head suspiciously.

"Not river water. Fresh from Dragonwell's condensers," said Albion. She took a long draught, then set to the leaf, popping four or five berries at a time. The fish she picked apart, flaking and hot.

When she'd had her fill, Albion asked, "Was there something in the ship?"

"Something, all right," she said, and filled him in while he set a smallish saucepan on the fire. She began with leaving Rosa Marija and the crew of the 'Berry, which he took stoically. His trust in his crew showed as total indifference to their plight, which was oddly comforting. When she got to the train wreck, Albion added a paper pouch of some brown powder to the pot, and bits and smidgens from some other envelopes hidden in his coat pockets. By the time she finished relating her one-woman airship raid and Hallow's betrayal, Albion was pouring some viscous, beastly liquid into a sturdy metal cup.

"I thought you were out of tea," Hargreaves said, scowling.

"Herbal tincture," Albion said. "Mostly Cantonese, with some Japanese Kampō touches and a dollop of honey for flavor."

"I didn't see you put in any," she complained.

He reached over to another leaf, wrapped securely with cord, and produced a fresh chunk of honeycomb, crumbly and sticky. "Roadside trader. Things are closer to their natural shape out here. Drink! It will help you heal."

At first, Hargreaves regarded the minging sludge as she might the leavings of a horse. The smell was cloying, sticking to her mucus membranes and befouling them. The stains felt permanent.

"I think I'll save this for later," Hargreaves said, setting the cup on a flat rock.

"No, you'll have it now. The doctors may have sewn you back together, but your insides need topping up."

Hargreaves winced. It was true; her guts felt like someone had taken a steamthrower to them. She remembered Rosa Marija once saying she had spent some time with the captain learning healing arts from a... What were they called? Some kind of doctor, in the Kowloon Walled City. Still, surely pirates had cause to appropriate medical knowledge that worked, she thought, with all the scrapes they fell into.

"It's best to hold your breath," Albion said helpfully.

Hargreaves sighed, pinched her nose, and downed the awful stuff in a single gulp. When she came up for air, scrabbling, Albion held the honeycomb just within arm's reach. The bitter taste couldn't be fully washed out, but the honey was fresh and floral, tasting slightly of orange blossoms. The combs were the same color as her bedraggled hair.

"It sounds to me," said Albion while Hargreaves laid waste to the honey. "It sounds to me like Hallow's plans can't be so simple."

"How so? Hallow's got his bloody Ghost Train to deliver the box anywhere he likes," said Hargreaves. "He could take over the country with his new army."

"We know Ubique funded him and helped build Alphonse along with this...Grimaldi monstrosity," said Albion. "His coffers aren't infinite."

"It makes sense, in a way," said Hargreaves. "This Ghost Train...I heard of it as a terrible rumor when I traveled America. It had shut down the rails of the North and I had to take plains crawlers to get through. So it had the run of the North."

"The Ghost Train created a rumor to protect itself. Hauntings and abductions terrible enough to keep people away from Hallow's moving laboratory," agreed Albion. "An armor of stories."

"Not just a laboratory. A manufactory," said Hargreaves. "I bet you his boxcars are full of flat-packed nightmare engines, ready to come to life once he infuses them with the Cook box's..." She struggled for a word. "Essence? But he can't go on making them. There isn't enough room on the train."

"Maybe more like his white automata...?"

"The Grimaldi..." Hargreaves muttered. She remembered the way its long, white fingers had moved when Hallow twitched his head. The casual way it had destroyed the airship, the way it had cast Hikawa aside like a rag doll. Despite being dry and close to the fire, Hargreaves shivered.

Albion took a deep breath.

"When I was swept aside by the floodgates under New York, the spider automata left me for dead, and stopped attacking. At the time, I thought it was simply leaving when the Cook box slipped out of reach. But it wasn't. It was avoiding something," said Albion.

"What could an enormous steam works spider be afraid of?" said Hargreaves.

"When I found my way out, it was through a municipal tunnel. New York's underground is a warren of blind corners, built layer upon layer like a giant stone cake. There are tunnels and byways in there that could hide anything, Hargreaves," Albion said. "What I saw was right on the surface, a passage into a government water processing plant. I could see people walking at the windows. That tarantula automata knew the place was there. It could have followed me in but it didn't want to lead me there."

"You aren't usually this verbose." Hargreaves' eyes narrowed suspiciously. "Are you...could you be afraid?"

"Yes, damn it, yes," said Albion, nearly spitting the words. His hands shook, but his brow was as unreadable as ever.

"What I saw..." And now Albion fell speechless, as if he wanted desperately to put the sight into words, but could not. Whatever had been in that room, behind the door in the water plant, Albion had brought it with him. It seemed to haunt him, as much as the specter of the Grimaldi did Hargreaves.

Instead of saying anything, Albion drew one last thing from his bottomless pockets; a package wrapped in waxed paper, the light, airy kind they used at photogram developing shops.

Hargreaves took them, and looked through them in the firelight. The first were of rooms full of steamcrafts, tinning machines, die machines and conveyor belts, meaningless churning cogs connected to powerful dynamos lurking in the backgrounds. Another was of stacks of cans piled high. Then she leafed through the great cauldrons, the holding pens seen from catwalks, each full of ragged, destitute people. She leafed through the photograms, and as she came to the rooms full of hooks in the ceilings, her gorge rose, and her eyes watered. The last photograms showed things that shouldn't ever exist, not so much charnel houses as the long, empty passageways of the soul made flesh.

It was funny, she thought, there had not been a single beggar or panhandler in those shining streets. There hadn't even been people sheltering in the dank tunnels, when she looked on them from the warmth of the 'Berry.

Suddenly Hargreaves had a vision of industry, that special efficiency capable of processing people by the pound and loading them in barrels onto Hallow's Ghost Train. People disappearing off the streets, being carted off in the dead of night, boxcars of the damned rattling away behind those beastly engines...All the rumors she had heard were falling into place like some terrible jigsaw puzzle. She imagined the huge manufacturing cars she had seen on the Ghost Train, crafting ranks upon ranks of dark metal sentries. Each one gutted and emptied, awaiting the impregnation of a meaty spirit twisted by the Cook box.

In the pictures, the machines were separating the bits into two conveyors. One led into barrels that looked industrial, probably bound for Hallow. The other led to a can packing machine, and the labels were shockingly familiar. She'd eaten from one of those cans. She'd been eating them ever since Appleton, at every diner and waystation. And after she retched, feeling the bitter tincture stick in her craw, she flipped to the last picture. The familiar cog-and-cam of Ubique was no surprise. The stars, stripes and eagles emblazoned on the cans were.

That morning found Hargreaves extinguishing the last embers of their campfire, as Albion slept on a pile of blankets on the hard ground. Though Hargreaves was sore, the morning dappling through the leaves seemed to cleanse her, and she took a walk toward the rails. She didn't know what she expected to see, but it felt good to stretch her healing body. Hargreaves walked a good mile, following the unwavering line of the rails. She kept a keen eye for Hikawa, who may have escaped or been thrown off the train. Bu she was wholly unprepared for what she actually found.

She turned on her heel and hurried back to Albion, trying not to run. He would not be roused until Hargreaves flipped him into the river. They trotted back to the rails, Albion leaving a trail of droplets.

When they reached the spot, they could scarcely believe their eyes. The Ghost Train had ejected its detritus as it passed through. Workmen had likely tossed everything not of use out of the moving car, leaving a trail of garbage along both sides of the track. Now the rail beds were scattered with broken crates and empty barrels. Lying amongst the wreckage, the Cook box sat, a tombstone jutting out of the shiny clinker.

Hargreaves walked up to it, and when she laid her hand on the smooth riveted surface the panels fell apart. She yelped, and jumped back. Between the Cook box's hermetically sealed sides, something had been hidden, and now the morning sunshine gleamed off its smooth length. They stood gaping at it, not quite believing what had been hidden with the box's contents. Albion stepped forward ran his hand across the object's surface, but jerked back as if scorched.

"Is it hot?"

"No, it...it's like it knows me..." said Albion, confused. He fumbled at his sodden hips, coming up with the Red Special, and tapped the butt against the surface. The aeon pistol rang a clear note. Hargreaves thought she saw a ripple of blue spread from the spot, in waves and patterns, like the surface of a still pond that had been disturbed.

"Do you know what this means?" asked Hargreaves. "That sly fox knew what I would do before I even thought of it myself!"

"Now that is hardly any way to speak of your matriarch," Albion said. Hargreaves covered her mouth. "Besides, it is too little, too late. Without Alphonse, you can't use this. Even Dragonwell wasn't built for something this large, he would never fly."

"Enough of your cheek," said Hargreaves. "Her Majesty predicted everything. To what other purpose is this if not to correct a potentially grave, catastrophic error?"

She gazed upon the gleam of its carving, at the words inscribed upon it, and the light glinting off the strangely opalescent surfaces. The etched words read "A Contrario" in a flowing script—Her Majesty's own handwriting, writ huge. This was meant for her, for Hargreaves alone. Maybe it wasn't a sign from God, but it was a sign from some higher power, the only one that mattered to Hargreaves.

Finally, Albion had to lay out the problem for her.

"Well then you tell me. How are we going to pull a ruddy, big sword taller than Dragonwell from a rock the size of Camelot? This thing is bigger than Rosa's butt."

STATION 12

Clean Slate

VERA JASPER KNEW SHE OUGHT TO BE ECSTATIC, DESPITE HER CUTS, bruises, and two broken fingers. It was no worse than practicing for the circus tricks she had done since beyond memory. Because of her unique assets, she could pull or wrench most of her hurts back into shape, but cuts were another matter, and the cold stung sharply. So she clasped her veil and her baffled goggles tighter across her face, against the gale winds howling into the observation deck of their Conqueror Worm. As the blazing sunset fast approached, her wounds inflamed, bloody and sore, she couldn't deny something had gone terribly wrong.

"Ugghhh..."

The pained groan snapped Vera out of her meditations. She turned, and seeing their prisoner awake, closed the observation deck's window. It hummed shut on smooth bearings. The groaner lay on a smooth metal bench, and he did not try to move. On the other side of the deck, his weapons had been neatly stacked. Vera did not begrudge the swordsman his betrayal; the man impressed her, as all men of skill did. He regarded her calmly. Though he had beaten her, his body was badly hurt.

"We don't really have cells," said Vera. "All the holding pens feed into the meat grinders. But if you try to escape from here, the sides of the car are smooth and round. You'll fall and be ground up by the tracks instead. Nod if you understand."

The swordsman nodded. Vera gave him a skin of water and some dry rations, before heading down the stairs at one end of the observation deck. She locked the heavy riveted door at the bottom.

Vera left the Oriental alone, and walked through the cars of their Conqueror Worm. The train's bulk was starting to bother her. It had started as metal and bolts, but at some point begun to develop an almost organic quality. The shadows crawled with writhing shapes. She passed the manufactory cars, stuffed to the brim with machinery. They took barrels of raw stock and processed them, pumping it to the storage cars further ahead. Vera didn't need to look up to see the scaffolds and holding pens that stored some of the fresher ingredients. They cursed and spat at her, the few who were awake.

In the storage cars, she passed row after row of insectoid carapaces, traveling through their mass on a catwalk path. The boxcar was packed full of them, top to bottom. The creations' limbs sat folded and compressed into asterisks, as if they were dead. Arachnid, mostly, with eight legs and glassy eyes. Their joints sprouted cogs and cams. Beneath their glass eyes they were hollow. Barrels marked with the cog and cam of Ubique lay stacked in the corners of the room, tapped to rubber nipples that fed into the pipes of the car. Vera shuddered, then passed from the storage cars into the deployment car. It took a long time.

On board the deployment car, the active automata had sat with pilot seats behind their eyes. The Scotland Yard woman had released them all. Vera passed these and continued to march forward, until she reached the car where the Grimaldi and Jean Hallow rested.

The room was currently being redecorated, but Vera ignored the workmen, marching straight up a short ramp to Grimaldi's collar. From this vantage point, she could see into the chest cavity, a dark pit she did not want to look into for long. Soft clicks and gushing noises bubbled up from it, in combinations too vivid to dare imagine. Jean Hallow's face peered from a den of madness.

"You let him live?" asked Hallow. His voice was but a wisp on the wind.

"This man posed as one of ours," said Vera. "I let him live. As you wanted."

"Yes," said Hallow. His face was parchment, impossibly paler than before. His shoulder was lost in an adder's nest of writhing shadows. "Who sent him?"

"He is to be bait?"

"Yes," whispered Hallow. "No. Maybe. I am not sure they will come for him."

"The derailment was likely their work," said Vera.

"Did you think I would overturn a train with myself inside it?" asked Hallow. "No, this kind of chaos could only have come from those wretched, scurvy-ridden Incognito."

His hate was palpable. Vera ran her agile fingers, tiny Lilliputian steps, over the intricate designs etched into the *Grimaldi's* helm. It shone a blazing opalescent in the arclight, but did nothing to soothe Vera's feeling of unrest. What lay beneath the shining façade made her the scarred skin of her back crawl. She knew a mask when she saw one.

"I would understand if it were a diamond, a painting, or a valuable aeon artifact like the Cicero Knife," said Vera. "The Incognito are pirates, thieves. What would they want with our Grimaldi?"

"They fancy themselves the shapers of their own destiny," answered Hallow. "And this is a shaper of worlds."

At that, the Grimaldi shuddered, and its chest groaned open. There was a cloak hanging nearby. For a brief moment Vera thought she saw a heavily muscled arm emerge, as if there was a strongman inside the machine. The arm was pulsing red. But then there was only Hallow, standing there like a scarecrow that had been slotted into an overlarge umbrella.

"I don't see how they can change anything," said Vera, recovering. "Without your investment and Burgess's connections, they would not be able to build any more. Only this train has been able to evade them all this time, keeping your creations hidden."

"My Conqueror Worm is an impenetrable fortress," said Hallow. "But they are bent on stopping us. In ancient times, the bow and arrow was the peak of the war artificer's talents. An army of those made Genghis Khan. The powder rifle carved out these lands below for the white man, and the steam engine netted the skies for the lone entrepreneur. What might have happened if none of these things were ever made?"

"What do you intend to do?" asked Vera. In all this time, Hallow hadn't trusted Vera with the fullness of his plan.

"This is about change, pure and simple," said Hallow. "This world has no place for our kind, so I will carve out a place for us. I am simply lighting the way."

A shiver ran across her back. There were, indeed, many things that changed in war. Vera might be brown as a nut, but if she acted in any way but English it was a facade she used to deceive those full of prejudices. Like that airship captain, Zampano, thinking her part of a gypsy band merely because she looked the part. Within her breast beat a heart green with Britain's merry land, a complex she recognized in nearly every Englishman who did not look English. It was a love-hate relationship, a desire to conform and a destiny of never fitting in.

Vera didn't want to put England into a war.

The twilit America passing outside the broken boxcar door confounded her with its rolling mountains and wild, free rivers. She didn't wish it ill either.

"A Balaenopteron's cannons can wipe out even an army of Grimaldis in an instant," Vera attempted to protest.

"Would you like a demonstration?" Hallow asked.

Without waiting for her reply, the Grimaldi's hand stretched out, a skeletal finger pointing outside through the broken car door. There was a hole in the palm of that hand, and from it shot a long, thin instrument, tapered at the end. A wand?

But before Vera could look at it more closely she got a fleeting sense of something terrible, like the smell of pain, or a feeling of red. There was the cobalt shock of a sparker going off, a thrumming like a plucked string in her belly. Trees outside shuddered at the passing of something immensely fast, and then a hillock outside exploded into a fountain of loam, a momentary landslide that set the birds and beasts howling into the night. Vera dashed forward, leaning out of the boxcar to watch the holocaust pass into the Conqueror Worm's rattling wake.

"Lord Almighty," said Vera.

"Perhaps," said Hallow, his voice softer than ever. "But it does not need to be divine. It merely needs to have the power to put things right."

"Right?" answered Vera.

"Come, my Orb Weaver," said Hallow. "It is time to see what has been growing in this cocoon of secrecy you've helped me weave."

Jean Hallow walked past Vera, past the workers who seemed a little bit afraid of their shadowy employer. Was he taller than before? Vera could not be sure. They walked through the storage car and back down the train.

"We are born into this world expecting to have choices. Why do we tell our children they can be aeronauts, or doctors, or discoverers of strange new lands?" continued Hallow. "We are not born into a world with choices. We are born into a world enslaved to the arbitrary rules of those who came before us, walled into a city of false hopes and dead ends."

Vera Jasper drew in a sharp breath as the forest in the train windows behind them immolated, lighting a bright orange to rival the sunset. They were going around a bend, and the sight of the Grimaldi's power struck Vera dumb.

They passed through the barracks and the various mundane areas of the Ghost Train. In the manufactory cars, the great engines that churned out sheet metal and cut delicate components were silent. Vera and Hallow crept through the tangled tightness of the pipes. At last, they reached the storage boxcars behind the manufactory cars, where the silent ranks of Hallow's host lay waiting. Their path led along a catwalk through the middle of the host, so they were surrounded on all sides, top and bottom by the creations. Vera felt, not for the first time, that she was inside an enormous egg sac. If so, then these were their brood; Vera's and Hallow's.

Innumerable asterisks of metal surrounded them in groups of eight, one set for each of the creations' eight legs. Vera had never liked how they were stored. They looked like enormous dead cockroaches. Each leg was a stake of metal, very sharp. Hallow reached out from beneath his cloak. It was his left arm, and it was very thin. He pressed his wrist to a sharp point, drawing a dribble of blood. The drops glittered like rubies in the half-light, then disappeared as they fell to the dark shapes of the creations below.

Hallow walked the length of the boxcar, casting his arm about as if he were blessing the car with holy water. Blood fanned out in droplets, smearing the perfect carapaces with gore. For a moment nothing happened. As Vera followed, she began to hear the groan and scrape of a thousand cogs turning, cables springing taut to life, and eight thousand legs begin to scrabble awake.

"They want us to play the game their way, because with their rules they always win," said Hallow. "I say, fuck them. Fuck their game. Let's kill them all and start over."

That was when Vera knew for certain Jean Hallow was insane.

STATION 13

Dragonslaying and Fried Chicken

Though Dragonwell could bear the weight of the sword A Contrario, there was no question about flight. Plucking the tip out of the loam was a tremendous effort. Steam spurted from its vents in billowing clouds. Finally, with a great sucking pop, the tip of the sword came free, flying up over Dragonwell and cleaving a bough off a stately elm to embed itself in the ground.

"This sucker is sharp!" Albion declared. He sheltered Hargreaves from the falling bough with one of Dragonwell's greaves.

"What an astute observation," Hargreaves said dryly as a sepia weir of autumn leaf threatened to bury her. "It would be a useful weapon, if it were not so unwieldy."

The sword was indeed unwieldy. Nearly twenty feet long, the pommel topped Dragonwell's head when they stood the blade straight up. It measured three feet across at the ornate hilt, carved with seven steel wings. The metal swam with whorls of layered colors, as if they had been poured in, folded together laboriously in some gigantic, infernal smithy. Dragonwell's oversized cutlass looked woefully inadequate next to it.

"This was made to slay dragons..." Hargreaves murmured.

Albion was dismantled his clothesline, and with the aid of a torn piece of balloon canvas, wrapped up A Contrario until it looked like a piece of mast wood. He threw the ropes over Dragonwell's shoulders so the automata could haul the heavy bundle onto its back. At zero lift, Dragonwell left deep dragging footprints in its wake. Even at full lift from the aeon engine, they were barely able to scale the great trough of the slope to the tracks. Unfortunately once there they did not know where to go next. The Ghost Train might be anywhere by now, and Hargreaves feared its unholy cargo.

"And where might we be going, Inspector?" Albion asked, once they were free.

"Why, Captain, I would have thought it obvious," answered Hargreaves, adjusting her scarf more tightly. Under her driving goggles, she dabbed a little grease from Dragonwell to protect her cheeks from the wind. It gave her the appearance of actually knowing what she was doing. "We go to call on Messrs. Hallow and Burgess."

"And the Orb Weaver," said Albion.

Hargreaves winced. She hadn't wanted to think about her.

Dragonwell did not have Alphonse's rolling wheels, but it could hop for lengths at a time over flat country. There was plenty of it, lush and vibrant, full of foggy meadowland and valley vineyards. Hargreaves' attention wandered over the wide wilderness. She marveled at the vast virgin country, often traveling miles without seeing the signs of humanity. The wondrous engine beneath them thrummed comfortingly. It reminded her of Alphonse, and soon she drifted off to sleep.

At three in the afternoon by Captain Clemens' pocket watch, they drove into a way station, purchased some flavorless sandwiches with more abysmal coffee, and changed places. Hargreaves sipped, and was surprised to find a rich, dark brew. The pasteboard cup advertised Hawaiian Kona, which explained the shocking price.

Three hours later, Albion curled up under his coat and Hargreaves pulled onto the road again. It was hard to tell when the sky ended and where the ground began. A velvety mist blanketed the hills and they rolled up into clouds lit orange by sunset. The faint scent of salt hung in the air, and she thought she could see the famed redwoods in the distance, vast trunks wreathed in mist.

They rode through the night, changing places once more so Hargreaves could get some sleep. Sometime around eight in the morning the mists parted over the hills and a quartet of shining red spires pierced the sky, as good or better for Hargreaves' drowsy soul than the erected wonders of Europe. Hargreaves started; it was the Golden Gate Bridge, spanning the doorway to the Lands Beyond. Past San Francisco, the world was yet unmade, civilization not so rooted and flowered. But here, the bloom flourished, enrobed in seaside grandeur. On the other side of the gray veil, the Lands Beyond waited, a vista of endless possibilities. If one sailed around the veil, one would arrive at the Orient—a world unto itself, birthplace of the Manchu Marauder Albion Clemens.

Nearby, the bay was obscured by what looked like a gigantic white cake. An airship hovered there, about a quarter the size of a Balaenopteron, though nowhere as whale-like as the city-ships of Britain. Other ships could be seen near the leisure yacht, flitting in and out like bees, taking up a berth or a tower here and there. They were traders, and raiders, and adventurers, all finding their fortune at the last waystation on the edge of the world.

"Why San Francisco?" asked Albion.

"Read a paper sometime, Captain. It's the center of Ubique's American operation. I don't know what Hallow plans, but the sundry barons will likely want a return on their investment double-quick," Hargreaves said. "Hallow said he needed their funding for the next stage of his plans."

"And they will know where to meet him," finished Albion. "Following the money. Well done."

The mention of Jean Hallow made her cringe. She had let the man into her work, her home. She had let him be alone with Cezette, and all the while he was a murdering guttersnipe. It was easier to label the man rather than feel the sting of the blade at her back.

They dared not take Dragonwell into the narrow side streets. Passing pedestrians and cramped market stalls made a quagmire for large vehicles, and switchback Lombard gave Hargreaves chills. Instead, they stood Dragonwell in a children's play park, where it blended in with all the slides and clambering things. The children seemed to take to the machine well enough, climbing, scampering and hollering with glee. Their parents, when present, regarded this as some sort of stunt, possibly by a picture firm. A few people took photograms, posing with the unlikely duo, who did look straight out of the pictures. Albion had taken to wearing a long black coat, darted at the waist, with his airman's goggles hanging off his neck and his cutlass worn on his back. And of course Hargreaves was every inch his equal, her hat canted at a jaunty angle. The captain retained the key bolt, so Dragonwell stayed motionless, popping himself cool as they finally sauntered out of the park.

From there, it was easy enough to board a clanging trolley. There weren't so many people on it in the middle of the day, but by chance they boarded a touring shuttle, and were forced to wait out the journey through an unfamiliar city. The buildings here were queerly constructed, perched on the hills as if they might slide away at any moment. Aside from this feature, the buildings retained the familiar collision of styles both of them had come to expect from American architecture. Cheerful row houses peered down on them like a colony of prairie dogs. Bay windows dotted the colorful pastel buildings like white-trimmed barnacles. In the more affluent districts, they passed familiar, sternly staring Neo-Victorian Queen Annes.

Hargreaves leaned against a window, cheeks in her hands, determined to fill the trolley with grump. They ought to be headed toward Ubique's headquarters in the shimmering heat of the city center, not enjoying the admittedly breathtaking beauty of San Francisco.

It took quite a while, but the steeply sloped streets slowly gave way to a busy port and wide main street. On one side, the vast Pacific stretched into the distance, though the blue was blotted out by a crowding of ships both in the air and on the sea. The Lands Beyond traders were relegated to the far reaches of the Bay, but nearer at hand were the gingerbread of leisure craft and the bloated caterpillars of plains crawlers. Facing the ocean was a tiny cul-de-sac where the trolley made a complete turnaround, creeping its way up on a steep, wide road. The road terminated at a sharp spire, which bore the familiar mark of Ubique. The letterhead at the top of the building was a gear-toothed "u" befitting the company slogan that it could make a tool for any purpose.

"Come on!" Albion said, swinging off the trolley's back as they passed it.

Outside Ubique's metropolitan ziggurat, Albion and Hargreaves faltered for the first time, unsure of how to proceed. Workers filed in and out of the rotary doors, but despite their hurried pace, seemed quite courteous. Everyone seemed to be on their best behavior. Even the street sweeps were polite in the marble-faced corporate square. The courtyard was dotted with conveniences; free telegraph nodes stood by, with attendants taking messages on typewriter keys. A clacking information board recorded the day's weather, the time, date, and local rail and omnibus times. There was even a brass button at its base that when depressed, announced in a clear voice a few issues of the day, and finished by advertising the Ubique product currently in vogue. The spotless elegance of the building belied the corruption within the company.

Finding no easy ingress and a stonewall at the front desk stall, Albion and Hargreaves were resigned to waiting it out for night to fall when they could plausibly sneak inside for a look. In the day, there weren't many clues to be had, so they boarded the trolley once more. Albion wanted to see the San Francisco Chinatown, understandably enough. Hargreaves was glad to see this side of him.

As they passed Chinatown near the water, the patchwork design gave way to a grand pagoda arch carved in the shape of a flowing dragon. It followed them across the rooftops for nine streets, and slowly Hargreaves noticed a subtle pattern woven into the scales of the dragon.

"My word, those are rail tracks," said the inspector.

"Yes. It was made to commemorate the Chinese workmen who helped to build the railroads of the West," said another passenger. She seemed to be an unofficial tour guide, the sort of leisurely old freeman woman who spent her days keeping the history of cities alive. She looked like she was made of parchment and slotted into a doll's tabbed clothes. Her shock of white hair was kept in neat braids that hugged her dusty black head.

"The Chinese worked here?" said Albion, clearly amazed.

"Many of them came looking for something to bring back to their families. They heard stories that America was a mountain made of gold," said their guide. She was warming to the topic. "And like my freemen brothers and sisters, many of them were paid in whippings and unfair wages. But with the rails came commerce. It breathed life into the West. When the airships came along many of them took to the skies, working as engineers. Why my brother ran a ship with four Chinamen who looked just like you!"

"And they set up base here?" said Albion. He stared at the tight streets, the pagodas and lion statues that were clearly many years old. "This is where they lived..."

"The rails all came here at some point," said the guide. "They say the Chinamen built all this! The trolleys, the streets. Even underground tunnels to hide their numbers, that lead all over the city!"

Albion and Hargreaves exchanged a meaningful stare that told her he'd come to the same idea. They leaped off the trolley, landing on the cobbles near an open-air fish market. A few crabs jumped, shocked.

"Thanks, old Auntie!" cried Albion as the trolley swung out of view.

It didn't take them long to become immersed in the myriad commerce of Chinatown. There were cramped streets full of wonders, little courts full of people playing Chinese chess, and children running through with paper pinwheels in their hands. As they ran, the pinwheels spun in colorful whorls. Stalls sold paper lanterns with small candles that Hargreaves had to fit into a tiny metal bracket to light. They were carried on long poles so they floated, pristine and colorful, over the street. The bakeries sold mooncakes, little brown squares that broke open to reveal a tiny moon of salted egg yolk in a night of sweet lotus paste. Albion mentioned in passing that these were all auspicious omens symbolizing reunion and togetherness. The Mid-Autumn festival was a festival of harvest, when the far-reaching Chinese got together and found family again. Hargreaves thought of her own family, and could only picture Arturo and Cezette. Albion seemed wistful, and disappeared into a liquor store for a moment.

"Want a tug?" Albion asked when he returned, fishing a bottle out of a brown paper bag.

"God yes," said Hargreaves, and took a good mouthful. It was rice wine, strong, but fragrant.

At length Albion sat down at Chinese chess with an old man who had staked out a table in one of the many courtyards. Hargreaves didn't know the pieces for they were all written in Chinese and moved strangely over a river drawn in the middle of the board. One piece was able to jump across the board like a rook, but only if another piece was between it and a target. But the aim was to capture the king, and Hargreaves knew tactics when she saw it. When Albion got up she took a turn, and lost spectacularly. But everyone laughed, and someone brought tea in paper cups. The old chess man had a pole with him that was hung with tiny bamboo cages, each with a budgie or a parakeet inside. It stood propped in a nearby tree. If asked, he would whistle and the birds would sing. They weren't for sale, they were his treasures that he showed off. Each of the old men at the tree-lined court had at least one birdcage.

Hargreaves was laughing with a group of old men as they showed off their prize birds when Albion tapped her arm.

"I've lost all our money," he said, laughing. But Hargreaves knew the Manchu Marauder well; he had lost on purpose. That was their cue to leave.

Two streets away, Albion sat them down at a street cafe that served potent tea and inexplicable waffles folded around peanut butter, tinned milk and sugar. Albion also ordered a dish of rice noodles dotted with something called "fish balls." Hargreaves, adventurous Briton, took a reluctant bite and discovered curry. Very acceptable.

"Have you found us a way into the building?" asked Hargreaves. It was hard to talk around the waffle. Albion had explained it was a Kowloon specialty, and she resolved to visit as soon as possible.

"Better," said Albion. He took a page out of his coat. It was a piece torn from a newspaper. "The old Chinese men love it when the youth take an interest in their affairs. He couldn't wait to tell me when I mentioned Burgess."

"What do you know? Burgess's sleaze reaches across the continent," Hargreaves said. Flipping the advert, the two of them looked at the sepia monograph showing Stevie Burgess's Darklight Cabaret, the toast of the West.

"Naked ladies are kind of important to old gents. Perversion to the rescue again," said Albion. Hargreaves gave him the stink-eye. He continued, "Old Zhao also said there's something happening out there tonight. There's been fewer shows for months, and they've been a little sad about it. But tonight they're putting on a big show, and guess what? The cabaret is playing host to a band of foreign dancers that have just arrived by train."

"This says the place is outside of the city. They have their own devoted shuttle and station to take guests out there," said Hargreaves. "That, pardon my French, smells like fish balls."

"They've chugged right up to the cabaret station and parked there," said Albion.

"Hallow must be making the deal there, if he hasn't already," said Hargreaves. "Burgess' cabarets are the fronts for his backdoor deals. The Darklight Cabaret is an ideal place for a meeting."

"Then, lack of an invitation notwithstanding, my good captain," said Hargreaves, "It appears as if we're going to a show."

———

The twilight found them sitting on crates outside the shuttle to the Darklight Cabaret, in the dry docks neighborhood of Hunter's Point. The cabaret being some ways outside the city, patrons usually entered by means of a free, hourly shuttle service. The train had pulled into the station. It was visible as a moving advert plastered with posters for all the different burlesque shows. It wasn't as exuberant as Burgess' New York establishment, but it retained the aura of pin-up debauchery. The passengers were discreetly hidden behind thick curtains, but there were two cars at the back with blacked-out windows.

Albion remarked on the profusion of slaughterhouses nearby, though Hargreaves still refused to make the connection between what he had found in New York's underground and what Ubique might want with a neighborhood full of abattoirs. It was abhorrent and wrong, and she felt sullied having been in Burgess's presence. Despite her denial, she had to admit those two cars at the back had only one conceivable purpose, and served as a means of clandestine entry to the cabaret.

"Any minute now," Albion reassured Hargreaves as the streetlights began to go on all around them. The gigantic sodium bulbs on the station marquee began to light up, hissing and popping one letter at a time. The trains were scheduled to arrive with time to spare for theatre seating, which meant the next train out was the earliest show. The clerks at the ticket booths seemed on edge; they worked quickly and wore expressions of strained consternation, waiting for some unknown calamity to occur. They behaved, in fact, exactly as if their boss was in town.

"He's starting up a burlesque," Hargreaves said. "My God, what if we're too late? What if he's sold it?"

"And...now," Albion said, as the final sliver of sun disappeared behind a low building.

The captain and Hargreaves strolled across the street into an alley where a few toughs loitered at the side entrance. Passing those, the pair turned into a darker passage. The captain's coat hid his customary trinity of guns, pocket glass and cutlass at his hip. Hargreaves caught sight of an enormous, red-stained grip in his belt—the Red Special. When she had first seen it, it had needed the strange aeon crystals from the doomed Jonah Moore to fire. That weapon was what Albion had been firing in the New York sewers, she suddenly realized. A gun that could deter one of Hallow's goliath spiders. Its presence on his hip comforted her now. Strangely, Albion's belt held not one but a variety of ammunition types.

Hargreaves had only been able to save one thing from her heavy carpetbag; the sparker from Firearms Division. The tiny device was jammed in a loop of fabric. San Francisco had yielded a serviceable Colt to replace her Browning 9mm. Hargreaves still had her hammered bronze dagger, and one more weapon; her curves, slotted into a loose cotton chemise and riding breeches. Probably not the most formidable weapon, considering they were about to storm a house of burlesque. But a gun and fresh clothes, not a bad day shopping.

They took the back way. With no Rosa Marija to gain access, Albion simply inserted his cutlass into the doorframe. He delivered a heavy kick to the handle and the door popped open. Inside, Albion gestured to the sharp-suited guard just by the shadow of the rearmost train car. He pulled out an empty absinthe bottle, placing it by his revolver muzzle, but Hargreaves rolled her eyes at this improvised attempt at stealth. She ran, full tilt like a cat, leaped up and captured the guard's neck between her thighs. The takedown was textbook, quieter than a church, and it only took another minute for the man's labored wheezing to change to the regular rhythm of sleep.

"The poor man's silencer doesn't work," whispered Hargreaves. "You'll blow off your hand before you give us away."

"Don't knock it," said Albion, grinning.

They made their way up a cargo gangplank, and found themselves amongst pallets of champagne, boxes stuffed with straw and crates well chilled with ice blocks. Experimentally, Albion cracked one open, and found it was a box of mushrooms. Chanterelle, if Hargreaves was not mistaken. The car was full of the sundry of a luxury lounge. Albion and Hargreaves were to sneak in with the daily bread.

Oddly, a large crossbar covered the door to the next car. They futzed with the lock, but could not get it open, and they weren't about to shoot it. The point was to enter unnoticed. They hid amongst the crates while workers rolled in a few more pallets. None of them were interested in more than leaving the items on the car as quickly as possible. Then they sealed up the loading door, sliding it into place with a clang.

Soon the train lurched, and presumably, began to pull out of the station. The jolly whistling of the tiny engine was unbelievably rude. It put one in the mind of catcalls. Then the rails began to rattle, and the clandestine duo relaxed against the boxcar's sides. The trip took perhaps twenty minutes, but once the train stopped, a line of men in white jackets came in and began to move the crates out. With so much to be moved, it was easy for two people to sneak out from the personnel door at the rearmost of the car. Small wonder the burlesque wasn't besieged by stowaway young boys. As they left, they remarked on a separate gangplank going into the partitioned area. The gangplank was completely sealed up with tarpaulin, its secrets impenetrable.

They found themselves on a lone platform carved out of a cliff, with raw rock and naked pilings everywhere. A pair of swinging doors let them into a back room which led into padded, velvety hallways that were all too familiar: cologne and old champagne, the pink smells of ladies' underthings, powder and glitter, the smell of theater.

The inside of the cabaret was damp, which suggested they were near water. The sounds of guests settling in the theater made it easier to orient themselves, and they soon discovered the layout was similar to the Luminescent Cabaret; a sprawling performance area, and behind it, little love nests secreted away in the nooks of the building. Hargreaves pressed to the walls and cleared corners. Albion walked along jauntily, his gun at his hip, cutlass in the other hand. Hargreaves scowled at this apparent laxness, but when one of the unmarked doors burst open, Albion had the upper hand. The door emitted a very satisfied-looking, corpulent man in disheveled clothes and a woman, even more disheveled in strappy heels. The guests must have been there from the night before.

Hargreaves might have fired indiscriminately from strung nerves, but Albion simply shooed the couple back inside. His smile disarmed them enough not to cry out, and for all they knew the inspector and the captain were just another amorous couple. Albion closed the door on them, putting one finger to his lips in a one-sided sign of conspiracy. Clearly, chaos was the man's natural habitat, improvisation as natural as breathing.

Further along the corridor. Albion stopped to examine an inconspicuous locked door. After a cursory inspection, he began to jimmy the lock with his cutlass like he did before. It was not apparent to Hargreaves why Albion chose this door. There was nothing particularly striking or unusual about it. Given his success at placating the native fauna, however, Hargreaves decided to trust Albion's instincts—and was rewarded when the door popped open to reveal a long switchback stair, leading down into a pit illuminated with dim arclights.

"Burgess' workshop I assume." said Albion. "He has one in New York."

They filed down the narrow stairs. The walls reminded Hargreaves of MAD: damp worked brick, crawling with scrabbling life. At the fourth landing, Hargreaves nearly pitted the wall with her Colt when a rat the size of a cat darted out from underneath a dripping pipe.

"Easy..." said Albion. "This whole area is tidal wetlands, the wildlife will be everywhere."

"Damn and blast!" hissed Hargreaves. "Why couldn't he have made his lair in a tower, like any self-respecting villain?"

They continued until the walls dropped away, revealing a cavernous space evidently used for storage. There were wooden boxes, and flat objects wrapped in waxed vellum. Myriad things lay apparently forgotten down here, including an enormous signboard featuring two-story high thighs in fishnet stockings. Albion scarcely sparred the board a glance. He seemed a bit down, and Hargreaves had to wonder, not for the first time, where Rosa Marija could be.

The duo turned a corner and found themselves in a very unusual corridor. Wood lined the stone walls and the path was a raised walkway over a channel of murky water. Like Albion Clemens, Burgess had found the best way of hiding secrets in a populous city; within the warrens of her very underbelly.

"If this place is anything like New York... yes," Albion said. They found a staging area, plausibly where the hidden goods from the barge wound up. Signs of recent activity lay everywhere: trails of cleared dust on the floor and the boxes lined up along the halls. Racks along the walls held Automata parts, bits of engines and jars for various chemicals, all neatly labeled and organized. Despite these indications of recent use, the place appeared deserted. The pirate picked up a glittering component from one shelf, made to pocket it, then looked with duper's delight at Hagreaves.

"Even on my best day, I wouldn't have a problem with you stealing from Burgess. He was...a dick. A loutish dick," said Hargreaves.

As they made their way down the strangely deserted tunnel passage, she recalled Burgess in the Luminescent Cabaret on the Bowery. The odd twitches of the fingers, the soft, cultured voice, and the curt way he dealt with those he disapproved of. The habits of a gentleman entrepreneur. Disturbing undercurrents had animated Burgess, writhing serpents under his mask of civility, and those seemed now to permeate this place. Judging from this dungeon of a workspace, he and Hallow were of a feather.

There was a discipline to the place that was unnerving, emanating from the well-appointed engine bays and neat workshops off either side of the hall. Despite the sorts of louts Hargreaves knew Burgess employed, everything was carefully placed, sorted, and labeled in big hands. Only compelling reasons could make muscle behave that way, for example a massive brothel debt. One ornate door with oranges carved in it looked to be Burgess' San Francisco quarters. Yet, not a single worker was to be found.

"They might be meeting here right now," Albion said, stopping beside the last engine bay in the hall. Beyond it, the path dropped clear out of the world, in a dizzying chasm a hundred feet across. The filthy water dropped off the edge and disappeared into nothing.

"This must be where he moves his wares to airships," said Hargreaves. "After he launders the Gear parts."

Albion drew his gun, and Hargreaves rolled her eyes when she saw the ridiculous bottle emerge once more. For one thing, it was bloody stupid. For another, their appearance would make any semblance of stealth a moot point. They were here to stop a deal with the devil, which meant aggressive negotiations. Hargreaves was prepared to do what she must.

"They might have left. There's nobody in these tunnels," countered the inspector, somewhat hopefully. "Not even a guard." It was like walking through the warrens of Burgess's hidden mind.

Albion reached out, grasping the knob. Hargreaves' instincts ran circles. They had the element of surprise, they had the sturdy rock doorjamb for cover...

"Snap out of it," hissed Albion, and yanked the door wide open. He dashed inside. Hargreaves spun into it, sweeping the room with her Colt, expecting a layout much like the bays they had crossed. She was kicking herself for letting Albion take point. There were too many blind corners, too many desks and shelves lining the walls.

"There's nobody here," Hargreaves said finally, putting her gun down. The room was like all the others save in two respects. The far wall was open to the pit, and it was much larger, accommodating a landing platform. The long tools on the walls and the bins full of parts were just as organized, but a few items were hastily scattered on the tables. There was a feeling of fervor here, and again a sense that these things were all recently touched.

Albion looked around, and began to poke into the corners, prodding aside neatly sorted boxes of parts with his cutlass. There was a raised portion of the room that appeared to be an inventory of pipes, valves, nuts and bolts on shelves like library stacks. Tellingly, there was a whole box of adamant Gear nuts. Soon Albion disappeared around some shelves of heavy equipment, and all she could tell of his whereabouts was the heavy clanging of metal being dashed aside. Vacuum tubes scattered from beneath a shelf like colorful marbles, shattering as they rolled off the lip of the raised floor.

"What are you doing? If Burgess isn't here, we're shit out of luck!" Hargreaves chastised. "Let's just get out of here before someone comes."

She loped over to a utilitarian desk, strangely set in the middle of the room, and began to pull open the drawers. "What about the government manufactory you found? Could he be there?" It was on the other side of the country, though, which meant they were days behind and the contents of the box were lost forever. Dread began to drip down Hargreaves' back.

"He could..." Albion's murmur was barely audible. It grew in volume as he rounded the other side of the shelves. "But the Luminescent Cabaret was never so rowdy without Burgess in New York."

"Don't be daft. The man has underlings to run things for him," Hargreaves said. She continued to move, making the most of her time exactly as she had been trained, while Albion stood there, touching a bauble here and there, never leaving the raised dais.

Why put shelves in the middle of valuable workspace? No efficiency, Hargreaves thought.

Having run out of places to look, Hargreaves joined Albion on the raised platform. The tools and parts here were well wrapped in tissue paper, and dusty. It stood to reason if Burgess spent his time on the East Coast as Albion implied, the operation here would hardly be touched. Perhaps it was used to refurbish parts sold on the West Coast?

Hargreaves stopped, nearly walking into Albion. Something had caught Albion's attention, and she wasn't sure what. He put one finger to Hargreaves' lip, shocking her with its gentle reproach. Carefully, he retraced his steps, one at a time, letting his body make the deduction for him. Was it the feel of the floor? The smell of the dust?

There. He had it. She saw it on his face. She moved closer. There was a spanner on the shelf, strangely free of dust. A triangular space had been cleared, like a snow angel, with the spanner as the hypotenuse.

"Albion. I think this is a switch," said Hargreaves.

"Care to do the honors?"

Hargreaves took a deep breath, and pulled. The end of the spanner came round, spinning by its jaws as if it were latched on to a particularly tough screw. Everything lurched. That strange lip around the shelves parted from the floor, and suddenly they were rising rapidly toward the ceiling. Hargreaves, struggling to her feet, unconsciously pulled back on the spanner. Their ascent lurched to a halt, becoming a gentle hover. The spanner had been the secret lever for some kind of elevator.

"Be ready for anything," said Hargreaves, easing the spanner forward. Slowly, they began to rise, and this time the ceiling slid apart to accommodate them.

The lift brought them up through a stone shaft. They could not see what was supporting their ascent, but the shaft itself was smooth, and other than the tiny, winking arc bulbs at the edge of the platform, completely black. By its light, Hargreaves kept them rising at a slow pace, until a dim rectangular space opened up overhead. Mindful of any braking noise, Hargreaves eased them up into a sort of lofty warehouse.

Whereupon they were blinded by the flare of a dozen arclamps. Hargreaves felt, rather than saw, Albion whirl, and the click of both the Red Special and Victoria sounded in his hands. Shots rang, and screaming followed. How could he have done in three men at once, blinded by the lights? Of course, the bottle; he had lobbed and shot the bottle, and the shards must have cut the men to shreds, exploding like ordinance. He must have done it by touch alone.

But all was in vain. There came a sharp double clunk, a clatter of metal on floor, and then a heavier thud. Hargreaves might have bet a quid someone had just brained the pirate captain with a cudgel. Dull, hard packing sounds of someone being kicked the shit out of filled the room.

The bright lamps could only blind for a fraction of a second, but Hargreaves had the impression of support beams curving away overhead, and a sense of unimpeded enclosure that suggested a large warehouse. She raised her sparker and the Colt, but unlike Albion, she was not a glutton for violence. Murder in recent days still weighted down her trigger fingers, and that was enough for something heavy to club the guns from her stinging hands. There was a strangely smoky scent that went away as soon as the burlap bag came down, shutting out the world, but she had seen enough for Hargreaves to conclude they were near the Ghost Train: Hallow's Conqueror Worm.

Then a familiar condescending voice rumbled through, accented by the clicks of multiple gun hammers being eased back.

"Why if it isn't my favorite mutton-shunter!" said Jean Hallow gleefully.

STATION 14

The Cavalry

UNBEKNOWNST TO VANESSA HARGREAVES OR ALBION CLEMENS, HELP was not far away.

A fisherman was returning in the early morning from two nights' successful haul. It was late in autumn, but the ocean had been thick with snapper, and his ice boxes overflowed. His keel rode low in the water. There had been good bycatch, octopus and sizeable crab, even a roughy, which he could not sell but would make good eating for his family. His was a multiple-use boat, and it had survived rather better than the trawlers or pelagic netters in a demanding frontier market.

As he headed back toward San Francisco, the open ocean had yielded more and more fish to the line, which let him replace the oldest catch unusually frequently. It was almost as if something was drawing the fish toward San Francisco, or as if the gray divide to the Lands Beyond was spitting more and more fish into the ocean, pushing them toward the east.

At the moment the junk was becalmed, but when the morning wind scattered the fog it would bring him along at a fast enough pace. It had been a good two weeks at sea. His daughter would be missing him. He was contemplating firing up the engine at the back of the junk when a sudden rumble overhead made him look up from the deck. Was it thunder? No flash of light came, but looking for lightning after thunder was as foolish as casting a line where the tide had once been.

The fisherman, whose name was Han, was understandably cautious. He had not braved the gray divide from the old country to die at sea and leave his family destitute. He saw what happened to the wives who had no husbands. There was demand enough both for fish and warmth in that city.

Han navigated his ship with extreme caution. He had to be careful of other seafarers this close to the city, and the dense fog in the air made this difficult. After a short time, the mist became too much, so he dropped anchor and took down his sails. Jing and Tung, his two crewmen, looked out with him into the mist, each man in a different direction. Tung periodically sounded the foghorn, but no reply came. Jing saw the shapes first.

"Amida Buddha..." he said, loanwords flavored in Chinese. "They are dragons..."

Han did not think they were dragons, but he had to admit the shapes emerging on their starboard stern were hard to reconcile. The westerners were fond of building big. The first iron-clad obelisk certainly fit the bill of the famed Balaenopterons, until the shape of it appeared behind. The back of the ship was a mere slip of a keel, like a beetle pushing along a rolling boulder of dung. Behind it followed a more traditional corsair, its gunnery deck scaled with cannon flaps. A three-pronged swift came howling at its back, its sails ragged as if worried by wolves. After that came stranger vessels, no two alike, but all seeming prepared for war. It was a procession of gunships. With a start Han realized none of the ships touched the surf, but floated some inches above it.

"It is a fleet of the dead!" sang superstitious Tung. "We are at the entrance to the underworld!"

"You dolt," said Han, striking his crewman over the head. If Tung was not also his cousin, he would never have had him on the junk. "They are air pirates, and they must have some dastardly purpose."

No dirigible ever flew this low, this close to the sea, not when they could easily avoid obstacles in the fog high overhead. In the distance, the mists parted for a brief moment, revealing another string of airships gliding over the water. Han watched the last of them pass, a bulbous shape like a swollen fruit, pitted and scarred, before letting out a deep breath.

"What do you think they are up to?" asked Jing, terrified.

"Whatever it is," Han answered, stoking up his engine, "I pity whomever chooses to stand against them."

Hovering at the city limits, the bulbous, scarred prow of the *Huckleberry* broke the foam of sea-fog for just an instant, before ducking back inside, a furtive animal testing the ocean surface.

"Let's keep it tight," a speaking horn thundered at Rosa Marija's elbow. She hissed, like a cat. An ether channel had been appropriated for communicating from ship to ship, and crystals distributed to fit in each ship's ether array. These were simple sugar crystals grown on a string, with water laced in aeon dust. They were easy to make, easy to get rid of if boarded, and impossible to duplicate. One had to have a piece broken off the same string to listen on the channel. It was simple expediency to swallow them or dissolve them in the sea if discovered, to keep the enemy from hearing their plans.

But nothing could stop the people on the other end from being utter twats.

"You there! Is a warm meal worth becoming crow food? Put out that galley fire before the smoke gives us away!"

"You idiot, we're in a real pea souper. Nobody's going to see."

The second voice propagating from the blade-like ether array was Gunsmoke Gilly, who seemed to have taken impromptu command. Rosa had found, soon enough, that no such thing as command hierarchy existed in the Incognito. Their very adherence to a group seemed anathema to them. Despite this, they all followed Gray Gunsmoke's lead, if not out of respect, then perhaps out of fear. He had other names: Old Ironclad, Skipper, and as the Viscountess Valentina insisted on using; the Stuck Pig.

Gilly continued. "Our men in the city tell us the enemy have mortar cannon, and a railway gun parked on the high hill. Stay behind the shield ships!"

"And my clairvoyants tell you the mist will hide us all the way there," answered a husky female voice on the line. The Viscountess Valentina was particularly touchy when she felt the women of Incognito were not being respected. She had a reputation of augury, promiscuity, and stringing men up by their delicates on her masts. "We know such things."

"I still do not believe there are real American guns on the hills," said another voice, gruff and cigar-scarred. Dante "Powder Monkey" Montalban was well known in the last war as one of the urchins who reloaded the British Navy's cannon, climbing the huge smoking guns with packets of powder. This was before steam-fed cannon were common, and often the monkeys would be burned, hit by the blowback or die of misfire. His survival was remarkable enough to earn him a medal, and a reputation for reasonable caution, nourished all the more during his illustrious pirating career. Life expectancy on Montalban's galleon, the *Loose Lady*, was reputedly eight times that of any other. Not that pirates kept decent records. Montalban himself strutted around decks like a cock, with his feathered hat.

"There aren't American guns," answered Gunsmoke. "The Americans would never openly support Ubique or their shadow auction. These are contractors. Mercenary companies. Guns for hire."

"I say we outbid them," said Montalban. "And not lose a single man."

"Are your pockets so deep they can hold your enormous ego?" said Valentina. "These mercenaries will never deal with us. They are legitimate! Respected. Businessmen! We are merely disruptive innovators at best, criminals at most."

"Bah! They deal with us when they need to throw a wrench into a competitor's trade! Mercenaries only ever follow the letter of the law."

"Enough! They've brought the *Tennessee Jack* up from Monterey. And if it's in the station when the fighting begins, you can count on the Ubiques to call for support. I need your heads in the game and your people at the cannons!" bellowed Gunsmoke.

The mention of the *Tennessee Jack* seemed to quiet even Valentina. Rosa knew the rumors. The all-too European Balaenopteron-class ships had been designed to travel with a retinue of smaller supply ships and escorts. For the vast stretches of wilderness that was America, that type of air superiority was unwieldy and impractical. Much of it was tornado and hurricane country. Unlike plains crawlers, large ships did not have water condensers big enough to cross large, dry distances. If a ship the size of Liberty Island was downed in Death Valley, nothing would bring it up again.

Instead, the railway gun slowly came to fore as the best way to bolster the Union's forces during its long territorial expansion. Each one had an enormous barrel like a chimney, hitched to a train of engines, boilers, and capacitors. The cannons rained down death and misery. They could be pulled west by conventional locomotive, by the Squamosa and the Maxima with their high wheels. More likely than not they were hitched to supply wagons and carried their own escort of troops and ironclads. When one pulled in over a hill, the barrel of the gun could clearly be seen hanging over the locomotive, sometimes eclipsing the sun.

During the Union's long Civil War, the guns laid waste to whole cities and stretches of battlefields, often with little to no warning. Their range was ludicrous, and battle commanders would often stage their camps twenty miles from the nearest rail, lest the death-knell of a whistling bomb come amongst them like the wrath of God. Only a few guns had been made, but exactly how many, nobody knew.

Each gun had been produced seemingly with no consistent plan, rolling out of the Union's manufactories in Detroit, Pittsburg and Tera Haute. The first and smallest was a nasty piece of work called the *Little Dickel*, and it had routed the southern batteries at Sewell's Point. The biggest of the rail guns was the *Kentucky Mark* (both Kentucky and Tennessee having declared for the Union after Sewell's Point). At Gettysburg, the Confederacy's forces half dead already, the Mark had been fired only once. Some argued the experimental incendiary shell did not need to be fired, since the war was reaching a turning point. Whatever the case, that shot left the ground of Gettysburg fallow for five years.

Rosa Marija had heard the stories from when she piloted dirigibles for a living. But the *Tennesee Jack* frightened her for a very unique reason, though the rail guns saw little use in times of peace. During the battles of Dragoon Springs, it had sown chaos on the battlefield for both Apaches and Confederates alike. Rumors could not be trusted, but the old colonel spoke of wights surfacing on the battlefield, of insects the size of dogs bursting in waves from the Jack's rounds, of weir clouds drifting out and seizing men, stripping the flesh from their bones.

"These pirates, they are mostly cowards, *non?*"

Rosa Marija sighed. Ever since she had taken Cid and the girl Cezette aboard, the girl had been excitable, belligerent, and overly familiar with the *'Berry*. After they picked the pair up, the Incognito man had given her a rendezvous location, and somewhere in the Pacific Northwest, they'd met with a ragtag army of air pirates. It was a formidable gathering, certainly, but not an army, and Rosa did not have the heart to tell Cezette this sobering fact.

Only some of the pirates, Gunsmoke and Monkey and the Viscountess, knew the stakes at hand. And they were all thinking the same thing: Ubique supplied America's already isolationist borders with arms. What might become of air piracy in the west if they had the contents of the Cook box as well? What might become of the trade out of the Lands Beyond? Whatever the box truly held, the pirates had come together to nip the thing in the bud, choke it off before it could be born, out of mutual self-interest.

Rosa was once more bringing the *'Berry* into the breach. What the hell was wrong with Albion, that he could so easily shoulder the weight of a world? Wasn't he happy with the home she had built for him? Did he have to cast it into danger? And worse still, they had brought children aboard. Rosa keened away from Cezette's exuberance, not trusting herself to it yet. But Cezette trusted this ship; it had saved her life after all. That had to mean something.

What might Albion say if he saw his ship held together by gaffer tape and aeon dust? Rosa gave a grunt of pain as she felt surface and pushed it down, into the furnace that powered her every move. Albion was strong. He would be drawn to where shit went down, and being here was the strongest chance of seeing him.

The Incognito, though anarchistic and disorganized, once summoned seemed quite adept at formations and strategy. By hovering at a distance from the city, they appeared either as distant travelers, high in the sky, or invisible against the horizon. This seemed a doubtful strategy to Rosa, until a squad of the Viscountess's scouts flew point and zapped the clouds with arc energy, drawing a thick mantle of fog around them.

"The traffic from the Lands Beyond being as chaotic as it is, the western shore is accustomed to strange airships," Gunsmoke Gilly explained over lunch later in the day. "More Incognito ships arrive each day. I hear your old mate Nessie Drake is coming with a new ship. It is best to wait and hide until our strength reaches its zenith."

Rosa shoved his feet down from where he put them on her dining table and set down Auntie's sandwiches. Gunsmoke grinned. His smile was without mirth, like a wolf baring its teeth.

Amongst the proud pirate captains, Gunsmoke was the one keenest to deal fairly, which might explain why he had emerged as leader. Unlike the others, his reputation was of being a gun for hire, or a bodyguard for merchant ships. It reminded Rosa that pirate in the functional sense was a loose definition, meaning only a person who had taken a vessel out to international waters without permission. Their ships flew no port of call but not all of them were brigands or thieves. In fact, several of the captains gathered here had tasted Gunsmoke's guns before—it was part and parcel of his command over them.

Rosa entertained the man in the 'Berry's galley, and she could not deny his tight fitting breeches held some appeal. Gunsmoke was gray at the temples, with the sort of callous attractiveness a girl might identify as a persistent father-complex.

"A shame. That Clemens is a lucky old dog," said Gunsmoke.

"Sorry," said Rosa, grinning. She hadn't even put on her best for dinner, choosing instead a hip-length one-piece that tightened around her thighs. If it were on a man they would be called overalls, but the material was perfect: soft to the touch, but difficult to remove. Since no Ubique fleet was coming to annihilate them, Rosa wasn't averse to Gunsmoke's lunch parley. His stories were good. Exciting ones, like the time he raided the Portuguese Navy's armory, or when he loosed a pack of wolves onto a rival ship. Tall ones too, like the ghost ship of La Noria, or the sirens of Dublin. He spoke at length about how he sacked the port of Santo Sangre for forty days and forty nights. At the end of it there was noone but women and children left.

"The children I put on the road with half a wheel of cheese and a jug of cider each."

"And the women?"

"We had been at it for forty days and forty nights, child. I could not withhold my men fair recompense. But the women had few places to go. The ones who got a bad deal took it out of my men's hides."

"And your fair recompense? You likely took it out of their backs."

"Only as indentured crew. My garden is lush, I have little need to pluck."

The man was Damascus steel, an edge colored by whorls of experience, shamelessness and manners. His tone cut at a moment's distraction. By and by Gunsmoke finished spinning his tales and came round to why he was there.

"The Incognito don't tell us why we are gathered," said Gunsmoke Gilly, like he was off on another story. "Why, the rascals haven't called a meeting more 'an once or twice in living memory. The first was to the defense of the *Straight Hook*, at the battle of Oslo against the Ottoman incursion. The second was at Revenge, with the contra-apartheid separatists. Now I hear there was some shindig over Moscow, but I wasn't invited to the ball, so to speak."

"Must have been lost in the post," said Rosa, suddenly overcome by an odd feeling. The way he was sitting, Gunsmoke blocked out the porthole so the room was enveloped in darkness.

"Now what strikes me as passing strange, so to speak, neither time did the Incognito uppity-ups see fit to inform us as to what we were fighting." Gunsmoke leaned forward, and Rosa's blood ran cold. She could see the porthole now, and Gunsmoke's ship, the *Remington*, behind it. It was a beautiful ship, she had to admit, all flying buttresses and ribbing. Rumor had it Gunsmoke's aeon lines were hung with dog tags and last words from the people who had died in his command. She saw all of the airship through the porthole, even the conservatory glittering with roses in the stern, but under the roses rode sixteen gun ports.

Gunsmoke continued.

"There's something they're not telling us. And make no mistake, child, the Incognito do not gather for anything but blood. Now seeing as we found your ship just drifting out in the middle of nowhere, as if you knew where we would be...well, I can't help but get the feeling you know whose throat we're all gathered here to cut."

"Hmph," said Rosa. At a signal, Gunsmoke could tear the ship to shreds. Not that he would, with him on it. The threat was empty, but present. She was glad she was resistant to his advances. There were advantages to monogamy after all...but Rosa would have to tell him something. So she walked over to the door and opened it, spilling the eavesdropping French girl onto the floor. Cezette looked up at them and grinned, her legs akimbo, and Gunsmoke out and out laughed at her, in big, throaty guffaws.

It took most of the afternoon to tell Gunsmoke everything. When they emerged from the galley it was to Cezette's disparaging glare. Gunsmoke merely winked, and blew Cezette a kiss. He briefly spoke with Cid Tanner, who had also arrived.

"I do not like him," said Cezette when Gunsmoke was safely off the ship.

"To Gunsmoke Gilly, that is a compliment," answered Cid. He started to light a small cigarillo, only to have Rosa slap it out of his hands, vanished with a little wiggle of her fingers.

"Old man, there have been some changes since you've been gone," said Rosa. "No smoking."

"Aye. And I see you went ahead and finished the Dragonwell, despite my warnings," said Cid. "And I hear you're acquiring Alphonse too, after all's said and done? What are you two planning after all this silliness, the rout of Buckingham Palace?"

Rosa tried to find something interesting about the deck to stare at, but for once the 'Berry failed her. Length upon length of charms hung on her pipes and there was never a distracting bauble when one needed one.

"Always contrary, Cid," said Rosa, and grinned. It was a pleasant mask. The airship force they had assembled was relatively small, disorganized, and as a rule quick to temper. The Incognito had been slow to act against Mordemere, who had left Europe pocked and scarred. One madman was dangerous enough. Now they had a madman with *corporate backing*. Ortega had been very clear about that with Cid and Cezette. There was every reason to think there wouldn't be anything left after.

Perhaps sensing Rosa's unrest, Cid's wrinkles loosened the tiniest iota. He grumbled uncomfortably.

"Not to say the idea of having automata isn't a good one. Come with me."

In the *'Berry's* patched and creaking hull, the draft had been held back from Elric Blair's workspace with sheets of sailcloth. Cid ducked under the first one, holding it up for Rosa and Cezette to pass through. Both women being of mechanical bent, the sight awaiting them drew a whistle from the helmswoman and a proud "*Alors! Le chevalier revenant!*" from Cezette.

Alphonse's knightly silhouette had grown wild and twisted. The only pieces they had been able to recover from the original machine was its sizable engine, and his frame with its accompanying black boxes. Those sat in sealed, bolted casings, squatting in Alphonse's guts like malign tumors. Their very indestructibility seemed to have protected the machine from further damage. His handsome chromed armor was gone, hopelessly twisted. Lesser parts like arms and legs had been found utterly mauled or inseparable from the melted locomotive parts.

From those dragon's teeth they had regrown Alphonse into something jagged and square, a monstrous hulk that would tower over the battlefield. His helm now sported a large under-bite, lending the automata an orc-like savageness. Cid had added a big, thick shield composed mostly of the dead locomotive's cow-catcher.

Hargreaves' steel fellow was imposing enough, but it was the shadowed figure behind him that made Rosa turn and slap Cid amiably on the back. A second Gear.

"There were enough parts left over. We'll need all of these we can get," answered Cid, shrugging. Grinning her inscrutable grin, Rosa turned to Cezette, who was running her hands over Alphonse's new shield.

"Do you know how to pilot an airship?"

The young girl's grin grew wider than the Seine.

STATION 15

The Factory Floor

HARGREAVES HAD A FAINT RECOLLECTION OF AN ECHOING TUNNEL, her wrists bound with rope, and the brisk clip of a hand cart or barrow. Soot on the air, metal pinging cool like a stopped locomotive. The Ghost Train was here, Hallow was here! Something rough banged up her knees. Blast! Batty-fanged and bound. That was the last clear thought before the veil of sleep fell over her again.

When the drug haze finally wore off, Hargreaves found she had been lain out on a bed. The linens smelled clean. Also there actually were linens, so she wasn't in a cell, or, thank God, one of the cages in their infernal manufactories. In fact the pillows had apparently been fluffed recently. Carefully, the inspector rose from the bed to give herself and the room a thorough search.

The first thing she realized was that most of her weapons were gone. Whoever disarmed her had not found the knife tucked in the lining of her left boot, though they had taken it off and set the pair at the foot of the bed. She was fully clothed. Evidently her captors had some decency after all.

Beside the four-poster bed, the room was rather plain. Not quite homely, but bland in a comfortable room-in-an-inn sort of way. A shallow wardrobe stood sentry to the left of the bed. At its right stretched a window with heavy curtains. A wooden door faced the bed. Locked. Perhaps she could jimmy it open? Unfortunately the lock was solid and the door emitted a depressingly thick, dull sound when gently rapped. Clearly this would not be a means of egress anytime soon. Hargreaves tapped her heel everywhere on the flooring, then stood on the modest nightstand and prodded at the rafters, but the bones of the place didn't seem to offer any way out. A chamber pot, a carafe of water, and a plate of sandwiches occupied the stand. She set them aside before climbing on it.

She next went over to far wall and swept open a set of thick curtains. Outside the window, she found a sheer drop of several hundred feet. The ocean waves pounded rhythmically onto the sharp rocks below. The night sky was clear. Stars and gibbous moon helped illuminate the surroundings. Peering out, she made out a road, and farther, the glimmer of train tracks. She breathed deep of the cool, salty air. Hargreaves deduced she must be still at the Darklight Cabaret. If it was the same day, then she could only have been out for a few hours.

Without any clear ways of escaping, she felt like a political prisoner, some hapless princess caught up in a coup. Grudgingly, the inspector had to admit, there was nothing she could do but wait. In the meantime she could speculate on her enemy's motives. What could Hallow possibly want in keeping her alive? It could not be for any sentiment. The fiend had tried to kill her once already. What was stopping him now? What end did she serve to him?

And what of Captain Albion Clemens? Where was he now?

———————

As Vanessa Hargreaves languished in luxury, Albion awoke naked, throbbing and aching. The left side of face in particular felt like it was on fire. Quickly he felt around, but everything else seemed to be in the right place. It was dark enough that he couldn't see his own willy, so Albion felt around.

Willy.

Yes. Okay, everything there. Priorities.

He reached up, and gingerly touched his temple. The agony was immediate—the touch of fingertips on his skin felt like red hot pokers. Albion needed to know the extent of the damage, and gritting his teeth, began to gingerly prod his face to determine what was wrong.

When his fingertips found a warm, wet hole, he nearly bit through his tongue in shock. He had been blinded. No, it was simply very dark, and the flesh had swollen over the left side of his face. A jagged piece of glass was embedded near the orbital, tearing a gash in his scalp. He had probably been hit with a bottle, or one of the shards from the one he shot as a distraction. Very carefully, he gave the shard a tug and was nearly knocked out again with pain. At least the bit sticking out of him was smooth and dry, and though it whinged when he pulled at it, came out. His left jaw felt a little loose, and the eye wouldn't open. A fracture, probably.

Albion groaned as nausea hit him suddenly. He began to heave, but nothing came up. Judging from the smell around him and the stains on his body he must have vomited sometime before, but could not recall when. Desperate for relief, he crumpled back into a pile and banged his head on something hard and cold.

Cursing, he felt around to discover what he'd hit and realized he was locked inside some kind of large cage. The floor and walls were large metal bars that felt gritty, pitted, as if soaked in the sweat and piss of the condemned for generations. The cage itself was claustrophobically cramped; there wasn't even room to lie down. The best Albion could manage was to pull himself into a fetal position. His back protested, hurting nearly as much as his head. At least the cold, moist bars soothed the pain in his skull. After a time Albion was able to take his attention away from the pain long enough to take stock of his surroundings.

His guns were gone. He idly wondered if someone would accidentally pull the trigger on the Red Special and blow out a piece of wall, facilitating his escape. It would be a good distraction. Had he reloaded it? With which ammunition? Depending on the color of the round the gun might burn the shooter to death along with whatever structure he was in, or jam harmlessly. Exotic herbs, aeon dust, grave dirt, those bullets were closer to witchcraft than guncraft. He wasn't actually sure what some of them would do.

The high pitched squeal of metal rubbing against metal dragged him back to reality. Albion realized his cage had been gently rocking back and forth. Looking upwards he saw the bars of his cage came together in a dome. From the dome's apex, a large chain trailed off to some unseen ceiling. Looking below, he strained to detect a floor, but there was only a black abyss. He nearly panicked. He had never done well with abstract distances and darkness. Clinging to rigging, no problem. Staring into a well? No thanks. As his eyes adjusted to the darkness, Albion realized he was not alone in this place.

The dim light and his busted eye made it hard to see, but he was able to discern a vaguely human shape floating nearby. His addled mind thought at first that it must be some dread spectre, a drowned ghost. The distended, bloated figure appeared to be levitating, naked, swaying gently back and forth. Pale flesh bulged out between flat bars. Sickeningly Albion realized that a morbidly obese person had been stuffed inside the gibbet next door. Their flesh pressed out on all sides of the cage. The figure's hair had been chopped off haphazardly, its head covered in large uneven patches. Though he couldn't be certain, Albion tenuously concluded she was a woman, based on the shape of the hips.

"Hey! Hey you," Albion called out.

The woman did not respond, but continued drifting back and forth languidly.

The sight of her filled him with mortal terror. Though mostly a relic of the past, some obscure colonies still used gibbets to punish pirates. The victims often took days to die. Mostly people weren't too original, and if the punishment ain't broke, the harbormasters weren't about to fix it. If Albion had been wearing pants he might have pissed them.

But there was no rain, no birds, and beside the discomfort, nobody was abusing him at all. His nose was stuffy from the swelling, but he caught the distinct odor of old piss and defecation, under some sort of humid, coppery taste. Curious. It looked like he had been left there to quietly rot.

There was a stout ring at the top of the bars, and a tightness to the metal that said this was where he was hanging from. Retreating from this exploration, Albion's foot slipped on the slick bottom of the cage, and he reamed his hand against the bar. He cursed a blue streak.

From somewhere in the darkness, a string of moans and epithets echoed him. When he looked, there was only darkness, but listening carefully, he thought there must be a line of cages, whining and creaking as the people in them moved. A man at the end was accusing him of extramarital relations with a donkey. The gibbets were probably clinging to an overhead bar, or trolley track of some kind, slowly trucking along. A terrible thought tried to surface, but Albion quashed it ruthlessly. Not what he needed right now.

After the first hour, his back could no longer be ignored. Fresh blood coated the sharp edges of the flat bars where he cut his hand. He could no longer stand the pain and the silence.

"OY!" He yelled, experimentally.

There was no reply, save the requisite cursing. He hawked up a wad of phlegm, that being the only missile available, and launched it at the pudgy woman in the next cage. She jerked reflexively, but that only set her cage swinging a little quicker before she settled. That gave Albion an idea.

"I wouldn't do it," a voice spoke up behind Albion.

"Do what?" Albion answered.

He pressed on the flat of the bars. He had to squirm, pushing his cramped, numb muscles into action, but eventually he discovered the wee old man crammed into the cage behind his. Stringy, but quite hale, with a trimmed beard, Albion might have placed him in a county fair selling fairy floss to children.

"Try to swing until something overhead gives," said the gentleman. Albion stopped immediately. The cage rocked to a standstill.

"Why not?"

"Judging from the screaming from the other fellow who tried it, the ground is at least a hundred feet away," answered the gentleman.

Like Albion the older man was naked, but his ebony skin was clean. As far as Albion could tell with his nose, anyway—the bugger was hard to see. "If you had woken in the previous room, you might have made it. The floor was only thirty feet there, but the sharp cans might have bled you dry before you made it to the door."

"This is some sort of factory?" Albion said. The black thought he had earlier now embraced him like a lover. "...a canning factory?"

"Mayhap the next room will prove more opportune," the gentleman added. "They can't keep us here forever. It's unsanitary." The gentleman was off putting. His cavalier detachment was completely incompatible with his dire surroundings. Albion wondered how long he would have to spend in the cage to turn into that fellow.

"How many—" Albion started to say, but was interrupted by sudden spark of light from down the line of cages, growing from a point to a line to a square. Albion blinked in the sudden brightness, the shadows of cages before him strange fruit in the gardens of Hyperion. It was a door, a vast door, and beyond it, the flames and the smell were almost too much to bear.

Not for nothing, knowing what everything did made the scene more bearable. Still, a little bit of wee did come out before he focused on the vast domed forges, crucibles pouring molten substances into molds, bubbling red tanks backlit through some viscous substance. Everything looked like it had been hastily unloaded and set up. The equipment was on rolling casters, and the space was something like a butcher's work floor, with train tracks through the middle for loading and unloading cattle.

Clear rubber lines ran from the tanks onto a couple of boxcars. The roof of one had been peeled back with the walls, like a fancy chocolate box. Instead of delicious truffles, the inside was lined with ranks upon ranks of sharp metal creatures. Their grubby carapaces sucked at the lines, gaping open and waiting. Tarantulas, yes, but also centipedes, and scorpions, hollow metal husks awaiting the gift of life. Albion suddenly thought he knew what Jean Hallow was doing with the contents of the Cook box.

The light came from a blazing fire at the far end of the room. A red glow lit upon a vast, bullish block of rust-red iron, shot through with square grilles and vented grates. Albion watched as from the other side of the room, a line of cages rocked back and forth on hooks over to the block. Each cage trundled over, catching some sort of mechanism in a track above. A brisk click sounded, then the bottom of the cage dropped open, and something scrabbling fell out of it, its screams cut short by the greedy gobbling of the machine as it burped and chewed and crunched. A thick red liquid bled from a grille below, swiftly swept down a line and into a ready tank, while at the other end the machine belched a dry mash into a trough that swept out to another room.

Albion looked back to the tanks, which were receiving the most attention. Each tank was far too large for a man to move, and they had domed tops ending in mismatched, asymmetrical ports. Dozens of them lined the walls, like sentries. They were plugged into a device with a seamless, egg-shaped orb attached to it on a plinth. Albion knew it instantly for the Cook box, even though he hadn't seen the contents.

In horror, the black thought fully descended upon him, shaking his limbs, chattering his teeth. He should have known. The trains free of hobos, the streets clean, the prosperous citizenry with the hunted expressions on their faces. That coppery smell had been human blood. He felt the punch of the aeon power in his gut, filling the room as people died and their intense, last moments of suffering were piped into the monsters on the boxcars. Liquid nourishment.

This was a killing floor that processed the poor, the addled and the destitute into canned meats. Now it had been transformed into a manufactory for feeding Hallow's machine horrors. There must be hundreds, thousands of these manufactories across the country, and Ubique had allowed Hallow's Ghost Train to use them to fuel his monsters. Albion's gorge rose as a fresh person dropped into the block.

They were going to make him into food.

And suddenly he was thrown against the bars once more as his cage lurched forward along the assembly line. As he approached, the top of the gore-streaked block came into view, revealing a set of gnashing metal jaws, row upon row of them roiling like a shark's maw. Below those, a churning puzzle box of razor-sharp gears indifferently turned, thrashing people into mince.

"Aye. I suppose there's nothing for it now," said the gentleman behind Albion, getting to his feet with an easy rocking motion. "But it was nice to meet you."

The gentleman gave a sort of twisting hop, and just like that the cage's ring jumped off its hook, plummeting some sixty or seventy feet. It seemed like an interminable plunge, a drop completely silent and free of screams, at least until the iron hit the first piece of machinery. There was a horrid squeal and crash of metal.

The workers were quick to respond, arriving with rakes and shovels and a barrow to move the remains into the grinder. And the assembly line moved on, taking Albion closer across the killing floor.

Back in Vanessa Hargreaves' room, she had come to certain conclusions.

One: Jean Hallow had business with her, otherwise she'd have been killed.

Two: If so, someone was coming for her sooner or later.

She wasn't quite so flexible as the Orb Weaver, but lying prone on top of a rafter with a length of bedsheet wasn't difficult to do. At least, it wasn't for the first thirty minutes. After that the wood began to grow uncomfortable and she started to feel very silly. With so many incidentals in the room, her captors clearly thought her worth the time to speak to. What if they had simply left her there for the morning? What if? Maybe she ought to try a little diplomacy.

When the first whisper-soft scuffle came from outside the door, Hargreaves was ready. As the door opened, she dropped a loop of cloth around the first head she saw and let the counterweight go, by putting her foot into the other end and jumping to the floor. She wasn't the equal of a whole man, but more than the equal of a man's neck, which snapped without fuss. She winced, watching the guard twitch on the floor.

He had a gun on him, a beautifully well-oiled, faithful Collier that made her think the man had been poorly assigned to room patrol when he ought to have been a fast draw at Hallow's side. Ornate without being obstinate, the handgun was almost a third the length of a rifle, with a heavy octagonal barrel and an eight-round levered cylinder that spun like it had been spoken by a politician. It took .357 ammo, and was a hell of a thing.

Outside, the air of the deserted hall chuckled with something perfumed and mildly celebratory. Hargreaves knew this hubbub, she had felt it before at Burgess' Luminescent Cabaret. It was the simmer of things proceeding as planned, the quiet of soothed consciences and dirty deeds done dirt cheap.

Then, quite abruptly she came upon the party; people everywhere in shocking finery. Perfume hung heavy in the air, libations flowed from fountains, and naked men and women in gold collars were openly being enjoyed by a variety of persons. Music flowed as easily as the drink and the flesh, but it was sickeningly sweet. Hargreaves caught something about good times and no worries, slapped on over a freeman water song rhythm probably intended as a liberating march from slavery. Some kind of sick abomination of sound, not music.

A man in an expensive suit reached out and draped an arm over her shoulders. He didn't bother with pleasantries, just started shoving her toward the back rooms where she had come from. He stank of cheap champagne and bordello funk. But Hargreaves knew how to fit into a society party. She let him get as far as the inside of a private room before she put the butt of the Collier into the man's left temple. The pig crumpled to the floor. She hastily closed the door.

When she attempted to hide the unconscious fellow in the wardrobe, she discovered a few of the burlesque's bordello costumes hanging there. They were clearly meant to be fetishist, but if she combined a few pieces, she had the makings of an outfit: black garters, leggings, a too-fluffy, diamond-patterned harlequin skirt and a fine brocade bodice. She added French maid heels, stuffed the Collier in the small of her back, and just for effect, threw on a black feather boa.

She breathed, looked in the mirror and took a step, nearly losing her balance as she wobbled on the unfamiliar heels. She was packed in like tuna up top and checkered like a picnic below, but looked like she had lost her proper clothes to an enthusiastic party guest. Good. Sex as a weapon; just her game.

If she was going to get out of this alive, Hargreaves would have to blend in, look the part. Somewhere, here, there would be an exit, and Captain Clemens, too.

To reach them, she was going to have to go undercover. That was something she could do very well indeed.

Having been under the engineer Cid's wing for most of his life, the young Albion had been subjected to grueling lectures in metallurgy, physics and mechanics as only an Oxfordian could deliver. Some of it, thankfully, had lodged in his head.

When his cage came to dangle over the churning maw of steely death, Albion had been ready with his fingers between the bars. As soon as the floor fell out from under his feet, Albion's body slipped out with it —but not his hands. Those he had placed just over the hinge of the floor panel, the place where the bars had been shaped to hold the drop mechanism. Its rounded form offered the only possible purchase. Simple physics; instead of falling, his body swung forward, painfully on his fingers. There was a terrifying moment as his toes dipped close to the chewing teeth. His fingers burned with the strain, his cramped muscles screamed, but the grime on his hands offered traction, and then he was dangling from the cage like a naked monkey. The lip of the block came within reach, and he balanced his toes upon it, letting go with a terrifying back-and-forth wobble before the workers could scrape him into the meat grinder.

Albion's foot slipped, and, with no small measure of guilt, he wished the woman in the cage before his hadn't been quite so corpulent. Vile stuff squished between his toes, and the air shivered with the gnashing of metal teeth. Then he fell the rest of the way off the side of the block, his poor abused face knocking the wits out of one of the masked, slick workmen.

But he was alive.

He did not have time to be politically correct, or mourn, or be sympathetic to anybody's cause. A thick crowbar lay nearby, and he took this up, smashing in every mask and lever he saw. Soon he was matted in foul-smelling ick, but the machine ground to a halt even as three more captives succumbed to a gruesome fate.

The smell, he found, was truly horrendous on the killing floor itself, sour and pervasive.

Thankfully, the fires now lapping at the machinery set off some kind of extinguishing system. Water began to spray from nozzles hidden in the ceiling. It was salt water, ocean water. They must be quite near the sea, still at the cabaret, perhaps. Albion let the grime sluice off of him, running into the drains, hoping it would befoul these monsters' disgusting product. The salt stung painfully, gratifyingly in his many cuts, as only life does.

One of the workmen came near, and Albion kicked him hard, the sort of kick intended to tip someone over the edge of an airship deck. The figure lurched backward, over a rail, and his foot caught in a floor trap. Much screaming and flailing followed as the blades in the trap chewed the man to pieces.

The workmen seemed intent on fleeing, which suited Albion just fine. He strolled along, naked as the day he was born, lashing out at the machines as he went and savoring the orchestra of gears grinding to dust. It was only a matter of time before armed guards arrived, but by then he had found the cage release, cheekily masked with tape and marked "free range."

A mob of subjugated outcasts tumbled off a receiving platform, cage after cage releasing a torrent of begrimed, naked people to be washed clean by the water to reveal black, brown and yellow skin beneath. They overwhelmed the guards who were unprepared for the naked abyss of teeth, nails, and rage.

Following the overhead gibbet track backward, Albion led his ragged band surging through the factory floor, brandishing the rifles and shock batons of the guards. These were cumbersome, with a backpack of coils to hold their incapacitating charge, but the batons' victims' uncontrollable waltz and voiding of bowels scared the piss out of the incoming guards. It made for easy pickings.

At one end of the machines stood a sorting facility with cans upon cans of vile product lying on pallets. They looked like graves, markers lying dusty and forgotten for months at least. It was a massive supply. In the next room, they came upon a mountain of grimy effects, which were being unceremoniously moved by steam loader into an incinerator. A collective moan emerged from the freed men and women, seeing the last vestige of their lives being shoveled into the ovens. Albion shocked the load engine's driver with a stun baton and ran the ugly loader into the flaming mouth of the incinerator, which drew a chorus of cheers. The blocked furnace began to smoke ominously.

In the saturnalia of reclamation that followed, Albion somehow made his way to a sorting room, where valuables had been separated from the piles of clothing. There were old heirloom watches, jewelry, even a gold dagger that had somehow evaded the pawn. On a shelf in the back for unsorted acquisitions, he found his long coat, with Victoria and the Red Special still inside. Someone thrust him some trousers. As he was tired of wet hair in his eyes, Albion grabbed a cloth from the next shelf and tied it round his brow. It hadn't occurred to him exactly how red the cloth was, or the way it hung off his head like a flag, or that his height and exposed chest set him apart from the mob. When he stood up again a man in the rabble cheered, and suddenly he found himself at the head of an army.

That was when the door at the end of the room opened, to reveal an extremely blonde person in an extremely low-cut bodice, her blue eyes wide as dinner saucers. An enormous pistol occupied one of her hands. The mob turned, the tips of their batons and rifles sparkling, their crowbars and pipes glinting off the murder shining from their eyes.

"Oh, hello, Hargreaves. How have you been?" asked Albion, cheerfully.

"The most difficult thing," Albion said a little later, "is keeping them from killing each other."

As he did, a couple of the stragglers at the back of the mob began to tussle over some of the nice things they had found in the private rooms.

"No! Leave it be," shouted Albion. He gestured at them with his gun. "Save it for the buggers further up!"

Albion's mob filled the hallway, which was thankfully quite grand, more of a common foyer than a connecting passage. The tussle stopped. There was still an air of relief at having their lives saved from the grinder. Albion was able to curb unnecessary loss of life, but as to the wholesale larceny and general mayhem, this he encouraged with aplomb.

"This is savagery! It's barbaric, not to be borne," said Hargreaves, watching a man chase down one of the escaped tarts, clearly without any intention of consent or payment. She had only just changed back into her riding trousers and boots, though she kept the bodice. It really looked very good on her. She had also appropriated a worn duster for her new gun and her knife, and now felt very much chuffed.

"The blood of the revolution is on the hands of the oppressor. You can try to stop them," said Albion. He gestured with a bottle of '89 La Fete in a philosophic way. "Or you can help me get to the good wines first."

They had come up from the killing floor to the crazed orgy party Hargreaves first encountered. She had wanted to go back to destroy the egg that now held the contents of the Cook box, but they discovered the doors to the killing floor were locked. Through it came the sounds of hasty men, probably packing away the box and preparing the boxcars to leave. The loading engine was crammed into the incinerator, now cold. So Albion and Hargreaves decided to go around, over the top to try to catch the Ghost Train.

Apparently Burgess' partnership had extended to building his pleasure palace on top of a Ubique abattoir, or as Albion suspected, the slaughterhouse below had been built specifically to service Jean Hallow's Ghost Train. In any case all hell had broken loose as the prisoners fell upon the guests. It was nothing Albion could stop. These people were destitute, who had never seen such opulence, and they had no love for these perceived oppressors. Hargreaves wanted to run in amongst them and scream that they were not hurting anybody responsible, not changing anything, but she knew it was a pointless effort.

"Burgess is a crook! Let the place burn," said Hargreaves, surprising herself. She took the bottle of wine from Albion now and had a good pull from the neck. She came up gasping. "But there must be something to be done about the savages."

"There is. They're doing it," Albion said, pointing to where a man was toppling to the ground, clutching himself painfully. The lady of the evening who had kicked him in the gentleman's area stood over him a moment. She spit in his face. Then she whooped, and joined in the looting. The girls only worked there, after all, and seemed to have no love for their employers.

"Democracy in action. Anarchy as order," said Albion, who clearly did not give a damn. Hargreaves stamped her foot, but it did seem, in this limited respect, the people could be trusted to do what needed to be done. Maybe this too, was uniquely American.

Albion had set guards at the party's doors while a core group looted the place for weapons. At his signal, they kicked down the double doors to find themselves in another large foyer cum hallway. They had been in only one of the party rooms, and it looked like there were several others branching off the foyer. It was too much celebration simply for a burlesque. Albion motioned for groups to split off and check the rooms. They were now deserted, though there were signs of a hasty exit.

"It bothers me we've seen neither hide nor hair of our captors," said Hargreaves.

"And why were they holding a party?" mused Albion. "Something must have been going on...Hallow or Burgess must have some purpose bringing all this society out to the cabaret."

"Why the devil do you suppose they went to the trouble? They clearly wished to preserve me for something," mused Hargreaves. The obvious had occurred to her; even covered in soot, her legs were shapely, her bust impressive. She supposed even if Hallow had no interest, his clients would. But that was a flimsy reason. He could certainly buy all the girls he wanted, here at the last waystation before the Lands Beyond. It bothered Hargreaves that Hallow had put her up in a nice room, and simply thrown Albion into the grinder. Were they so different?

"I suspect," answered Albion after a moment, "simple prudence. That hidden hold must have been built to supply the Ghost Train, and made for a convenient dumping ground for anybody Hallow or Burgess wanted to get rid of. It was best to dispose of me, who had seen their faces, and imprison you. You have sway with the Queen. The cans are probably a side business...waste not, want not."

"What cans?" Hargreaves asked. When Albion described in detail what was under the mansion, Hargreaves had to run and retch for ten minutes into a plant. Then she came back, and they drank, and no more was said about it.

Albion led them through the Darklight Cabaret, which was now completely deserted. They stormed across the stage, kicking aside props and scenery. Someone knocked over the ghost light, which set flame to something backstage. Hastily, Albion led them out through the front doors, to emerge onto a large cul-de-sac which served as the cabaret's front entryway. A gilt archway stood nearby, the entrance to the shuttle station back to the city. They could see the platform was deserted. Where was the Ghost Train?

Just as the last of their survivors exited the cabaret, the ornate windows burst outward. The flames had finally reached the front rooms. Now the elegant mansion began to burn to the ground, hopefully taking the hateful abattoir with it. Albion looked at the mob milling around in the manicured grounds, then turned to Hargreaves and shrugged. She knew the gesture for what it was. He had freed them from the abattoir, but he was no revolutionary. He was just a pirate.

Hargreaves found herself thinking on what she had seen, and the more terrible things she hadn't. There had been a terrible elegance to the modest proposal found in that underground factory. In secret, the placeless had been quietly put to use, kicking and screaming, to nourish the rest of society. The abattoir was, in a gruesome way, understandable to Hargreaves, and that made it worse.

Albion and Hargreaves watched the cabaret burning to the ground. They sat and they drank, and as they drank a thick fog rolled in over the flames, giving it a warm halo. Hargreaves squinted. For a second there she thought she saw something in the darkness, where the smoke and the firelight met.

There!

There it was again!

"Albion, do you...?" said Hargreaves, only the pirate captain was on his feet, his guns in his hands. He pointed them up at the air between the burning hulk and the thick cloud of smoke. Hargreaves jammed her eyes open, even though the air was dry and her eyelids felt like sandpaper.

There *was* something there, something parting the veils of smoke and fog. The ornate, burning cabaret looked a little like a stage, and it seemed almost as if a hand was piercing the curtain. Knocking on the world's door. Wanting to make an entrance...

"There's something in the fog, no?" Hargreaves said. Was it an airship? A gust of wind, perhaps?

"I don't think that's just fog..." whispered Albion.

It was eerie. The fog was moving back and forth swaying, almost like... Hargreave's breath caught in her throat, but it was Albion who put action to words.

"You there! Look out!" Albion screamed at the nearest knot of escapees.

They looked up at him, perhaps deafened by the crackling of the mansion, and they waved, smiling at their leader. And perhaps it was better that they were too far away to see Albion's look of horror as a pale hand came down and crushed them out of existence. Only a red slick remained, sticking in strings to the hand as it lifted away, back into the mystifying fog.

Jean Hallow didn't think it was important to count how many were crushed under his right hand.

It was of passing interest the hand operated well, certainly, but that was to be expected. Hallow had designed it himself, as he had designed automata for the Queen, for Ubique, and for a time, Mordemere. He had brought a medical perspective to the fleshy apparatus so favored by the aeon particle. Unlike Mordemere, who had hidden the flesh in a cocoon of steel gilt, Hallow had held it up, embraced it, intertwined it within his machines. Raised columns of it, erected monuments to it.

Seated on his throne of flesh, his will now reached every clattering limb and every inch of the throne, this seat of the soul he called the Grimaldi. Alphonse had been a sophomore effort, extraordinarily gifted by the powerful will of Vanessa Hargreaves. He had been sad to hear it had been destroyed.

Outside, Hallow had crafted a body to rival any dirigible gunship, an impenetrable, steam-driven figure of absolute terror. This shell of his had the bulk and power of a dirigible warship, and with the Cook engine back at the Grimaldi's heart, it moved at the speed of thought. He was aware of the egg-shaped device, a warm, pulsing thing somewhere behind his back. Sealed in a chamber of arc-controlled flesh, he had surrounded himself with a warm, safe womb. He wondered if this was what if felt like in the warmth and nurture between a woman's thighs.

Not so different from a man, then. He'd had lovers, but none he could speak plainly to. His thoughts horrified them, he had found, and were best kept secret.

While Hallow had all these thoughts, he was also methodically, absent-mindedly crushing out the vermin on the lawn of the cabaret. A shame—he had admired the Darklight's classic architecture. All of the meat would have to be destroyed, of course. It was important to use many of the Grimaldi's weapons. He had to make a good show of it.

When he had killed enough of them, he flew the Grimaldi back up to the high cliff side where his Conqueror Worm was parked on its tracks. He had swiftly herded his guests into the train's party car, and gotten them out of harm's way. Now they were perched on the cliff where they had a clear view of the meat dying.

Hallow landed Grimaldi inside the open party car, and his guests cheered as he stepped out of it—behind a silk screen of course. When he emerged, he was strikingly handsome in a decorative cape that covered everything but his face and one pinstriped sleeve.

"Is all of this necessary?" complained Stanley Burgess as Hallow mingled through the crowd. "My cabaret... "

The dealer, Hallow thought disdainfully. The one whose usury and sin banquets had so gleefully funded this vision. It was Burgess who had taught Hallow to entertain these creatures in the first place. Soften them up, so to speak. Hallow felt disgusted by Burgess' oily presence.

"Do not mourn your lost pleasure palace, Burgess," said Hallow. "You will be able to build ten more. Enjoy the facilities. I assure you they are every bit the match of your cabaret."

Hallow had to be careful. His head was growing fuzzy from being connected to the Grimaldi for an extended period of time. Yet, his arm was not quite healed, and if he left it for too long he would bleed to death within minutes. The throne, while comforting, had a warmth and coppery scent too irritably Freudian. The nuisances had to be borne, or dealt with. To business. The Ubique man was near. Hallow had to make a good show.

"Ubique wants a demonstration, and they will have it," concluded Hallow. He stepped through the party.

"You will reimburse the cost yourself, Hallow," grumbled Burgess.

"It will be my pleasure," rumbled Hallow, and was pleased to see the other man shy away.

What was intriguing to Hallow was Burgess's and some other guests' apparent enjoyment of his display. Beads of sweat stood out on Burgess' forehead. Hallow did not care what was happening. It was unfortunate for the rabble, they were going to die sooner or later regardless. Whether it was by his hand, literally or otherwise, was of no consequence to him. But he understood Burgess' bloodlust when he saw it, and it was disgusting.

"Mr. Anderson?" Someone was trying to speak to Burgess' neighbor, some contractor or another working for Ubique.

"Oh? Oh, yes, I was just watching that rather corpulent buck trying to escape. His leg is rather crushed."

"Ah, the large dark fellow there."

Hallow idly wondered how corpulent Anderson's bank account was. He found it irritating that of the people assembled in this room, Hallow and Orb Weaver were the only ones under forty million in wealth, and under fifty in age. The dancers and the molls did not count. It tested his calm to think it had taken pleasuring all of these fat, depraved ticks to do what needed to be done. All these people were doomed, and only he and Orb Weaver knew it.

A fireball suddenly filled the windows nearly disrupting Hallow's calm. A cry of excitement rose from the hall, followed by a titter of laughter. Part of the festivities! It was all a grand show. Breathtaking. But Hallow recoiled. *Who dares?* Hallow stalked back to the Grimaldi and climbed back in as a razzle of lightning lashed across the Conqueror Worm's insulated flanks. It was no easy task, but his guests were distracted by the light show.

The Grimaldi shook from head to tail. It was difficult for Hallow to reassert control. His awareness was key.

Soon Hallow had his balance, and lifted off gently. He shifted the great lenses of Grimaldi's eyes to bring something very small into view. It was Vanessa Hargreaves! And her pirate friend. That was right, he had left her in the mansion. Silly of him, really. Hallow respected Hargreaves, he hadn't wanted her to die if she didn't have to. Now that little mistake seemed to have cost him. The pirate raised something in his hand, and there was a flash. This time it was invisible, but in a moment he felt it viscerally; a smattering of fog water pulled into a swarm of bullets, searing painfully across the Grimaldi.

Pain! Oh, accursed pain. Pain screamed through his body like it had when he was a boy undergoing his father's treatments. Part of him, the alchemist part, was stunned; an aeon reaction that drew moisture from the air, and forced it at an enemy. Most impressive.

Hallow lashed out with one of the wands at Grimaldi's disposal to crush the bluff the pirate stood on. He imagined it would be like one of San Francisco's famed earthquakes on that cliff now, the earth losing its cohesion, dumping them into the sea.

"Now, where were we?" said Hallow, his voice rumbling out from the Grimaldi's seat of power. "Ah, yes. Mr. Anderson. So there's the potential of the automata. Shall we see what the train's cannons will do? I have a hankering to do in some pirate scum."

Down below, Albion gawped at the enormous white shape coming to crush them out of existence, and he dropped the round he had been trying to load into the Red Special.

"Clemens! Buck up!"

Hargreaves pushed him over the edge of the bluff, near a decorative gazebo perched on the edge of the grounds. The grass of the cabaret ran right over the edge of the rocks, with hardly a barrier to keep one from falling over the edge. Now Hargreaves did it on purpose, and just in time too. The ground roiled, like an upset table with them on it, and the gazebo tumbled away into the ocean. It didn't make a sound as it disappeared into the waves.

Albion fumbled, feeling for the next round from his coat pocket even as the world came all topsy-turvy. At the last moment before they hit the rocks below, he locked the whammy bar, slotting the round into the chamber. Mere feet from the ground he pulled the trigger.

The resulting blast of wind blew everything away, rocks, dust, and the hearty lap of the Pacific tides. It also buoyed them up, just enough that he and Hargreaves slowed to a painful tumble in the stones instead of dashed to death upon them.

Albion opened his mouth to scream, but all that came was a wind-blown gargle. The Red Special was a glowing brand in his hands, kicking like a prize stallion. If he let go, he was sure they would be crushed by aeon forces run wild. These chord rounds had been Cid's halfway measure, a blend of rare aeon dust and ground up bric-a-brac. Even Cid hadn't been sure what firing one would do.

It suddenly tasted very salty in Albion's open mouth. Overhead, boomed a sudden thunder, and they gaped as a glowing line seared through the fog. Something was being burned to cinders on the road overhead.

"No!"

Vanessa Hargreaves' voice was an alarum in the murk. Albion came out of a red daze, his eyes open wide. There was a round in his left hand. His right hand was aimed up at the white shape overhead, like a spirit looming in the dark. The Red Special shook in his hand. Hagreaves must have feared he had been about to load it and fire, heedless of the innocents that would be caught in the ensuing blast.

Hargreaves came stumbling on a cascade of pebbles and shoved him into an alcove in the cliff, seconds before a thunder wave rolled through the night. A clod of dirt came down almost on top of the spot where Albion had been standing. They hid in a slight overhang while the rain of sharp rocks died down. Thunder came once or twice more, but eventually the assault ceased. After a minute a distant whistle sounded, followed by the rattling of a train's engine. There fell a deep, oceanic quiet.

Across the frothing sea, there was only soft opaqueness. The fog was impenetrable, and what light came from the burning mansion was fading fast. They looked up at the sheer bluffs, a blank craggy wall marked by the high water.

The barnacles stopped an inch over Albion's head. By either pirate or Briton reckoning, it could only be an hour or so before the tide came in and drowned them both. The fog made it impossible to be sure, and its sable depths threatened to give one bad dreams. They might as well have been at the edge of the world.

"A rock and a—"

"Don't you say it, wanker," interrupted Hargreaves.

The relief flooding through him when Albion found a foothold and began to climb felt a bit like the first pint after a long day. It was an elation only surpassed by the dread of slipping twenty minutes later. Hargreaves slid two feet down the sheer cliff face, only stopped from smashing on the rocks by the improvised tether of the belt from her duster. Recently reclaimed from a pile of destitute refuse, the straining material was barely strong enough to hold her. She made a Hail Mary grab for a wet handhold and just barely caught it.

She clung there, letting the damp cover her. Meanwhile, Albion was trying to separate the rush of the waves from the pounding of adrenaline in his head. Six minutes later he came tumbling past her in a slide of loosened rocks. The belt broke then, snapping at the cheap buckle. This time Albion clung to some deceptively sturdy scrub brush. It held fast.

After that it was a matter of slowly crawling sideways to find handholds, before they reached a gentler slope and collapsed on some loamy cliff grass. Compared to the hard rocks, it was a feather mattress.

"Isn't there...one of those...blasted bullets...that can make this... easy?" gasped Hargreaves. They lay prone on the ground, spent.

"Why...yes...I'll just...pop it in here...and we'll be...on our way," answered Albion, tossing the empty Red Special over. It hit her in the solar plexus, eliciting a grunt. The point of a gun was to cause pain, after all. Maybe it was the thick, wet air, but Albion wondered if she felt a certain affinity. Guns were tools only to punish, to contain. Never to save, and speaking with Hargreaves, she was of the opinion she had done little saving, which was why she became a police officer to begin with. Then there was the name always at her lips when she thought nobody could hear: Maple Cross.

Climbing the cliff took them the rest of the night. By the time they emerged onto the road above, the tide was well and truly up, the fog banished, and Jean Hallow's monstrosity had gone. The rank smell of smoke and seared flesh hung in the air, and a sunrise just began peeking over the horizon in a smattering or oranges and purples.

"Did...did anyone?" Hargreaves gasped.

The pair looked for survivors, but found only dark smears and charred powder. An open bottle of champagne rolled slowly down an incline, drawing a wet line across the gravel.

"Hargreaves! Help me!"

Albion's deep-throated cry shook her out of a stunned torpor. Not far away there was a man trapped under a charred pine trunk that must have been blasted off the landscape. The man was still conscious. The pair grasped him firmly under the arms and pulled, extracting only a tortured scream.

"Aughh, no, no, stop! There's no way," the man cried. It was as much vitality as could be got; the man's eyes were unfocused, and his lips dry. The mahogany skin under the grime was slowly going gray.

"There's a bleed," said Hargreaves. "Something under the tree must be torn. If we move him he'll die." She stood in the middle of the road, where the scars were showing by the morning's light. The ground was pockmarked and cratered, the dirt underneath fleshy, brown loam.

"Listen, we're going to get help, we're going to find something to tie off your leg," Albion said. The pirate had his hands at the place where the deadfall held down the man's waist. He was tying off the trapped leg.

"Albion, by the time we—"

"You're going to be just fine!" And Albion grinned his big daft grin, the one that scrunched up his eyes. The man under the tree laughed, a soundless, weak laugh, and then he was gone.

"I told you so," started Hargreaves, but she choked when she saw the tears rolling down Albion's smiling face.

STATION 16

Fog of War

LIKE MOST CONFLICTS, THERE WAS NO OFFICIAL SIGN FOR THE BATTLE to begin. Rosa Marija had never served in any army, but she had a feeling traditional forces had hierarchy for this very purpose. The value of officers was to be idle enough to realize when the first volley arrived. To announce the charge, loose the dogs.

Certainly the ships of the Incognito might have used a chain of command that day, a hierarchy better suited to lead the drunken Powder Monkey or the Viscountess Valentina. Even Gunsmoke was only able to rally by his brilliant use of a cat-o-nine-tails, the screams broadcast over ether crystals singing at the head of every ship.

Gunsmoke could hardly be blamed. A minor band led by the plains pirate Sam Walker had had a mutiny during the night. They'd lost three ships to the entrepreneurial crew and the remaining ship flew Walker's head high on their mainmast as a standard. Apparently the late captain's wife Felicia Walker had caught him abed with one of the Viscountess's girls and had started the mutiny, earning her the nickname "The Nutcracker." Mutiny and insubordination were common enough when dealing with pirates, but that one was set to go down as swashbuckler lore.

Rosa knew it was not in the nature of pirates to coordinate. In fact only the vague threat of the Incognito's power kept them together now. It had been the Incognito man Ortega's promise to find Albion with their vast, shadowed connections that brought Rosa to the front line. In exchange she would assist MAD and Vanessa Hargreaves. The fact Hargreaves was her friend did not seem to factor into Ortega's calculations.

Even Gunsmoke Gilly found it difficult to climb out of his bed once the first cannon fire reached his ears. That was part of the problem. It wasn't immediately clear if the Incognito were under attack at all. With the fog gone, the pirates had hidden themselves amongst the traders from the gray divide, shutting their anchor launchers and cannon behind the false livery of Ubique, of Albatross and Ursine. Gunsmoke ran the flags of the Prince of Nigeria. It was common practice, running false colors, and more than one pirate doubled as legitimate traders depending on what latitude they sailed. Needles in the haystack.

But either their attacker had other means of telling pirate from trader, or they didn't care which was which. When the first reports sounded across the bay, the crows nests lifted their goggles and peered across the dawn-lit harbor to see the first schooner explode in a gout of flame, quickly consuming a plains crawler dirigible that had been taking on cargo nearby. Shreds of the last remaining fog ballooned out from the fire and dispersed. The congregated airships, at the docks for grog and women, scattered as if before a strong wind, and it was finally clear they were indeed under attack.

"Jesus Christ!"

"Well pork my momma, look at that fireball go!"

"Goddammit Leeroy!"

"Blast! Was it one of ours?"

The chatter over the ether was confusing, but the general consensus was it had occurred in the northern end of the bay, and their one small casualty was a no-worth schooner that had only ventured there for the whorehouses. Once lookouts had their scopes pointed in the right direction, it wasn't hard to make out the gleaming snake circling the high hills, the huge wheels of the engine pulling the guns, and the thunder of cannons fired from a rail-mounted platform.

"What in seven hells!" Gunsmoke's voice came over the din. "Fight back! Wesson! Shelby! Cormorant! Bear on that train and fire on my command! "

Once the order was given, Gunsmoke's own ships fired a volley upon the hill, raising up huge clods of dirt. His *Remington* led a phalanx of corsairs that laid on a barrage from all over the bay with far-reaching guns. Seeing their success, a few opportunists turned their heavy keels in the air, and then the pirates were all firing upon the glimmer of silver on the hillside.

"Idiots! You'll give away which of you are Incognito!" hissed Rosa as she watched from the *'Berry's* deck.

Before the dust settled, half of the pirate ships suddenly erupted into flames, blown out of the air. A dozen ships fell before some sensible commanders halted the assault, turning the ships bow-forward toward the enemy that had flanked them. One corsair, her captain perhaps frightened by the scale of the conflict, turned to flee and was immediately blasted to pieces. She wasn't simply destroyed—she was spread across the sky by something moving incredibly fast, ripping her bow out through her stern and dragging a purple cloud of foulness behind it. Something crackled within that cloud and the gas burst into flames, sick purple-black flames that continued to burn as they hit the water.

From the South, the *Tenessee Jack* rode high on the hill.

Train cars full of ammunition trailed behind her. There were ten times the crates as there were men to load them, scurrying back and forth in the scopes with heavy Gatling guns and wing clipper guns on wagons. Mercenaries, hired by Hallow, no doubt.

"There's no escape," said Gunsmoke. "All ships, all hands, prepare to engage the enemy!"

Gas escaped in clouds of blue as Gatlings tore into the sides of the pirates. Some of the older ships still flew with gas envelopes and balloons. Deflated, the sinking hulks rammed into each other, their hulls careening into the bay. New fires shimmered into being, raining down upon the few who survived. *The Tennessee Jack's* gun spat its gas, which pooled on the surface of the water, igniting into a foul, smoking slick. Men fell through the smoke and were devoured by the tide of flames, a blighted shadow floating across the bay. Later, survivors would tell of the tiny clockworks in the purple clouds, the clicking whirligigs that were released by the rail gun's rounds and sparked as they turned in the air, igniting the purple gas.

It took Rosa two minutes from the time she saw the cannon flares to tell what was happening. Fire haunted the air and smoke tasted bitter in her mouth. She ran from toggle to toggle in the bridge, until the other ships dropped away and the 'Berry fell back with choked hiccups of her forward vents. She saw a golden arch of Gatling bullets dip in a deadly column, a finger of death to tear the ship apart. Then followed a varicolored flash, and the heavy *thunk* of towing anchors latching to the 'Berry's hard points, dragging her away from the gunfire.

"*The Papillon Nancy!* Alice! My wife is out there!" came the voice of Elric Blair, hollering through the ship's horns. The whooping came from the outside, where Alice and her crew were carrying on. Sleeker than a dolphin, the *Nancy* pulled the 'Berry just out of reach, accelerating her out of the space of sky that now held only death. Not out to sea, but down, near the water, where they could steer around the falling gas and wrecks that came down like pillars in the sunless lands.

Alice was only the spear tip of a reinforcing force. A swarm of ships that included Nessie Drake's unmistakable *Morcego*, which hadn't been seen in ages and was the subject of myriad rumors. Its arched lines and brooding sails held banks upon banks of anchor launchers, which she used to gather every airship within reach and yank out of the fray.

Prissy Jack was there too, and he had somehow transformed his flying roti restaurant into an elephant-headed shield ship: *Ganapati, Remover of Obstacles*, trailing a thick fog of spices and rich aromas. Behind thick armored flanks, freighters and corsairs sought refuge, and were able to escape a group at a time over the ocean and out of reach. The other shield ships followed suit, bouncing the terrible clippers off their thick shields.

It was in the midst of the maelstrom that Cezette Louissaint appeared on the bridge. Rosa gestured wildly at a shivering lever. The girl lunged across the tilting deck, managing to get a hand on it. Her heels squealed to a halt, fast against the deck.

"Hold, and unfurl the port sail. Yes, that's it!"

"*Oui, madame!*"

The ether *dague* still blared its song of the dead and the dying, and the *Huckleberry* wove between all of them, dodging the plumes of seawater and the falling, burning ships. One of the Incognito ships drifted too close to land, its captain busied with the flames sinking his ship. In an instant the dirigible burst apart, ripped to shreds by the dreadful white figure that hovered close to the water.

"Oh god, oh god!"

"My arm! Somebody pick up my arm!"

"The other gods! The elder gods! The gods of the outer hells that guard the feeble gates of Earth! Oh...! "

"Don't look at it!" Rosa screamed. "Just look at the controls!" The sight of Hallow's Grimaldi teased at the fringes of sanity. Rosa didn't know what it was called, but she knew to stay away from it, even from looking at it.

"*C'est horrible!*" cried Cezette, her eyes averted from the scopes.

The Grimaldi sailed over the destruction it had wrought, turning its great limbs in a lazy spiral. Trying not to look at it, Rosa watched the train writhe, and instantly regretted it. Perhaps it was the gas, or the fog of war, but the train seemed to be animating into a sinuous shape, no mechanical creation but some sort of organic creature. Chitinous plates slipped over and under each other as it moved, the slithering of a millipede, or some other loathsome creature. Slowly it met up in the distance with its other half, and now it was a unified worm, eating its way through downtown San Francisco.

Aboard the 'Berry, there wasn't enough time to gape or even utter some profanity. Cid labored at a bank of switches in the engine room, squeezing every ounce of power from the 'Berry's strained engines. In the hold, Elric Blair and Cockney Alex clambered over a dozen pipes, drawing thick straps across tarpaulin-covered loads. Just as they clipped the canvas into place, a wing clipper round tore through and the weight tipped into the strap. Fortunately it held, preventing the heavy cargo from ripping through. If it had, a dozen decks and the bottom of the ship wouldn't have stopped its fall.

And so it continued, no time for rest, each breath gasped desperately, harsh and dry and possibly the last. The fight went on and on, and still the Worm continued chewing its way through the Incognito, stopped only by the contrary nature of the pirates. The rogues of the sky were unwilling to gather and die in a group. Still, the Worm seemed insatiable, unstoppable.

A sprinkling of airships broke away from the crowded spread in the bay. The 'Berry led them all, paving the way with her intact manipulator arm. Some were merchantmen and freighters glad to break free of the sudden holocaust. Others were ships of the Incognito, flying the discreet black mark of their kind. Amongst them was Viscountess Valentina, who had lost three bracera in the first barrage. Their wide hips had been built to hold audiences and bedchambers, not cannons, and they had fallen at once. Each had been full of courtesans, warrior princesses all, and spirit sisters to the Viscountess.

"Blasted pirates!" Gunsmoke Gilly's voice drifted through the ether. "Get back here and finish the job!" The *Remington* had taken a blow to the screw, and limped along at the fringes of the chaos.

"Maybe those cowering bastards have bit off more than they could chew," Rosa muttered through gritted teeth, though Gilly could not hear her. But the questionable morals of the Incognito could be called into doubt later. Something was happening.

As the Worm drew close to the shore, a shimmering flower bloomed from its flanks. One of their airships had plummeted into the Worm's side, and its flaming death dealt a blow to the thing's armor, ripping up the tracks underneath. When the smoke cleared, the Worm was motionless, just a train blasted off its rails once more: no chitinous surface, no warbling, sinuous movement. No cannon thunder. Just a big hole and boxcars lying on their sides.

"*Magnifique!* It is stuck! Derailed!" cried Cezette in the 'Berry.

The shock arrived a moment later, a thunderclap that shook the knick-knacks from the shelves. They were close, too close. It knocked Cezette Louissaint to the ground, despite her firmly braced legs. Dazed, the girl struggled to clear her head. She braced herself on a control panel, barely aware of the tempestuous chaos outside. Meanwhile the chatter of the ether was returning, this time filled with shouts of triumph.

"Cormorant! Wesson! Shelby! What? Shelby's dead? Smith, take over!" Gunsmoke's orders came fast and furious. "I want a tight banana on the rail gun!"

Cezette struggled to the viewport, the ship's scopes shivering with Rosa's violent piloting. It didn't take long to sight Gunsmoke's hastily assembled group of airships. They were aligned broadsides, the dull muzzles of steam cannon points that formed a flat crescent. Of course, with the Worm out of commission, the rail gun was the biggest threat. As one, the airships fired, briefly engulfing themselves in a cloud of white steam.

In true pirate fashion, the Incognito ships had little enough regard for human life. Their staccato of steam eruptions left the ears ringing and a score of rooftops on the ground gored through. Cezette covered her ears at the cacophonous whine of dozens of missiles soaring across the sky, leaving long trails of white steam.

Seconds later, ammunition exploded into orange and black plumes of incendiary bombs, engulfing the *Tennessee Jack*. The missiles were stuffed with cheap fuel packed into munitions canisters and lit with lucifer match heads crammed into the ends. They burned notoriously hot, and could melt chrome steel. The glimmering lines of Gatling fire immediately halted as groups of mercenaries burned to death.

Cheers went up over the ether *dague* until the leftmost point of Gunsmith's crescent detonated in a purple fireball.

"Regroup! Regroup!" came the call of Gunsmith Gilly over the ether. But it was perhaps too late, as most of the Incognito forces were either destroyed or run away. The ether was strangely quiet when moments before it was full of people running about, crying out when the ships were hit; the sounds of war.

Then, suddenly, there was an altogether different sound over the ether *dague* and Cezette, at least, knew it wasn't just war any more.

"They're coming out of the breach!"

"What are they doing? That one, it's picking somebody up!"

"Oh god, its eating them!"

At first Cezette could not believe her eyes, let alone the horrified voices at her ear. She dashed forward, leaning against the deck, her fingers gripped white at the knuckles. A corsair streaked past, crumbling into a meteor shower of smoke and flame.

"Oh move! Please move!" she cried. But when the ship fell away so did Cezette, horrified. On the ground, the Worm had been derailed about a mile from the *Tennessee Jack*. Where once the silver length of the train had lain, crippled, now the ground was alive with moving, terrible things. Cezette did not want to look, but she knew, somehow that she must, and when she did, she saw an army of clockwork spiders, of scorpions, of things that had no natural analogue that swept across the city. It was as if the Worm had been disgustingly pregnant, and now it was birthing these clacking, scrabbling things from its side in a swarming wave.

And yes, they were eating people.

"They are...indiscriminate," whispered Cezette. She almost wished the *'Berry's* scopes functioned less admirably, her windows less clean. Young or old, suits or rags, women and children...the army's appetite could not be satiated. It was even eating the men paid to defend it, as it reached the rear car of the *Tennessee Jack*.

The recovering mercenaries turned their guns on the wave of death swarming up their hill, and the barrel of the *Jack* itself turned too, far too slowly to be of any use. The city slowly succumbed to the army of horrors, its picturesque houses crumpling before the wave of metal. Horror of horrors, the creatures were even righting the Worm itself, and soon there was a terrible whistling that could be heard throughout the bay. All aboard! This train was headed to hell.

"Cezette." Rosa's voice cut through the fugue as if it were a church bell.

"*Oui!* I am...all right," answered the girl. Her hands shook at the controls, but she could still grip them.

"Good. I'll need you to take the ship now," said Rosa, placing Cezette into the helmsman's chair. She buckled the girl in.

"Now?" protested Cezette.

"It is wrecking the city...and Albion and I need this city," said Rosa. Cezette looked at her quizzically, but Rosa merely smiled. "Now take his ship, and I'll see about carving Hallow a new privy hole. He's wrecking that chocolate factory down there. Where else will Albion take me once all this is over?"

And before Cezette could protest, the helmswoman was gone, leaving the bridge empty save for Cezette and the screaming in the ether.

At the edge of the city, Albion was finally getting the hang of the trolley.

"And on your right, behold San Francisco's iconic Chinatown, currently full of fleeing locals. Hello locals!" he said over the miraculously functioning speaker horn. For good measure, he gave the bell a couple of rings. Then the tracks veered violently, and everyone in the car clung to the rails. If they didn't, they'd be thrown through the trolley's open entryways. Mostly the tourists aboard had come to terms with the hijacking, as it seemed like they were avoiding the worst of the burning things falling out of the sky.

"Good God!" one clearly devout old woman cried. "You're leading us back towards the fire!"

"I left something back there!" answered Albion.

"There! The dragon arch! I see its tail!" said Vanessa Hargreaves, just a hair's breadth beside him.

Albion saw it too, the commemorative dragon that had been built to honor the Chinese rail workers. It meant Dragonwell was close. With his free hand, he slipped Victoria out of her belt, tumbling the pistol to cock the hammer. A snap and a bang later, the trolley rolled on a new track.

"But that's impossible..." said Hargreaves, gaping at the hole resting dead center in the switch. Albion knew it, too, in an uncanny way. That tiny piece of lead could not have shifted the heavy switch. Perhaps, if it had been teetering on the brink, or rusted through in a particular component...but Albion knew it wasn't so.

Just like the bus that had broken down conveniently by the road so they could get to the city, and the trolley sitting abandoned on its ring, ripe for the taking. Maybe those things had been someone behind the scenes, helping them along. But maybe that was one too many coincidences for any secret society. More likely it was the aeons, those mysterious particles that suffused their world like particles of sun-bright dust filtering through a window.

Albion himself, having briefly been enveloped in the cloud of aeons known as the Laputian Leviathan, and he knew the aeon effects better than most. He had had an aeon crystal embedded inside his shoulder. Even now the particles seemed to gather about him like a cloud of peevish, fickle fairies. Aeons were useful, certainly, but they made Albion nervous sometimes. If a few pebbles of aeon stone could lift an airship, what could lots of them do?

But perhaps it was already a moot point. The aeons had been behaving strangely ever since Mordemere's false Leviathan exploded in the night sky over Europe. Pirates had been eking out more and more from their lift compounds, flying higher, steaming harder. Arc energies whirled through cities. The steam age was pulsing with aeons like blood in the veins.

Following the scales of the dragon, it was easy to get to San Francisco's Chinatown. They put the trolley in the hands of a freeman old woman, who was a surprisingly adept driver. .

Albion and Hargreaves set off through the streets, the rolling thunder of destruction a quaking backdrop behind them. The peaked roofs glowed orange with firelight. Albion wondered if Hargreaves found the city alien, its colorful streets inhospitable. Labyrinthine. The word's rounded syllables seemed appropriate, calling up the rusty, dripping corners of Kowloon. That had been a true warren, its passages warped and narrowed, its turns sharp enough to cut. In places the *feng shui* of the place demanded a narrowing of the walls, funneling one into a space not large enough for a dog to pass. It was not uncommon to find a corpse trapped in those crevices, let alone a monster. San Francisco's Chinatown was just like a labyrinth flattened and poured over the hills, but within these hills there were real monsters. Albion felt it in his bones.

Once in those narrow, deserted market streets, it was easy to trace the scent back to the park where they had left Dragonwell. But nothing could prepare them as they rounded a corner and found themselves in a hail of crossfire, dust rising in lines that nearly cut Albion's toes off.

"Down, blast it, down!" Of course, it was Hargreaves and her police training that saved the day. She pushed Albion roughly against a hawker's stall. Dry almond biscuits rained on them in a crumbly deluge, but they were safe from bullets behind the solid cinder blocks someone had appropriated to build the damn thing.

"What is it?" Albion asked, as Hargreaves peeked over the top of a block. He listened to the regular chatter of the weapons, the heavy thud of the bullets tearing up the street. "Hell. Mercenaries."

"Oh bollocks, what's got them so jumpy?" cried Hargreaves. Even for paid guns, they were hot on the trigger. Something had them spooked.

A deafening boom sounded. The sudden clap clipped the steady sound of bullets neatly in half. Opaque clouds of cinder dust drifted through like wandering ghosts. Then the gunfire began anew, only not at them. Albion crawled to the edge of their little pocket of safety, and poked his head above the stall. He could just see through his goggles and the dusty air a suggestion of thick, chitinous legs.

Mercenaries were shooting at the legs, picked out in unadorned dark uniforms. Albion began to count the number of the chitinous legs before realizing there were lots of them, too many to count. Red splotches stained their various limbs, tinged here and there horribly with scraps of cloth. It was easy in that changed, misty street, to think them something fallen out of a rip in the world.

"We have to go. We have to go now!" hissed Albion.

"Where?" asked Hargreaves.

"Dragonwell! Where else? There seems to be something very appropriate in which to sheathe your Majesty's royal pricker."

"You insufferable! Oh, you mean the sword."

They picked their way through the street from cover to cover. The troops seemed to have weaned off their attack, occasionally taking potshots answered by the walloping boom and sizzle of steamthrowers. Ghastly, and all too familiar.

As they ran, Albion couldn't help but wonder. Where had the monsters come from? What did they want? The Ghost Train was here, he could feel it. Aeons? Something much darker. Something old, and rotten, like a bitter, festering cesspool.

They reached the play park, tripping over the merry-go-round as they went. Albion turned to shoo a wayward child away from the oncoming storm and missed Hargreaves clambering up Dragonwell's knee and into his cockpit. Before he knew it, the lumbering bulk of canvas and enameled steel was nearly atop him, dragging the sword A Contrario out of its canvas wrapping. In the dust, it was like watching a highland warrior emerge out of the mist, claymore in hand- especially because the blasted blade couldn't get more than a foot off the ground.

"It's too heavy!" Albion was more worried for Hargreaves than for Dragonwell. If Hallow's host saw her!

The first of them appeared almost right at the entrance to the playpark. Up close, Albion saw thick mandibles, and the long, tapered limbs ending in neat pads. It was built on the lines of a hunter-killer, a species of spider that regularly killed birds or small mammals- Albion had nearly had his nose chewed off by one in Brazil. It would lay in wait, and when the prey of choice appeared, it would propel itself in any direction on its spring-like legs and crush its prey with powerful jaws. He had a terrible, sinking feeling that whoever designed it had a similar plan for this metal beastie.

Before Albion could do anything, the hunter-killer leaped for Dragonwell, its splayed legs snapping it forward in a violent arc. It launched itself like a very ugly trebuchet, dripping mandibles snapping together as if magnetized. For a moment it hung there, motionless, ready to sink its fangs into Dragonwell's neck and the vulnerable Vanessa Hargreaves inside. And then it stopped, as if it had hit an invisible wall surrounding the play park. Its legs scrabbled for purchase, its eyes swirling madly.

By chance, the sword A Contrario was in an upswing, Hargreaves bringing the heavy length of steel out in an underhanded arc. At the peak of its parabola, the sword seemed to weigh no more than a tree branch. Its point caught the hunter-killer, and cut through like the creature's armor was butter, straight into what would have been the abdomen of a real spider. Then Dragonwell fell back, the hilt bracing against the ground, and the sword slipped through the back of the monster with no more difficulty than poking a piece of paper.

Something screamed, and Albion could not see what it was. There was only the flailing arms of the wretched thing, stuck like a pig, Thick limbs banged on Dragonwell's tricorn head, scratching the paint, but doing no real damage. Albion dove, rolling under a leg that reduced a set of swings to rubble. Ichor washed out of it, a black filth rupturing from the hunter killer's abdomen. A rank smell filled the air, both metallic and rotten, like sour cheese and old pennies.

Then the creature went still, the tips of its legs folding quietly to its thorax, dying without any more fuss. The thing had barely given up the ghost before the sound of many feet drummed from around the corner. Albion began to run toward Dragonwell, which now knelt motionless on the ground.

"Hargreaves! Hargreaves! Wake up, damn it! There's more of them coming!" But there was only the thrum of feet that left no tracks, in that ruined children's playpen.

The *'Berry* was still far too injured to participate in the battle, but Cezette kept her close enough to watch San Francisco unfold into crimson flowers. Whole neighborhoods folded away as the Worm crawled its way forward, flattening the buildings, plucking up the fleeing personages and feeding them into its star-shaped mouth. It had long since left the tracks, traveling instead on the backs of its clattering brood.

A quiet burst of orange fire interrupted the eternal blue sky of the California morning, a sun being born five-hundred yards off their port bow. The corpse of a downed ship spun into view, gored through by the Grimaldi high in the air. Death was a beautiful thing, slow red lilies against a lapis backdrop, but the voices sounding through the ether underscored the confusion and pain aboard the Incognito's ships.

"What hit us?"

"I don't know, I don't know!"

"Get to the bloody launches!"

"The launches are on fire!"

The vibrating ether *dague* nearly plucked itself from its mount in the compass deck with the urgency of its keen. Soon enough those frantic voices gave way to true screams as the fired hulk dropped out of the sky. Cezette watched the ship dip below the waves, vanishing into the San Francisco Bay. Sapphire flashes lit the water, dying breaths of the ship's engines, lighting the salt water beneath.

The other ships took up the position, maintaining a more or less constant barrage against the Grimaldi, and the Worm, and the host below when given a chance. Having run out of proper shells years ago, the pirates' ammunition consisted mainly of unpleasant things packed in ham-cans. Their impromptu shells traced a parabola arc to shatter in clouds of flammable tar, glass, rusted tea-tins, anything that would leave a mark.

The Grimaldi raised its eldritch limbs occasionally to deal devastating retribution. Only the thick shieldships at the fore offered some protection, but those oases of sky was taken up by injured dirigibles. Once a ship left the safety of the thick shield, they fell from the sky as easily as kites in a crosswind. The shieldships lit up in flares of blue, rivers of molten steel running from their prow as the hands gestured at them like a magician's flourish. Cezette took the 'Berry low, and the crew tossed knotted lines overboard for floundering aeronauts to climb. It was more prudent to keep moving, but Cezette knew every moment counted—there were many taken to the sky who had never learned to swim. She took up the speaking horn, directing Cockney Alex, Elric Blair and Cid Tanner to the worst cases.

"There, that man! He is going to be dragged under!" She pointed the airship's prow toward the keel of a downed corsair beginning to sink below the waves. There was an aeronaut heroically battling the drag of the sinking ship, but already his limbs had stopped making a difference before physics. Cezette had nearly given up hope when the ether dirk trembled a reassuring cry—Rosa's voice!

"Don't worry your pretty little head," Rosa's voice tittered. "I've got him."

And so she had. Before anyone on deck could react, a pink blur fell from the clear blue sky, and suddenly the man was launched clear out of the water, landing near one of the knotted lines with a splash. It was close enough for Cezette to see the spittle sputter from his lips. His fingers found a fast hold beside other grateful men and women and the 'Berry began to winch them in.

"Was it flying?" one of the men scrambling aboard asked, near enough to a speaker horn for Cezette to hear. On cue, the pink blur flashed through the sky again, landing with a thump that tipped the ship's bow briefly into the waves. A frenzy of mauve, fuchsia and circus-striped lavender came into view, panels of sailcloth, tin and painted ship's wood.

Cid and Elric had managed to cobble together hourglass-delicate hips from salvaged bits of train, married to what parts could be spared. Exposed gears and sprockets peeked from the canvas at the joins. The heel tapered into a sharp stiletto point. Its wooden face was scavenged from a ship's figurehead, originally a sculpted likeness of some sainted matron, and it was softly framed with naked ship's cable. Rosa had insisted on painting it with lips and eyes.

Directly beneath, Rosa Marija peered out between ersatz breasts, her view unfettered. Along the edge of that crow's nest, in cursive script, Cezette had stenciled its name: Keemun Cassis. As it stood against the bright of the day, Cezette thought of Joan of Arc, or Jeanne Hachette, whose statue in Beauvais Cezette had seen once in a book.

The cable-wire attached to the Cassis' wrist made a whirring sound as it withdrew, terminating in a thick harpoon that clunked back into its mounting. No, the Cassis did not fly, but swinging along its stout cable, she might as well had wings. Elric Blair clamped a thick refueling line into the small of the Gear's back, right at the kidneys, as Rosa hopped nimbly down and made her way to the bridge. The Cassis had no engine of her own, relying on the 'Berry to supply pressure, but the work of riding her left Rosa's skin glowing, droplets of sweat pooling in her cleavage.

"If I didn't have to stop every ten minutes, I could make short work of that white automata," said Rosa, hopping into the bridge through one of the broken windows.

"A harpoon straight to the heart!" agreed Cezette.

Cid was also in the bridge, helping Elric coordinate with deft flicks of his papery, roughened hands. Now he spoke up, gesturing at Cezette to stop her exuberance.

"Don't be stupid," said Cid. "I can scarcely believe we worked next to Hallow for months and suspected nothing. Do you not think he is ready for anything we can throw at him?" They had learned of the betrayal from the Incognito. Cid had emitted a stoic grunt, but Cezette had taken it hard, refusing to believe her tutor was capable of such things. Up until that moment she hadn't allowed herself to think of her dear Jean inside the terrible automata in the air, picking off her beloved air pirates as if it was swatting gnats.

"Our guns only warm his backside," complained Cid.

"A backside ready for a spanking," said Rosa. "Gunsmoke's ships can't turn worth a damn, but I can drop Cassis right on top of Hallow's head. Then he'll get a face full of stiletto!" She turned to Cezette with a guilty look, but the young woman at the wheel was resolute, her fine heels planted in the deck.

"A mere pinprick. A length of alloy ground to a point. My work is only as good as the material I am given! If only Alphonse could fly!" cried Cid. "Then we might hope to pierce that dreadful armor."

"I can pilot Alphonse," said Cezette, but her voice was a note away from breaking. "I've done it before. I...I want to talk to Jean. There must be some mistake."

"Then who will fly the *'Berry*?" asked Rosa. She took the girl's hand, jittery and still youthfully slender. "No, there is no way. I am sorry, Cezette. I was caught up in the moment. There's no need for you to see him again. We're more good to the people in the water."

Elric Blair came in trailing a band of ragged, wet survivors. Rosa snorted, but with the Gear on deck still filling with pressure like a clock needing winding, she could only pace, and help distribute some hard ship's biscuits and tea.

Eventually Rosa boarded Cassis once more, and in a while Auntie appeared, with a heavy milking jug and a basket of bread.

Cezette looked out on the deck, where Rosa flashed past, firing her cables like a croupier dealing cards. Rosa flung them in rapid succession, stuck fast in the ships above. Then she swooped through the falling wrecks, scooping people up or tossing them toward the *'Berry,* never once unsheathing the stiletto at Cassis' side. Rosa was right, of course, the work here was as important as fighting with cannons and swords.

Maman might have done it with a cooler head, perhaps with a better bedside manner. But the thought only raised Maman before Cezette like a ghost. No. It would not do to dig her a grave before seeing the body. Cezette had to believe Vanessa Hargreaves was out there. She had already lost her first maman. She would not lose a mother twice.

Cezette banked the ship now, taking her low to avoid the Grimaldi's attention, trailing their lines in case a straggler was overlooked in the water. One of the Powder Monkey's galleons with its heavy catapults exploded into a meteor shower of pieces, beautiful despite the fragmented lives it burned through. She flew toward it, aiming close to where it would drop. It wasn't just wood and engine components, no matter how badly Cezette wished it. There was life aboard, people who had parents, or were parents, someone who maybe liked the same books, had the same dreams, who were perhaps putting their lives back together just like she was.

For now, Cezette Louissaint could only pick up the pieces.

Vera Jasper's life was falling apart.

She stood behind the bar, watching the Grimaldi come in above the fat gray hogs to land at its place of honor at one end of the boxcar. Streamers and balloons had been hung over the open roof and side wall. The car had been separated from the rest of the train and deposited high over the city, near the limits, for the best view of the demonstration. Vera herself wore a sari over her usual flexible performer's suit, and she sparkled with real jewels and glitter on her exposed skin.

Beneath the counter, a bottle of red vermouth stood open, the sickly sweet smell mixing with the harsh herbal smell of the gin. Vera had never enjoyed negronis. They tasted vile and made her think of stuffy country clubs.

The air had a crackling quality to it, as if Vera could feel the wheels in Jean's head turning, machinations of its own device threading dreadful punch cards. She looked at the fires and the swarms raging through the city, at the people fleeing. What genius could possibly justify all this? Vera did not know.

She desperately wanted a reprieve, but she knew outside the box car the hills were full of party guests. She'd passed a cluster of trees earlier and heard someone say in a raspy, broken voice, "You look like something I'd want to eat." Vera had kept walking. The tents their workers had set up were full of guests at their games: roulettes with people pinned to the wheels, whips snapping, pins clicking, the sound of arc power striking between points. Screaming. Grunting.

Worst of all were the faces of the guests in the darkness. Most displayed profound ennui, but a few showed wanton lust, if the entertainment was novel. Their sounds and smells ran together in her head, creating an unwanted image of their diversions. Like keraunography- lightning scoring the silhouette of terrible things behind the veil. There was something wrong with Jean's guests. They had a kind of madness that seemed to grow as the party went on.

"How we keep these dead souls in our hearts. Each one of us carries within himself his necropolis..." whispered Vera. Gustave Flaubert. It felt oddly appropriate. The first time she had read it was at a lonely waystation in the Cornish rias. They were burying a circus member who had been mauled by the tigers, but he was not a Christian, and they were not allowed to use the church graveyard high on the cliff. They'd had to put him in the potter's field. Water welled up when they dug too deep. Surely the ground was de-sanctified and foul in these guest's hearts as well.

One of the guests approached the bar reeking of alcohol and sex. Without looking at Vera, the guest extended an empty highball glass and waited, as if service was his birthright. Vera gingerly took the glass and began to prepare his cocktail in a fresh one. Her fingers shook as she garnished the rim of the glass with the perfect rub of citron peel. Just so.

Earlier that day she'd gone to the cells in the back of the train, past the clicking, whirring contraptions that gave her nightmares. She'd taken a key to the observation deck and sprung the swordsman with the machine eye.

"Go. Go to your masters now," she had told him. "There is nothing they can do to stop us anymore."

The swordsman was weak, but had been hale, and he could still hobble. Vera had given him food through the tiny porthole in the deck door. She had handed him his bundle of swords.

"Soon there will be nowhere to run to," said the swordsman as he buckled them on. There was a moment when he stood there, perfectly capable of running her through in the blink of an eye. But he only said, "Your master is mad," before he bowed once. Then he was gone, through the train car and off through the cabaret's tiny station.

Vera Jasper did not know why exactly she set the swordsman free, but it made her feel a little better. It was a small thing. Jean would likely throw him into the cannery after torturing him on the pretext of learning about the Incognito. Still, she wondered why she had released the swordsman. It wasn't like her.

The pitcher of negroni was just another in a long line of things that didn't sit right with her. Hadn't Jean wanted to change this world? What were they doing with these bottom feeders, these parasites who thought themselves kingmakers? Weren't Vera Jasper and Jean Hallow out to rewrite things so this pestilence wouldn't exist? These captains of industry inhabiting the parlor, they chatted about what developments they might raise on newly vacant lots and how much they would have to pay to acquire them.

Her stomach lurched.

She remembered speaking to Jean before about these men, these benefactors who made his plans possible. Jean had scoffed then, saying, "benefactors? More like beneficiaries. They grow fat, like ticks, on the worship of their lessers. And yes, it is worship. What else would you call people who continue to revere and serve their tormentors but the faithful?" Vera had been impressed by the insight. Their guests were not sadistic demons, they were bored gods, capricious and indifferent to suffering. Lulled into unfeeling by plenty. That had assured her Jean had wanted no truck with them,

At least, she had convinced herself as much. Jean had grown distant after. Ensconced behind the Grimaldi's implacable grinning mask, gesturing with its limbs, speaking in its voice. How was she to know if Hallow was still in there, or if he had been re-forged by this crucible? Remade in a steel womb? Vera fumed quietly. Her stomach churned as the gentlemen around her grew more inebriated. Below her, in the city, a group of mercenaries were falling back under a wave of Hallow's creations. Unaware that their client had set these contraptions loose without a care for their lives, they hadn't thought to secure their flank against Hallow's host.

A series of shocks rocked the party deck they stood upon. Jean brought up a view of the locomotive-borne rail gun on a clever lens aperture. The device swung out of the Grimaldi's hands and displayed the views from the automata's telescoping eyes, reflected in mirrors.

The *Tennessee Jack* sat perched on a high hill, firing upon Hallow's host in bursts. The mercenaries had regrouped, contractors coordinating with the privateers, the sub-contractors and sub-sub-contractors. Turning their expensively leased toy on their former employer. Hallow gestured, and the host in the distance swarmed out of the purple gas clouds, scrabbling over the gun. They couldn't see the blood under all the metal limbs. Then their Conqueror Worm arrived and latched its end to the rail gun, its silvery carapace opening to clamp on to the gun's tremendous boiler cars. There was a cheer amongst the watching guests as the *Tennessee Jack* became part of the Worm's writhing mechanical body.

"And now the auction begins!" cried Jean Hallow, in a booming voice she had never heard him use. Vera's blood ran cold. "How much will you pay to own everything you've seen here?"

An auction. A sale.

Jean was making a sale of everything he had just shown. He had destroyed San Francisco to sell these men the Conqueror Worm and all the power of his creations.

Vera didn't even register the high-velocity voice of the auctioneer, nor the frenzied bids that rang from every part of the party. Guests began to gather at the dais, people coming from the hillside to shout numbers at the auctioneer. In the midst of this saturnalia, Jean glided up to the bar. He wore a wry smile on his face. When Vera made no move to look at him, he frowned, then reached under the bar with his one thin arm. He drew out two glasses and a bottle of whiskey.

"This?" asked Vera. "This was your huge plan? You wanted to sell them your brainchild? What will they do with your army, destroy a few more cities, build up the flattened neighborhoods only to raze it all to the ground again? The Host of Jean Hallow, reduced to the service of usurers and cheats. Congratulations, Jean; you've succeeded in utterly confounding and disgusting me."

"Every monster has one weakness," said Jean, pouring both of them a double measure of whiskey. "No matter how thick its skin or how sharp its teeth. Even if it can stone with a gaze or poison at a touch...if it eats too much..."

"It explodes. You gave them this so they would destroy each other," said Vera, aghast. "They're going to put your host to conquering the world."

"Their greed will be their downfall. These people are too drunk on gin and aeon mist to notice, but my auctioneer is making them all winners," said Jean. He grinned. "My needle in their eyes. All of them will have my Cook engine. My host. Once a steamcraft is out there it is out for good. Eventually someone will figure out how to make it."

"You've sped that up by decades," said Vera, in shock. "They're going to go back to their manufactories and commission millions of your clockwork monsters. You just handed all of these wealthy fucks the means of cannibalizing anything they want. Clean out a waterfront slum to build picturesque hotels. Burn down whole fields to drive up the price of corn. Destroy railroads and sell iron. Nobody would know it was these captains of industry."

"Wreck an airship port and rebuild it bigger! Take apart a city street by street and buy it piecemeal!" said Jean. "Eventually they will go to war. My clockwork army will be too fast, too uncontrollable for traditional militaries. Once the Cook material makes it into automata they will be unable to resist the swarm. The automata will simply be part of the swarm."

"The parasites grow fat on what's left...only to realize their mates are doing the same thing. There will be a tipping point when they've burned everything, left nothing of value," said Vera.

"Nothing to rebuild with. Nobody to sell to. Boom!" said Jean, and he blew out his cheeks like a bullfrog, before letting loose a rollicking peal of laughter. He downed the whiskey. "By the time they realize the armies will all obey my blood bond with the Cook engine, it will be too late. They will have done the work of making a clean slate, and I will finish them off. Then my army will rebuild from the ground up. From the ghosts of civilization will come a new, clean world."

Vera was quiet for a moment. Then she poured Jean another double, and clinked her glass to his.

"Cheers, Jean. To a new, clean world."

"Cheers to that, my Orb Weaver. Your cocoon hatches into a glorious future."

STATION 17
Priceless

WITH AMPLE PREJUDICE AND A FAST CUTLASS, IT WAS SHORT WORK FOR Albion to dispatch the others scampering into the park. It didn't take long to figure out these new creatures were unmanned. Hallow had taken out the human element out, leaving a feral swarm. As they climbed through alleyways, over roofs and along walls they left a wake of punched-out footprints and crushed bystanders. The sword A Contrario had to be left impaled through an enemy's middle, immobile, and Albion made his way by ten feet of Cid-forged steel. The blade hummed with aeon steam, wicking off the edge as a sparkling mist.

From the children's park, Albion with Hargreaves in tow fought their way through Chinatown, upending market stalls and cleaving great chunks from the winding dragon sculpture. Plaster innards, fish, and fruit showered upon the guts of the spider things. In close quarters Dragonwell had the upper hand, cutting through with ease. Hallow's machines, varying from one to two stories tall, kept catching their sharp tips on canopies and telegraph cables. Albion seized one of them by its daddy-long legs and cast about, hammering its wretched shape against its fellows until his truncheon resembled a spider crushed by a teakettle.

There was a large body of water just down the slopes of the city, a municipal park or reservoir. When they reached it, fighting through hordes of scrabbling creatures, Albion submerged Dragonwell's arm in it up to the elbow. With a slick gurgle, the Gear's tanks filled, and Albion and Hargreaves flew up on a cloud of bluish vapor surging from Dragonwell's vents.

The pair might have escaped but for a mass of the spider things linked together mandible to thorax. It reared high into the air, moving together from some malevolent agency, striking down like a giant's hand. Dragonwell struggled to stay aloft, pushing as the horde pressed down on its form. The weight of them buckled the steel and cracked the automata's armor, sending razor-sharp enamel chips flying.

In light of Albion and Hargreaves' peril, Rosa Marija's sharp scimitar could not have come at a better time.

"Get it together, baby!" she thundered, unmistakable, a voice from the heavens. Her blade fell upon the closest of the enemy, severing the pseudopod of linked creations. A pinkish razor wind hewed a forest of spidery legs from existence. Several more of the dreadful machines were cleaved into sparkling scrap before Albion began to laugh, and then to Hargreaves' consternation, join in.

"Come and get your love!" Albion crooned at the top of his lungs. He took his cutlass and stabbed all ten feet of it through the nearest hunter-killer.

"Oh dear god, you're a duet..." Hargreaves moaned. Another of Hallow's brood fell, its innards staining the water. "And you're out of key!"

Once they had attained a relatively safe height above the swarm, Rosa wound her harpoon cable round Dragonwell's shoulder, latching Keemun Cassis there like a lover. Then she climbed across to press her face to Albion's. Hargreaves looked away as they stayed stuck together, in midair, while the battle raged on the ground and in the air over the bay. The Ghost Train was using the *Tennessee Jack* on the remaining pirates, who were putting up a heroic battle.

"Come on you two," Hargreaves griped after what seemed to her was an indecent time. "The longer we're up here, the more likely those things will find something to throw at us."

Albion came up for air. "We should cut these things off at the source. Jean Hallow."

"Clobber his stupid face!" cried Rosa with glee.

"I was thinking sabotage? Personal grudge or no, there are only two of us," said Albion. "Two gears, or autos, whatever." He glanced at the Cassis, all pink striping and quiet grace. "When did Cid whip this up?"

"She doesn't have an engine," said Rosa. "But she's a hot tamale. Look." She pointed, up where Albion Clemens' *Huckleberry* flew high in the sky.

"Well butter my biscuits," said Hargreaves.

"You've been through the South, haven't you?" noted Rosa.

Once they landed aboard the *'Berry*, the stocky, gray figure of Cid standing on the deck made Hargreaves weak in the knees. She ran up to him and clasped him to her chest. He was a little shorter than her, and complained huffily. His beard scratched at her skin like a favorite wool blanket.

"An old salt likes his sugar," said Cid. "But this is a mite sweet for me."

"Whoa there. I've a family," said Blair, blushing, as Hargreaves turned to him. Distant thunder echoed through the hold. "I expect those are her cannons."

"You must tell me all about her when this is all over. Tea? Crumpets?"

"You've met! Alice Hanson."

"Not a fling after all. Well done." But just then she caught a glimmer of the hulking shape on the deck. Scarcely believing her eyes, she dashed across to it.

Standing there, rather plainly and all the worse for wear, was the Alphonse she'd brought all the way from merry England. He'd been patched square with thick panels. A thick portmanteau of cow catcher and hopper siding rested like a hussar's shield against his shoulder. It looked like a furnace grate had been recovered to rebuild his mouthpiece, and all the steel surfaces were rough, grainy without the smooth, hard enamel. But it was her own dear Alphonse, squat frog helmet and all.

"And the black boxes?" Hargreaves asked, trepidation writ large. She remembered the arm they had recovered when Alphonse was destroyed. The writhing appendage had been branded with the Ubique logo. She looked down on the swarm that was chewing through the remaining mercenaries on the ground. "Will Alphonse get all...tentacles...once I have him walking?"

"Your blood is with him now," said Cid. "Like Dragonwell and Albion. I'd bet my wrinkled hide he's your man."

"Think of it this way," Rosa said, coming up and draping an arm possessively over Hargreaves. "We can use all the help we can get. Alphonse here might be the only muscle we have that has a hope of reaching Hallow. And if you had to be tentacle groped, there are far less savory choices." They both stole a glance at Cockney Alex, whose hairy maw was working diligently at a sandwich he'd gotten from somewhere. His hands looked like bear paws.

Hargreaves had to take a deep breath to stifle the giggle, but it was one of those rare times when Rosa was the most sensible person aboard. Hargreaves felt that undeniable connection to her big steel friend. Perhaps Hallow hadn't understood the forces he was tampering with when he laid them into Alphonse's bones, but Hargreaves thought she might. She'd traveled with the galoot across the rugged bluffs and wild plains, and now she'd bled into his veins. Alphonse's father might be a Machiavellian puppeteer, but his family had been MAD.

"Right. Carry on then," said Hargreaves, and the passages of the 'Berry echoed with cheers.

STATION 18

Haven't You Heard? We're Getting the Band Back Together Again

IN RETROSPECT, THE BATTLE OUTSIDE HAD BEEN CHAOS FOR A LONG time, but now there seemed to be some kind of reckoning. Hallow's creations simply swarmed over the streets, overrunning gun emplacements and penetrating their sandbagged batteries like wildfires consuming dry brush. Routed in the open, the scattered mercenaries took refuge in the thick buildings and hills surrounding the city. From the decks of an airship, it was easy to see the squadrons' frenzied darting from building to building as they beat a hasty retreat from the black swarm.

But as the crew of the 'Berry observed, the mercenaries slowed, surging into homes and public spaces to bring the fleeing city with them to safety. From cowardly guns for hire to chivalrous knights, in the blink of an eye, it was a capacity Hargreaves admired in the American people, and had admired since Appleton. Many of the mercenaries had been in military service, that was clear from their movements, and it seemed they had taken an oath no amount of money could erase.

Gunsmoke Gilly, who was likely exactly this breed, ordered the pirates who were left to herd the swarm of horrors away from the fleeing citizens. The Ghost Train had slowed, joining the swarm's rout of San Francisco. It wove through the black swarm as a silver worm, consuming anything in its path and occasionally birthing new waves of monsters to swell the ranks.

Unaccountably nightmarish, the Host of Hallow was no longer composed merely of the arachnid. There were ten-legged things in there, swirling like millipedes. There were steaming things with far too many eyes, wriggling limbs jointed the wrong direction. Grinding metal maws tore into the men wrong-jawed, dribbling bits all over the streets. The abominations were countless in their variety, impossible to pigeonhole into a coherent design. It was as if whatever infernal engine Hallow was using to assemble his creatures had mixed up the plans, punched the wrong card, shuffling teeth, eyes and legs willy-nilly. Strange, because those who knew Hallow knew him as a fastidious architect. This host was not of Hallow's design, not completely.

In all the ruckus, it would have been hard to notice the trio of specks being dropped into the devastation that was downtown San Francisco. Hallow's creatures had long since passed the playpark that had held Dragonwell, raging their way out from disused buildings and tunnels in the hillside. But soon, those specks were impossible to ignore, and the rear guard of Hallow's host found themselves defending against something routing their ranks without mercy.

A pinkish shadow swooped down, quickly striking at legs and vulnerable thorax joints, before ascending into the heavens. Great streaks of the host began to disappear in the explosions that followed. In the east flank, a blue shadow dipped in and out of the tide of monsters like a hunting seabird, with similar results. And in the west, a vast swathe was consumed in a harvest of flame.

High above the fray, Hallow gaped at this sudden turn of events. The auction was not yet done, and already the might of his host was being challenged. That would never do. No nation on Earth should have been capable of withstanding his mechanical army. Yet, inconceivably, their horde was being struck down. His plan depended on the host being invincible to close the deal.

It was a disaster, and Hallow said so, only to find himself alone with the cannery princes and land baronets. Where was Vera? Where was his Orb Weaver? Frustrated, he climbed into the Grimaldi amidst the scattered hoots of his guests.

Once inside, he felt the Cook engine embrace him with a wet pop. Hallow didn't need to fly to be able to see the battle. He focused upon the left flank, borrowing from his host's many-faceted eyes, but the vision cleaved suddenly, unceremoniously, split by some vast, tremendous weight. There seemed to be a certain arrogance in the blow, a certain "Fuck You" in the poetry of a strike.

In a fury, Hallow flew high up, high enough to aim the Grimaldi's wand down to incinerate the whole block in a blaze of aeon power. He looked upon the ruin he had wrought, an ocean of fire, but the speck survived, darting back and forth through the wrecks. Surely nothing on the ground had such power!

"An automata, clearly. But how?" Hallow said to himself.

He did not understand why, and so when his own craft came under blows, it was as startling as a needle to the eye. He lifted away from the ground, from a wasteland of blows in mushroom puffs of dust and rubble. A portion of the airships had trained their fire upon Hallow and his engorged ship.

"ENOUGH!" said Hallow, and swept one of the craft's hands in a terrible arc. The attacking airships blew apart in a conflagration of orange flame. Flaming wood and molten gears rained down. His missing arm trembled, pain surging through as the Grimaldi's power moved through him. Hallow drew the weapon across the earth as a hot finger, sending waves of thermals rising to upend the remainder of the airships. It formed a wall of rippling heat between the Grimaldi and the pirates, a shield of sorts.

There. Let the moneyed princelings marvel at that. But from the inside of his throne of steel and flesh, he could not help but wonder:

Who dared to oppose him in his moment of glory?

And where, oh where, was his most trusted right hand, Vera Jasper, his Orb Weaver?

———

At some point near twilight, a mysterious squadron of kites descended over the hills. A boy of nine or ten, whose name was Paul, sighted them from his family's home at the foothills. They had stayed despite the burning and the looting because Paul's aged grandfather was confined to a wheeled chair, and it was damned difficult to move down the warped wooden stairs of their San Francisco home. Paul's father wrestled the heavy chair, while Paul's mother and sisters helped the old man climb wearily, step by step. His youngest sister, Anna, huffed while the others moved stiffly. She had the whooping cough, and the smoke was not helping.

They'd all seen the swarm of black things from their windows, and later from the roof of their home. Paul was a scrawny lad, so they sent him running for this and that, putting him to use so he would not be afraid. He hadn't seen much, but he heard the older girls gasp. He had been upset- the ruckus had begun just as he heard the ice cart come jingling down the street. It was bad for Anna, but she and Paul both adored the frozen slushes with their fruit syrup drizzled on top. They hadn't had any since last summer, and their Christmas had been disappointing, with only a hard fruitcake to whet the pair's insatiable sugar craving. He had wanted to go get Anna a tall lemon ice, but that had been when Paul's mother raised the alarm.

Paul had always been protective of his youngest sister. He had sheltered her in his arms, carried her across the country on the woolly bears when his family moved from the East.

Anna was too young to have known the tribulations of crossing, though the cough had given her an unequal share of troubles from the start. Still, she was a cheerful child. Her lungs were full of ilk but her head was full of the latest hat ornaments and the young florist's boy from down the street. When Paul's father reached the bottom of the steps, he reached for Paul's grandfather, and the family let out a little chorus of relief. The street looked clear, and the hill free of hansoms and rickshaws. The family's cabriolet would hold them all. Maybe Paul's sisters would have to cling to the outside, but they could rest their feet on the running boards. His father would drive slow, at half steam. When Paul's grandfather set his foot on the last step, the family cheered.

Paul looked, forlorn, across the street. The ice cart was just there, not even upset like some of the sedans further in the distance, but just sitting there, abandoned. He looked at Anna, who chirped, not alarmingly but expressively. Was there time? Paul looked meaningfully at his father, busy ordering everyone to fit in the cab. There was smoke in the sky, Paul remembered later, and it matched the exasperated cast to his father's face. Twilight lit both of them orange.

When the grizzled patriarch nodded, Paul ran to the other side of the street followed by. Anna. The ice was still cold. There was his favorite strawberry, and enough for everyone, stacked two-deep in huge beige cartons. Anna dug deep while Paul held her waist, past the pasteboard cylinders of rainbow, pistachio and vanilla. She was almost waist deep in it, and his hands were cold holding on to her. When he looked back he could see his family lined up like one of those fanciful portraits at the barber's parlor down the street. They were grinning, waving for him to join them.

That was how he would always remember them before the fire rained down from above, consuming the little knot of people and making orphans of the two children at the ice cart.

The kites cared little for the people below. Each had two men aboard, a pilot and a bombardier, encased in a thin coppery frame suspended between the gliding wings. A tank of steam sat near the back, which the pilot used sparingly to ascend higher. Swooping low, the kites began to pelt the pale host below with firebombs, heedless of the dribbling flames slipping onto the heads of those hiding from the conflict. When there was a chance, the bombardiers dropped from them on lines to notch mining charges in devastating places. But their aim was not to slow the host, or to wound the Conqueror Worm. No, their aim was Jean Hallow, and their bombs were only to carve a route toward the pale automata in the midst of the host, behind the rippling wall of heat from the fires at its feet.

Meanwhile, hidden beneath the rubble and unnoticed by the host, survivors poured out of rat holes as the straggling mercenaries drummed Gatling bullets over their heads. Many of the people on the ground were injured or burned by the firebombs. The smell of spilled blood and the cries of dying monsters drew the scattered swarm back from the front lines, eager to feast upon the dead and the screaming. So the mercenaries kept up the barrage, sending those marauders back whence they came.

The kites harried Hallow's great white machine, using the heat of the bombs to climb high on rising thermals before lobbing their deadly arsenal once more. It looked as if they could be winning. In fact, the Grimaldi screamed as the firebombs dribbled glowing orange pitch over its form. Its weapon wavered wildly, ripping into the buildings and the clouds overhead. At least, it looked like the kites were winning, until the whirring host underfoot finally took flight. The lightest of them shivered, shedding bits of armor to unfurl iridescent wings, before chittering up to the kites to chew on their riders. The grounded swarm climbed up the Ubique tower, the Golden Gate Bridge and the high dragon's head of Chinatown to pounce on to the closest of the kites. Kite riders fell with muffled screams, faceless in goggles and leather masks.

Vanessa Hargreaves, swinging the sword A Contrario with Alphonse's truncheon arms far below, knew the gliders for what they were. The cross-shaped wings and liquid flames were unmistakable. Her Majesty's Lillenthal Dragoons were here, the stuff of schoolboys' fantasies, legendary in the savage Indian subcontinent. Originally assembled to combat Portuguese gun platforms on the high seas, the kites were flown by hardened daredevils and designed to glide into enemy territory to set their enemies alight. In the chaos, the bombardier would go through the flying gun platform, garrote the crew and blow the gas reserves, tipping the bloated hulk into the ocean. Why were they here? Who had ordered them deployed? Regardless, seeing them fall brought her heart into her throat.

Hargreaves tried to tell the rest of the 'Berry's crew all this through the ether dague stabbed into Alphonse's controls. She tried to relay the locations of the survivors she saw. Her damned sword was a handful and a half—her hands were full just clinging to the controls before her. It was a bastard length in Alphonse's hands, and couldn't make up its mind if it was a claymore or a poleaxe. In the end she simply grasped it a third of the way up and started bludgeoning the hordes, driving the sharp edge in as if she were bunting at cricket. Unwieldy, yes, but the edge seemed almost like the mystical Excalibur, cutting through armor with a single touch. *Thank you, ma'am*, Hargreaves quietly genuflected.

The snicker-snack of Hargreaves' sword traveled across the battlefield, where the Keemun Cassis and Dragonwell fought, blades shivering. Rosa grappled for the few pirate vessels overhead, swinging through the air upon twanging cable. She fired bolt after bolt from the sprung bow in Cassis' arm, their detonations flinging hot flechettes every which way. Then Rosa dove down to sink the tip of her stiletto into the nearest abomination, kicking out Cassis' needle-sharp heels into the nearby creatures.

As she dealt with the swarm on the ground, Albion gave her cover from the largest of the clockwork horrors. His cutlass laid low the creatures' limbs, and when a monster was simply too big, Albion seized whatever projectiles he could lay Dragonwell's hands on, be it a sharp bit of airship ribbing or a heavy anchor hurled through the streets. The pair of them cut a swathe through the enemy, a corridor where the survivors could flow back toward waiting aid.

But the fight was far from won. While the pirates could retreat and resupply at the 'Berry, their stamina was not unlimited. Soon the blades in their steel hands were no better than clubs, save the A Contrario, which was not dulled at all by its use. But Alphonse was showing wear and tear, his sturdy train parts covered in deep, feral scratches. Soon even Albion resorted to Dragonwell's fists and feet, and the Red Special, unloading bursts into the eyes and mouths of the abominations from his open cockpit. Under fire from the Red Special's strange shots, the host's inner bits variously melted, froze, and blew out of the contraptions' skulls in fans of wet, glittering clockwork. Still they swarmed and seethed, uncountable.

When even the Red Special lay smoking at the bottom of the cockpit, Albion loosed his ace in the hole, the triple-barreled Gatling cannon hidden behind Dragonwell's eyepatch. The rounds were a much larger caliber than the mercenary's pitiful wagon-mounted peashooters, and they punched deep. But they were costly, burning Dragonwell's noggin red-hot. Soon the mechanism jammed, and the endless beasts began to close upon them.

The sun was a sliver on the horizon when they regrouped with Hargreaves, standing back to back.

"There's no end to them!" screeched Rosa over their ether *dagues*. The devices rang in their cockpits, shivering with voices where they were stabbed into various instrument panels or framework.

"I'm sure Hallow did not intend this. This an unmitigated disaster!" said Hargreaves, perhaps a bit optimistic about her former friend's intentions.

She decked the closest arachnid, shoving Alphonse's high hussar's shield into a thing of pocked faces and slapped-together limbs. It leaped back, its broken machinery screeching steam from all its seams, as if possessed of nothing but the faculty of hate. As she watched, the downed beast was summarily torn apart by its fellows, its bits ripped apart and stuck on wherever they happened to fit. Black slime coursed through the seams, animating the new limb until a new mass of horrors stood before them.

"They're cannibalizing their dead," said Albion, finally catching on to the host's ghoulish recovery. "This is not Hallow's doing. This reeks of Mordemere's madness. I doubt even Jean Hallow understood the thing he loosed from the Cook box."

"What use is that now?" yelled Hargreaves to the glowing *dague* in her instrument panel. "We are surrounded. Watch them! Try to find a weakness!"

"What weakness?" Rosa cursed, thrusting Cassis' spindly arm into a creature's maw. She let fly two bolts, killing the creature, before the arm was ripped off and swallowed in its death throes. Grease and steam sprayed a brackish cloud, and the Cassis fell to one knee, unable to recover its lost pressure without an engine.

"Climb to me!" said Albion. On a wing and a prayer he thumbed the trigger to Dragonwell's gun, which sputtered into life enough to spray the nightmarish wall with hot metal. The creatures fell back, holed through, but the gun guttered and caught. There was a final death knell of delicate machinery grinding to paste, and the scrabbling wave washed over the Cassis- but Rosa was safe, having climbed over to Dragonwell's cockpit.

"And now we are two," said Hargreaves grimly.

"And they are legion," finished Rosa, gasping for breath.

None of them knew how exactly they survived the onslaught. Exhausted and dirty, each of them would recall in their own unique way how the anarchy ensued. Rosa's account was easily confirmed, as everyone had watched her leaning out of Dragonwell's cockpit with her boot planted on his armor, wielding the Victoria and firing like she was downsizing a major manufactory. Albion recalled only the sting of the ichor as he pounded away at the horde, drops of it burning as they touched and turning the skin an angry red. Hargreaves herself only recalled the feeling of her cotton bloomers sticking in unfortunate places as she whirled with Alphonse inside the hot cockpit.

It was only when they emerged, their furnaces nearly spent and Alphonse's boiler bone dry, did they realize something was deeply wrong with Hallow's host. The dragoons had disappeared from the purple sky and pirate airships still limped along at the periphery, picking up straggling survivors. But where Hallow's host was once an unstoppable horde, it was now reduced to straggler bands, limping along amongst their dead fellows, ignoring the living. There was a quiet to the twilight that was disturbing. Eventually even the last of the host slowed to a crawl, and then to a stop, their surfaces steaming like cooling lava slicks.

Scrabbling over the rubble with her lace hem not two feet from the ick, Rosa kicked at one of the sickly contraptions with her boot. No response. The claws had stopped clipping, jaws ceased to masticate, and all was still. The smell of them was pervasive, rank and chemical, like a hospice.

Hargreaves stood Alphonse up, reaching down to scoop Rosa from the sizzling ground. Bits of plate rained from him in chips and enamel flaked from his chest. Knackered, shot, pierced and battered, it was a wonder the automata knight could stand. Dragonwell had fared no better. His cape hung in strips over a score of holes, and the bones of him showed, like the captain of a ghost ship. It was a relief when the *Huckleberry* appeared from behind a building, even if it bobbed along like a diabolo.

"My ship! The blazes happened to her?" cried Albion.

"Sewer spelunking and combat with legions of darkness, you silly man," said Hargreaves dryly. "Your Rosa's been working overtime to get her air worthy."

The helmswoman in question looked sheepish, and Albion was about to say something apologetic when an anchor with a thick cable hooked to it slammed into the ground nearby. Showers of rubble rained down on everyone, and when it cleared, there was the distinct sound of someone rappelling down the cable on a sprung grip. Hargreaves shielded her eyes against the strange half-light enveloping the city to see her ward somersault the last few feet, end over end like a circus act.

"Cezette!"

"Maman!" cried the girl, landing as well as a spring-heeled jack.

"Bloody Nora!" cried Hargreaves as Cezette came in for an embrace. She was decked out for battle, with sharp spurs on her knees and heels that made holding awkward. The skirts were rather too short for her liking, but they freed those deadly talons, like thorns on a rose's stems. But her top half was soft enough, a leather camisole over sharp ship-pressed linen that made her look quite cavalier. Hargreaves held onto that awkwardly.

"What are you doing on the ground? You must withdraw, immediately," said Hargreaves.

"Did we not go over this at the hospital? I am no good with the *'Berry* like this," said Cezette. "And there is to be a reckoning, *oui. L'habit ne fait pas le moine.*"

Albion looked her them both quizzically, but Rosa only snorted, her face a wide smirk.

"She's after the bloody spider," sighed Hargreaves. "The Orb Weaver that put me in the hospital."

"With typical French flair, I might add," said Rosa approvingly.

"You are no Edmund Dantes, young lady!" said Hargreaves.

"Non," said Cezette. "Violet is not herself. She is hiding! She is..." and she emitted a frustrated string of French, in which could be heard clearly *"Merde!"* several times.

But before Hargreaves could give her customary lecture about the pitfalls of wroth, something moved in the street, a twitch of a leg, the glimpse of a stained claw. The group whirled to face it, weapons drawn.

The bones of a creature on the ground shifted, and some panel opened in its recesses, spilling a grimy figure from its depths. Bedraggled and dirty, the figure doubled over on a clean patch of street and vomited right then and there. But when he stood up, even the indignity and smell couldn't hide the bobbing platinum coif of Arturo C. Adler.

"Arturo!" cried Hargreaves.

"Hello old girl," said Arturo, wiping the sick from his face. "How does my hair look?"

"Oh, you stupid toff! You're hurt!" Hargreaves cried. She sighed, looking from her hurt friend to her adopted child. Rosa was pluck-plucking at Cezette's outfit, giving her tips on where to slip weapons or pull back to show a distracting glimpse of skin. Hargreaves shared the role of parent with Rosa, she remembered. It wasn't her place to reel the pair in, or to send Cezette packing to safety. And if she was coming along, then Hargreaves felt better if they were all prepared for the worst. "I suppose a spot of rest and recovery is in order," she allowed.

At a nearby café that had somehow survived the destruction, they righted a table and harvested the spoils of war: a tin of amaretti wrapped in waxed paper, and some bottles of pop, cold packed in ice blocks and sawdust in the back of the pantry. There were also innumerable cans of meat and a haunch of ham, but none of them had the appetite for such delectables, not after what they had seen. But there was bread and, wonder of wonders, a packet of silken pouches in the back of a drawer; Vanessa Hargreaves had found tea.

"Oh dear, it's almost as if I'm having my constitutional in Rome," said Arturo fondly. After a little toast and some hardy black ship's tea, he recovered quickly enough and was much his old self. "Save the scenery, of course."

"There is the Conqueror Worm," said Hargreaves quietly, unable to tear her eyes from the sinuous shape of Hallow's machine wound around the Ubique tower. It was now impossible to separate the legs of the creatures holding it up from the original boxcars of the Ghost Train. The thing may well have been birthed from an egg sac, not welded together from steel plate. Somewhere in those coils lay the Grimaldi, where it had retreated after destroying the dragoon kites.

"How did you come to be inside that creature?" asked Rosa. She stared at Arturo.

"And who is this luscious creature?" asked Arturo, oily as sin. He continued to munch on a biscuit in quite good humor, as if the destruction all around them were only Hyde Park at high noon. Rosa glared at him, but Hargreaves could see the weight of what he knew upon his brow. Arturo was contrary when he needed space.

"How *did* you wind up there?" asked Hargreaves eventually.

Arturo took the time to finish his cup before answering.

"What is it I do best, Inspector?" asked Arturo with a long sigh.

"Drink," said Hargreaves immediately. "Smoke. Gamble. Patronize brothels."

"Quite right. And?"

"I hate to say it," said Hargreaves. "Oh all right! Insufferable as you are, you are first and foremost, a first-rate detective."

Arturo seemed pleased, and surprised, which made his words direct. "I was investigating the cockpit of the creature that pursued us not so long ago. You will recall, I bid you go on ahead. What happened after you left, by the way?"

Hargreaves filled Arturo in, briefly.

"My, my," said the detective. "And I thought I had difficulty sneaking into Jean Hallow's Ghost Train." They all snapped to attention, turning with wide eyes to catch Arturo's every word.

As it happened, Arturo had discovered return coordinates in a sealed glove box of the machine that had terrorized them on the road. It had been encoded, but Arturo was quite fond of puzzles. As his father would say, it was elementary. Of course, the way Arturo told it, only a master mathematician could have done better.

"I traced the address to one of the stops of the Ghost Train. Hallow calls it his Conqueror Worm. Poe. How melodramatic," said Arturo. "The facility you found under the cabaret was only one of Hallow's laboratories, devoted to the manufacture of these horrors you see around you."

"I wish I had stayed to watch the show upstairs instead," said Albion. Gallows humor, but Rosa pinched his cheek anyway.

"I had a good long run through the place before the train began to move, and I hid myself in one of the creatures thereafter." continued Arturo. "There were so many, all deactivated and hanging on brackets. They seemed empty, like dolls awaiting a soul. Hundreds of them in the train. I snuck into the stations and stole food, water. I saw terrible things."

"Ubique's people, most likely," said Hargreaves. "Harvesting the destitute for Hallow's furnaces."

"I saw cargo containers and documents from Mordemere's atelier in Leyland," continued Arturo. "But I also found plans that were laid with Her Majesty's firms in Scotland, the ones that made Alphonse and his black boxes. Hallow is a master engineer. He has been designing these automata since before we knew there were automata... I daresay he is the father of this particular steamcraft, operating as a clandestine second or third party at every step, leaking vital innovations where he needed them. His entire existence at Scotland Yard must have been to facilitate the creation of the Cook box and his nightmare army."

Everyone looked up at Alphonse, before Arturo continued.

"Unfortunately, his designs needed an aeon power source to move his creatures. I believe he approached Mordemere and his research into aeons to obtain it. Then he variously solicited the British government, Ubique and private investors to gather the funds for his army."

"That blackguard!" said Hargreaves, fuming.

"That shiny-headed fancy boy is absolutely barking mad," came a voice across the wasteland of corpses. "He is also absolutely correct."

"Violet!" cried Cezette, who had sunk into an exhausted torpor after her string of expletives, and now sprung up like a freshly wound clock.

"The Orb Weaver," hissed Hargreaves, and threw out her arm to stop her ward in her tracks.

But the sight of the Orb Weaver was not what any of them expected. Vera Jasper approached with her hands held out, and she had no sleeves in the cold to hide any weapons. Her hair blew loose in the wind, and there were tiny gems in it, accenting the glitter dusting her brown face.

There were streaks in the makeup—she had been crying. It looked like she had just come from a party.

"Just Vera," said Vera. "I have so many names...Vera is as good as any. Please, I've come to talk."

"You tried to kill my 'Zette," accused Hargreaves. "You nearly killed me."

"Maman! Vera was only—*ah, ça me saoûle!* I have not the words!" cried Cezette. She spun, getting in between the group and the deadly girl before them. She turned to look at Vera. "*C'est vrai? C'est cela l'amour, tout donner, tout sacrifier sans espoir de retour,*" said Cezette.

Arturo's head perked up then.

"Is it true?" said Arturo. "You...you love Jean?"

Vera's eyes shone for a moment, and something passed between them. She took a step forward.

A sliver of light flashed from behind her and pinned a length of sari to the ground. Vera stopped in her tracks, glancing down at the throwing knife not two inches from her foot.

"No farther. The next goes in your head," said Rosa, and Hargreaves could hear death in those words. She was surprised. It seemed the helmswoman had formed a bond with the French girl as well. But then Rosa had helped Hargreaves save Cezette, pulling her from the belly of Mordemere's iron monster.

"What do you want?" asked Albion to Vera before his helmswoman could stick her like a pincushion. He alone hadn't tasted the Orb Weaver's treachery. A moment passed, and when the Orb Weaver spoke her voice shook.

"I am sorry," said Vera. "Cezette. And you, inspector. I was...not in my right mind. I believed Jean wanted the best for all of us. But...I am sorry."

"Something's gone wrong," said Arturo. He rose from his seat.

"This thing...this Grimaldi...it is killing Jean. Slowly, painfully, in unimaginable agony. It's drinking his mind dry," said Vera. "I know it as surely as I know he was kind to me, once, a long time ago. Please, it's making him do something terrible. I...I'll take you to him. You have to help me stop him. Save him."

Almost clipping her words, a dragoon kite struggling to stay aloft crashed nearby, sending up a plume of smoke and debris. It turned heads and served to hide Arturo's expression, and no one except Hargreaves, who had to look past Arturo toward the kite, saw the pain there.

Before anyone could stop her, Cezette had crossed the few steps to Vera's side, and had her by the shoulders. And just as suddenly, she burst into quiet tears. The cocoon had broken to reveal a girl child, not a monster. The others stood around rubbing their heads and hiding faces behind empty cups.

"What did he want?" asked Rosa after a while. "Doing all this, it defies comprehension." She looked first over the ruin of San Francisco, then at Vera, accusingly, expectantly.

"It doesn't matter. If Jean is not stopped, this will go on," said Vera. "Please. You have the…the means. The trickery, the power, I don't know. Please." Vera Jasper sank a little lower, and then Albion was there, holding her up with Cezette while Vera sobbed quietly. It left the two other women and Arturo together. Arturo slowly maneuvered to turn his back to Vera. His platinum coif looked umber in the beginnings of sundown.

"So we kill Hallow," said Rosa to Hargreaves quietly. There was a finality to it.

"Your pirate captain hasn't the stomach for it. He's too kind," said Arturo.

Neither have you, thought Hargreaves. That's why Arturo was asking. He knew Rosa could do it, was itching to do it, and the notion of Arturo manipulating his allies to confound his heart was almost too much to bear. His affection for Hallow was clear as the glass in her hand.

"God forbid Cezette should do it. So it leaves us," said Hargreaves, giving Rosa a meaningful look. They had known each other long enough, and the other woman gave an imperceptible nod. But what of Vanessa Hargreaves? This was no longer a simple self-defense killing. This was premeditated, homicide in its purest form. But the look in the inspector's eye was even, at peace with herself.

"Agreed," said Rosa, watching Albion pluck her knife from the ground.

"We stop Hallow. We stop him and the monster doesn't come back," said Arturo.

"Oh, it will be back," said Hargreaves, surveying the ruin around her. "It always comes back. I'll see it on my desk every day. But it won't come back like this."

The impromptu siesta lasted a little longer, but after Vera's revelation the pop was a little less fizzy in their bottles. The coils of the Conqueror Worm were still visible, a great serpent with the city in its clutches, gleaming in the last sun before twilight. Somewhere inside it, Jean Hallow sat waiting.

"It's now or never," said Hargreaves, watching the light cast the city ruins in shadow. "We can walk right up to Hallow." She left the next part unsaid, for Arturo's sake.

"We know where he is. Why do we need you?" said Rosa to Vera, a bit hatefully.

"I will get you to Jean, and I will do it without you being seen." Vera offered. She seemed as anxious to move on.

Vera led them through narrow alleys, tunnels through wreckage and side streets just wide enough for a person to pass. She had hidden a grappling hook in the rubble a few yards back, which launched with a quiet hiss and buried itself into the rubble high over the ruined chasms of fallen buildings. It held the promise of crossing the divides by the expediency of swinging across. But to do so required someone to cross first. If Vera did anything to the hook, or held out a knife as someone landed on the far side, they would fall to the mess of twisted steel and rubble far below.

That is, for everyone but Cezette. She simply hopped across, light as a feather.

"Well? What are you waiting for?" she mouthed across the gap, though they were still far from the Ubique tower. She was bursting at the seams to help everyone, even someone who had threatened Hargreaves' life. Vera shrugged, as if to say, "How do we argue with that?"

Because they were all nervous around the contortionist and assassin Orb Weaver, they hung back until Vera had crossed and tossed the hook handle back over the gap. Albion was the first to try it, and even he hesitated, inspecting the grappling mechanism for any tricks. Eventually he swung across, legs pin wheeling, and the two young women caught him with open arms on the other side. When Hargreaves landed, she gave Vera a piercing look, but saw only sadness there. In the half-light and with her posh garb, Vera didn't look like a seasoned killer. She looked like a sad girl who had been ejected from her own birthday party.

As they made their way through a quiet, deserted canyon formed by scorched gap-toothed row houses, Arturo walked abreast of her and they shared a brief exchange. Vera began to speak, just loud enough to hear.

"You have guessed rightly. Jean needed to sell his army to Ubique and the other wealthy investors to move on with the next stage of his plan. But when you destroyed the Darklight Cabaret, you rather put a bee in his bonnet," said Vera. She stopped to indicate a turn. "He had to suppress the insurrection as efficiently as he could, so he unleashed his horrors far too early. They were still malleable, in the crude minds he crafted for them, and in the clockworked flesh, as well. Like children, newly born."

"Because they are children," said Rosa. "I saw the early work in a church in Maryland. Horrors hatched in the bowels of a holy place, corrupting innocence into creeping evil. And you, Orb Weaver, you spun the sick web that holds his plot together."

Hargreaves thought of the things they had seen in New York, the half-made spider creatures that sang with taut, steam-driven cable as well as with the apparatus of a human throat, and she shivered with the nausea that sprang to her throat.

Vera stopped, turning, and Rosa paused mid-step to see the wet trails like rivers through the earthen brown of Vera's determined face.

"They just keep coming," said Vera. She touched the tears, as if they weren't her own. "The only way I know how to atone is to stop Jean."

"Then all this, this is just a prelude?" said Albion. "He means to spread this evil to other places? Sell them to armies and...what?"

"I know not," answered Vera.

"That means he is sitting in that coil, waiting for us to strike," said Rosa. "You're leading us into a trap."

"Would that stop you from going to him? I would have you go into the Conqueror Worm and parley with Jean," said Vera.

"With no automata," repeated Arturo now. "How will we parley when he holds all the cards?"

"It does Jean Hallow no good to destroy us as we are," said Hargreaves. As much as she hated to admit it, Vera was right. "Jean needs to destroy us at the peak of our strength to prove to his buyers that his is the superior steam craft. The automata would have been our doom." That simple realization put her back on solid footing. Logic. The promise of sense. It was the lifeblood of an Englishwoman.

"*Tres bien*," said Vera Jasper, climbing higher into the rubble.

Soon they were within the shadow of the Conqueor Worm when Vera held up a hand, calling for them to hold. They stood near the Ubique tower, the great corporate courtyard that served the front of the building. The signboards were empty of rail times, and the telegraphs stood silent where they hadn't been ripped out by the Worm's passage. The Worm itself wound around the building's front and up several stories of the tower, leaving a thin sliver where it was possible to enter the building. There were no signs Jean had noticed them. In fact, under the clutching legs of the monster train, all was calm and peaceful. It felt a bit like everything had died in that courtyard.

"So he is here, then," Albion said. He turned to the rest of the group, nodded, then walked forward.

"Whoa, wait!" Rosa protested, but Hargreaves stayed her hand.

"He will come to no harm," said Hargreaves. She followed.

"Come out, you bastard!" cried Arturo. "You've had your blasted fun. Inspector Hargreaves might not have had the heart to shoot you but I've got a bullet for you right here!"

"No! We've come to parley!" cried Vera, but Rosa came up behind her and struck her temple with the pommel of one of her knives. The Orb Weaver went down, in a pile, looking surprisingly fragile. No response came from Jean Hallow.

Albion held up Victoria, but from behind him, Hargreaves saw the Red Special in his other hand. He might not have the heart, but he had the gumption. And too late Hargreaves realized the raw energies in the aeon pistol were their best shot of stopping Hallow. Hargreaves fumbled for her Collier, and patted her pockets for the sparker she had brought all the way from England, retained through all her adventures. Blast!

Where had it gone? No, she didn't have it. But the Collier was at least reassuring in her hand.

They walked right up to the building. A chill wind blew in from over the ocean and swept up the debris in the court. It suddenly felt much colder, and the silent telegraph podiums stood like grave markers.

The blow that found Albion took him completely by surprise. Arturo, at the front of the group, whirled, parting the thick air with a slim gun barrel that seemed to have leaped into his hand. But the shot that rang out missed by a mile. One second the court was empty, void of movement. The next, as quietly as a mouse, the Grimaldi's arm had plucked Albion from the floor like a rose. The sky was occluded by its collared jester shape. The Cheshire grin of its face hung in the air like a crescent moon.

They all heard Albion's arm break, no clean snap but a wet crunch, surely splintered into a million pieces. Albion screamed, all the time he was in the air. Hallow threw him across the cold court and into a telegraph booth, where Albion lay gasping.

An answering scream followed, and a rattling tinkle of knives—Rosa, crying in rage. Her blades rattled as they struck the Grimaldi's impenetrable skin. A thump sounded as the machine's leg found the nimble helmswoman, and a sick scraping sound as she slid across the court as well, coming to a stop near the Worm's terrible bulk.

"*Hum gah!*" Hargreaves watched Albion try to say something in his native tongue but all that followed was the gurgling bawl of an infant.

Now the Grimaldi dangled Victoria like a boiled sweet for a moment before crushing it between its giant beige fingers. Bits of metal tinkled to the ground. It leered, and took a step toward Hargreaves, shaking the floor with its enormous mime feet. Its toes were pointed up at the end of its long, thin legs, as sharp as stakes and horrifyingly close. Hargreaves began to fire at the white beast, round after round, expending all of the Collier's eight chambers. An echoing ring, as Arturo unloaded another blast into the sheer cliff of metal before him to no avail.

Cezette! Where was Cezette? Hargreaves craned to see, but the terrifying shape suddenly filled her vision. She had let it get too close!

"Hey!" a hoarse gargle came from Albion, and the Grimaldi turned a second before it was upon her. "Bollocks to you!" And then there was a riot of thunder, as the grim white specter lurched sideways, thrown a good twenty feet into a quiet signboard. The court was filled with the tinkling of tiny tabs and cogs burst free from their mountings.

Fumbling southpaw, Albion had aimed the Red Special and squeezed off a shot. It was a beautiful shot, a dull vibrato that left the barrel shuddering visibly in his hand. Even with Albion's terrible aim and dragging his smashed arm, the white cliff of Grimaldi was impossible to miss.

Hargreaves didn't doubt the blast could have gone clear to walls of the tower. Yet when the Grimaldi stood up, it was completely unharmed.

Albion cursed a blue streak.

Hallow's creature leaned forward now, and made a motion with its long, creepy fingers. The Red Special jumped from Albion's grip and flew away, as if hooked by a celestial fisherman. Then it slowly made the flicking motion at each of them that were up, the tinkling of guns hitting the floor like sleigh bells. When it hit Hargreaves she felt the passing of a massive train, like a parade of the dead knocking her clean to the floor.

Threat of bullets gone, the Grimaldi's chest opened like a flower. The petals of white enamel were a fleshy pink beneath, blooming in increasingly sickening layers. Inside the stamen, Jean Hallow squatted like an insect. His whole lower body was sunk into the automata's flesh, melted, wrong-looking. Splotches of raw red dripped clear onto the floor. Whatever had befallen his mighty host had struck at Hallow himself; that much was clear. His face was haggard, the stump of his lost arm wretched and blackened where it was just visible sunken in the mess. The machinery inside still pumped and dipped through the flesh, but it shuddered, haltingly, as if its movement had broken off a few teeth.

A high-pitched scream, a different voice now, Vera, awake and, huddled in a corner of the court, shivering.

"It is a shame you did not bring the automata," Hallow said in a hoarse gasp. "But Inspector, what made you think I would not still make mince of you all? I can throw the broken dolls in on top of you."

Hargreaves groaned, the pain blinding now, paramecium creatures eating up her consciousness. She had fallen badly, and her old wounds were seeping between her stitches. She struggled to stand, and succeeded in leaning against a telegraph.

There was a thunk in the court now, solid.

It took everyone a moment before they noticed the cutlass sticking out of the red mess where Hallow's leg should have been. Albion had thrown it, end-over-end, lobbing the thing as if from a catapult.

"Ah, very good," said Hallow, watching the blood pump from the wound. The fluid welled up, dribbling in a throbbing river, then a stream, and finally dwindled to an ooze as the substance of Grimaldi sealed the wound. The cutlass clattered to the floor. Then the Grimaldi was near Albion again, moving so quickly they could not follow. It picked up the pirate by his broken arm.

Albion's screams echoed afresh.

"You're an abomination..." hissed Albion, clutching at his shoulder. His arm dangled uselessly from the Grimaldi's delicate fingers, and now it was bleeding a thin stream.

"No abomination. Merely..." Hallow tilted his head, musing. "Evolution, you might say. Darwin revisited, if you will. I've merely sped up the work of centuries a bit, and reached a form few have dreamed of. Even Her Majesty's little present is nothing, I will be rid of it shortly." He twitched, and a few splotches disappeared from his skin, healing.

"You're rambling," said Albion. Hargreaves knew what it was; he was grasping for his familiar banter, a ward against the blackness closing in. He was bleeding, not just hurt, but broken somewhere inside. Outside, a thundering boom echoed. Was it an illusion Hargreaves just saw? A ship, so close to the Worm and Grimaldi's terrible reach? They had told the damaged 'Berry and Blair to fall back. It would not be here.

"It is of no use," said Hallow through parched lips. "Now...Inspector. If you will be so kind. Bring us the automata...the one with the sword. Yes...the Queen's other present. Bring it here so I may rip it limb from limb, or watch me do it to your precious pirate captain."

"Fuck you!" said Albion, and this time he struck hard enough to rip the cloth at his shoulder, freeing himself. He tumbled to the ground, rolling and stumbling away, clutching his arm like a mewling babe. He slunk into a cramped space beneath some rubble too small to fit Hallow's abomination.

"I'll just have to come after you then," said Jean.

"Captain!" said Hargreaves, and tried to get up, but was laid low by a wave of terrible nausea. There was the stench of the slaughterhouse to it, like the Grimaldi was sweating the stuff, keeping her down. Hallow was going to eliminate the greatest threat. He was going to kill Captain Clemens, and Hargreaves could do nothing to stop him.

"Jean?" Hargreaves heard Vera's shaking voice ringing through the ill wind. But Hallow ignored her.

Horror of horrors, now the Grimaldi's substance began to push out of itself, to extrude and writhe hotly in the air. Tendrils of it reached out, as if tasting copper mist from the blood on the floor. Hallow reached one fleshy arm out of the gore and braced against the edge of the opening. Then he stepped out of his suit of demon armor, jumping lightly to the ground.

If Albion was posturing before, now they knew he had inadvertently spoken the truth. Hallow had become an abomination. A nest of serpents had wrapped itself about Hallow's shoulders, digging into his skin. Kraken tentacles draped across his back, pushing the muscles of his slim form outward. His deltoids exploded to meld with bulging pectorals. Hallow's biceps were great hams. His missing arm was now a turgid surging mass, terminating in a round, shiny tip, phallic and grotesque. Worst of all the head that sat upon those shoulders was Hallow's own face, the same sallow, drawn countenance Hargreaves first met in the case archive under Scotland Yard. It sat on the mountain of flesh, enveloped and swallowed by it. Hallow had become a monstrous caricature of masculinity, a strongman skinned and wrapped about a scarecrow's bones.

Hallow picked up a nearby chunk of shrapnel and threw at Albion a few steps away. Striking Albion's shoulder, the pain must have been exquisite, like being clipped by a cannonball. He shrieked. A second missile clipped him where his head was already injured, and his face was suddenly covered in dark, shining blood. Hargreaves smelled the copper of the blood over the terrible stench of this place.

"Fuck you," Albion said again, gargling a little. But he went down, crumpling on the spot.

"Hah!" said Hallow. He looked Albion up and down, appraisingly. "Perhaps I will." One bulging, throbbing leg took a wet, slapping step toward him.

"Wait!" cried Hargreaves. "I'll... I'll do what you ask!"

Tendrils of flesh were already creeping round Albion's ankles. But Jean Hallow stopped, and turned.

"You will bring the sword-carrying automata," said Hallow. Even his voice was different, deeper and harsh, as if the worst part of every man possessed his spirit.

"Yes," said Hargreaves, sobbing freely now.

"Or I will rip this fellow open."

"Please. No!"

Hargreaves stood there, clutching her own wounds, watching as Hallow's unutterably loathsome form stood over her friend prone on the floor. Albion was still moving, his chest rising with some difficulty. But Hargreaves had no cards to play, nothing to save him. Even if her gun wasn't out of ammunition, Hallow's tenebrous form was beyond anything that could be harmed by mortal weapons. The tentacles were gibbous, not thinning out toward the tips but bulging in obscene musculature. He reminded her of something pre-Cambrian, something accustomed to battling the giants in the dark for its survival.

Just as her fingers loosened on her Collier, a voice rang out over the court.

"Who are you kidding, Jean? Clemens is a lout. You prefer the gentlemen, do you?"

Hallow turned, his mouth open, frozen in a moment of glib reply. That was when the bolt of lightning struck him in the shoulder, every bit as terrible as the one that knocked down the Grimaldi. It set all the tentacles writhing in pain. Little arcs danced between all the surfaces, and the Grimaldi twitched, exactly as Hallow twitched. The pair of them jerked uncontrollably as uncanny flesh burned, bubbling like hot treacle. A terrible oily smell hung in the air. Hallow screamed, lurching back, and there was Arturo, limping along, clutching Hargreaves' sparker in his hand.

"You wanker! So it was you!" cried Hargreaves, patting the spot where she had it stowed just moments before Arturo nicked it.

"Alby!" cried Rosa. When Hargreaves looked, she was dashing across the court to retrieve her captain, who was awake and getting a grasp of the situation.

Before the detective could get off another shot, Hallow leaped into the air, landing a yard from Arturo. A tendril shot out and knocked him to the floor. The arc weapon tumbled from his grasp, sending off little static charges across the stained flagstones. As a bolt of stray lightning tweaked Hargreaves' leg, she felt a cocktail of emotions: regret, affection, and the bitter taste of betrayal. Arturo had been holding back, but the aeons didn't lie. The sparker had translated all of Arturo's feelings into a deadly arc of energy.

"Adler! You!" Hallow cried. The pain was from more than the sparker; that much was clear. She could see it in his eyes. Empathy just took the piss.

Hallow took two steps toward Arturo, and he seemed to recover his composure. He sneered.

"Did you like our hot, turgid night together? Well, look at me now!" All the tendrils waved, cheerfully.

"Oh, it was him, then."

Jean turned, once again. He winced as if expecting pain. And there was pain. Standing there was Vera Jasper, her pose slightly askance, one leg in front of the other like a glamour model. Her voice shook, and tears streamed down her face. Cezette Louissaint stood near her, legs twitching uncontrollably, reacting to something beyond her. But her face was drawn in determination, and she was handing something to Vera Jasper's outstretched hand.

"I knew you had taken a lover, but to treat him like this. I am glad we never..."

"Dearest Vera. Have you been with me so long and still clung to that hope? How silly of you. How utterly...woman."

"Oh, I think you've been very silly yourself. Haven't you heard?" asked Vera Jasper. "There's naught in hell like a woman scorned. Burn, you cur. Burn!"

She raised her hand from Cezette's nested fingers, already unfolding as she teetered away from the weapon. The iced-cream gleam of the sparker she had picked up from the floor was already glowing and sending out little tendrils of energy, something inside developing a fault.

And when she squeezed the trigger, Hallow's look of horror was priceless.

STATION 19

Conqueror Worm

MADDENING SHAPES PEELED BACK LIKE A RABBIT BEING SKINNED, revealing the non-Euclidian clockwork of the horrors driving the Conqueror Worm's movements. Hargreaves believed enough in the aeons to know this wasn't some fever dream or madness. Her eyes felt as if they had been turned to ice. A surety came over her that if she'd glimpsed the vision for more than a moment she would have gone mad. Then the airships ruined the perspective, and the illusion dispersed.

Years later, when asked about the events of that night she would only recall an impression of suffering, of many hands holding up a throne reeking of wet shit and sour meat.

"What is it doing?" Cezette's voice shook Hargreaves out of her torpor. She stood on the bridge of the 'Berry, with her hands in the gloves that controlled the ship's manipulator arms. As the Worm came around close enough to snap at the pirate airship with its terrible jaws, she threw open the throttle. The ship lunged away, as a deep sea diver might from an incoming horror of the deep. The Worm howled, a caterwaul of rage.

When Vera Jasper launched her frenzied sparker assault at the foot of the Ubique Tower, the court immediately filled with a branching, frenzied lightning. Arturo's sparker bolt had been loaded with his complex of feelings for Hallow, like a champagne cork giving way. Vera's was ten years of rage and unrequited love that had burst in a torrent that filled the court like a searing acid bath. She fell, her hands terribly burned. A fragment of the sparker had cut her deeply. Now both she and Arturo were unconscious. Hargreaves would later find a keraunographic pattern etched red into her skin, which would not fade. For some days afterward people complimented her on the tattoo of a tree she had gotten on her arm, so much that Hargreaves got fed up and had an oak detailed over the scarring.

When they managed to see again the Grimaldi was gone, and the Conqueror Worm that had once been the Ghost Train was slowly rearing up into the sky, uncoiling length by length from the Ubique Tower. At its head was something truly terrible; the Grimaldi, its white frame fused into the substance of the Worm. Its collar was unfurled into something like a lizard's intimidating flaps, and its chest opened to reveal a terrible mouth, with a single wet eye staring out of its center.

"Don't just stand there like a lump, go in closer," Rosa said. She ran toward Vera, ripping a cloth from her blouse to staunch a brilliant flow of red blood at the prone girl's side. Rosa spared a glance for Albion, who looked actually kind of okay. He was breathing, and there was no sign of blood save for his poor arm.

"Distract it!" cried Rosa to Hargreaves. She jerked her chin upward, and the Worm was so big there could have been nothing else she was indicating.

"We'll distract...that?" gaped Hargreaves. But as she asked the 'Berry appeared in the sky, no mirage but real and solid, and ready to pick up her crew. Ceazette was at the helm, threading skillfully through the few buildings that remained standing, getting close enough for people aboard to throw lines.

"There's our girl," Rosa had said, smiling.

"Oh, 'Zette, bloody good timing!" Hargreaves had cried.

"*Oui, madame!*" answered Cezette, her high voice tinny over the speaking horns.

Vanessa Hargreaves, not satisfied to lay low while others went to fight, had been the one to drive the 'Berry's fists against the Worm, leaping into the controls with abandon. She could not allow the Worm to reach the survivors below, some of whom were too injured to move.

Now Hargreaves braced her hips to deliver a huge, pugilistic blow. Her stitched abdomen hurt abominably, and the scale of the fight was unbelievable to someone accustomed to a tussle in Whitechapel's narrow alleys. Each arm rushed past the bridge's windows like a freight train, and when they connected it was to the cacophony of a million plates falling.

Hargreaves might have kept up the fight indefinitely, save for two things. The 'Berry hadn't fully recovered from her ordeal in New York. The left manipulator arm was already severely damaged, moving sluggishly even at high pressure. Worse still, the blows seemed only to make the Worm angrier. One terrible eye spun wildly, and its teeth chewed at the 'Berry's fingers. When the left arm ripped off in a spray of splinters and steam, Hargreaves lunged for the wheel, with Cezette at her side. They put all their weight upon it, and the 'Berry surged forward, her screws up to ramming speed. Hargreaves whooped a terrible war-cry, quite out of character, before flipping all the throttles to maximum.

"Ahhhh!" cried Cezette.

"Ahhhh!" cried Hargreaves.

"Squee!" came Blair's voice over the horns, choked by the weight of the turn.

By sheer chance, or through damage as the left arm was ripped off, Hargreaves had left the right arm in a straight-out position. Now that arm locked in place, flying out ahead of the ship like the fist of God. Fist-first, the ship dove into the Worm's mouth, breaking off teeth and wedging inside the creature. With a tortured groan of supports, the 'Berry's last arm sheared off at the elbow, and the ship broke free.

"Ah. The captain won't like that," said Hargreaves from the floor. But at least she had bought them a moment's reprieve, as the Worm writhed in the sky, its treacherous eye blinded by wreckage.

───────────

Speaking of captains and eyes, at that very moment Albion woke up in the courtyard below the fight. Somehow the falling debris managed to miss falling upon the pirates, though it did crush a nearby telegraph booth in spectacular fashion.

Rosa Marija heard Albion groan, and she rushed over from where she had finished binding Vera's side.

"How in the blazes...ahhh," wheezed Albion painfully. "Watch my eye."

"Why, where is it?" said Rosa, but her gallows humor felt forced, painful. "Oh just look at your arm...how will you hold our child now?"

"Ch...child!" Albion cried, and nearly swooned again.

"You're just shipshape," said Rosa, pulling him up in a sitting position.

"Are you...did we?"

"You idiot. There's plenty of time for that later." She began binding his arm to a straight piece of railing she had found, but her touch was gentle, her ministrations effective. His blood stained her ruffles and tight bodice—she had dressed expecting to see him.

Just when she was done, another groan came from the figure besides Vera. Rosa had dragged Arturo C. Adler closer, and he hadn't seemed to need any medical attention. But now he struggled awake, and didn't try to sit up. He was trying to say something.

"What is it?" said Rosa, annoyed she had to leave her captain.

Arturo hacked, and tried to spit out something that sounded like "...marshmallow bread."

"Do you need some water?"

"No....Is Hallow dead?" Arturo finally said, fighting through his cough.

"No," said Albion grimly. He was hurt worse, but he could talk just fine. "It was the girl, Vera. The Orb Weaver. She hurt him, but she didn't kill him. He disappeared inside the Grimaldi thing again."

"It doesn't matter," said Arturo, finally clearing his throat "He's spent too long inside it. Nobody should dwell too long in the seat of the Grimaldi's soul. Do you have any idea how much aeon energy is stored aboard? He's going to lose control and destroy everything for a hundred miles."

"Oh bollocks," said Albion. He looked up at his ship, valiantly battling the writhing Worm. It seemed to close in a vice grip around the 'Berry, but at the last moment the ship gave a spurt of bluish steam and jetted from its grasp. "We have to get the survivors out. While Hargreaves has Hallow distracted."

"But the *'Berry's* hurt," said Rosa. "What will happen to her? She's our home!"

Albion softened for a moment, but his eyes stayed hard.

"We'll call Gunsmoke Gilly, Alice Hanson and the others. They can help evacuate everyone before the *'Berry* gives out," said Albion. "Even if she does, we can get out with the Gears and the longboats."

"I have a better plan," said Rosa. She leaned forward from her kneeling position by Albion. "We're pirates! We take what's ours and get the hell out!"

"Rosa," said Albion gently, wincing through the pain. "There are children down here."

Rosa sat back onto her calves, defeated. Then she pulled from the depths of her bodice a short, thin ether *dague*—the one from Keemun Cassis.

"I'll tell Hargreaves," she said, and stabbed the *dague* into the ground. It quivered, ready to receive Rosa's voice.

———————

"I can't hold her!" Elric Blair's voice trumpeted throughout the bridge of the *'Berry* a few minutes later. He needn't have said it—everyone aboard could see the gauges trembling like wheat before a storm. The whole ship shook with the effort, straining to shift the struggling weight of the Worm. It was still blinded, and Hallow's voice streamed out of the thing in a continuous high-pitched din.

Outside, one of the bundle of anchor cables linking the airship with the terrible Worm snapped. It twanged like a broken guitar string, lashing wildly through the sky. It slapped against several other lines, anchors fired from the *'Berry* to secure this dread thing from destroying the rest of the city. It joined others that were linked to other straining airships, and together they held the Worm immobile. Rosa's warning had been taken to heart, and many of the airship crews here had family in San Francisco. The Conqueror Worm looked like a snake that had been tangled in a child's balloons.

The cut steel rope slashed down, digging a huge furrow out of a nearby barbecue restaurant that had, until then, somehow escaped the fray. In that instant the Worm whirled, pointing its great mouth full of wetly churning gears, and engulfed one of the airships nearby with a flaming plume of sick greenish smoke. Its breath was an unnatural marriage of the *Tennessee Jack's* ammunition: steamthrower acid and something else that seemed more evil than alchemical. The wood of the airship's hull shriveled away from ribbing turned red with rust. As the airship rotted away, its cables snapped as well, freeing the Worm further.

Someone aboard the *'Berry* unhitched the loosed cable and fired another, which looped over the Worm's form until it was lashed securely, pinning the dread mouth closed. Inside the *'Berry,* her crew scurried through her bulkheads, patching the shuddering pipes as best they could. A scream echoed as Cockney Alex became the victim of a bolt shot from a ruptured capacitor. It was only a flesh wound, but that meant Auntie was out of commission caring for the big lug.

In the cargo bay, the crew had set up an impromptu telegraph junction. The voices of Gunsmoke Gilly, Alice Hanson and Prissy Jack amongst many others echoed from a grove of ether *dagues* stabbed into the bulkhead. A wild wind whipped through, kissing the crew with a salt mist. It whistled through the places where *'Berry's* hull had been breached. The cargo bay was just as good as a viewing deck now, peppered as it was with bullet holes. As they watched, one of the anchors ripped free of the Worm, pieces of carapace raining down onto the fleeing people below.

"What the hell are Gunsmoke and the others doing?" cried Hargreaves, her fingers dancing over the panel of ether *dagues*. When flicked with a thumbnail, there was a brief moment when she could speak directly to a certain ship. The others kept up a constant susurrus of voices that Blair and Cid complained was confusing, but Hargreaves took it as a means to run the helter-skelter mix of airships still in the Bay area. She had immediately begun coordinating the efforts far better than Gunsmoke Gilly himself.

"You uppity child," Gunsmoke's voice grumbled through a *dague*. "I was commanding troops when your mother was trying on her first garters. I'll respect you for one thing, though. You've a sound head for deployment."

"Oh, I never!" said Hargreaves. To Cid, she said, "Who is this Gunsmoke anyway?"

Even so, it was soon abundantly clear the plan had come too little, too late. The shadow of the Worm was escaping their steel net, and far too quickly for everyone on the ground to leave.

"We'll never keep it up long enough to clear the city!" shouted Rosa, her voice echoing through the cargo bay. "The *Berry* will fall apart before we do!" She was right. Another pipe burst, and Hargreaves momentarily suspended in the air, dropped two feet as the *Berry* lost her grip on the ether. There was a clatter of dropped tools, and a chorus of curses from all over the ship.

"She'll never hold. Isn't there anything we can do?" said Hargreaves. "The anchor mountings are about to rip apart!" Her voice came accompanied by a tortured, crunchy wailing of timber from somewhere in the ship.

"What about Dragonwell's engine?" Blair's voice echoed from the engine room.

"Dragonwell is down in the streets. Besides, that aeon crystal's the size of an ether *dague*," protested Hargreaves. She'd seen it when they pulled it out of Albion's shoulder, way back when the pirates fought Mordemere. "It's never going to produce that much—"

"That might work!" interrupted Cid. "The energy in the crystal is very dense. As long as you believe in it strongly enough, it will bear the strain. If we use the Queen's sword as well...it just might be able to stop this beastie from killing us all."

"That last shot..." said Hargreaves, thinking of Vera Jasper. If they wanted it strongly enough, then maybe...

"At least it will gum up the works," said Blair. Turning, Hargreaves was shocked to see the lean Briton's sweating, half-naked body leaning full-tilt on an enormous lever. With a click, something gave inside of the ship and they surged forward. Outside, the cables drew tight, and there was another horrible scream from the entangled Worm.

"I could feel something down there, with all the monsters," came a voice weakly over the ether. It was Arturo, using Rosa's *dague*. "They craved the life above their heads. All those tortured souls wanted to live again, to be free of their iron maidens. The blood in the Worm yearns to be in the world once more."

"I thought you didn't believe in this aeon stuff?" said Hargreaves.

"Seeing is believing," said Arturo simply. "Whatever remains, no matter how impossible it may seem!"

"I won't be responsible for what happens with Dragonwell," added Cid. "There's never been a collision of so much crystal amplification and so much raw..." He stumbled on the word. "Humanity. It might detonate the whole affair, or it might rip a hole in the world. It might make a nice cuppa. We just don't know!"

"Cid!" cried Elric Blair, who was trying to reach another lever while holding down the first. Cid did not hesitate, leaping to the lever indicated with his old, rambling gait. When they had locked it down, the old engineer turned to another part of the ship, moving unhurriedly but efficiently.

"All right. Undo all the limiter bolts on the undercarriage of the cockpit, and open the auxiliary steam lines, numbers four through six. Then you need to—"

"We can't expect Albion to pilot in his condition," said Hargreaves. Into an ether *dague*, she said, "*Morcego*, your anchors aren't holding up the east side! *Papillon*, start grabbing everyone under Nessie's ship!"

"But who else can go?" said Rosa through the *dague*, breathing hard. There was a regular groaning, squeaking, rattling noise. It sounded like Rosa had found a wheelbarrow or something, and was pushing violently. "I should go in Dragonwell."

"I'll take the Gear and endeavor to stop the Worm," said Hargreaves. "I can get to it on the '*Berry*."

"I don't think so. I'll do it. The ship needs to keep the Worm held. The Cassis was built from Dragonwell's spares, I can ride it just as well," said Rosa.

"You can't leave them down there!"

"Albion and Arturo are awake. Arturo is starting to get up."

"I brought the Cook box to America, I will take responsibility. You must—"

"Oh that is just like you, Hargreaves, it's all about you and your fucking guilt!"

"Excuse me?" screeched Hargreaves, immediately hating herself for doing it. "You just want to keep your precious hubby out of danger. What will you do when he loses his Randy Rosy?"

"You! How the hell do you know that name? That is a *private* name! If you've been at my closet!"

"Oh it's not like you two keep the blasted door closed! The whole deck can hear you!"

"Look, it's not weird, it's a souvenir from the Monte Carlo flying circuit!"

"I've never seen leather cut that thin, that's just stupefying."

"So you *have* been in my closet! Wait, something's happening."

"Don't you dare change the subject!" cried Hargreaves.

"No, wait. Albion isn't there," said Rosa, and from her tone of voice, something else was definitely happening.

Rosa Marija turned her head for one second and Albion was standing in the middle of the Ubique courtyard, his intact hand stretched to the sky. Far above him, the clouds had turned an unnatural red color, lit by the Conqueror Worm that was its source. The serpent wound through the sky,

"Alby!" Rosa cried, but she had both hands full moving Vera's unconscious form across the court in a beer barrow. Vera's hands were terribly burned, and Rosa had to lift her by her armpits. Beside her, Arturo lay groaning. But her own Albion Clemens stood a ways from the wagon. He seemed to be transfixed by the sight of the Worm in the sky, and the wind brought his words to Rosa's ears.

"Come to me. Come to me..." murmured Albion. He seemed not to hear his lover's call.

Impossibly, something was happening around the pirate captain's body. There was a sort of bluish glow that gathered around a soft spot at his shoulder. His good arm was raised in its black sleeve, his coat billowing out behind him. Pointing the Red Special up, he held it for a moment and the glow suddenly intensified. Starlight whirled around the pirate Captain as if drawn to him, and the air hummed with energy, as if each brilliant point was a fairy singing to the man who had summoned them into the world. Motes of light appeared like moths, drawn to the gun that was no longer a gun. Now it was a beacon, and there could only be one thing it was calling.

"Now!" Albion cried, and pulled the trigger. "Come to me!"

At once the gun exploded in a brilliance like a supernova, and the entire court was filled with blue light. It was hard to look through it, but in that light something was coming, something that fell from the heavens, cracking the smooth corporate pavement of the court. When the light faded, Dragonwell was kneeling there in a massive crater, with one fist in the ground, ready to receive his captain. Beat-up, battle-scarred Dragonwell, his bones showing, looking more like a scurvy-ridden sea pirate than ever. At his back he held the sword A Contrario, and every one of its seven wings stood open, outlined in the blue glow of the blade.

Now at the foot of the Ubique tower the glow was scintillating, a galaxy contained in the depths of Dragonwell's gears. Silhouettes shone through the splintered armor: the straight telegraph pole of a femur, the buttressing lattice of the rib cage, big triangles of joint cups notched like nautical sextants. Albion turned toward Rosa, one foot aboard Dragonwell's outstretched hand. He mouthed something, and he smiled, a warm embrace that traveled the distance of the court. It would have traveled the world.

"Albion?" whispered Rosa, in awe, but in the next blue flash, both Albion and Dragonwell were gone, leaving only a blue streak arching up into the sky.

STATION 20

Peace

LATER, NOT A SINGLE PERSON WOULD AGREE ON EXACTLY WHAT IT WAS that happened over the city of San Francisco. With pieces of something indescribably horrid raining upon them, it was a small wonder they did not look to the heavens for salvation. What glimpses of the Worm writhing in its bondage turned into stories of an impossible serpent, a demonic force, a clockwork dragon. Even the pirates, gathered later at the pubs, burlesques and dirty underground saloons could never find a story they agreed on, so like a myth or a legend, the thing grew arms and fangs and extra heads, becoming more and more deformed until no one could be sure what had happened.

What everyone could agree on was that it had brought peace to the hills of their city.

As best as they could piece together, something had come from Downtown and risen up to meet the horror in the sky. No one on the ground knew for sure, but they could all feel the doom that would occur if the horror was allowed to touch down. They held their loved ones close, even though the armed men insisted on herding them away. They must have known their hopes now rested on the blue speck flitting back and forth above their eyes. There was no communication between the pirates and the mercenaries, but they all stopped at once, and they stood, an anxious audience to the theater above.

Witnesses reported a blue streak grasping the nose of the horror. Differences in opinion always escalated at this point. Some said the shape was small, just a man ascending like an angel, to answer the prayers of the poor sods on the ground. Some said it was a horror itself, an old god from the depths of the ether come to rectify its confederate. The old pirates mostly agreed it was some sort of Gear, and that it had worn the badge of the Incognito: the skull and bones of the Jolly Roger, the grinning mask and the eyepatch of their swashbuckling forebears.

Whether or not this was true, ever after the airship pirates enjoyed a certain respect amongst all who tread the skies. Patrols let them off lightly, hardly a one was ever hanged, and some said merchants gave away their wares cheerfully when boarded, though that was likely mischief, without a grain of truth. The suspicious amongst the audiences considered perhaps this was a story cooked up by the Incognito, intended to further the ease of highwaymen antics in the skies. But the practice of gibbeting was banned on most shores, that much was true. It was a pretty good story, and it wasn't below the Incognito to bend the truth in their favor.

"Balderdash. I'll tell you the secret of the Incognito," Gunsmoke Gilly would say, if the story was told in his presence. He'd lost an ear in the Battle of the Bay, which he had covered with a feathered headpiece. It lent him a presence some described as "dashing." Rosa called it "bumptious," "cocky," and on happy occasions, "preening." If allowed, Gunsmoke would continue to talk.

"There isn't any inner circle of Incognito. There aren't any secret coffers on any deserted island, no barrels of jewels in the depths of the *Straight Hook*. Nobody making up stories to be spread like the clap. No, the Incognito were always a volunteer organization. Enough people work together and they can do just about anything. Democracy in its purest form, straight from the teat. You want something? Do something. That's why the story goes on. That's why it can never be killed, *because everyone wants to hear it told that way*."

Gunsmoke's ranting wouldn't stop the storytellers. They would go on to illustrate how the good ship *Huckleberry* finally gave out, its screw spewing smoke and flame instead of steam, toppling aside and falling like a stone. They would sing of how the blue streak at the Worm's face thickened then, deepening in color as the figure deep inside girded his loins, or whatever gods and machines do to prepare themselves. Like a comet in the twilight sky, a portent of something no one quite understood, its tail reached from the heavens to the Earth, and pushed the horror back up, as if it had said, in a great bellowing cry:

"No. Not this day, nor any other day!"

And others would throw empty bottles of grog at the bard, laughing and jeering at this melodrama. Or sometimes full bottles, if they thought he had told it in a particularly rousing way. But the queer thing was most of the bards did tell it this way, and each more dramatically than the last despite the broken glass. Their hats were full of coin, excellent liniment for their hurt brows.

Some bards claimed they saw the Gear crumbling deep inside the blue streak. They saw its arms and legs come apart under the titanic forces at work, until all that was left was the shadow of a man with his hands clenched tight around a shining blue point, like the unbearably bright part of the sun.

And then it vanished.

The comet, the figure, and most of all the enormous horrible "thing" hanging in the air over them was simply gone. It disappeared without pomp, without celebration, perhaps in a final burst of cerulean that could have been added by an addled old pirate, baiting an audience to keep his back teeth afloat. All they knew was the danger was gone, and the skies clear and the proper color once more. The stars were out, and how beautiful they were, the constellations peeking from behind the silhouettes of the airships. Suddenly the world seemed to enlarge, to puff up from held breath exhaled from a million mouths.

Suddenly everything that had seemed impossible was, for an inscrutable reason, possible.

Still, the thing that stumped the bards and the pirates and the storytellers was this:

What had become of the captain of that fateful ship Huckleberry? He who might have given a firsthand account of the whole thing was nowhere to be found. Had he been the one inside the blue streak? Had he perished in the flaming comet? Even his crew could not be persuaded to answer, and the beautiful, golden-haired pirate who had commanded from the *'Berry* was even more tight-lipped than most.

What had happened to the Manchu Marauder, Albion Clemens?

TERMINUS

Maple Cross

"Tell me about Maple Cross," said Rosa Marija.

She'd found Hargreaves sitting on a stone in the midst of the finally quieted triage, in the ruins of the city. Nothing more than a collapsed school in what had been the richer part of San Francisco, the place had filled from midnight to noon the day after the battle. Treated patients were replaced by new ones in a stream of wounded that kept Hargreaves elbow-deep in field dressings. Until just now, when someone handed the sweating, dark-eyed Hargreaves a drink and made her sit down.

High above, Cezette, Prissy Jack, and Alice Hanson still ferried supplies in to treat the wounded. Bandages and ampoules arrived daisy-chained from airship to airship from as far as Tacoma, Santa Fe, and Nevada. From the settlements beyond the gray veil of the Lands Beyond that could hear the call came stranger remedies, potent salves and tonics saved for the critical case patients. From those ephemeral places came glowing wands that mended bone with a pass, and artifice skeletons that clipped on over a person's broken body, holding it up while the flesh healed. The Lands Beyond was mysterious and dangerous, Hargreaves felt, but the people in them probably no different from herself: they offered help to those who needed it.

But for now, the task of healing was better left to those fresh and unscarred by what had happened. Rosa and Hargreaves had a moment to themselves, and a bottle of wine between them with a cloth across the broken neck, to catch the glass.

"Well?" said Rosa.

"Maple Cross," said Hargreaves. "Why not? It was dashed stupid of me to mention it."

They propped two chairs together high on the roof of the school, and watched the nurses go from patient to patient in splotched aprons, significantly less hectic than before. Most of the black ichor had been hosed down by fire engines, and the streets were even beginning to look, if not clean, at least cleared. Lorries could pass unobstructed, and their rumbling recalled the long trip Vanessa Hargreaves had taken across America.

"Maple Cross was a mistake, I see that now," said Hargreaves.

She was too tired to be anything but honest. Her fingers shook as she poured down the wine, and she felt swampy under her linens. Unattractive, but it felt like good, honest sweat. "At the time I was torn between duty and…maternal feeling I suppose. Some peasant weakness, I thought, some inability to let my betters dictate proper station." But even this was a dodge, a way of avoiding the problem. Rosa did not push, and they sat there, passing the bottle back and forth. After perhaps two minutes, Hargreaves spoke again.

"It was a ship full of all kinds of people. Young, old, boys, girls. But mostly it was the girls," began Hargreaves. Rosa tensed, but said nothing.

"Some as young as nine, others nearly women. All sorts. They were to stock the brothels from Shetland to St. Agnes. The gang who held them was ruthless, but the raid had been planned for months, and we managed to arrest them without losing constables. The gang had picked the hideout for easy airship landings, but that meant they had nowhere to run when we sprung the trap. Open country. All in all it was a feather in the cap for a detective inspector fresh from academy, her pips still squeaky clean."

"But?" prompted Rosa.

"But, some uppity-up decided it was too much expense for Her Majesty's government to house five hundred mouths and tamp two hundred quims once a month. Something had to be done. Someone had to pay for it. So those girls were put to work in the asylums, in Bedlam and Hanwell and Marylebone. Scrubbing, cooking, and resented for being a drain on the country. Getting beaten and shoved into closets for the night. Working their fingers to the bone. Blinded by dim sculleries lit with guttering tapers, instead of by schoolbooks. Nobody raped them; too many witnesses. But if the girls said anything, asked for anything different, they would be thrown into the cells, and accused of hysteria, or madness, or worse. Easy enough for an asylum. The abuse would still happen, only with straps cutting their wrists bloody."

"And you had to sign the order."

"No. I was the poster child of the raid. When I found out, it was only by the grace of God and an accusatory article in the *London Times*. My head was full of the good of the country. Everybody has their station, each cog their place. But there was no excuse. I knew what institutions are. All that sanitary green, boiling pots of lye, the bloodied bedclothes and flung feces."

"Oh my gods. Maple Cross was an asylum."

"They put me in after my parents died in the carriage collision when I was six. It's why I'm so good undercover, you see? Learn what the doctors and the orderlies want to hear, and you can pass for anything, even sane. They put me in Maple Cross Asylum for the Mentally Disturbed. That was the institution I was in for two years. I went back there, when I read the article five months after the raid, to see the women sentenced to that hell. That day, two of those girls had stolen bottles of strychnine. Downed them together in a back room."

"I'm not going to tell you there was nothing to be done," said Rosa, her face implacable. "And I don't think going back to Maple Cross was a mistake."

"You don't have to," said Hargreaves. "I watched the shame cross the faces of everyone who worked at Maple Cross as they carted out the bodies of the girls. In many ways I think going mad would have been kinder. But I didn't go mad. I have lived with the memory of it all these years."

"You decided to be a champion for them. You wanted to rise to a position where you could do some good," said Rosa.

"No. That was the person I was pretending to be. Maple Cross was where six-year old Vanessa Hargreaves pretended to be someone else. I tried so hard that I think I actually became one of them for a while. Walked around with faith in Queen and Country stitched to my collar. But soon enough someone in that world goes into a back room and drinks enough poison to turn blue, because it's not a proper world, Rosa. Maple Cross taught me what the world is under all the rules and propriety I lived so hard to uphold. It's an asylum, Rosa. You can only get yourself out."

"Is that what you want? To be like us pirates, fighting tooth and nail to be outside the tide of dying mayflies, trying to live the way we want by sheer force of will?"

"That's people, isn't it? That's the aeon. It's in the ether, the wave-front of the species inflicting its will across the Earth. Like Hallow's host, consuming everything...but giving back, too, building things in nature's place. And you pirates, you jump in and out of that current and let it take you where you need to go. I bet if you went to Mars and attempted to ascend on an airship it would be impossible. Simply impossible."

"No people."

"No desire."

In truth she'd known this revelation only when one of the surviving Lillenthal Dragoons alighted nearby the triage and handed her an ether *dague*, bejeweled and carved with the arms of the House of Hanover. The crystal of his ether *dague* was protected from the wet with parchment and oilskin.

Once unwrapped, Her Majesty's voice was carried from signal crystal to signal crystal, buoyed across an entire world. There were sounds in the background, heartrendingly familiar. The clink of a cup on a saucer, the clip-clop of hansoms in Soho, drifting in through Her Majesty's conservatory. The sounds of home. In an abandoned schoolroom above the triage, the Queen's final lesson rumbled into Hargreaves' ear.

"Ma'am," Hargreaves said. Her lips were parched, difficult to move.

"Hello, Vanessa," said Victoria the Third. "Congratulations on completing my mission. Good show, my clever friend. Was the sword to your liking?"

"It was quite adequate to the task, Your Majesty," managed Hargreaves. She nearly choked on the next word. "But..."

"At this point, I've no reason to hide anything from you."

Hargreaves swallowed.

"It was you, wasn't it? What happened to Jean Hallow's host?"

The Queen fell silent. Hargreaves said nothing.

"I told you about Doctor Snow, Hargreaves," answered Her Majesty after a moment's hesitation. "When we had Mordemere and Hallow build an engine of flesh and steel, all those years ago, it was in the hopes of freeing ourselves from coal and peat. Of relying on foreign peoples in far-off colonies to feed us and clothe us. Paying them in modern conventions and modern debts..."

"You didn't trust Hallow," said Hargreaves, not letting herself be swept up in rhetoric.

"Naturally, I devised a contingency. A pox to stop his engine dead."

"It was a mistake," allowed the Queen, with hardly a break to breathe. "We should have known the cost of such an engine, but we were foolish. Not even Valima Mordemere realized the obvious: any artifice of flesh must subsist on flesh. But Hallow knew, and he embraced the darkness."

Hargreaves drew in a long breath.

"Mordemere's final solution, in the grips of madness, was to build a factory of limitless flesh," continued the Queen. She was speaking of the *Nidhogg* now, the false Leviathan. "A flying city, endlessly working to churn out more bodies to feed into the hopper."

"And Hallow's?"

"I suspect to change the nature of flesh altogether."

"Beg pardon?" said Hargreaves, confused.

"Hallow was a sodomite. Such a creature abhors women, has no use for women. There is potential in his research for certain barbaric applications...to usurp woman's proper place in creation. But happily, we shall never know what they are."

Hargreaves did not think so. Actually, she thought the Queen sounded far too biased. Hallow's closest confidant, the Orb Weaver, was a woman. Even now Vera Jasper wore the scars of their partnership without complaint. Hallow had taught Cezette, a girl-child, faithfully, without bias or dark doings. And, most of all, until his betrayal, he had been a trusted companion of Hargreaves herself.

Rather, Hargreaves thought, Jean Hallow had been driven to madness because of a world run by normal men and women. People who would happily throw their fellows into the meat grinder so their streets would look a bit neater. Such things had been around before Hallow and would go on after him. Jean Hallow had merely sought to turn the machine against its masters.

"But our solution to Hallow…" said Hargreaves.

"After Mordemere's Calamity, we offered him the dish on a silver platter, well-seasoned, of course, with a plague of our own making. His host fell, and there was no Doctor Snow to save him."

"What if it had spread? What if it turned San Francisco into a plague pit?"

"We were willing to risk it. The Cook box was the key to Hallow's plans, my dear," Her Majesty the Queen said. "His lynchpin. We had to manufacture a plague to get past the his machinations. And it worked. Not only did the plague we added to his infernal engine destroy Hallow's host, the threat of his dominance destroyed all those dreadful Incognito. And the red herring of a devastating weapon was useful. Simply the rumor of it forced the Ottomans' hand. We've crushed them in the Falklands, pushed the Argentines back. When the Ottomans made to strike at the motherland, our Balaenopterons were ready over the Channel. Not diverted, merely hiding. Once the threat was gone, the Falklands were ours."

That small cluster of islands an ocean away from Buckingham Palace held a fortune in aeon stone, lightly mined. With one stroke, Her Majesty had crippled a major threat and ripped away a crowning gem for her Crown.

It didn't make events sit any easier on Hargreaves' mind.

"America was your model. You wanted Britain to be self-sufficient, to be isolated and protected by miles of ocean, only that wasn't possible, so you created an ocean of fear," accused Hargreaves. She didn't care that the dragoon stood near, hearing everything that was said. "But I've seen what they must do to satiate the appetites of the masters here. Nobody here is independent, not yet, though they fight valiantly for it every day. How easy was it for Jean to convince you to build his monsters?"

"Violence and physical colonization cost too much gold and too much English blood. It's a vulgar habit. Today we buy our enemy, or we allow them to destroy themselves. I won't ask you to approve, but we have to protect ourselves from the seeds we've sown. The days of imperialism are over, Vanessa," replied Her Majesty. For the first time, the Queen sounded shaken. Unsure. It was slight, but it was there- and that more than anything solidified Hargreaves' resolve.

"Not from where I'm standing, ma'am," said Hargreaves. "Begging your pardon, but consider this my letter of resignation."

Before Her Majesty could say something eloquent, Hargreaves took up the shivering *dague* and broke it over her knee. Then she removed the nugget of tuned sugar crystal inside, still quivering with the Queen's voice, and popped it into her mouth.

The very idea of what Her Majesty had done sent a wave of revulsion through Hargreaves. She thought she had been dragging a spectre of war across America, when all the while the box contained only a trap set for one man. A death sentence, not a world-killer. A booby-trapped present for the tick at England's neck, Jean Hallow.

Let the Queen worry about her congress of shadows. Vanessa Hargreaves had had enough.

———

After their conversation with Rosa atop the school, Hargreaves dove into the care of the survivors of San Francisco. By the time she returned to the wreck of the *'Berry*, late in the evening, Auntie was speaking with the owners of the building they'd landed upon, and there were rumors of turning the whole arrangement into a thematic inn. Certainly the ship would never fly again; her vital engine had been ripped clean out in landing, dashed to pieces. Rosa's room was stripped, save for a pack of tarot cards for Hargreaves left on the desk. Their edges were soft pasteboard—regular tarot, not Rosa's specialty throwing ones. There was no reason for Rosa to stay—this was no longer Albion Clemens' *Huckleberry*.

It took nearly three weeks for Hargreaves to make up her mind to find Rosa Marija in the roiling pot that was America, but once she began looking, she discovered just how easily a worldly airship pirate could disappear into the ether. Rosa Marija left no sign anywhere on the coast, but Hargreaves did a tour of the dives anyway, traveling from city to city, knowing the pirate favored such dingy, comfortable watering holes. She drew tarot cards from her pack when she was unsure of where to go. As she looked, she kept hoping to run into someone with wide shoulders a very tall Chinese with a penchant for whiskey.

In a relatively small mining town turned pirate port, Hargreaves paid a local a pittance for a room, over the open-air market, and settled in for the long haul. There was a good waystation, and easy ether connections at the telegraph office. She didn't have to run around bodily, not when airships carried information about Rosa to her doorstep. The outpost was so far removed from civilization that pirates could speak openly, deal plainly, and even traded in their own coin. Mostly they ran people from one end of the country to another, less pirates than shuttle pilots.

To pass the time, Hargreaves put a stop to a local bandit. Then another, then an arsonist, and then the neighbors came by regularly, for their small quibbles, their lost cats and to sue their government for small offenses, like fixing their roads. No inspector any more, she still possessed a crack shot and a reluctance to use it: the best credentials a lawman could have.

In February of that year, she somehow got swept up into the Lunar New Year celebration in the local Chinatown, briefly becoming the midsection of a dancing dragon, and got famously drunk. For a month afterward, not a single person who passed her in the street would fail to give her a knowing smirk or shout "milkmaid!" On St. Patrick's Day she was outdone by a firebrand named Maddy O'Halloran, who outclassed her by two corset sizes and a half-pint. That was the year they made the flash contest official, and set a prize for it.

Finally, with the first spring flowering, Hargreaves traveled to a San Francisco in the midst of rebuilding. The neighborhoods were not so stylish or tall, nor worn comfortably by history any longer, but the people were hardy, and used to labor. There was grain spirit in plenty, good company in the saloons, and most of all a unity of purpose that had red Indians smoking with brown Italians. Southern belles sung alongside negro pianists, with the good old boys clapping rhythm alongside. Lenders rubbed shoulders with vagrants, who were not vagrants at all, for they had jobs and slapdash addresses and new friends to care for them.

She missed Funny Goat.

In the Chandler Hotel against the knees of the city's famous hills, she signed for a room, found a fairly good-looking, dusky young man in the bar and slept with him. When she left in the morning a bored-looking desk clerk delivered Hargreaves a missive that had crossed and re-crossed the western edge of the land. Like a hound on a scent, it had followed her travels for some months, missing her by days in San Jose and nearly burned up by an airship disaster in the Napa Valley. The thin pad of paper would have gone up in flames, only it had been waylaid by a week even before that, by a roundsman's strike in Las Vegas.

But the envelope had found her at last. It bore the thick scale of postage that was the evidence of multiple post ships, dark cloakrooms and even one sprawling stamp that suggested the thing had done a loop through Mexico. Inside the envelope, there was only a pasteboard card, of the kind found in the tourist kiosks, and sold on the trolleys.

It was a cheap postcard, a view of the Golden Gate Bridge and the Pacific. A mark had been scrawled on it, bright red even though the edges of the card were starting to soften to yellow from wear. At first, she thought the mark circled the red peak of the bridge. On closer examination, the mark was off-center, and actually went round the ocean itself.

"That's bloody clear of you," the inspector cursed. It took her a moment to realize that, yes, it was. Beside the floating seafood restaurants, the fishing junks, and the trader dirigibles circumscribing a languid route to the Orient, there was only one thing left out there worth any interest.

It was fearsome. It was daunting. It was also the last place not already found, not claimed by some robber baron, persecuted religion or outlaws seeking another life. It was clean, and it was still, despite folks' best efforts, mostly a mystery. Not the last, but certainly the next frontier.

...the Lands Beyond.

She turned over the card. The missive read, simply:

He's out there, Inspector. Why don't you come catch us?

THE END

Thank you for reading! Did you enjoy?

Please Add Your Review! Catch even more science fiction fun with the Children of the Uprising novels! Turn the page for a special sneak peek of book one, UNREGISTERED.

UNREGISTERED SNEAK PEEK

Bristol Ray did not exist.

At least, not according to official records. The back of his left wrist, where his assigned watch would have lived if his birth had been important, was bare. There was a lump under the skin of his right hand where a tracking chip had been inserted, but he was pretty sure that was there just to scare people like him. He wasn't being tracked. His left hand was ringless, and the skin around his fourth finger was consistent in color and texture to the others. His teeth were hopelessly crooked, his brow prematurely creased, and though the lessons from his mere five years of formal school had faded, his mind was bright with life.

He stood in a shadow, clutching his homemade paper stencil to his chest, and surveyed his work on the brick wall before him. He'd painted a figure that could have been a nun. A slouching, ancient woman dressed in long robes, slicing her chipped hand open with a cross she held in the other. Getting the blood to drip from that hand hadn't been easy. For weeks he had sketched as he watched water drip from faucets to catch a glimpse of that line, that light, and once he'd seen it, his incinerator ate the drafts and roared with rejection. If his incinerator were here and had the ability to destroy whole walls, even this nun may have met her doom.

Eventually, though, the nun and her blood had to go out into the world, fully ready or not. He stepped back from it, still safely out of range of the disabled street camera. One could never be too careful.

One last glance over his shoulder was all he allowed himself. She could be there for another week, or she could be gone in a few hours when the morning sun revealed her to the commuters and schoolchildren and stunned police. He packed his stencils and paints in his backpack, kissed the air in her direction, and started home.

Bristol zigged and zagged along the dark streets in the way he always did to avoid the detection of the street cameras. He wore a glove on his left hand with an ice pack slipped inside to cool his chip, just in case. Now that it was no longer activated by his body heat, he was free from all surveillance. The only thing an unregistered person had to lose by breaking curfew was his or her life, which could happily be taken from anybody stupid enough to be caught.

A notice fluttering on a telephone pole read:

WARNING
Any persons not assigned to the artist vocation are prohibited from painting, sculpting, drawing, or working with any other mediums in the attempt to imitate Art. Violators will be prosecuted.

He hesitated a beat, snatched the notice, and added it to his bag.

His sister Denver was waiting for him at the window when he reached the house. With one of the shoddily soldered bars missing, he easily squeezed through into the bedroom they still shared. He returned her smile and handed her the notice.

"A violator you are," she said.

"And intend to stay."

"We'll have to get rid of that," she said, but he'd already taken the scissors to cut it into ribbons. She sat on her bed and yawned. "How did the blood go?"

"Not bad. It was better on the last outline, but it's done now, and I can't think about it anymore."

Denver nodded at the shreds of paper. "Better incinerate those before Mom gets up."

"She'll kill me if I don't. You're lucky."

"What, that I'm getting married?"

Bristol nodded. "And moving out."

Denver laid down and pulled the blanket to her chin. "It's not like I have a choice. And Mom's fine to live with, you know, as long as you don't have any sneaky habits."

"I promised to keep Mom out of it."

"Good. She's made a lot of sacrifices for you."

"I know." Bristol kicked softly at his backpack on the floor. He wasn't sure if Denver was trying to make him feel guilty or not, but if that was her purpose, it did the trick. "Did you get your letter today?"

"Don't change the subject."

"I really want to know."

Denver sighed and shifted. "Not yet, but that's okay. I'm sure they're going to pair me with a Four."

"A Three with a Four? You're studying to be an architect. You're saying you could end up with, what, a nurse or data-bot technician or something?"

"I'm sure Metrics will match us in other ways, personality and all that. I know they don't like to mismatch Tiers, but they'll do it in situations like mine."

"What situation?" Bristol asked, but realized the answer as the words came out. "Oh."

"Don't say oh like that."

"Sorry." He unzipped the backpack with a little more force then necessary, took out his stencil, and ripped small pieces from it. The pile containing the bits of the notice grew larger. "It's just that sometimes I forget that my life is always wrecking someone else's."

"My life is not wrecked. I can still be an architect—I'll just have to live in Four housing and stuff. My kid can still be a Three if they do well enough on their four-year-old exams."

"Yeah." Bristol mindlessly ripped away at the stencil. "It's weird your kid won't have a brother or sister."

"I know. I was thinking about that tonight." She propped herself up on her bony elbows. "Do you realize that at the end of our lives, we'll have known each other the longest out of anyone?"

Bristol sat silent for a moment. "What about Mom? You technically knew her a year before you met me."

"But Mom will die when she's seventy-five. Then I'll have spent fifty years knowing her. But then when *I* die, I'll have known you for seventy-four years! You don't know anyone that long unless it's a sibling."

"Lucky us." Bristol gathered the damning notice and piles of confetti that had been his stencils, walked out of their room, and tossed them into the incinerator. He stopped a moment to watch the flames snatch and lick their prey, reducing weeks of work to shapeless ashes that could have been anything else—a recipe card, an ad, a pamphlet on new and exciting ways to save energy. They all became the same once the fire was done with them. When he came back into the room, Denver was already dressed.

"Almost time to get up anyway," she said. "Bristol, does that scare you?"

"What?"

"Mom dying?"

"No." *Yes.* "Everybody has to do it."

"You don't have to worry. I'll take care of you."

Most people, both registered and unregistered, avoided this topic. At the same time, these kinds of thoughts were intriguing—direct thoughts about privilege shared across the divide. Even from Denver, it felt simultaneously coarse and comforting, though they'd never talked in length about their differences in Tier. He didn't like to think about it, and he certainly didn't want to talk about it. Why would she bring it up now?

She's getting married soon.

"You can live with me," she said. "I'll—"

"And what about this new husband of yours? What is he going to think of marrying someone who has a brother? I mean, what are the chances he's even *met* an unregistered? Not good. What's he going to think of you just taking care of me?" A hotness laced his mouth. "I'll tell you what will probably happen when Mom dies. You and me, we'll look at each other and remember seeing the other one in a smaller size, but we won't really know each other as we are. And you'll care more about your new family than me."

They caught each other's eyes. Denver walked over to the mirror and began brushing and pinning her hair. For several minutes, neither spoke.

Bristol rubbed his sore eyes. "It won't be your fault. It's no one's fault. That's just how the world works, Den."

The sun had begun to soak the curtains, so Bristol stood and opened them to let more of it in. With a click, he turned their blue-tinted overhead bulb off and let his eyes adjust to the color of natural light.

"Thank you," Denver said, her fingers still braiding.

"Do you think Fours have blue lightbulbs too?"

"Everyone does. These units were built right after the uprising, so they're designed to only allow the color blue for lighting."

"Why?"

"It was right after the uprising," she repeated. When Bristol made no indication of understanding, she glanced at the holowatch on her wrist. It was silent, so she stood, pushed in her desk chair, and continued quietly. "People were unhappy. Blue lights make it harder to see your veins."

Bristol nodded. Metrics underestimated how much some people needed an escape and would just invent new ways of getting drugs into their bloodstreams.

Denver sat next to him on his bed. "Listen, while we're on Metrics—"

"I know. I have to stop."

"You *have* to. You've been lucky, but it can't last forever. I don't know what Mom would do if—"

"I know, Den."

"You wouldn't have to stop drawing. I'll still bring you paper when I'm married. You can still make things here."

"You know how careful I am." He closed his eyes. For as unlikely as her offer to let him live with her had been, he could see it had been honest. *Be nicer.* "But I see your point. I'll stop someday."

Denver stood and lingered by the doorframe. "It's got to be soon. I'll see you after work."

She walked away, and an idea for a painting flashed just behind the space between Bristol's eyebrows. Though his body begged for sleep, his hands, suddenly animated by some unconscious energy, fumbled under the bed for a sketchpad and pencil. He crouched over the paper, hoarding the white space and the possibilities it offered, clutched tight the idea in his mind, and began drawing.

Don't stop now. Keep reading with your copy of UNREGISTERED available now.

Want even more sci-fi adventures? Try Children of the Uprising by City Owl Author, Megan Lynch!

Living the ideal life is a human right, unless you're unregistered.

Living under the watchful eye of the Metrics Worldwide Government has its perks. Citizens are assigned a life, so they don't worry about finding schools, jobs, or spouses for themselves. They're even allowed to have one child, enabling them to focus on raising an ideal son or daughter and experience an optimally satisfying family life.

The only people left out are the unlucky accidental second children, called the unregistered. For 20-year-old Bristol, this is the only life he knows. But he can't shake the feeling that something is wrong with his world, and spends his nights painting controversial murals in low-profile parts of town.

Metrics doesn't like the murals, or the frustrations of the unregistered citizens they represent.

They enact their long-debated unregistered solution: publicly, they announce the relocation of all unregistered citizens to far-off desert states. But when Bristol and his friends discover the dark truth behind the plan, they must work together to escape the clutches of their motherland, and survive long enough to discover an unknown world.

Innovation, Creativity, and Affordability, check out City Owl Press at www.cityowlpress.com.

ABOUT THE AUTHOR

KIN S. LAW is a Chinese-American author who looks to include diversity, representation, and truth in his steampunk. Instead of a historical fiction where one event has changed things, his worlds represent what could have been, what should be, and what always was. He draws from a life lived in multiple cultures, but always with a love for everything weird and geeky. voxvorago.tumblr.com

facebook.com/kinslawauthor

twitter.com/VoxVorago